ROEE ROSEN

KAFKA FOR KIDS

Kunstmuseum Luzern

Sternberg Press

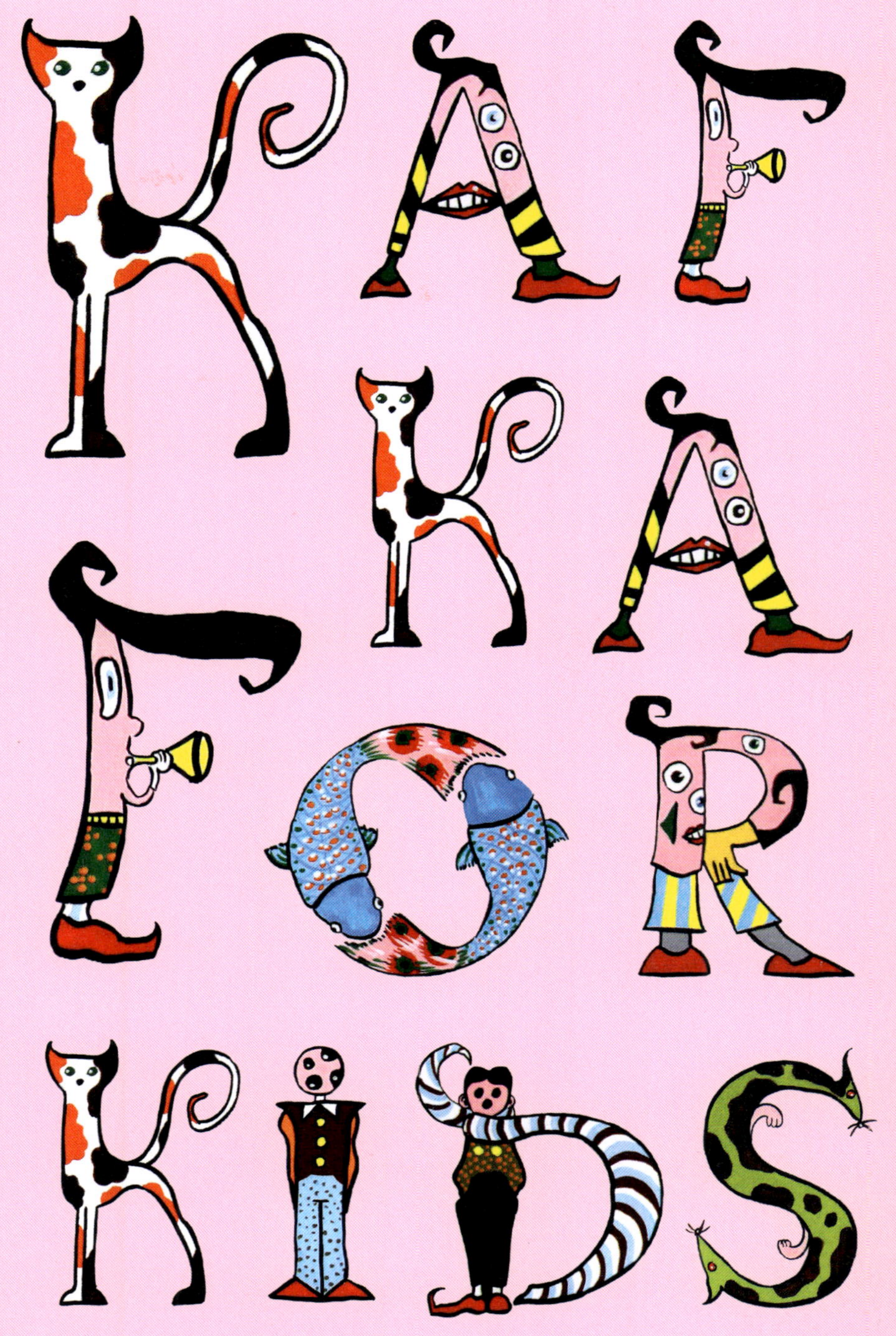

KAF
KA
FOR
KIDS

TABLE OF CONTENTS / INHALTSVERZEICHNIS

7 **Kafka for Kids, The Script**

83 **The Escalation**
Fanni Fetzer

88 **Roee Rosen: Literature, Fictionality, and Blindness**
Sergio Edelsztein

98 **K. for Kids**
Jean-Pierre Rehm

113 **Kafka for Kids, Das Skript**

189 **Die Steigerung**
Fanni Fetzer

194 **Roee Rosen: Literatur, Fiktionalität und Blindheit**
Sergio Edelsztein

203 **K. wie Kinder**
Jean-Pierre Rehm

ROEE ROSEN

KAFKA FOR KIDS

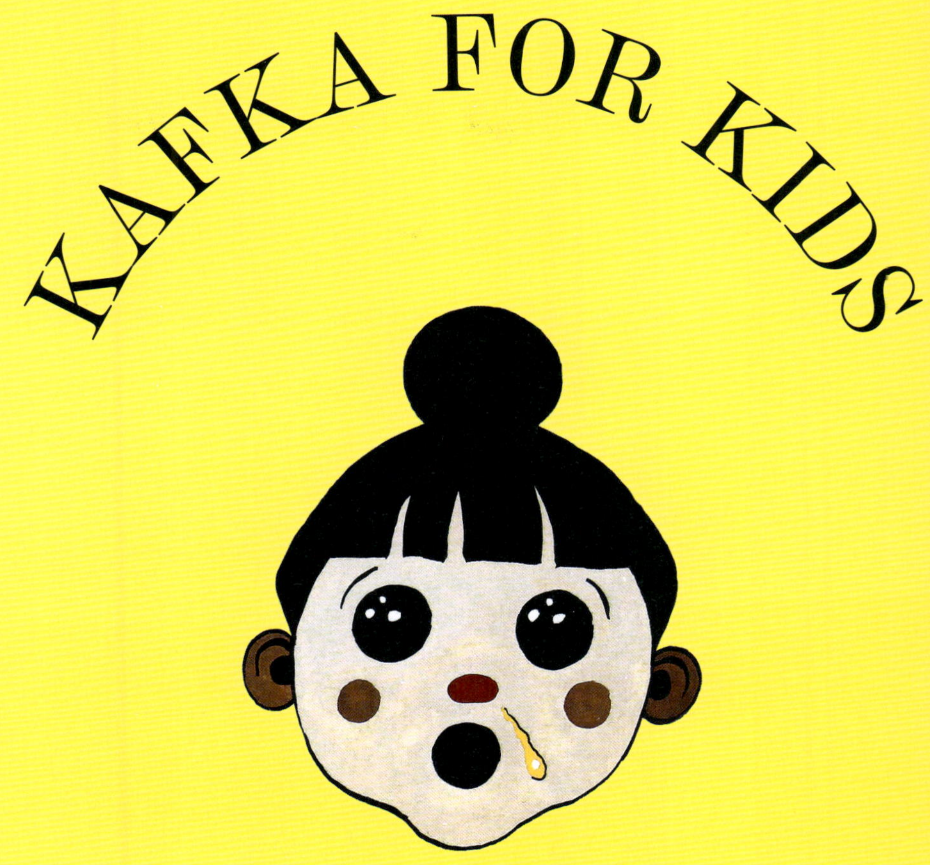

THE SCRIPT

CAST

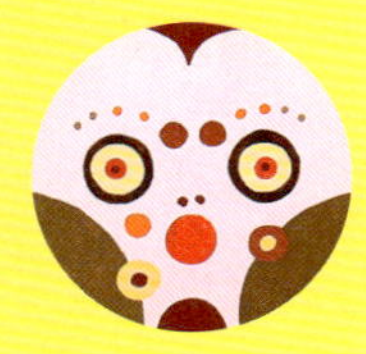

Storyteller—Jeff Francis
Child/Legal Expert—Hani Furstenberg
The Bearer of Bad News—Eli Gorenstein

Choir:

In the Living Room:

Mr. Table (doubling as the voice of the *Clerk*)—Hillel Benjamin Rosen
Mrs. Closet (doubling as the voice of the *Charwoman*)—Nadya Kucher
Mrs. Lamp (the voice of *Grete*)—Yifeat Ziv
Mr. Ball (the voice of the *Father*)—Yiftach Mizrahi
Mr. Chair (the voice of the *Lodger*)/Female Announcer—Ayelet Robinson
Mrs. Chair (doubling as the voice of the *Mother*)—Orna Katz
Titorelli's Painting—Yum Umi

In the Bedroom:

Ms. Left Pillow—Ayelet Robinson
Ms. Right Pillow—Nadya Kucher
Ms. Blanket—Yifeat Ziv
Mr. Bed—Hillel Benjamin Rosen
Mr. Ball—Yiftach Mizrahi
Ms. Light Blue Blanket—Yum Umi
Ms. Pink Blanket—Orna Katz

Toy Orchestra Players

PROLOGUE

SCENE 1—IN THE MAGICAL STORY HOUSE

The Storyteller and the Child are seated at the table, on which the book awaits. Inside many of the objects in the room are actors whose faces (painted to match the objects) are visible through holes; they are Mr. and Mrs. Chair, Mrs. Lamp, the painting on the wall (aka "Titorelli"), and the other members of the Choir.

Storyteller: Good morning.
Child [with a shy hand wave]: Hi.
Storyteller: Do you remember what we planned to do today?
Child: Ah-ha.
Storyteller: Today, for the first time ... [waits for the Child to complete the sentence].
Child: Ah-ha.
Storyteller: ... Do you remember why?
Child: Ah-ha.
Storyteller: ... Why we are all excited? [Pause] We're excited because we'll start reading the stories of ...
Child [after a pause]: Ah-ha.
Storyteller [gently]: You can say the name, sweetie.
Child [hardly believing her good fortune]: I can?
Storyteller: Go on, tell all of our friends in the magical story house [gestures around], and even our friends outside, like the farmers, and the doctors ...
Child: ... and the stones, and the pilots, and the midgets, and the mice, and the windows, and the doors, and the stones ...
Storyteller: ... and the children, and the legal experts—tell them all that we are going to read one of the astonishing, funny, and sometimes scary [performs a cheerful "shivers" gesture] stories of ...
Child [quietly]: Fr-hanz Kar-fka. [Musical emphasis.]
Storyteller: Franz Kafka! For many years Franz Kafka brought great happiness and pleasure to grown-ups, and now it is time for kids to share in the fun too. And we will start today with one of Kafka's most famous tales. It has some funny moments, and it has some weird moments, and it has some *scary* moments [they both do the "shivers" gesture], but in the end it has ...

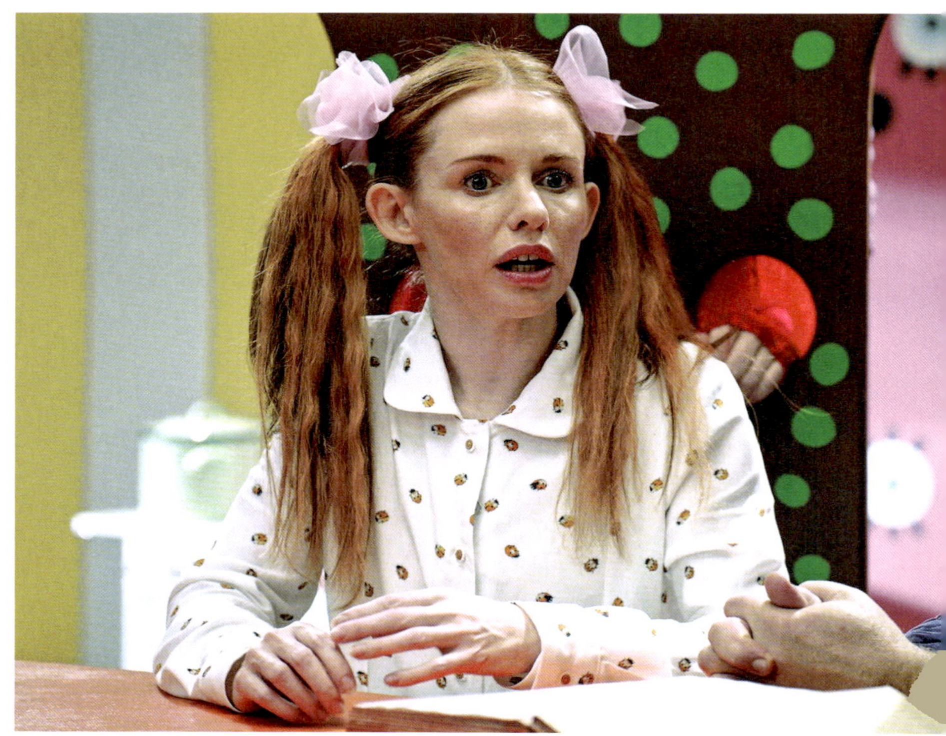

Child [hesitantly]: A *happy* end?

Storyteller: That's right. Like almost all of Kafka's stories, this lovely story has a happy end. [Opens the book.] ... And the name of the story is *The Metamorphosis.*

Child: The *what*?

Storyteller: It sounds like a difficult word, but it is really very simple: a metamorphosis is, when something becomes something else. Do you understand?

Child: Oh, OK. Like, when an egg is boiled.

Storyteller [happily]: OK! Or ...?

Child: And then it is not wet inside anymore, you can hold it in your hand and eat it.

Storyteller: OK ... Can you think of another example of a metamorphosis?

Child: I once ate three boiled eggs. Three [raises four fingers]!

Storyteller: Very well ... but can you think of another metamorphosis?

Child [after a short pause]: When a pilot becomes a boiled egg [Pause]. Or when a farmer dies.

Storyteller [cheerfully]: OK, then. A metamorphosis! Without further ado, let us begin.

Opening "Kafka for Kids" Theme Song

A cheerful tune performed by the Choir as letters of the Kafka Alphabet dance, fill the screen, and finally create the film's title.

Ka, Ka,
Ka, Ka,
Ka Ka,
Ka ka ka ka!

Ka, Ka,
Ka, Ka,
Ka Ka,
Ka ka ka ka!

Ka-*Wo!* Ka-*We!* Ka-*Boom!*
Ka ka ka ka!
Ka-*Oh!* Ka-*Oi!* Ka-*Ooh*!
Ka ka ka ka!

It's Kafka,
Kafka for kids.

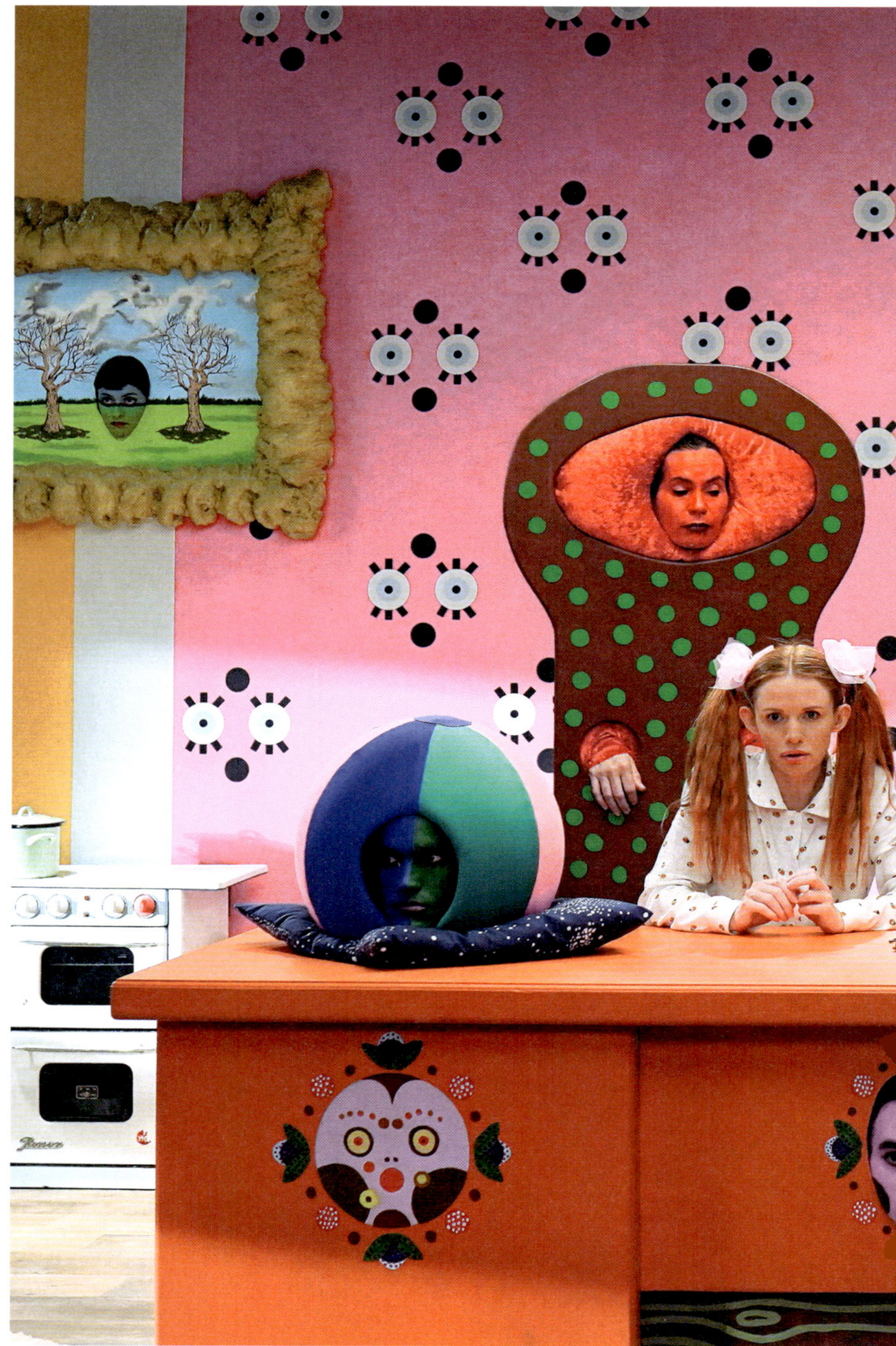

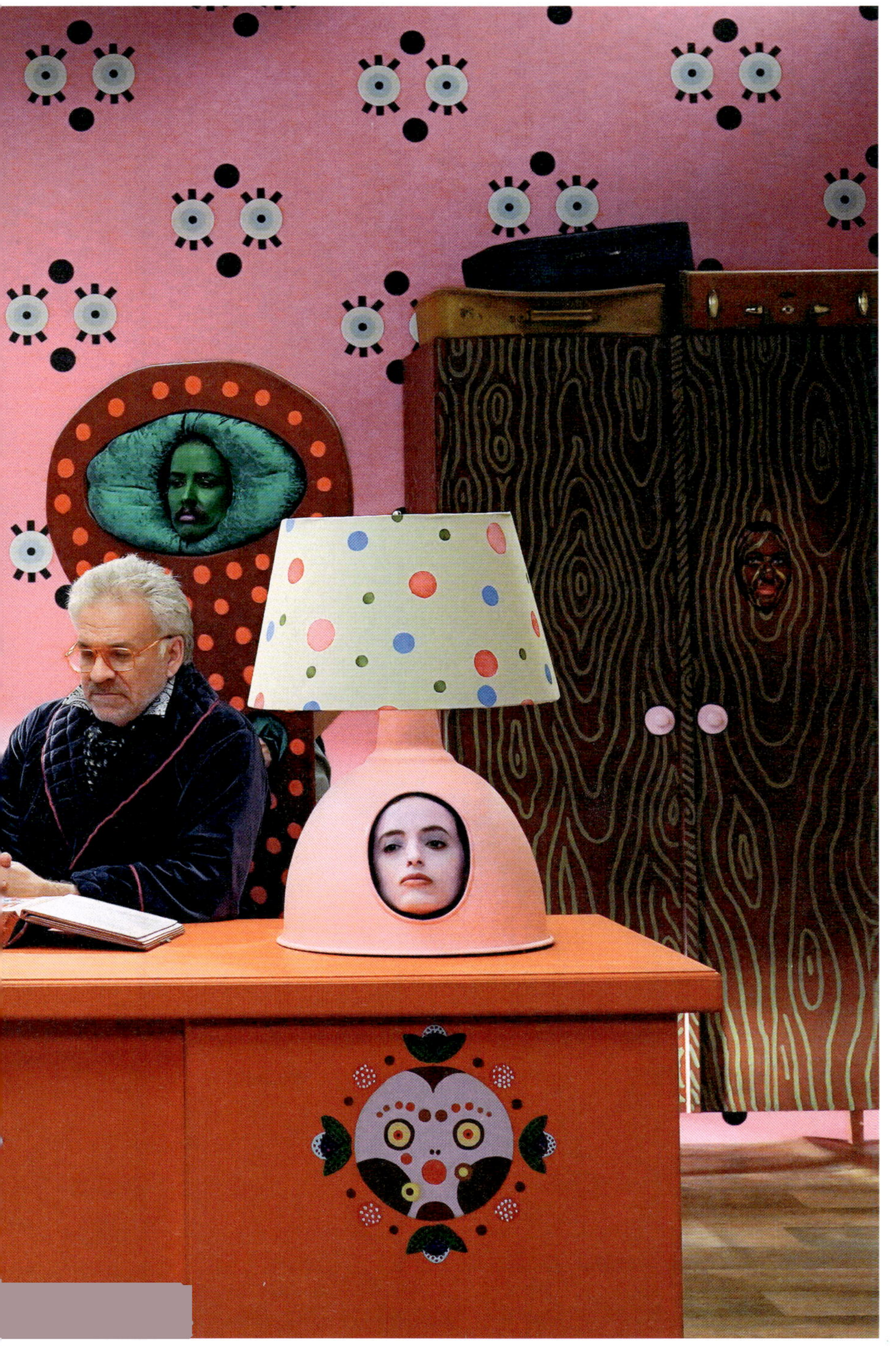

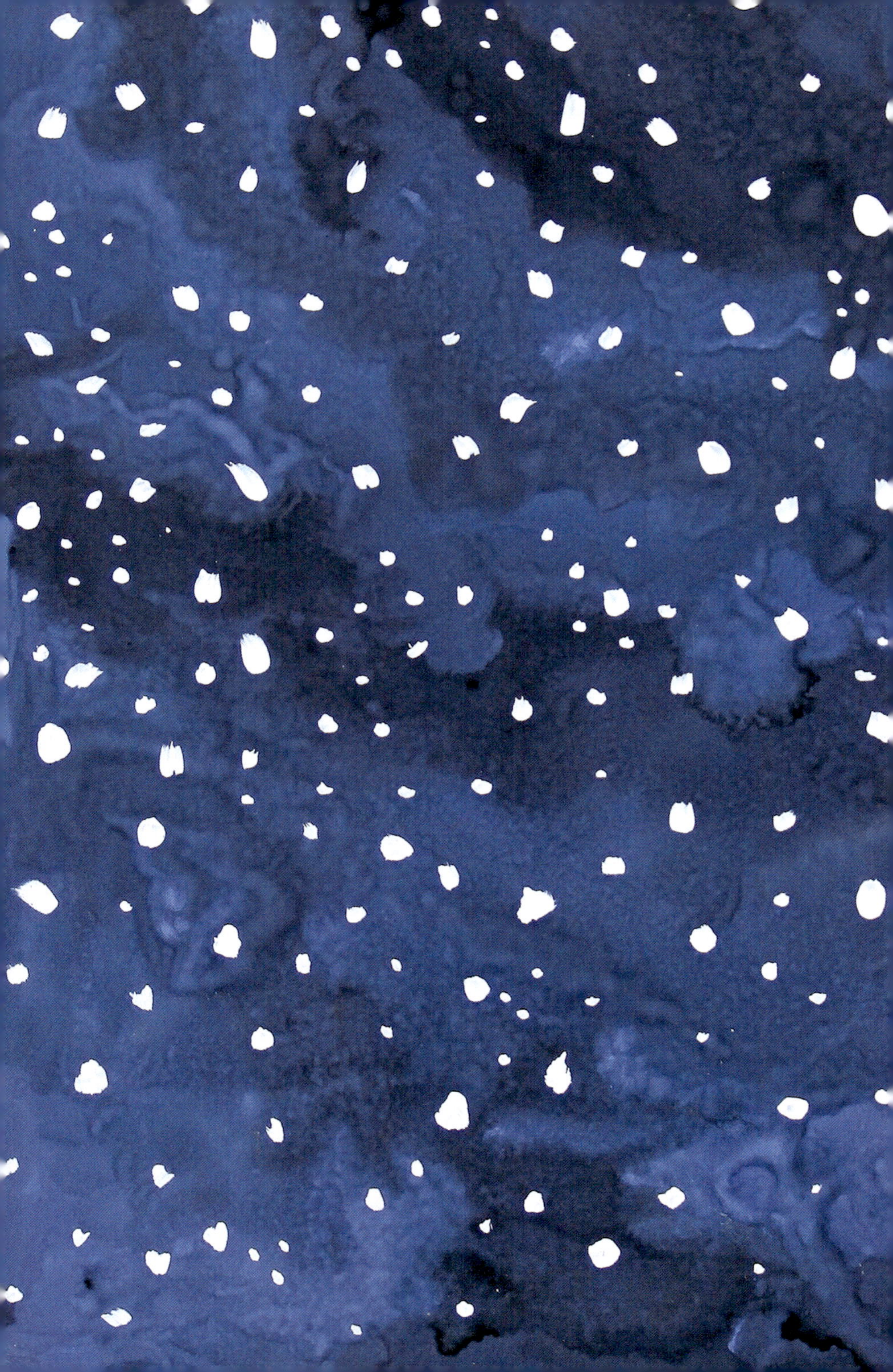

CHAPTER

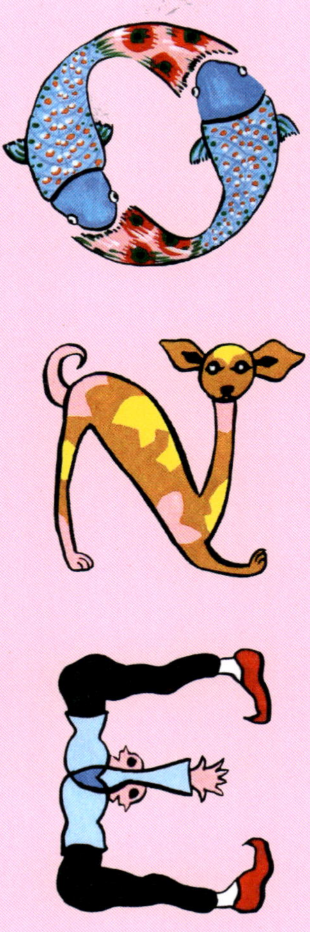

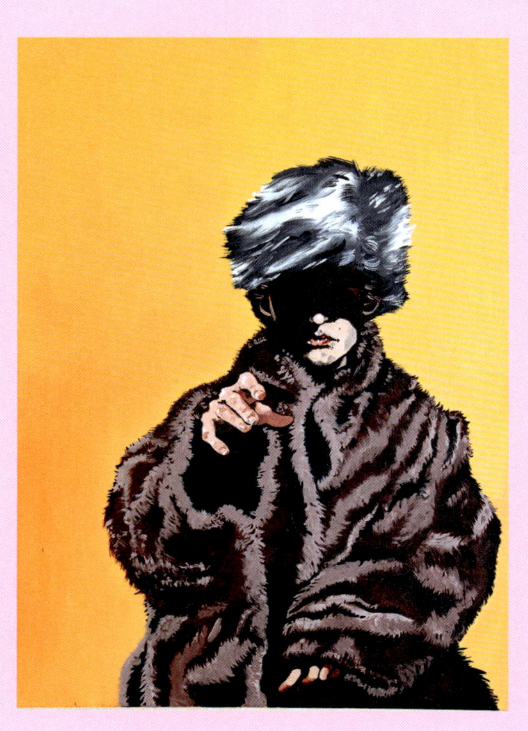

SCENE 2—WAKING UP

A painted pattern appears on the screen; the camera pans left slowly; the music stops as the Storyteller proceeds.

Storyteller: One morning, a man, whose name was Gregor Samsa, woke from his dream and found that he had changed into a gigantic insect. [The pattern is revealed to belong to the quilt covering Gregor's body, and the camera now shows his face.]

Child [delighted]: I wish *I* could change into a gigantic insect!

Storyteller: Well, at first Gregor thought he was just dreaming, but it was not a dream. [Animation: the camera zooms out from Gregor's face to arrive at a long shot of the bed, as well as the walls and the floor of the room. A continuous pan to the left will provide a 360-degree continuous tour of the room's four walls, showing details corresponding to the narration.] "Perhaps if I could sleep a little more," Gregor thought, "I'll wake up again and everything will be as it was. This getting up early makes one pretty stupid."

Child [giggling]: "Stupid ..."

Storyteller: ... But it was not to be. Gregor looked out the window and saw that it was light out. He looked at the alarm clock on the chest and was amazed: he had set it to four, and it was already six-thirty! [The alarm clock is shown.] Gregor was a busy traveling salesman. He had to wake up early each morning and work hard because his father owed lots of money to the chief of his office, and he had to pay it all back. Samples of the fabrics he was selling were on his desk. And above the desk, there was a photo of a beautiful woman in furs extending her arm. Gregor liked it so much he made her frame all by himself [the pan halts for a moment as the camera lingers on the picture]. But it was so late! The chief of his office will be worried and send someone over to check on him. He had to hurry up. And Gregor was also very hungry. [The pan completed, the insect is seen again; the quilt is now on the floor.] And—his belly was itching. Then he heard his mother calling from the other room.

Mother (Mrs. Chair) [Intercuts between the closed, white double door and Gregor]: "Gregor? It's quarter to seven. You have a train to catch."

Storyteller [as Gregor]: "Thank you, Mother, I am getting up now." [With his normal voice]: Then he heard his father.

Father (Mr. Ball) [same door intercut]: "Gregor! What is wrong with you?"

Storyteller: ... And his sister joined in, from behind the other door.

Grete (Mrs. Lamp) [second door intercuts with Gregor]: "Gregor? Are you well? Do you need anything?"

Storyteller [Gregor's voice]: "I'm almost ready!" [Normal voice]: He really had to turn over and get out of bed. But how do insects roll over?

SCENE 3—GETTING OUT OF BED

Animation: Gregor is rocking and rolling; the movement is highly repetitive and simple except for the twitching of his eight legs which is somewhat more complex. A 2/4 rhythm; musical instruments and voices join in a crescendo.

Storyteller: Gregor rolled from side to side—one, two!
Again, he rolled and tried to turn—
Storyteller and Child: One, two!
Storyteller: Rocking, rocking all his body—
Storyteller and Child [with more enthusiasm]: One, two!
Mr. and Mrs. Chair [shown for the first time behind the reclined backs of the Child and the Storyteller]: Keep on dancing, dirty darling!—
Storyteller, Child, and Chairs: One, two!
Mr. Ball and Mrs. Lamp: Keep on rocking, creepy-crawly—
Storyteller, Child, Chairs, Mr. Ball, and Mrs. Lamp: One, two!
Mrs. Closet and Titorelli: Hurry up, the clock calls seven—
Storyteller, Child, and Full Choir: One, two!
Mr. Ball and Mrs. Lamp: This is fun; it's like a game.
Storyteller, Child, and Choir: One, two!
Mr. and Mrs. Chair: Rocking, rolling, battle beetle—
Storyteller, Child, and Choir: One, two!
Mr. Table: Careful not to crush your feelers—
Storyteller, Child, and Choir [enthusiastically; bell rings now accentuate the words]: One, two!
Storyteller [responding to the ring]: Oh, no! The doorbell's ringing!
Choir: Oh, no! Who's there?
Storyteller: Go, go, one more push—

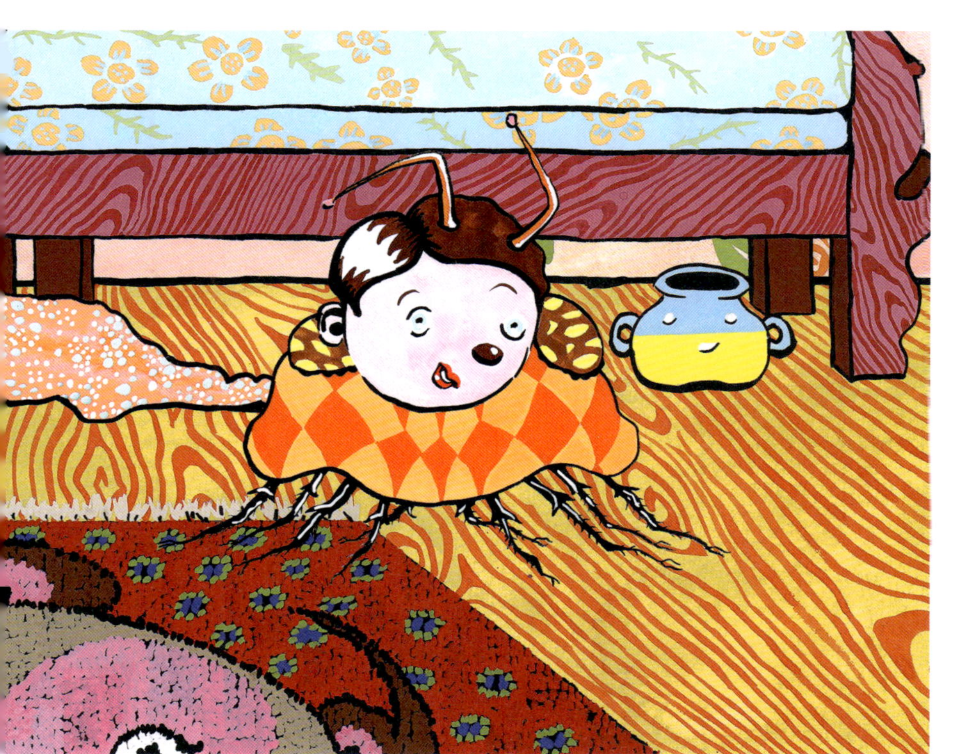

Storyteller, Child, and Entire Choir: One, one!

Storyteller [as the music stops]: And *PATOOF!* Gregor swung straight out of bed! But just as Gregor landed on the floor, he heard the voice of the Super-Clerk who was sent by the chief of the office to see why Gregor was so late.

Mr. Table: There was something falling down in there, in Gregor Samsa's locked room. [Pause. A ring is heard again.]

Mrs. Closet: Oh, no—the Super-Clerk is here! [Another, more insistent ring.]

Titorelli: Oh, dear me—the Super-Clerk is here!

Child [puzzled]: The door again? But the Super-Clerk is inside! He heard the animal falling from the bed. [Another ring.] So who is ringing?

Choir: It is him, him, him! Stop the story!

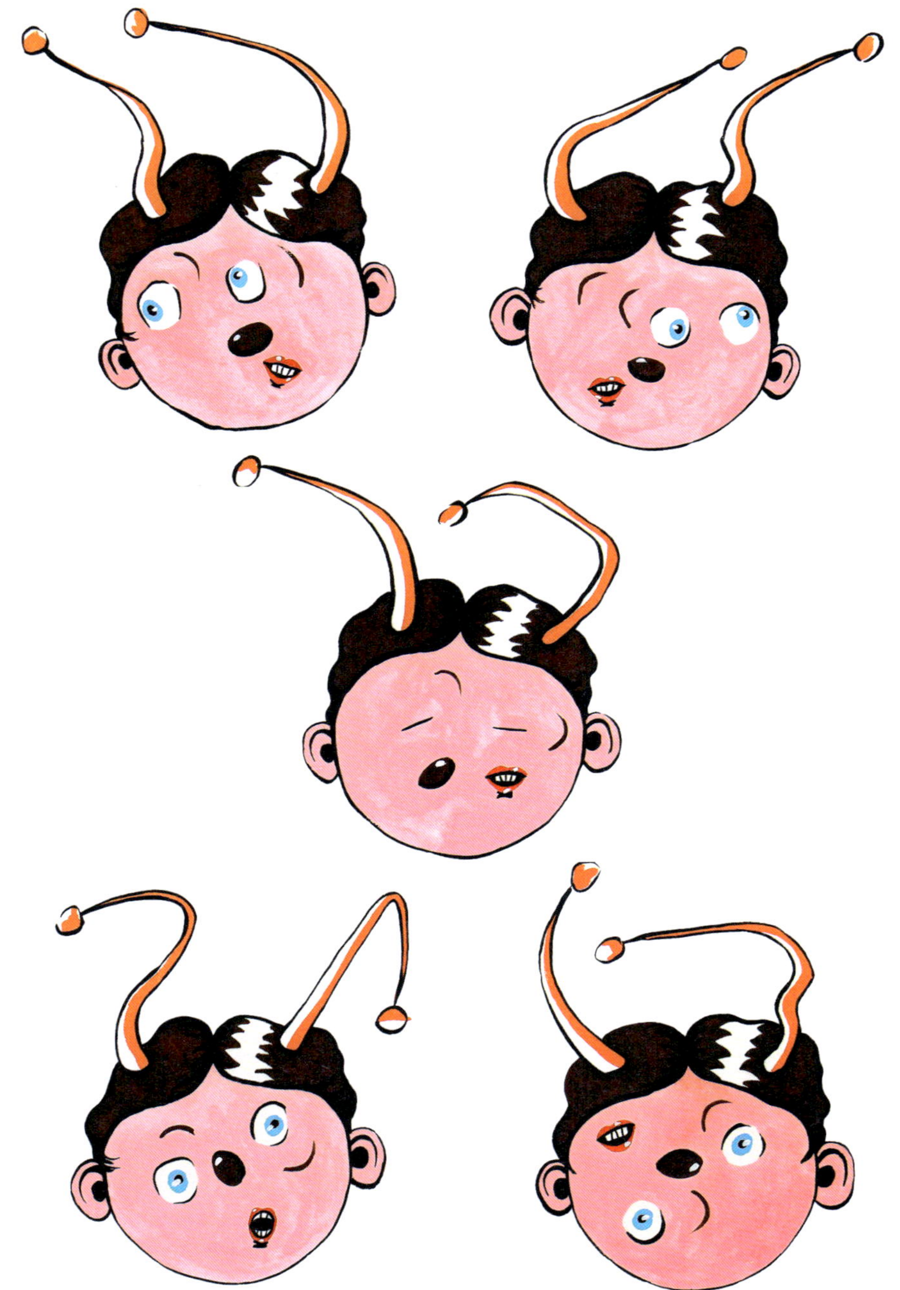

Child: Who? Who? Who?

Choir: It's The Bearer of Bad News! [The *Bearer of Bad News Song* plays as he enters wearing a doctor's white robe, with a stethoscope as well as a hammer and a pair of pliers hanging from his neck.]

SCENE 4—THE BEARER OF BAD NEWS

Bearer of Bad News Song

The red bikes that Becky wanted,
Will not be her gift this year,
And in the car crash now reported,
Her sister lost her cellphone, and her daddy lost his ear.

Doris—you'll be ditched by Alice,
Lonely Lee—you'll get no mail.
Kindness shall be met with malice,
And little brother Abed—will stay a year in jail.

I am the saddest of the sad:
The news I bear is always bad!
[Choir]:
He is the reason we are scared,
The news he bears is always bad!

I wish I could skip work,
And stay all day in bed.
[Choir]:
We wish he could skip work,
And let us stay in bed.

Look at happy Mrs. Taylor,
Smiling gaily by her window,
As I tell Eve Katz, her neighbor,
Mister Katz dropped dead, and she is now a widow.

But Mrs. Taylor smiles no more,
No schadenfreude and no humor,

When I knock on *her* front door,
To tell her that her tiny lump, is actually a deadly tumor.

I cry all day, I cry a lot,
My dismal job, my lousy lot!
[Choir]:
We cry all day, we cry a lot,
As he reveals our awful lots.

I wish for once I could amuse,
Both Mrs. Katz and Mrs. Taylor.
[Choir]:
Run away, dear Mrs. Taylor,
It's the Bearer of Bad News!

The Bearer of Bad News!
The Bearer of Bad News!

The Bearer: Good day, kids. I hope you are enjoying the story. I am so sorry to be the bearer of bad news, but as you know, I *am* the Bearer of Bad News.

Child: Ah-ha.

Storyteller: We know, and we love you just the same.

Child: Ah-ha.

The Bearer: Thank you. That means so much to me.
[They hug. The Bearer wipes his tears and blows his nose.]

Storyteller [smiling emphatically]: And what is the bad news that you bring us today?

The Bearer: I'm afraid the bad news is very bad. [Pause] We may have to stop the story and cancel the program!

Child: Stop the story? No! No!

Choir [sounding quite happy]: Cancel the program! Yes! Yes!

Child: Cancel the story? Why? Why? We've only just begun!
[She performs a little rage Ur-dance in a circle].

The Bearer: I know. I feel the same way. [Sings, as if to himself, and is answered faintly by Titorelli.] *I cry all day, I cry a lot, my dismal fate, my awful lot.*

Titorelli: We cry all day, we cry a lot, as he reveals our awful lots.

Storyteller: But what is the problem? Why will we need to stop the story?

The Bearer: You see, many years ago, when *The Metamorphosis* was printed as a book for the very first time, Kafka heard that there would be a picture on the cover, so he immediately wrote a letter to his publisher, Mr. Meyer [he pulls out of his pocket a piece of paper], and in this letter, Kafka writes [he reads]: "The insect itself must *not* be depicted. It cannot *even* be shown from a distance."[1]

Child and Choir: Oh no!

The Bearer: Oh, yes! Kafka himself prohibited *any* drawing of the insect, and in our program we have *many* drawings of the insect. It is clearly wrong, perhaps even illegal, to go against Kafka's wishes. One must never see how the insect looks. It's not just illegal, it's even bad, too! [Looks at his cellphone.] But excuse me ... I have to run. I have so many bad news, lots and lots of bad news, to deliver to other people. [Pretentiously] So, Adieu!

Storyteller [to the Child]: That means "goodbye." [The Bearer exits.]

Child and Storyteller: Adieu! [They wave their hands as the Bearer's theme is heard.]

Child: So what do we do? What do we do, what do we do? What do we do? What are we to do? What shall we do? What is to be done? *Chto delat?* What now? And how? We cannot have a story without pictures. We need to see what happens in the story! And we already saw the insect! Oh, my goodness, this is bad news. [Pause. Looks at her hands, thoughtful.]: I wonder if my hands belong to me. Are my hands on loan? Will I have to return my hands one day? [Looks at the Storyteller.]

Storyteller: I'll tell you what we need to do. The Bearer of Bad News is not our only friend. Do you know who we turn to in difficult moments, when problems are complicated?

Child and Choir: Who?

1 Franz Kafka, letter to Georg Heinrich Meyer, October 25, 1915, quoted in: Franz Kafka, *The Metamorphosis*, Norton Critical Edition, edited by Mark M. Anderson (letter translated by the editor) (New York: W. W. Norton & Company, 2014), 65.

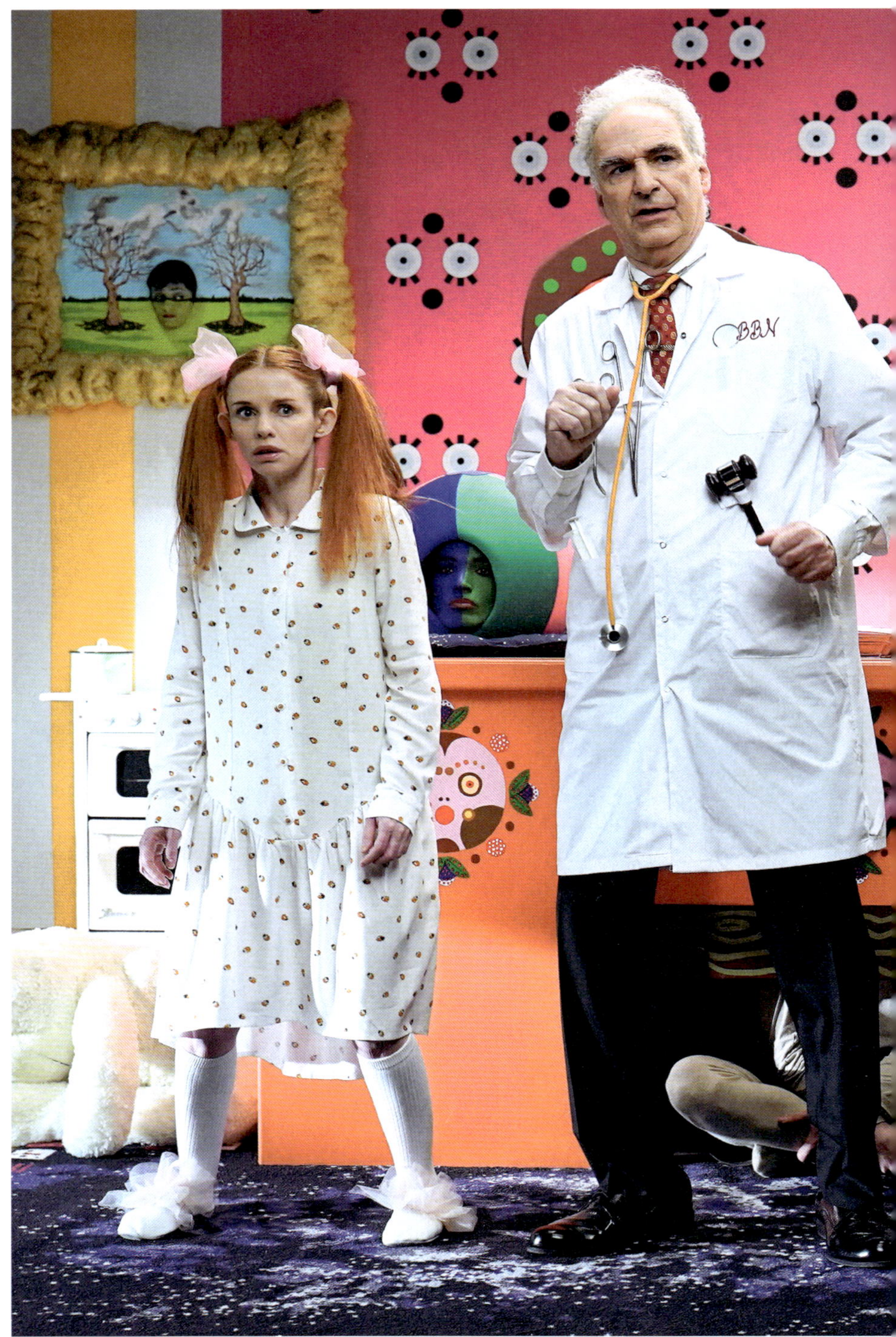
BBN

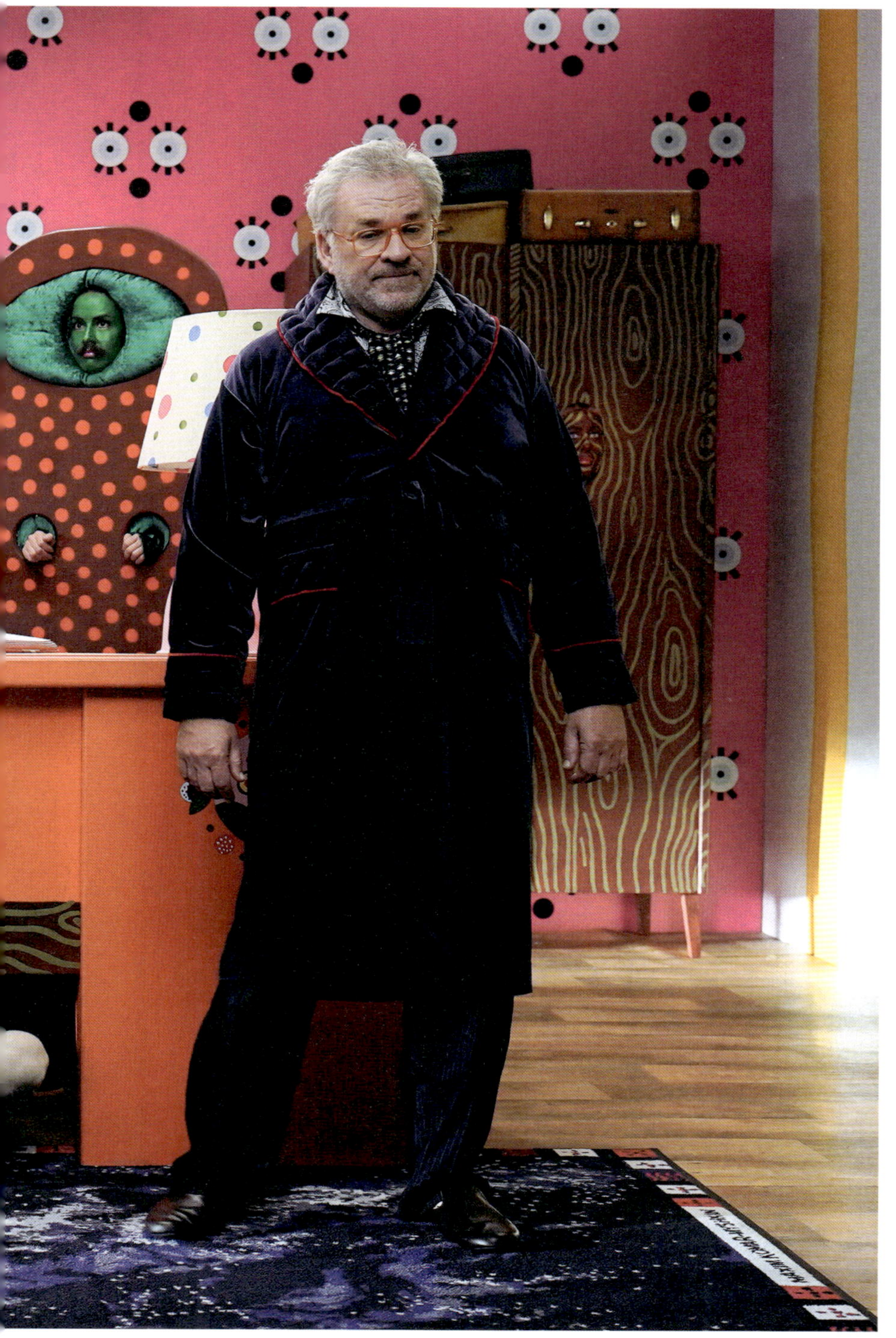

Storyteller: We seek the advice of our wisest friend, someone who was very, very, very close to Franz Kafka in real life. Who is it, that can find a way out even when all seems lost? Who is the smartest friend in our entire magic story house? Who knows the most, *especially* about Franz Kafka?

Child and Choir: Who? Who?

Storyteller [after a pause]: Our smartest, godlike friend is ... Kafka's shoe! [Child and Choir gasp as the Storyteller lifts from behind the desk a man's shoe. *Kafka's Shoe Song* starts.]

SCENE 5—KAFKA'S SHOE

Kafka's Shoe Song

Kafka's shoe, Kafka's shoe,
When trouble comes it's tried and true.

Kafka's shoe, Kafka's shoe,
It is a friend to me and you.

Kafka's shoe, you cunning Jew,
Tell me quickly what to do.

Shoe-Jew-Chew-Jew-Shoe-Do-Do,
Tell us quickly what to do.

Child: Is this really Kafka's shoe?

Storyteller: It sure is. It is a classic-cut left shoe, for the left foot. Kafka wore it and walked in it every day to his office, where he delighted in being a great legal expert. In fact—he was even a *Doctor of Law*.

Choir [astonished]: A doctor for the law?

Titorelli: Was he treating the law when the law was ill?

Storyteller: In a way, yes, that's exactly right, and he specialized in problems related to work accidents insurance. Kafka was a good and successful Doctor of Law, even though he was also a Jew ...

Choir: A Jew!

Storyteller: A Jew like his shoe ...

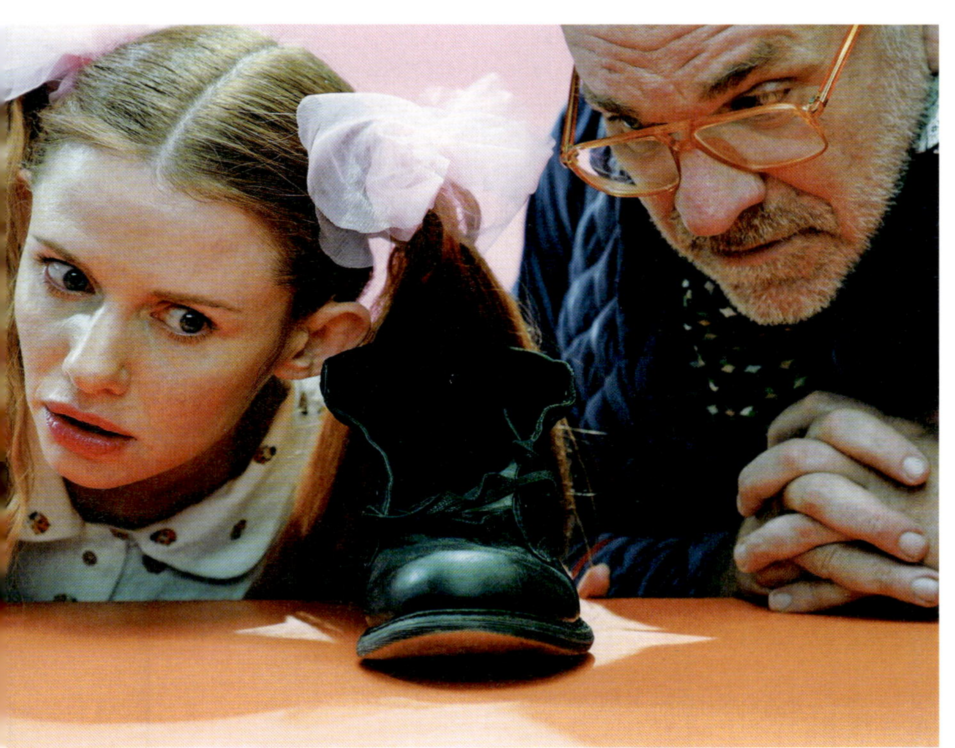

Choir: His shoe!

Storyteller: ... And business in those days was very restricted for shoes, I mean for Jews. Anyhow, Kafka loved this shoe dearly. It was almost a part of his body.

Child: It is so ... black.

Storyteller: Yes. It is a black shoe. [Pause.]

Child: Is it worth a lot of money?

Storyteller: A tremendous amount. [Child and Choir gasp.] Everything related to Kafka is very sellable. But we will *never* sell it.

Child: Can I ...

Storyteller: What, dear?

Child [shyly]: Can I smell Kafka's shoe?

Storyteller: Yes, you can. [Looks approvingly as the Child sniffs the shoe slowly and thoroughly.]

Child: It smells so good!

Storyteller: Yes it does, doesn't it? I think so too! What does the smell remind you of?

Child: I'm not sure. Schnitzel, perhaps?

Mrs. Chair: Yummy! Schnitzel! [She licks her lips.]

Child: Can I ... May I lick Kafka's shoe?

Storyteller [apprehensive]: No. You can smell Kafka's shoe, but you cannot lick it. At any rate—do you remember why we summoned Kafka's shoe?

Child [pause; it is difficult for her to articulate the issue, and she employs hand gestures as she thinks and speaks]: Ah-ha. Cockroach ... Picture ...

Storyteller: That's right! Kafka prohibited depicting the vermin, and we are afraid the show may have to be called off. And now we shall listen to Kafka's shoe very closely, and the shoe will tell us whether we can go on or not. [He holds the shoe between them. Tense music in the background. The camera zooms in.]

SCENE 6—LIVING ROOM SUITE

6A—PROBLEM SOLVED

The Storyteller and the Child are listening intently to the shoe. Tense background music. A smile glows on the Storyteller's face. The music stops.

Storyteller: Yes! Yes!

Choir: Hurrah! Hurrah! The shoe said yes!

Storyteller: Kafka's shoe permits us to freely use pictures of the vermin! As you remember, Father, Mother, and Sister Grete urged Gregor to open the door. The clerk was losing his patience and becoming upset—and so Gregor tried to speak and calm him down ...

6B—ANIMAL SPEECH SONG

In this song, Gregor's incomprehensible voice is represented by a dissonant, screeching string instrument. The words appear as if on a karaoke screen. Front view of Gregor, with his moving mouth shown intermittently with

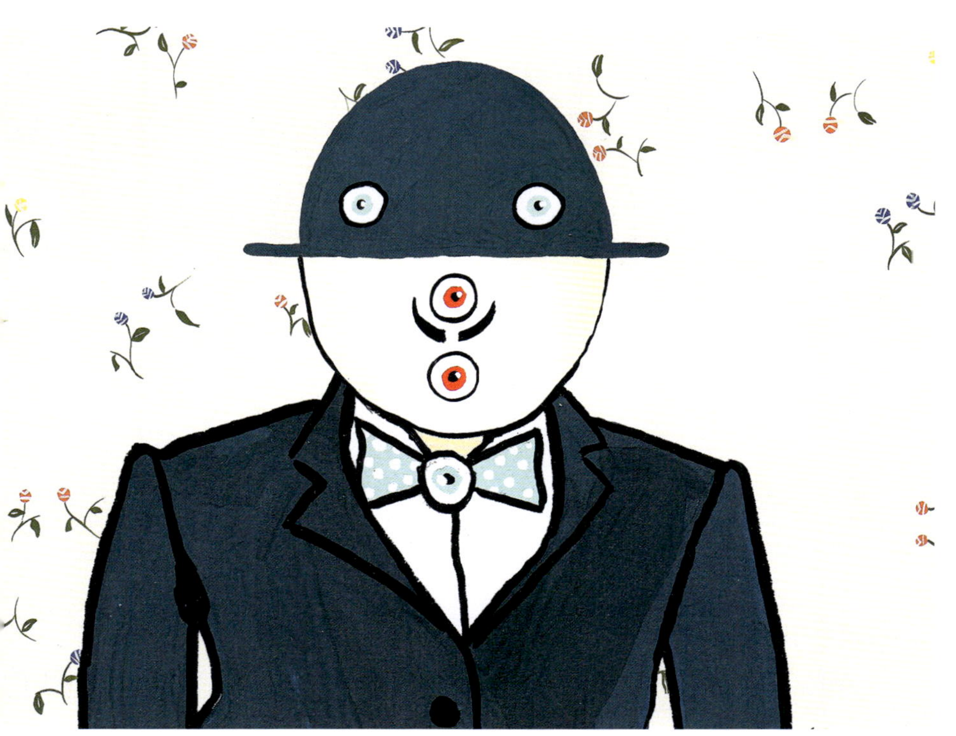

reaction shots of the Father, the Clerk, the Mother, and Grete.
Each time Gregor is shown, his facial features are differently assembled.

******, **** ***, * *** **** * ****** ***, * ****** *****,
(Please, Dear Sir, I was just a little ill, a little dizzy),
**** *** ** ** **** ** *******, ********, ********* *** *****,
(Soon I'll be my best of selves, upright, disposed, and fizzy),
** ****** **** ** ********, * ********,
(Be gentle with my parents, I implore),
**** *** ** ****** *** **** ** *** ****,
(Soon I'll be myself and open up the door),
** **** *** **** *** **** * **** ***** ** ****,
(Be kind and tell the boss I will delay no more),
**** *** ** ******, **** ** * *** ******.
(Soon I'll be myself, just as I was before).

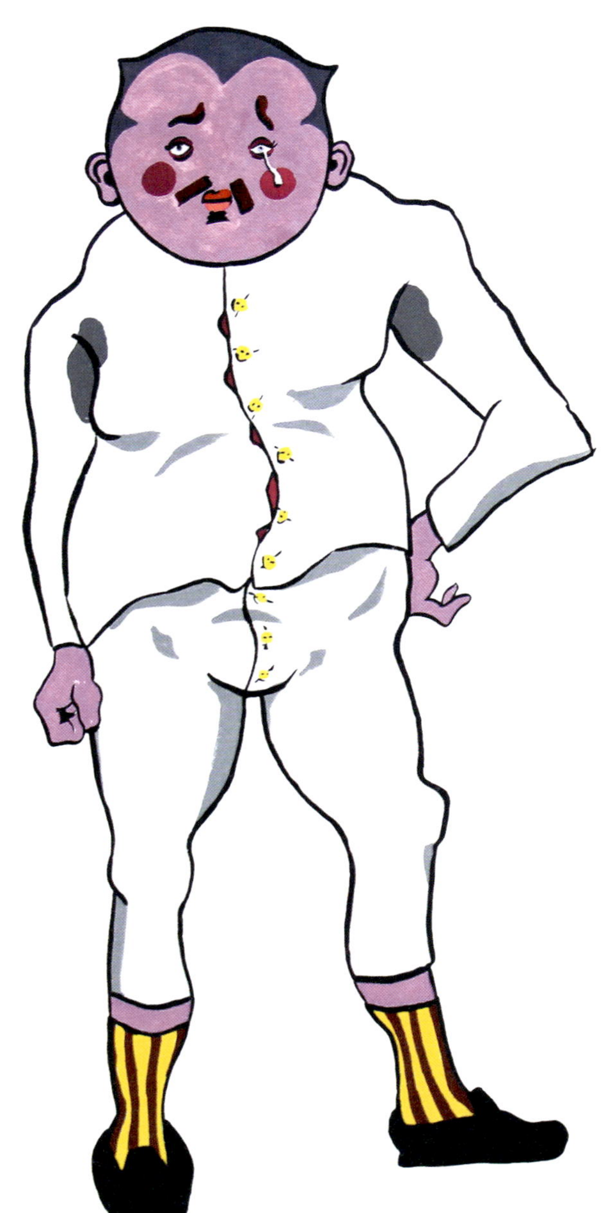

6C—GREGOR APPEARS

A different, dramatic melody evolves from the preceding song. View of the living room; Father, Mother, and the Super-Clerk frame Gregor's closed double door.

Clerk (Mr. Table): Did you get a single word?

Mother (Mrs. Chair): Dear God, he sounds ill! Grete, darling daughter!

Choir: Hurry, Grete! Hurry, Grete!

Grete (Mrs. Lamp) [from the right]: Mama? Mama?

Mother (Mrs. Chair): Hurry—fetch the doctor, quick!

Choir: Hurry—get the doctor, quick!

Father (Mr. Ball): His lock is stuck—Anna! Anna!

Choir: Hurry, low-paid maid—Anna! Anna!

Maidservant (Mrs. Closet) [from the right]: Master? Master?

Father (Mr. Ball): Hurry—fetch the locksmith, quick!

Choir: Hurry—fetch the locksmith, quick!

Maidservant and Grete: I go! I go! [Both girls enter the picture from right and make their way across until they exit left.]

Clerk (Mr. Table) [quiet and ominous]: He sounded like an animal. It is an animal's voice!

Choir [mockingly repeating the line by imitating Gregor's chirps]: ** ******* **** ** ******. **.**.**.******* *****.

Storyteller [recited]: ... Gregor strained to turn the key with his jaws. He tried so hard!

Choir: How hard?

Storyteller: So hard he hurt his mouth badly and brown juice began to flow, but finally he managed to open the door. [The white door slowly opens, the music maintains its tempo, but a diminuendo indicates the tension. Gregor peeps from between the doors. The music regains full force, with a melody echoing the "Kafka for Kids" theme song.]

Clerk (Mr. Table): Ka-Oh!

Mother (Mrs. Chair) [crying]: Ka-Ay!

Father (Mr. Ball) [shaking his fist]: Ka-Ooh!

Choir: Ka-Ah, Ka-Oi, Ka-Ooh!

Storyteller [Imitating Gregor's voice]: *** *** ** ***** *** *****, *** **** ***** ** ****.

(I'll put on pants and shirt, and will delay no more).

Storyteller: Gregor did not want to show his naked body ...
Child [giggles]: "Naked!"
Storyteller: ... but when he saw the clerk was about to leave, Gregor forgot his caution, and leaped out into the living room! [Gregor is fully revealed. The Super-Clerk, aghast, exits in a rush.]
Clerk: Ka- Oh! Oh! Oh!
Mother (Mrs. Chair): Ka Ay! Ay! Ay! [Mother leaps twice high up in the air, then collapses by the table. As she falls, her skirt flies up and her panties are revealed.]
Father (Mr. Ball): Ka-Ooh! Ka-Ooh! [Grabs a walking stick.]
Storyteller: Father tried to make Gregor retreat into his room. Gregor wanted to, but he was too afraid to turn and ...
Choir: Roaches cannot walk backwards!
Storyteller: But finally he did turn, and Papa delivered a mighty shove with the stick and sent Gregor flying into his room, bleeding profusely, the door was slammed shut, and everything was still at last.

End of Chapter 1

SCENE 7—FIRST ADVERTISEMENT BREAK

7A—FOOD

Top view of a plate of food. Ethereal music. A slow zoom provides an extreme close-up of the food's texture. Images of other foods are superimposed, creating an unidentifiable yet highly tactile mass.

Seductive female announcer: Mmmmmm ... This craving you almost always have, whenever your stomach is feeling healthy, to pile on *delicious* food—and dare to do terrible deeds. First, relish the label on an old, hard sausage; bite into it with all your teeth; mmmmm ... ahhhhh ... and now swallow quickly, regularly, and thoughtlessly, like a machine. Go ahead. Increase your haste. Shove the long slabs of raw rib meat into your mouth without even chewing, then pull it out again from behind, ripping it through your stomach and intestines. Cram yourself with herrings, pickles, and all the old, acrid foods. A hailstorm of bonbons pours into your mouth from tin boxes. You are

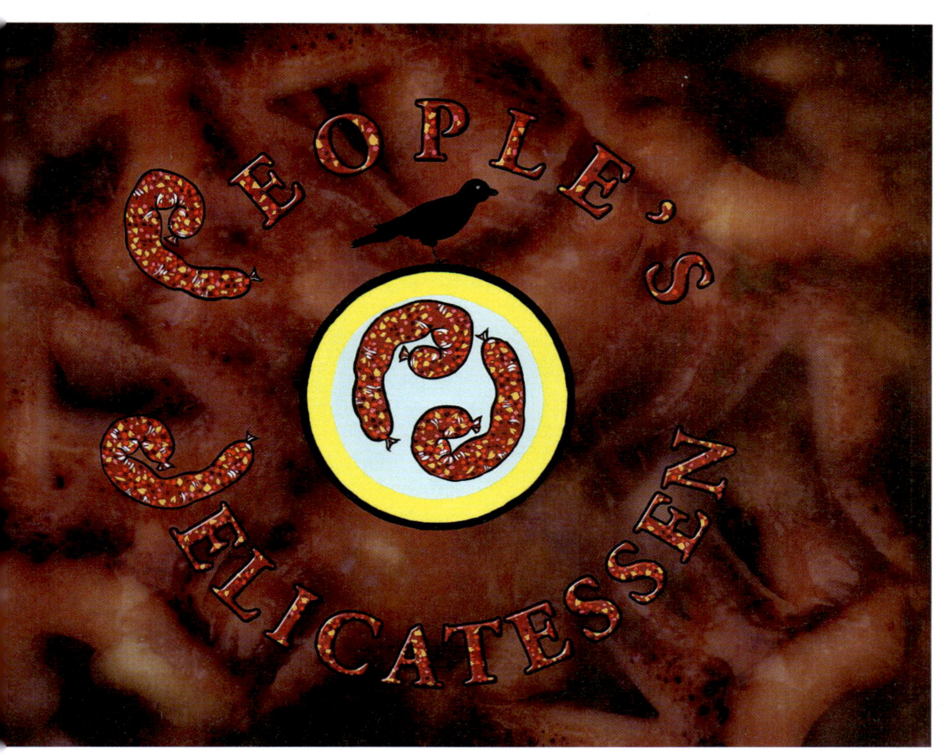

a good, tender child. Papa loves you! You deserve no less than *The People's Delicatessen*.[2]

7B—BOKI-POKI

Two cell animation: fast-tempo, rhythmic music accompanies the round-faced, crazy-happy Boki-Poki, who resembles the face on Gregor's carpet. Boki-Poki rolls his eyes, and sticks out his tongue, all to the rhythm of the music. The background displays a dizzying and constant flow of concentric rings whose colors blink in blinding combinations. Boki-Poki changes color as well.

2 Based on an entry in Kafka's diaries, October 30, 1911.

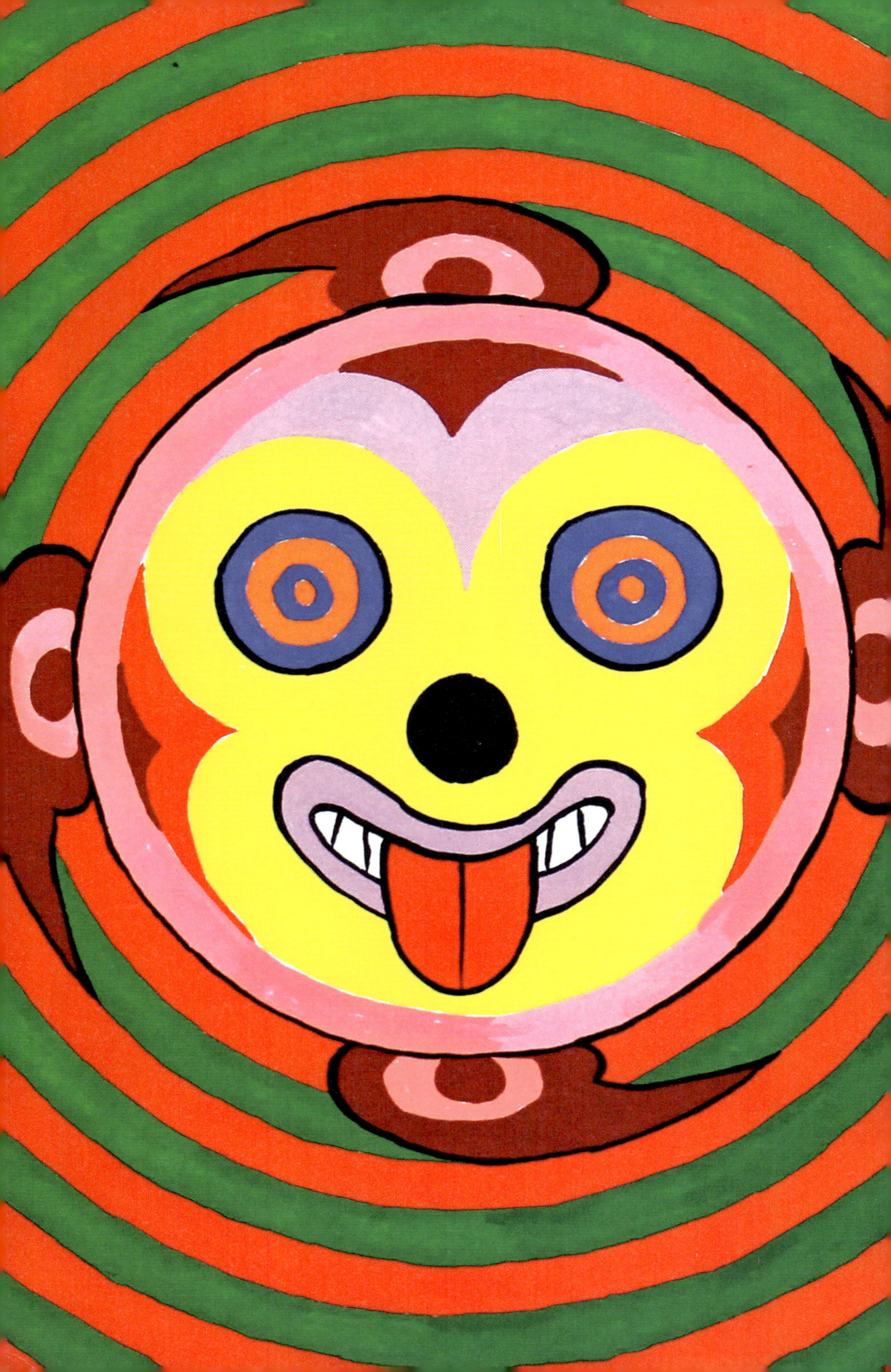

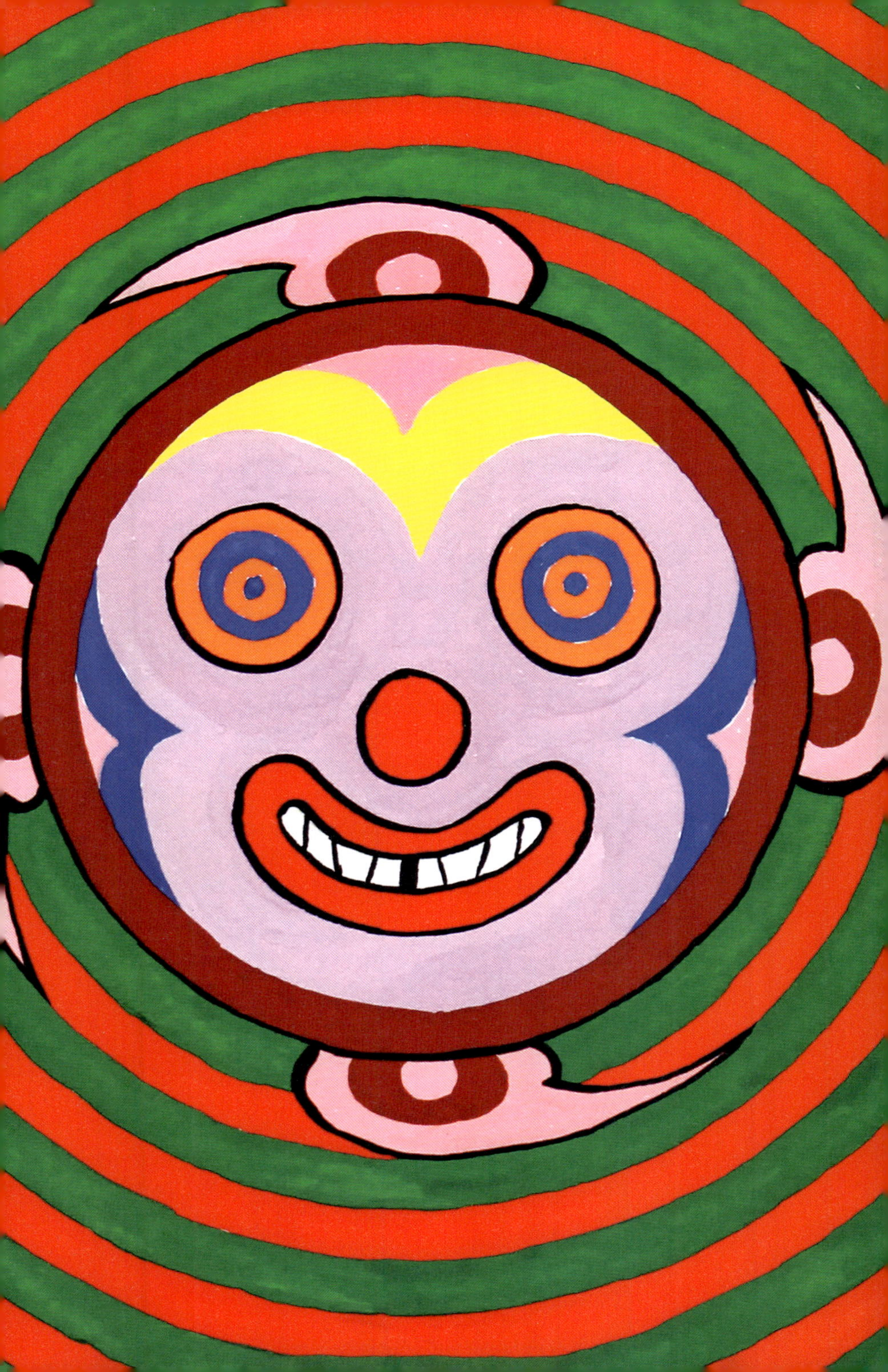

Choir [in unison, to the music's rhythm]: Boki-Poki! Boki-Poki! Boki-Poki! Boki-Poki! Boki-Poki! Boki-Poki! Boki-Poki! Boki-Poki! Boki-Poki!

A Happy Announcer: Tomorrow, on the best children's channel.

7C—COMING SOON TO *KAFKA FOR KIDS*: THE BUCKET RIDER[3]

Animation with intercuts of reaction shots of the Child, the Storyteller, and Choir Members.

Seductive Female Announcer: In an upcoming episode of *Kafka for Kids* ...

Storyteller: It was so cold! In search of coal, I straddled my bucket, my hands on the handle, the simplest kind of a bridle, and up, up, up my bucket ascended, flying magnificently in the skies!

Child [straddling a bucket, hands spread like wings, trying to move herself forward as she imitates flight]: Weeeeeeeee! Weeeeeee!

Choir [responding without enthusiasm]: Weeeeee! Weeeee!

Storyteller: I fly on my bucket in the freezing air until I float in front of the coal dealer's door and cry out: "Coal dealer! Coal dealer! Give me a little bit of coal! When I can, I'll pay you!"

Coal Dealer (Mr. Chair): Do I hear correctly? A customer!

Wife (Mrs. Closet): What's with you, husband? It's nothing! There's nothing there. Let's go to sleep.

Storyteller: But I am right here, and I am very cold. Please, please spare me some coal. [Jets of tears flow from the eyes of the rider. The "Kafka for Kids" theme song plays, and the program's logo fills the screen.]

3 Based on Franz Kafka, "The Bucket Rider," in *The Penal Colony*, translated by Willa and Edwin Muir (New York: Schocken Books, 1961), 184–7.

CHAPTER

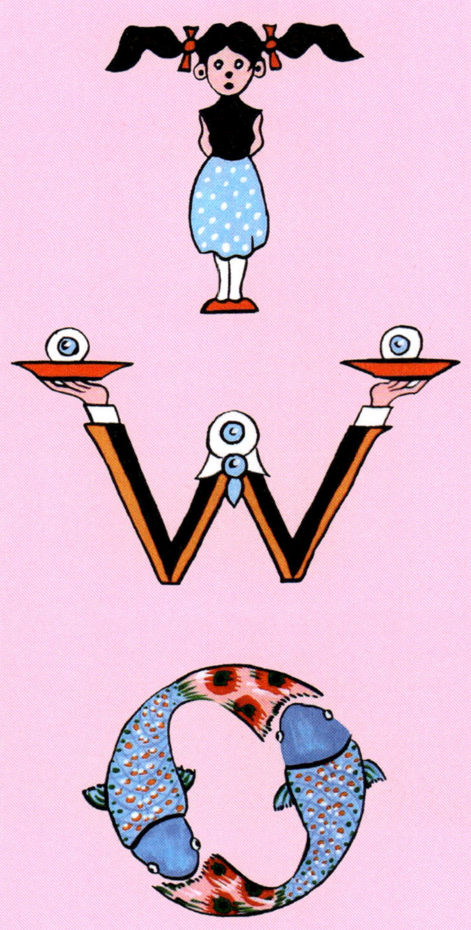

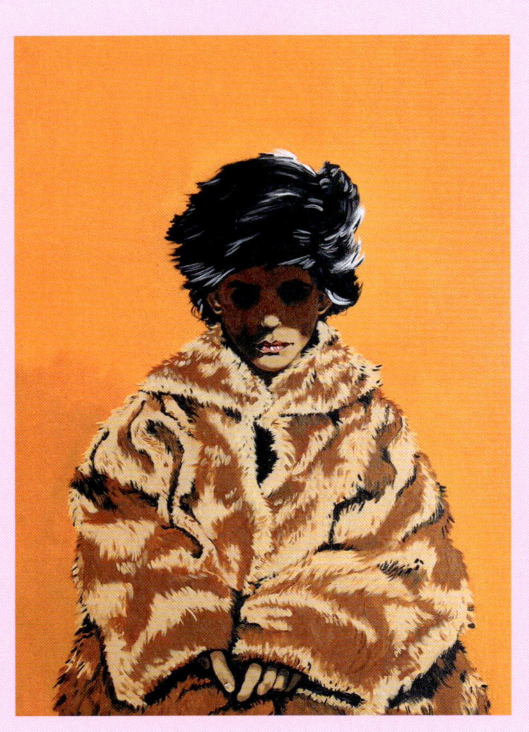

SCENE 8—GARBAGE BREAD

With a few adjustments, the story house living room is now a makeshift kitchen. Close-up of the Storyteller's hands as he kneads gooey dough. As the camera zooms out, it shows that the table is partially covered by a white tablecloth, half covering Mr. Table's face.

Storyteller: Aren't you happy that we finished the first chapter?

Child [distracted by the Storyteller's busy hands]: Ah-ha.

Storyteller: ... But also a bit sad? ...

Child [a short pause]: Ah-ha.

Storyteller: ... A bit sad because the story will soon be over ...

Child: Yes; I am sad because the story will be over.

Storyteller: But there is no reason to be sad, silly! Kafka wrote so many more stories! And I will read you all of them, each and every one!

Child: But you *wanted* me to say I am sad. [To herself, quietly:] This is such crap! [Back to staring at the dough:] What is that?

Storyteller: I am making a special garbage bread. You see, much of the second chapter is about food. Gregor was very hungry, and the only person who understood this was the one he loved most.

Titorelli: Who? Who?

Mrs. Lamp [as Grete, in a cloying manner]: His beautiful little sister, Grete.

Storyteller [kneads vigorously as he reads]: ... That's right, Grete was the one who finally dared come into the insect's room to give him food. Now, Gregor sensed that he was too disgusting to be seen, so he quickly hid underneath the sofa. Grete brought a bowl of his favorite drink—warm milk—and quickly left so that he could drink it in private, but as soon as the milk touched his jaws he was disgusted.

Choir: He didn't *like* warm milk!

Storyteller [stops kneading]: And so, the next evening—what did Grete place on the floor instead of milk?

Choir: What?

Storyteller: Grete left a whole selection of foods, arranged in a neat line, and then she quickly left and locked the door so that the insect could take his pick of the menu. [The Storyteller turns to a line of products that are now assembled on the tablecloth.] There were half-rotten vegetables, leftover bones in white goo sauce ... [The Storyteller scoops the sauce and adds it to the dough. Some of it spills over the face of Mr. Table, who is already disgruntled because of the tablecloth.]

Mr. Table [to himself, quietly]: This is such crap ... [to the entire world, angrily]: This is such crap!

Storyteller: ... Some raisins and almonds, a piece of moldy old cheese, a dry piece of old bread, a slice of buttered bread, and a slice of bread with butter and salt. Gregor immediately devoured the moldy cheese.

Choir [each responding with a different cry of delight]: Mmmmmm! Delicious! Yummy! Moldy! Oooooh!

Storyteller: Exaltation! And he gorged on the rotten vegetables as well. [The Storyteller adds the vegetables to his dough. The size of the dough-ball becomes visibly larger.]

Choir [in unison]: Mmmmmmm! Delicious, cram yourself!

Storyteller: ... And Gregor also loved the nasty old sauce.

Choir: Mmmmmm! Ahhhhhh!

Storyteller: The fresh food, on the other hand, was utterly repulsive to Gregor.

Titorelli [the painting chews vigorously then spews out a chunk of food with an expression of repulsion]: Fresh food—God, save us all!

Storyteller: And now it's time to put our dough in our magical story-house super-speed turbo oven [he puts the dough in the oven]. Gregor was really full. His belly was swollen. [Animation: Gregor's belly is swelling up to the point that most of his legs have to be fully stretched to reach the floor, while the shorter ones dangle in mid-air.] Gregor was so fat that when he heard Grete turning the key, he barely managed to cram himself underneath the sofa.

Mr. Chair: *Now* Grete knew exactly what he liked, and she came every day to feed him.

Mrs. Chair [addressing the Child]: So sweet, that little Grete—just like you!

Choir: Just like you!

Child [looks around at the Choir]: Like me?! How so?

Mr. Ball: Well, she was also a little child.

Mrs. Closet: Pretty but fragile ...

Titorelli: Happy yet sensitive ...

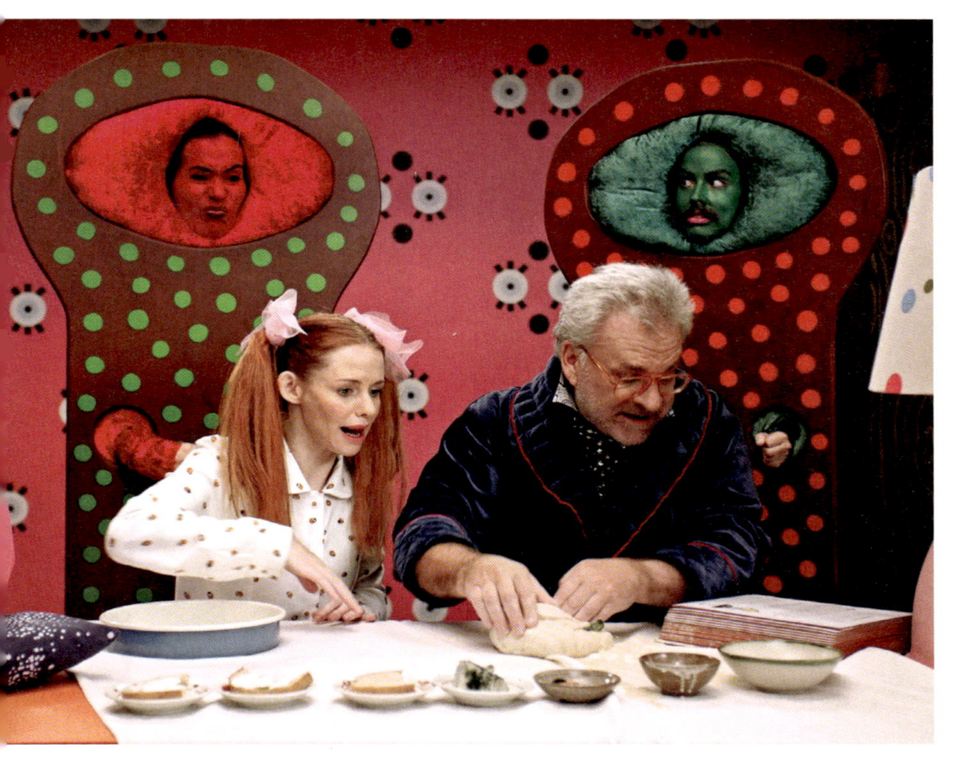

Mrs. Lamp: Gifted but confused ...
Mr. Ball: Short but not too short—
Choir: A child! A child!
Chair: Only seventeen!
Child: Wait, what? *Seventeen*? Seventeen is still a child?
[Song begins.]

SCENE 9—WHAT IS A CHILD?

A gentle waltz. The Child seems to fall asleep during the last verse. Animation: During the instrumental breaks of the song, Grete appears three times: first, her full body hovering romantically in the skies; second, a close up of her face, with the triple pupil circles in each eye moving slowly, as in an old screen saver; third, one eye ball fills the entire screen with the same screen-saver-like movement.

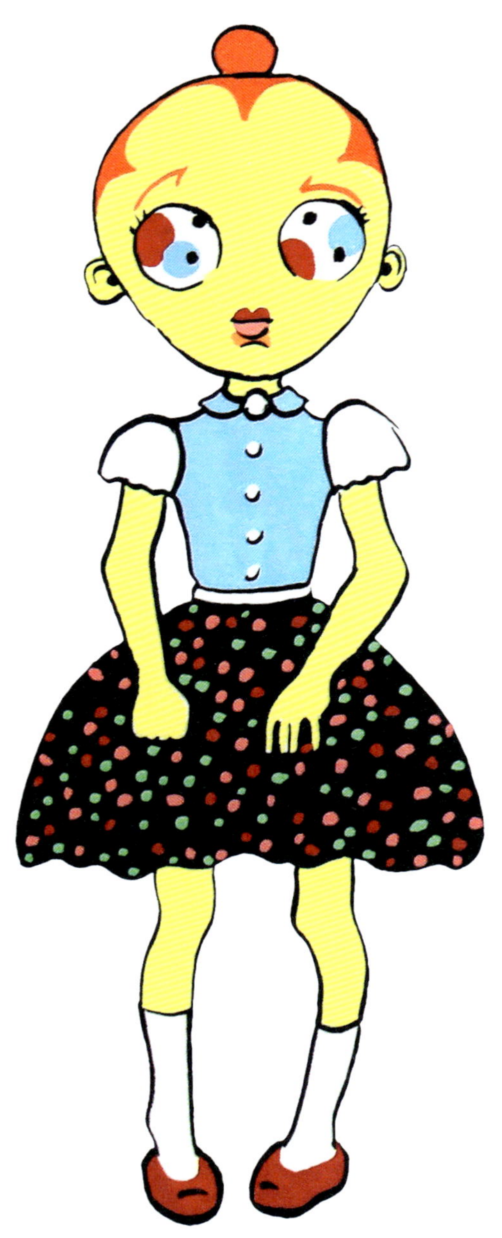

What is a child? What is a child? The smell is sweet and clean,
Perhaps one day she'll practice law and play the violin.

What is a child? What is a child? It's really hard to tell.
A child is ever growing, but only for a spell.

Till when a child? Till when a child? Seven? Twelve? Fourteen?
When will it flip from plump and pink to wrinkled aubergine?

A child is happy promises of futures spread ahead,
A treasure box inside of which lies someone old, then dead.

SCENE 10—ROUTINE, MONEY

An alarm bell startles the sleeping Child.

Storyteller: The bread is ready! [He takes out of the oven a perfect, appetizing loaf of bread. He happily tears off a chunk, bites, and spits it out immediately.] This is nasty, rotten crap! [Different Choir and Orchestra members are shown spitting out the bread.] And so, the days passed. Gregor would eagerly eavesdrop on the family's conversations in the other room, and had some happy surprises. Before, when he was still a man, he thought that his father had lost his entire fortune, and that the money Gregor provided was speedily spent each month. But now he learned that his father had some savings stashed away, and that there was also interest on this money.

Mr. Ball: An interest is a reward that people with money get for having money, and the reward is more money.

Storyteller: It was not a fortune by any means; Mother, Father, and Grete all had to work now, but, still, things were not half bad! They found nice jobs: Mother sewing dresses, and Father—[animation of the Father] he became a bank porter.

Choir: A bank porter! [A small smile appears on Father's sullen face, then vanishes immediately.]

Storyteller: ... and had a beautiful uniform ...

Choir: A uniform!

Storyteller: ... with golden buttons ...

Choir: Gold!

Titorelli: Gold! I am going to faint! Hold me! I may fall off the wall!

Storyteller: Now that Father had such magnificent uniform, he never, ever took it off. Yes, there were exciting changes in the family. But no less exciting were the changes Gregor himself was undergoing. And he was still evolving.

[*The Merry Vermin Song* begins.]

SCENE 11—THE MERRY VERMIN SONG

This song is accompanied by dynamic animation that is startlingly different from the lethargic animation shown thus far. Gregor is dancing and swirling on the walls, leaving behind him green trails. These green lines assume rhythmic and abstract changes, and Gregor's own body multiplies, elastically convulses, and changes into abstract, dancing shapes to the rhythm of the music. The Sister's puke mentioned in the lyrics is also integrated as an abstract painterly element in this sequence, as are nostril-like black ovals, sardines, and other elements; but the main recurring figure is that of Gregor on the wall, scuttering in circles with great speed.

[Gregor]:
When Sister smells my smell, she feels repelled, she wants to puke,
I smell like poo, unclean latrines, and soggy, green sardines.
Her disgust is impolite, but I keep still, I don't rebuke,
For in the kingdom of the smell I am the reeking king.

[Choir]:
He is a very merry vermin,
Merry, merry, very vermin,
We are green with envy,
Of the sniffing reeking king.

[Gregor]:
When little Sister saw me, she turned green and nearly fainted,
And while I'm seeing less and less, I'm smelling more and more.
And I don't mind becoming blind, for sight is overrated,
Stench is a sincere embrace, vision a cheating whore.

[Choir]:
He is a very merry vermin,
Merry, merry, very vermin,
Myopia is a blessing,
There's nothing much to see.

[Gregor]:
I'm dancing freely on the walls, I'm hanging lightly from the ceiling,
I leave behind thin sticky trails of greenish liquid muck.
She gags, but maybe it's a jealousy that steers her sickly feeling,
Her eyes are set so high—but on the floor she's stuck.

[Choir]:
He is a very merry vermin,
Merry, merry, very vermin,
He freely rises, lightly soars,
While we are prim and stuck.

SCENE 12—FURNITURE

Storyteller: Gregor's room was now *so* slimy. Grete came in as little as possible, and whenever she did she immediately rushed to open the window. She noticed, of course, Gregor's crisscrossing green trails on the floor and on the ceiling.

Titorelli [shouts]: Nasty! Nasty!

Child [shaking her finger at Titorelli]: Titorelli, hush!

Storyteller: ... And so, Grete thought: why not remove some of the furniture from Gregor's room so that he will have more room to move about, especially the big pieces, such as the desk and the wardrobe?

Mr. and Mrs. Chair: An insect does not need chairs!

Mr. Table: A millipede doesn't need a desk!

Mrs. Cabinet: A cockroach doesn't need a closet!

Mr. Ball: A beetle doesn't need a wardrobe, or even a ball.

Titorelli: Shitty shit beetle!

Choir [except Titorelli]: Titorelli, hush!

Mr. and Mrs. Chair: What language!

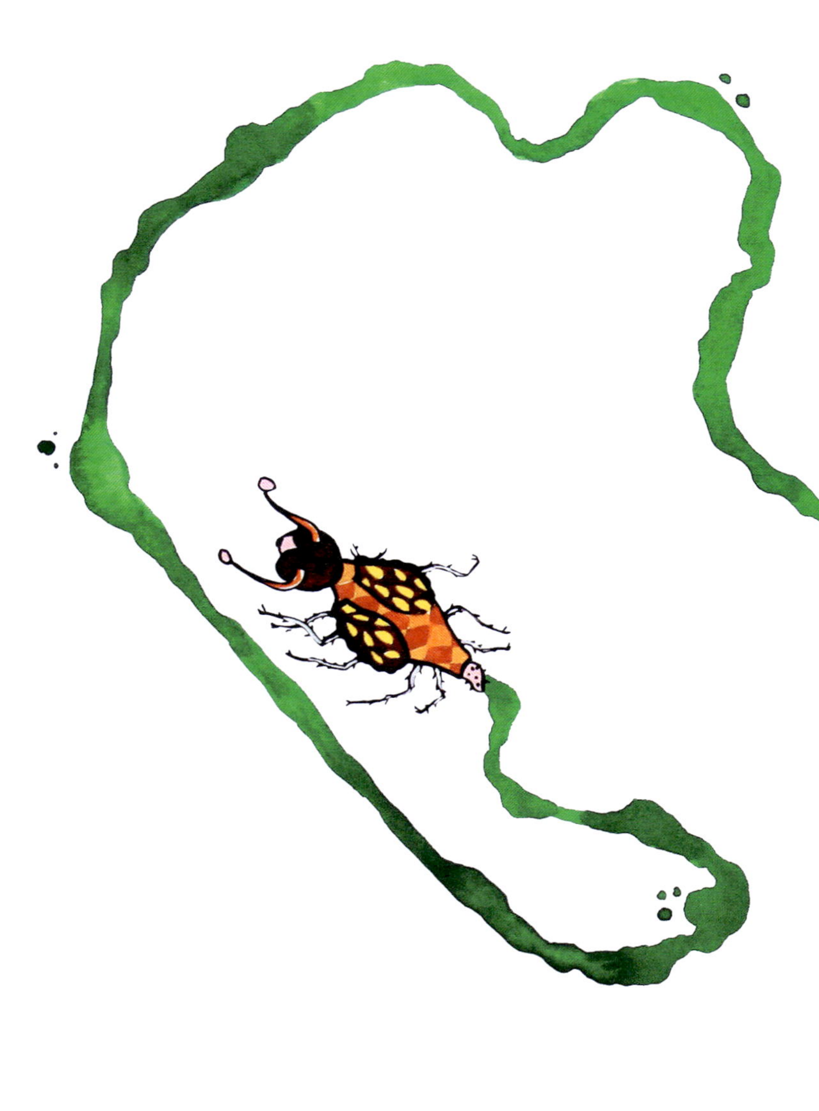

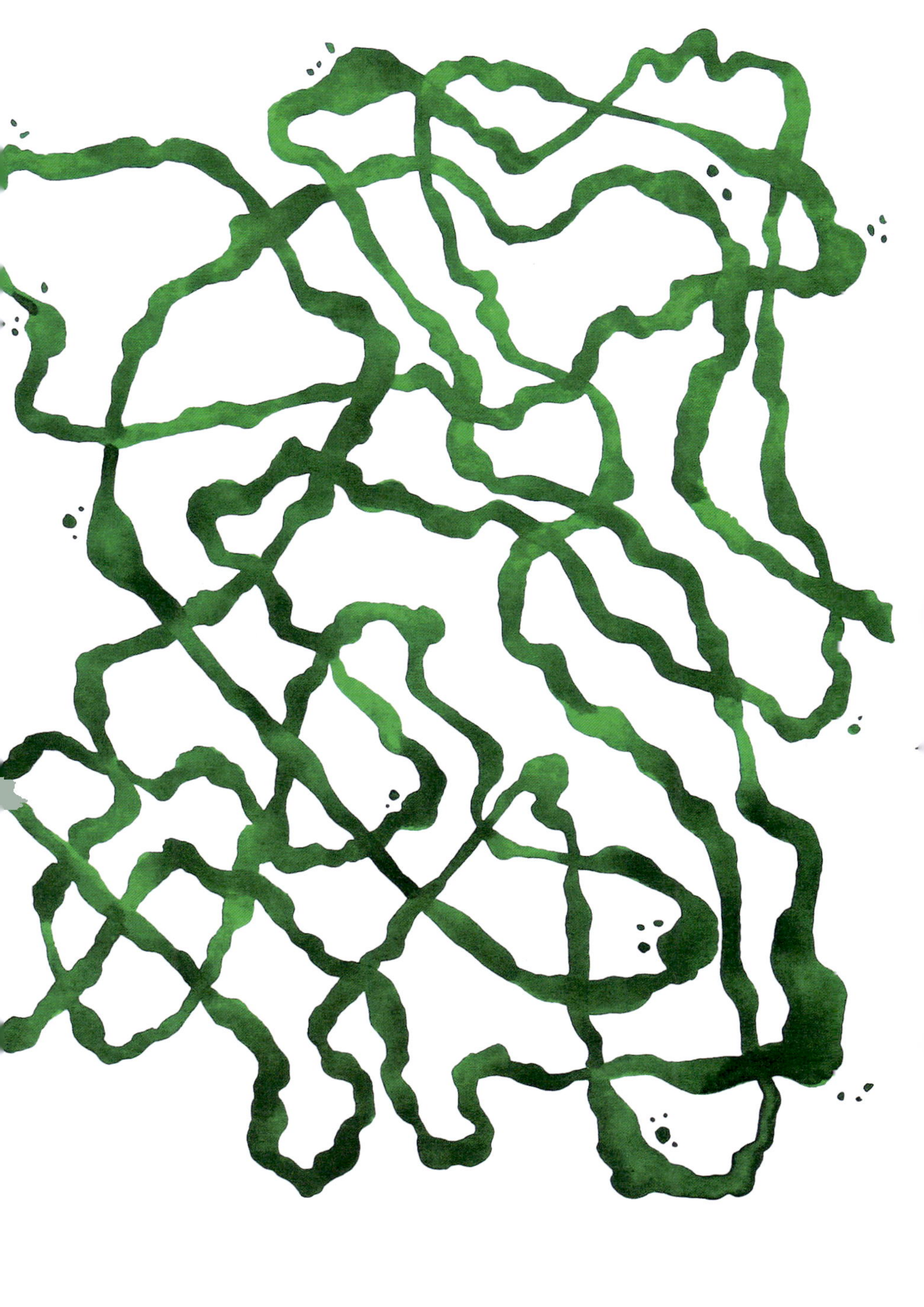

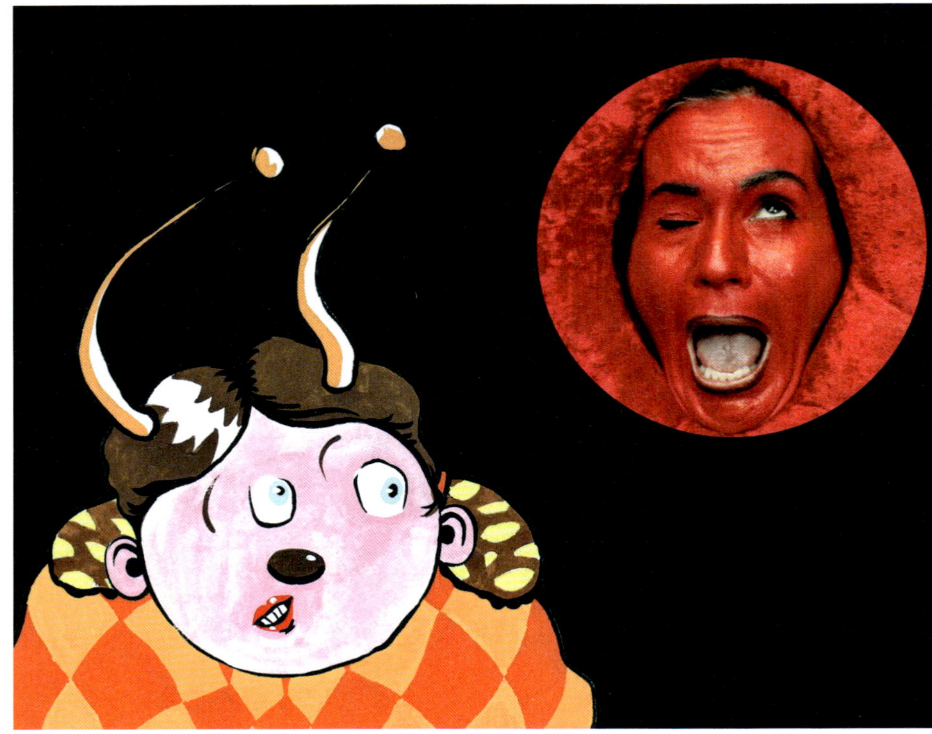

Mr. Ball: What is wrong with you today, Titorelli? Don't you know that paintings should be silent?

Mrs. Chair: Yes—good paintings do not need words!

Mr. Chair [with a sense of importance]: Real paintings are beyond words!

Titorelli: Shitty shit shit.

Choir: Titorelli—hush!

Storyteller: Now, Grete could not move such heavy pieces of furniture all by herself. She did not dare ask Father, and so she waited until he went to work, and then asked her dim-witted mother for help [animation of the two women].

Mrs. Chair (Mother): Yes! I will help, and finally I will get to see my handsome son again. [Mother smiling.]

Storyteller: But as soon as the door was opened, she was a bit afraid. [Mother's expression changes to apprehensive.]

Mrs. Lamp (Grete): Don't worry, Mother, you won't see him; he always hides underneath the sofa.

Storyteller: And so the two began moving the furniture out, pushing and shoving. [A variation on the music that accompanied Gregor's attempts to turn around in Scene 3.]

Choir: One, two!

Mrs. Lamp: Shoving, pushing.

Choir: One, two!

Mrs. Chair: I cannot breathe.

Choir: One, two!

Mrs. Lamp: Keep on trying.

Choir: One, two!

Storyteller: But the wardrobe was so heavy! [Music stops.] As it was stuck in the middle of the room, Mother had second thoughts.

Mrs. Chair (Mother): Wouldn't taking away Gregor's furniture mean that we've lost hope of finding him a cure? Perhaps we better leave his room as it was.

Storyteller: When Gregor heard these words, two voices began arguing inside his head ... [Gregor's face is now at the center of the screen; two circles frame his head and show the prospective Choir members representing his inner conflict.]

Mr. Chair [for the insect side]: I need more room to dance and be the happy cockroach that I am: Wooooo! Weeeee! Waaaaa! All around, take the junk away and burn it down!

Mrs. Chair [for the human side]: How could I forget I am a man? Oy! Ay! Vey! I need a decent bedroom, not a den!

Mr. Ball [insect side]: No room, no room! You vex me, go away! Get out, get lost, and let me play!

Mr. Table [human side]: They cannot take what's mine, my table and my chair! It's indecent, it's uncivil, it's illegal—it's not fair!

Mrs. Closet [insect side]: Get rid of the dreck—it's the Reeking King's lair!

Storyteller: Yes—Gregor was both alarmed and moved by what his mother said. But Grete was upset with Mother's idiotic thoughts, and was more determined than ever to empty the room.

Choir: Everything must go!

Storyteller: The two women went for a moment to catch their breath in the other room. Gregor, seeing he was alone, got out and ran around several times to catch his thoughts. Then, his eyes fell on his most cherished treasure ...

Choir: His woman in furs!

Mr. Chair: He cannot let them take her away! [*The Woman in Furs* musical theme is heard; it continues during the following sequence: the Woman in Furs is slowly changing in cross-dissolve from second to third phase, then to the fourth, growing dirtier, darker, and furrier. Fade out.]

SCENE 13—SECOND ADVERTISEMENT BREAK

13A—BOKI-POKI

A Happy Announcer: Tomorrow, on the best children's channel. [Animation: Boki's music and crazy-happy figure are now much more dynamic, his face swirls, moves closer and farther, multiplies, and changes colors. Internal frames appear and disappear, each containing unrelated children's products: a pencil case, girl's shoes, a candy, and a unicorn toy.]

A Happy Singer: Boki-Poki! Boki-Poki! Boki-Poki! Boki-Poki! Boki-Poki! Boki-Poki! Boki-Poki! Boki-Poki! Boki-Poki!

13B—FOOD AD REPRISE

A seductive Female Announcer: You are a good, tender child. Papa loves you ... mmmmm ... you will never be alone ... ahhhhh! You deserve no less than *The People's Delicatessen*.

13C—REAL TITORELLI AND FAKE TITORELLI

Animation of Joseph K. and the painter Titorelli.

Seductive Male Announcer: In an upcoming episode of *Kafka for Kids* ...

Mr. Ball (as the Painter): Indeed, Mr. K, you stand accused by the court, but rest assured that I, the painter Titorelli, who spent more time than anyone painting portraits of litigators inside the court, I will tell you all you need to know about your chances of acquittal ...

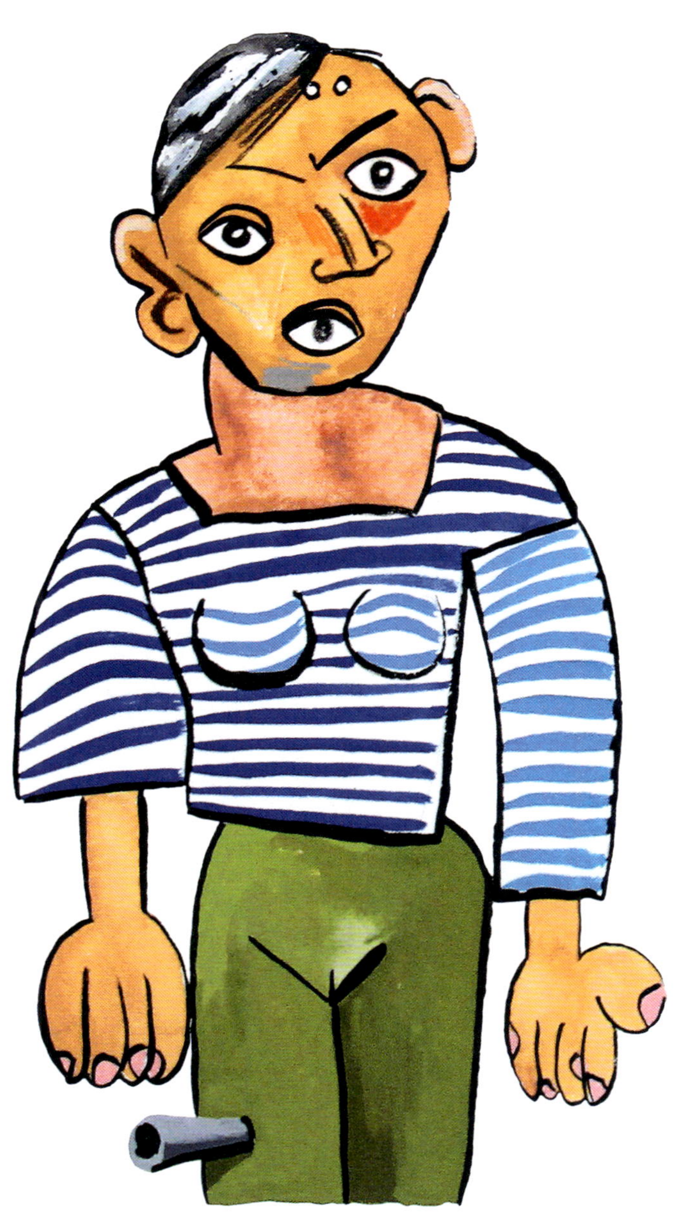

Storyteller [to the Child]: That means "not guilty."

Mr. Ball (as the Painter): ... But first—won't you buy one of my landscape paintings? [Shows a picture with two trees, similar to the character Titorelli.]

Mr. Table (as K.): Fine. Being that I want to know how to end my trial, it will make sense for me to buy a landscape painting.

Mr. Ball (Painter): Or perhaps two? [The two figures are shown with two identical paintings behind them.]

Mr. Table (K.): I can find room on my wall for two landscape paintings.

Mr. Ball (Painter): Almost free! For not much more—a whole series? [A full view, with the wall behind filled with identical paintings. A short pause.] Settled, then. And now, about acquittals: you are standing trial and you are innocent, so it stands to reason you want to be acquitted. But I need to ask you: what sort of acquittal do you want? There is not one, but three, three kinds of acquittal. First, there is absolute acquittal! [Musical emphasis.] Then, there is apparent acquittal! [Musical emphasis.] And finally, there is deferment [musical emphasis].[4]

Choir: Deferment!

The Bearer of Bad News [entering with a wrapped painting in his hands]:
I am the saddest of the sad:
The news I bear is always bad!

[Choir]:
He is the reason we are scared,
The news he bears is always bad!

[Bearer]:
I cry all day, I cry a lot,
My dismal job, my lousy lot!

[Choir]:
We cry all day, we cry a lot,
As he reveals our awful lots.

4 Based on the chapter "Lawyer, Manufacturer, Painter" in Franz Kafka, *The Trial*, trans. Breon Mitchell (New York: Schocken, 1999)

The Bearer places the wrapped painting on the oven near the Orchestra, so that it is somewhat lower than Titorelli.

Bearer: My friends, I am afraid that I have some bad news. [pause.] *Your* Titorelli painting [close-up of the painting as he eyes the Bearer, visibly alarmed] ... is a fake!

Choir, Storyteller, and Child: Oh!!!

Storyteller: Are you absolutely sure?

Bearer: As proof, I have brought with me a *real* Titorelli. You will immediately be able to tell the difference between fine art—and forgery. [The Bearer pauses dramatically before unveiling the real Titorelli. It is almost identical, but the head nested in the picture is upside down; he positions the painting the "wrong" way, so that the face is straight, the ground is down, and the sky is up. The Child carefully examines both paintings.]

Child: I don't see the difference. [She examines the paintings further, and the camera partakes by shifting between them.] They are exactly the same.

Bearer: It appears that way to you simply because you are a sweet, innocent child, unaccustomed to tricksters and cheaters. Now, I know that during the time you spent together, all of you grew fond of the old, fake Titorelli. He is almost a family member. But the bad news is that he has to be punished, and the badder news is that there is no choice in the matter but the harshest punishment. [pause.] This is a serious crime. And the worst news is that the fake Titorelli ... [pause] will have to be burnt!

Choir: Fire! Fire! Fire!

SCENE 14—MOM AND THE WOMAN IN FURS

The Woman in Furs is transformed in cross-dissolve morphs into her dirtiest, darkest, and furriest incarnation.

Choir: His woman in furs!

Mr. Chair: He cannot let them take her away!

[A series of close-ups: the Child is looking ominously at Titorelli. The Painting returns her gaze silently. The Child shakes her head. Titorelli is terrified by the gesture. The Child signals a throat slicing with her finger, then performs a hanging-by-the-neck gesture, and finally mimics

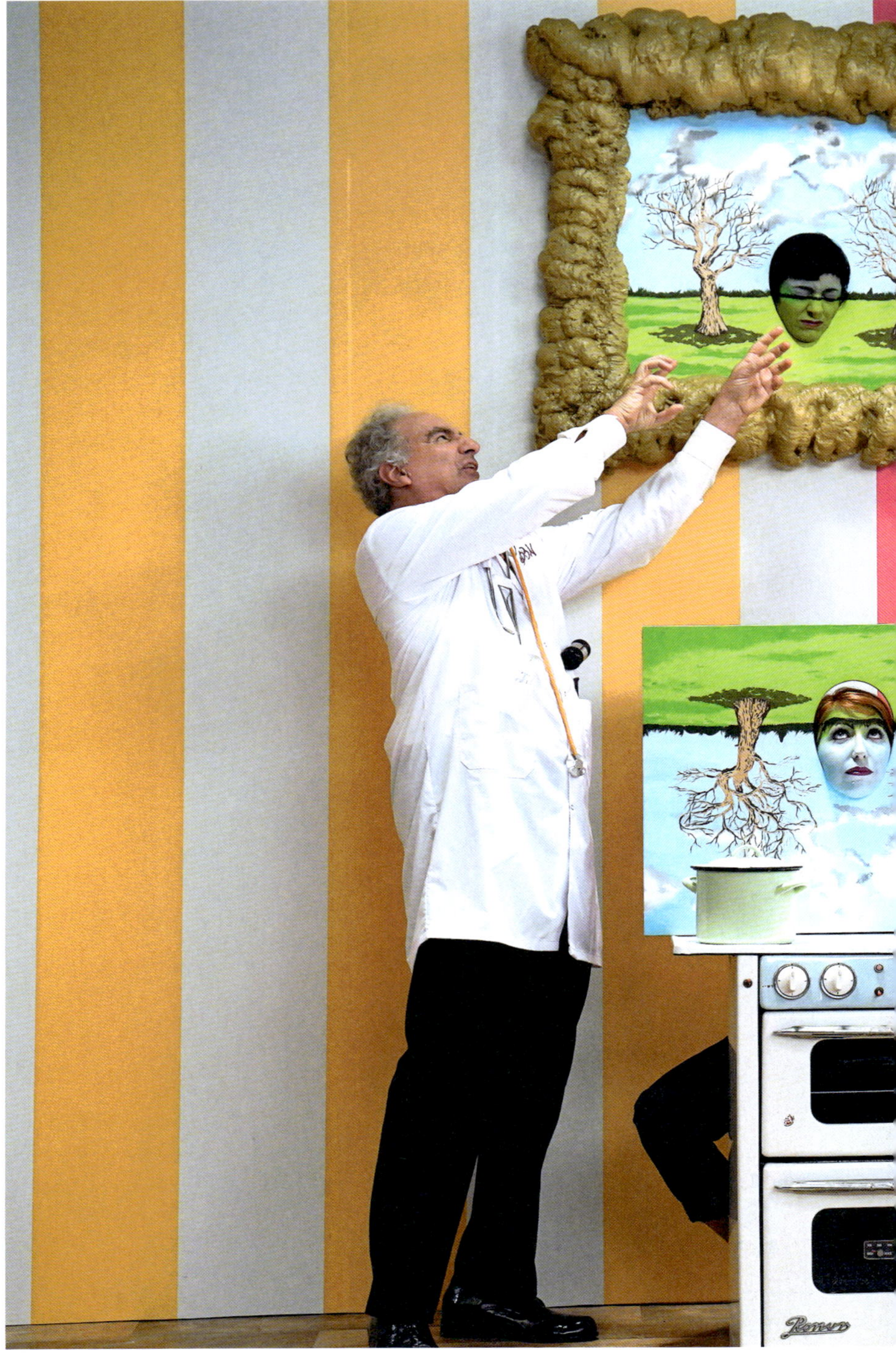

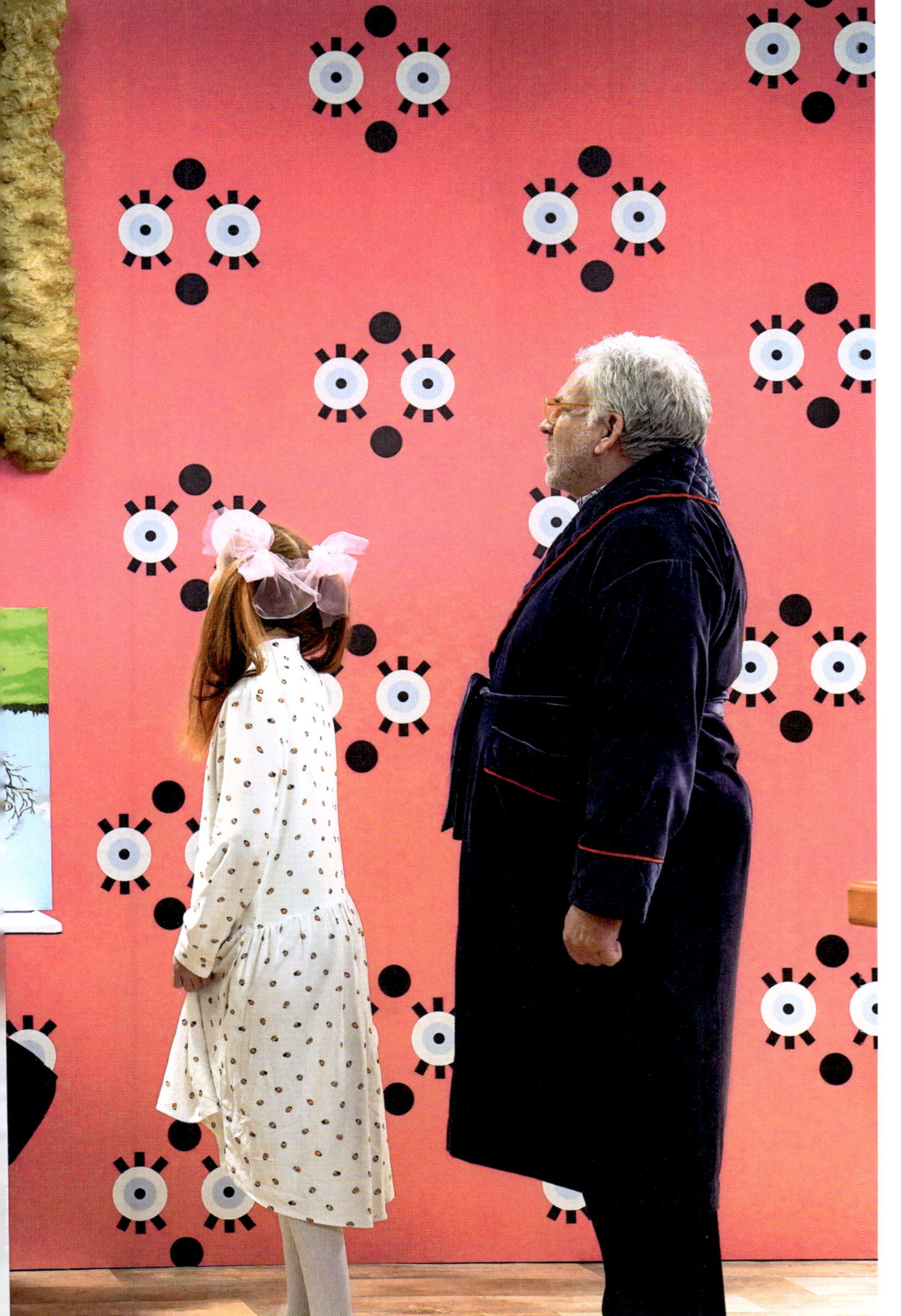

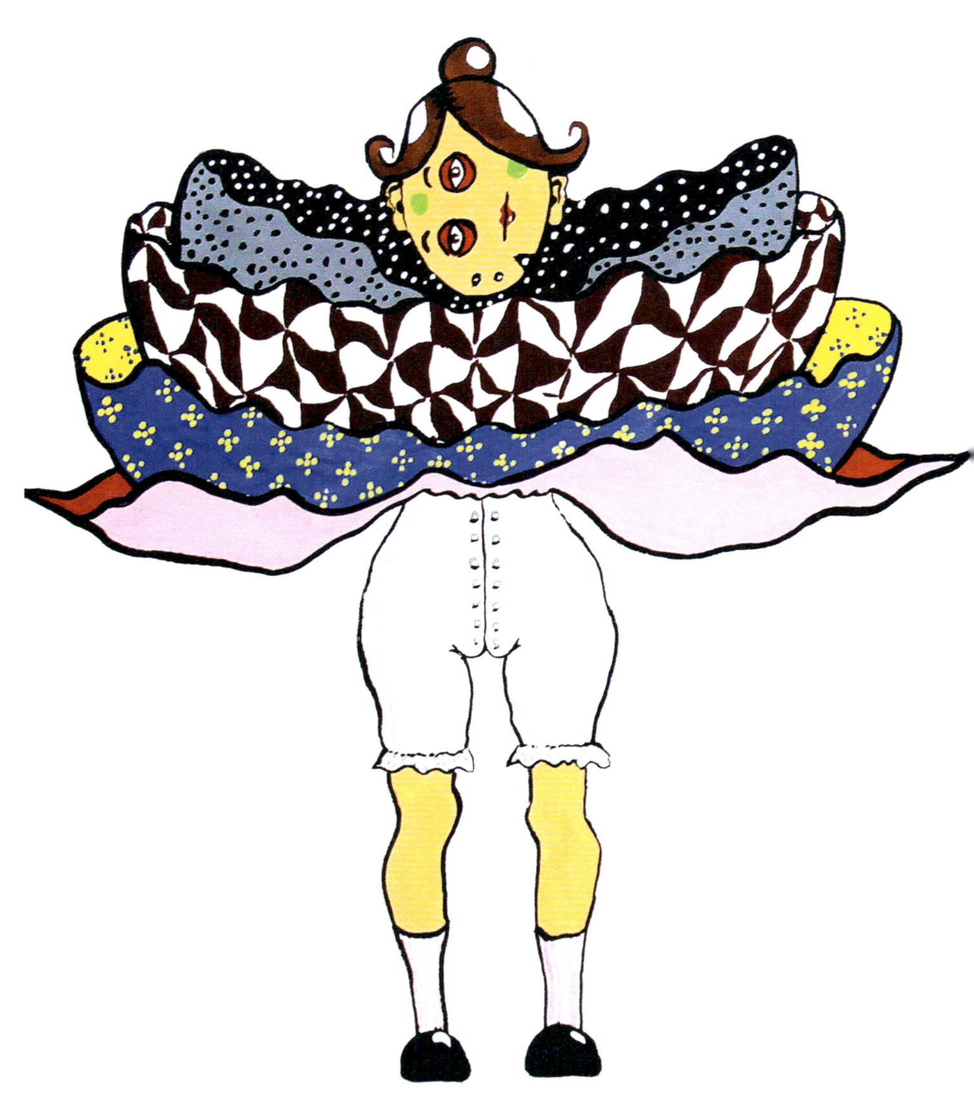

strangulation and death thralls. Titorelli is crying profusely, his tears visible as trails of streaking makeup on his cheeks. Continuous shot as the Storyteller, oblivious to all this, continues the story.]

Storyteller: His beloved lady in furs? No way! Gregor was *not* going to let them remove his lady friend [the picture is seen on the background of the flowered wallpaper of Gregor's room], and so he quickly climbed on the wall—and ... [Gregor's body covers the picture almost entirely].

Choir: *PLOOP!*

Mr. Table: The icy-cold glass felt so good, stuck to his overheated belly.

Choir [except Titorelli, as if in transports of pleasure]: Mmmmm! Oooooh!

Mr. Ball: Oh, how good that picture felt! It is *good* to be alive!

Choir: Mmmmmm! Oooooh!

Titorelli: To be alive! Alive! [Titorelli bursts out crying again.]

Storyteller: ... and now—the two women headed back to the room, Grete first. Her eyes quickly met Gregor's. [Intercuts of the two staring at each other. Grete's eyes change from dispersed to focused mode. Her face quivers with anger.]

Mrs. Lamp (Grete): Why don't we go back to the living room for a second, dear Mother?

Storyteller: Now, Mother, as you already know, was a bit stupid—but she was not a complete fool, and Grete's words only made her look up for what her child did not want her to see ... and she was shocked!

Choir [in a mocking—giggles are heard—and somewhat chaotic imitation of Mother's response]: Shocked! Shocked! Oy vey! [Mother falls on the sofa, as if she's fainting, her undergarment exposed again.]

Storyteller: The girl rushed to the kitchen to find some drink or drug that would help Mother feel better. Gregor saw that his mother was ill, and he also wanted to help, so he pried himself off the Woman in Furs, which was not easy, because his belly was gummed to the glass with all that green goo he was secreting; but, finally, he fell to the floor and rushed after his sister, out of his room. Grete, her arms full of different bottles, didn't even notice him. One of the bottles fell, smashed to pieces, and a shard scratched Gregor's face. Then Grete ran back to his room, closing the door shut with her foot and leaving him all alone in the living room.

Choir: All alone! First caged inside—now trapped outside!

Mr. Ball: Gregor crawled thoughtlessly.

Choir: Hither and thither.

Mr. Chair: Floor, carpets ...

Mr. Ball, Mrs. Lamp, and Mr. Table: ... walls, ceiling ...

Storyteller: Finally, he fell smack on the table, and laid there, exhausted.

SCENE 15—APPLES

Pause. A ring is heard.

Choir [a burst of song in Pavlovian response to the ring]:
Run away, dear Mrs. Taylor,
It's the Bearer of Bad News!
The Bearer of Bad News!
The Bearer of Bad News!

Storyteller [reproachful]: No! [Choir members' expressions of confusion.] It was *not* the Bearer of Bad News this time, you are *wrong*! [Ashamed expressions of some Choir members.]

Mr. Chair: It was Titorelli's fault!

Choir: Titorelli! Fire! Fire! Fire! [There is a lynching atmosphere.]

Storyteller: Please, guys, silence. Someone rang, and Grete opened the door.

Mrs. Lamp (Grete) [dejected]: Hi, Father. How was work? Gregor escaped. Mother fainted.

Mr. Ball (Father) [his anger mounting]: I told you this would happen, but no—you women do not listen. I kept telling you. I kept telling you. I kept telling you. I kept telling you.

Storyteller: To show he only meant well, Gregor rushed towards the closed doors of his room and stood there, making it clear that all he wanted was to go back in.

Mr. Ball (Father): Ah-ha!

Storyteller: This time, Father had no walking stick with which to push Gregor, but he found something even better.

Choir: What? What?

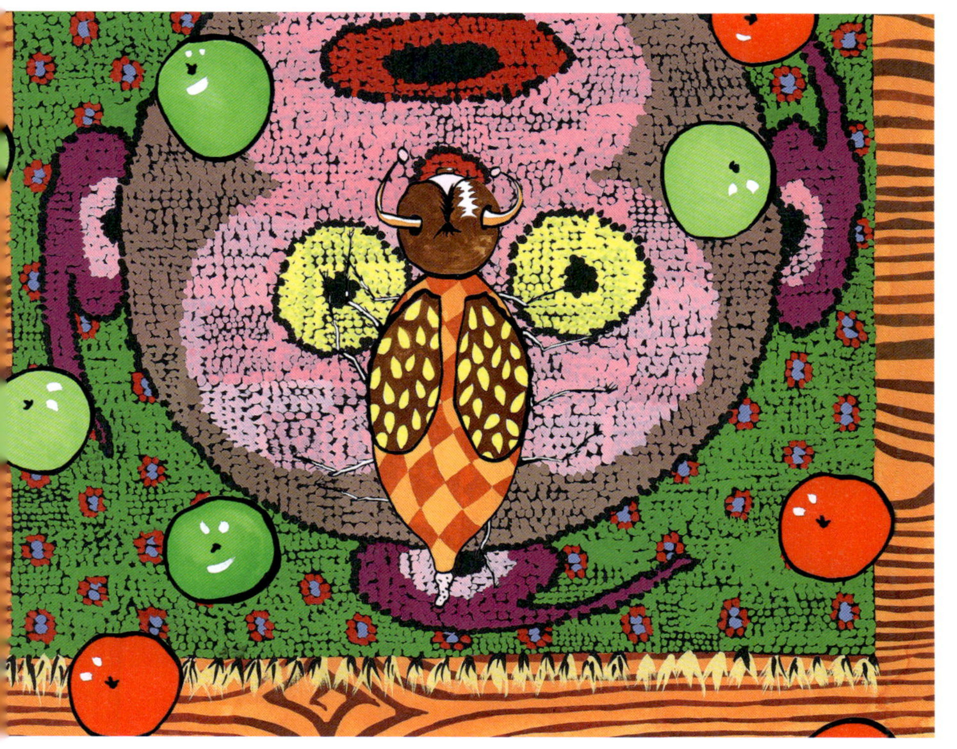

Storyteller: A bowl of apples! And he started throwing the apples at Gregor, one after the other ...
Mr. and Mrs. Chair: *Bang! Poof! Padam!*
Choir [happily]: *Bang! Poof! Padam!*
Choir and Child [elated]: *Bang! Poof! Padam!*
Storyteller: Gregor simply didn't know where to run, and the apples kept coming and coming!

Apples Song

Tart and hard when green,
Sweet and moist when red,
Cuddled in a bowl,
They are playing dead.

Biting apples, throwing apples,
Afraid of being eaten, that's why they're playing dead.
Better eat them young,
Apples green and red,
Eat an apple-son,
Lest it shrivels like your dad.

Peeling apples, rinsing apples,
Better peel an apple-boy than rinse a rotten dad.

Storyteller [as the music plays on, and the Child is dancing]: Father may have been strong and had beautiful gold buttons, *but*— he was not very good at this game. He missed Gregor time and again. Apples were rolling around all over the floor. But then, Father made a truly excellent shot: he hit Gregor in the back so strongly that the apple plunged deep into Gregor's body, and stuck there. [Music stops; Storyteller and Child sit; an image of the apple stuck in Gregor's back.]

Mrs. Chair: ... And the last thing Gregor saw before he passed out, was his mother, her undergarment exposed, jumping on Father to make him stop. [Still animation: Mother with raised skirts on top of Father. "Woman in Furs" musical motif.]

End of Chapter Two

CHAPTER

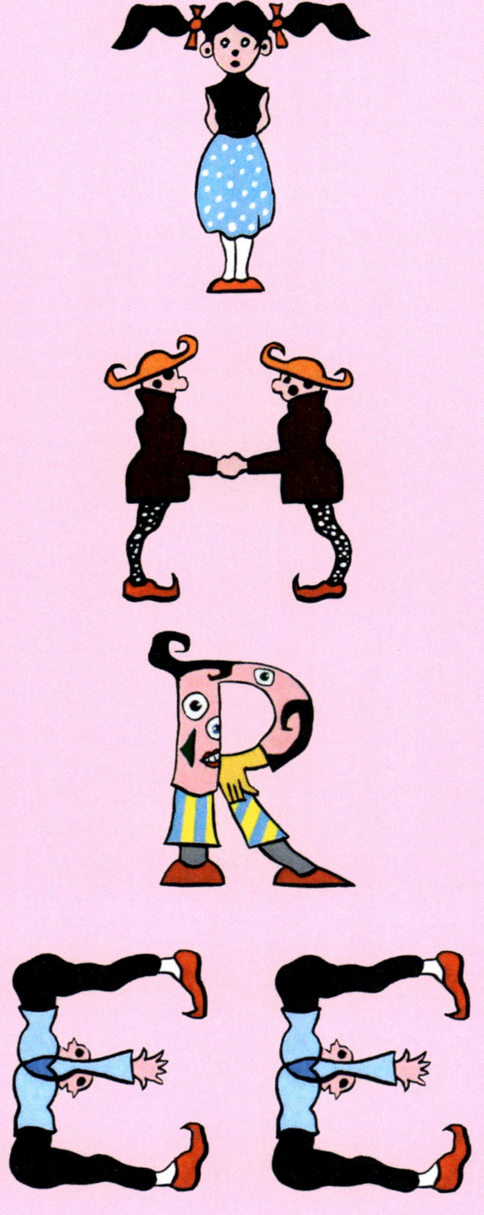

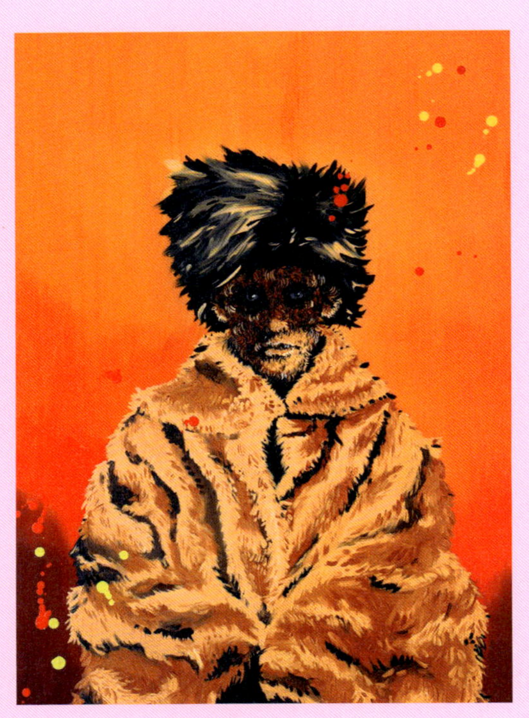

SCENE 16—THE FAMILY BUSINESS

Close-up: the Woman in Furs' last, darkest, and dirtiest phase. Still animation: Gregor.

Storyteller: The apple that hit Gregor remained lodged in his flesh. Now he walked very slowly. Climbing on the walls was out of the question. But things were not all bad. Now his door was always left open in the evenings so that he could observe his dear family. The household was a busy little business: Grete working in a shop, Mother sewing women's underwear, Father never taking his uniform off, and every now and again they sold a piece of jewelry. Gregor watched all this like a silent partner; after all, he was once the family's sole provider.

Child: What is a provider?

Mr. Ball: A provider is the one who brings in the money to buy the things a family needs or wants.

Child: But ...

Mr. Ball: But what?

Child: But that doesn't make any sense.

Mr. Ball [after a pause]: You are right, in several ways; lots of questions can be raised about provisions and work, such as why would someone work for the benefit of others even if they are, let's say, old, enfeebled parents, or little children? And there are other complicated issues—like, for example, how should the money that was provided be divided—which, incidentally, is a topic Kafka, as a Doctor of Law dealing with insurance, was a great expert in. So, you are right to point out that being a provider doesn't readily make sense.

Child: No—I mean it doesn't make sense that *Gregor* made money.

Mr. Ball: Why not?

Child: It doesn't make *any* sense. [Pause. She chuckles as if encountering an evident absurdity.]

Mr. Ball: And why?

Child: Because he's a cockroach. A cockroach does not make money. [pause.] Unless you sell it. [pause.] And even then, someone else makes the money.

Storyteller [after a pause, gentle if a bit disheartened]: But you remember, right?

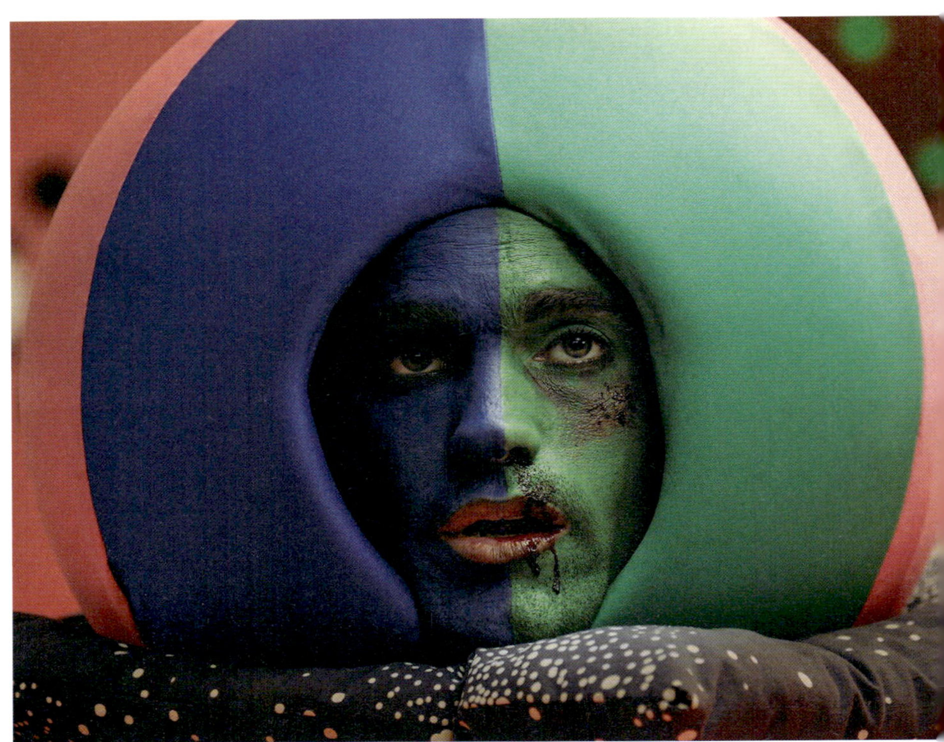

Child: What?

Storyteller: That Gregor was not always an insect.

Child [doubtful]: What?

Storyteller: He became a woman, I mean a vermin, in the beginning of the program.

Child: OK.

Mr. Ball: OK, then!

Child: If you say so. [Mr. Ball smiles. In a sudden burst of rebelliousness and anger, the Child picks up the ball with both hand and throws it. The effect is of a beheading. The ball flies in the air, and rolls on the floor. The Storyteller picks it up, wipes away a bloodstain with the sole of his shoe, and places the ball's head back on the table.]

Storyteller: Gregor's room had not been cleaned in weeks. Gregor tried to draw Grete's attention to all that dirt by standing defiantly in the slimiest corner, but she ignored him. Once his mother came in to clean. She had to spill bucket after bucket of water. But when Grete came back from work—oh, how angry she was!

Mr. Ball (Father) [visibly bruised and hurt]: This nonsense cannot go on. We will hire a cleaning woman.

SCENE 17—THE CHARWOMAN

Storyteller: ... And so, they hired a cleaning lady, and things became even better. Whenever she entered, she would fondly say to Gregor ...

Mrs. Closet: Come here, you dung beetle!

Storyteller: Or, she would say ...

Mrs. Closet: Just look at this old dung beetle!

Storyteller: Gregor charged at her one day, to see if he could scare her. But by now he was so decrepit that his running was merely a slow limping and hopping. The cleaning lady just raised a chair with her strong arms, and Gregor was scared. These were the little games they could now play every day. She was poor, of course, as dirty and as disposable as used toilet paper, yet this cleaning lady was *magnificent*.

The Charwoman Song

A stately chant that begins with the male singers becomes a duet with the women's section and ends with a diminuendo. A slow upward movement begins with the charwoman's feet, and concludes with her head towards the end of the song. Her features are made of orbs which constantly change in position, size, number, and function.

A great woman who had seen it all,
  A great woman with a bushy white mane,
A great woman, many-years-old,
A great woman whose wrinkles are real,
A great woman, upright and tall,
A great woman, her shadow is long,
  She knows how to handle the broom,

A great woman with muscular thighs,
She knows how to squeeze the wet mop,
A great woman whose odor is spiced,
She knows how to master the stick,
A great woman whose shoulders are broad,
She knows how to punish the dirt,
A great woman with peering black eyes,
She knows about beating the dust,
A great woman whose voice makes you swoon,
She knows how to brandish the brush,
She knows about bristles and prongs,
She knows about squeezing the sponge,
She knows about lifting the chairs,
She knows about taming the muck,
She knows about vermin and all,
She knows about squeezing your heart,
She knows about kneading you soul,
She knows how to handle the broom,
She knows how to handle the broom,
She knows how to handle the broom.

SCENE 18—THE THREE LODGERS

Storyteller: Now that Gregor was hardly moving, the family could store all sorts of stuff in his room: broken chairs, discarded heirlooms, worn-out carpets. Gregor was hardly eating. He only took a little morsel once in a while and held it in his mouth for a few hours before spitting it out when the nurse of the ward wasn't looking.

Child: We are all garbage.

Mrs. Chair: Garbage.

Mrs. Lamp: Crap.

Storyteller [ignoring the disruption]: And so, with all the old junk stored with Gregor, a small room became vacant, and the family could make extra money by renting it out to three lodgers. These were three clerks who brought in three beds and three little lamps. As the lodgers liked to have supper at home, Gregor's door was usually closed. But one evening the cleaning

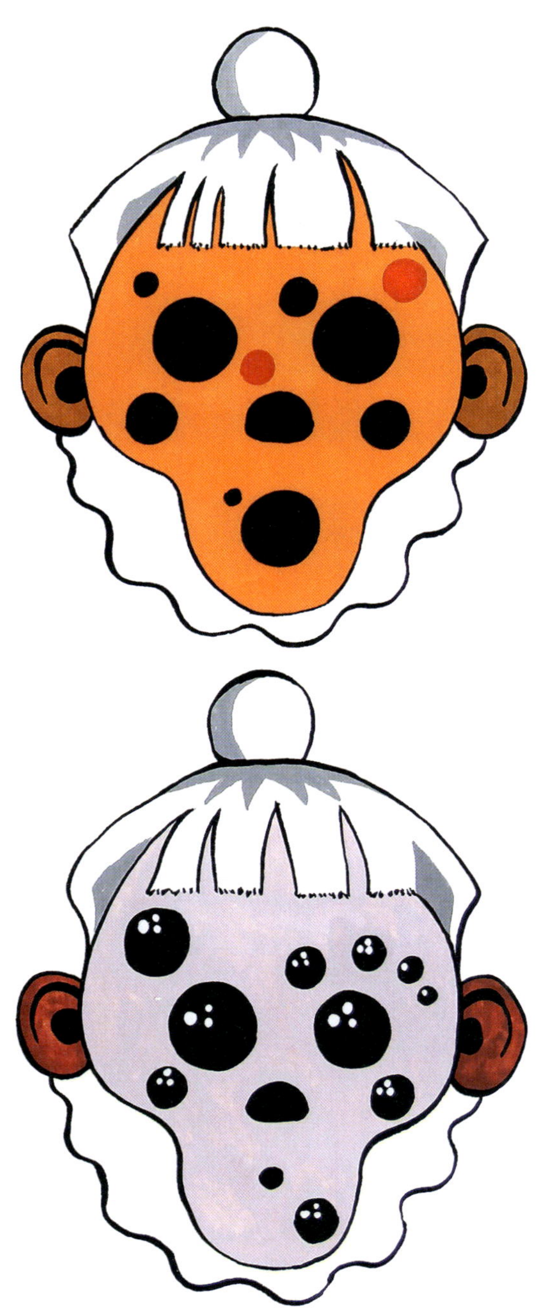

woman forgot to shut it, and Gregor could see the three lodgers sitting down in the living room to eat [corresponding animation of the lodgers at the table with raised knives and forks].

Mrs. Lamp (Grete): The potatoes—soft enough?

Mr. Chair (Lodger): Soft enough. [Father appears in the picture.]

Mr. Ball (Father): The meat—tender enough?

Mr. Chair (Lodger): Tender enough. [Father disappears from the picture. The food disappears. A newspaper appears. They read. A violin sound is heard faintly and tentatively; it is the same as Gregor's voice in Chapter 1.]

Mr. Ball (Father): My daughter is practicing her violin. Is the noise bothering you, gentlemen?

Mr. Chair (Lodger): Not at all, why doesn't the girl come and play here? My colleagues and I appreciate culture. [Grete appears. Pause. She starts playing the same melody.] We are disappointed. We do not find the music entertaining at all.

Storyteller: But Gregor, on the other hand, was very moved by the sounds. [Close-up of Gregor's face, quite dirty.] He hadn't heard Grete playing for a very long time. He decided to crawl over and encourage her, perhaps even to invite her to play in his room. And so he went, even though it was hard for him to move, and even though he left behind a trail of stinking scum—he was merely a tiny pile of pollution at this point.

Choir: We are all crap.

Storyteller: Gregor crawled slowly into the living room, all the way to Grete.

Mr. Chair (Lodger) [pointing]: Mister Samsa! In light of these disgusting circumstances, unclean apartment ...

Choir: Crap, crap!

Mr. Chair (Lodger): ... And unwholesome family, I give notice on my room, effective immediately.

Choir [shouting]: We give notice on our room effective immediately.

Mr. Chair (Lodger): Needless to say, I will not pay for the time spent here.

Choir [shouting, happy]: Needless to say, we will not pay a dime for the time.

Mr. Chair (Lodger): In fact, I may pursue you with legal claims! [The lodgers disappear. Father, Mother, and Grete, slouched in their chairs.]

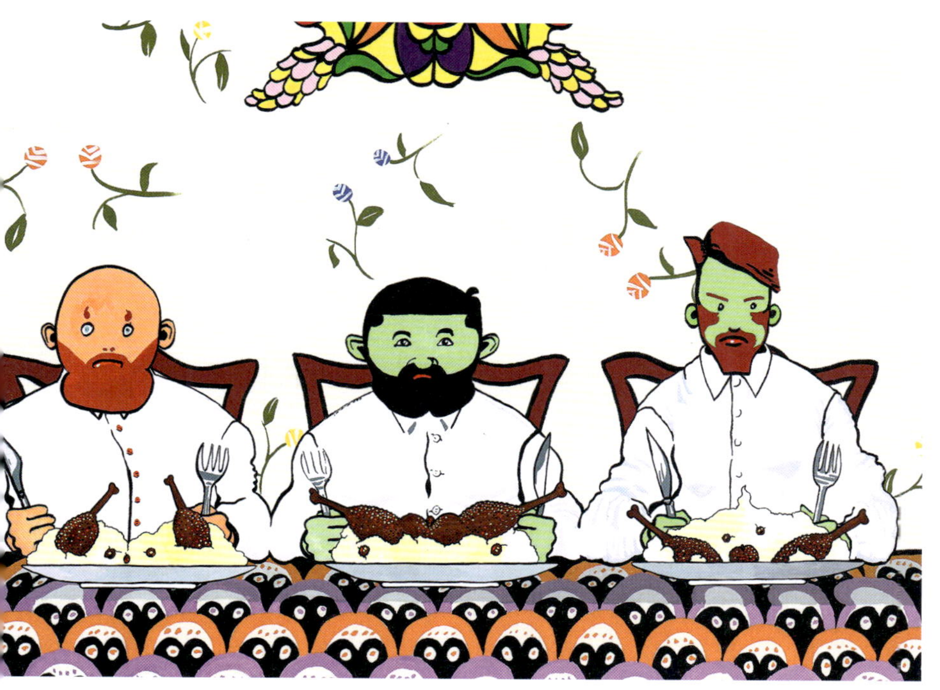

Mrs. Lamp (Grete) [after a pause]: We have to get rid of it.

Mr. Ball (Father): But what can we do?

Mrs. Lamp (Grete): We must find a way to get rid of it.

Mr. Ball (Father): You are right, but what can be done?

Mrs. Lamp (Grete): Oh, look! There he goes again!

Storyteller: And indeed, Gregor now moved a little. He just wanted to go to his room, but the way back, now that he was so thin and weak, was very long. As soon as he was in, the door was slammed shut behind him and locked. And so, the vermin closed his eyes for the very last time.

Child [yawning]: I'm also tired.

Storyteller [looks at her fondly]: I will put you to bed, and we can finish the story there, before we say goodnight.

SCENE 19—THIRD ADVERTISEMENT BREAK

19A—BOKI-POKI CANCELED

Boki-Poki's face appears degraded, in very low resolution, and without music.

Announcer [sounding a bit concerned]: Due to circumstances, Boki-Poki will *not* be broadcasted tomorrow. We are all united in hope that the allegations against Boki-Poki will be dropped, Boki-Poki will be released, and will join us once more. Please follow our schedule to learn if and when you may see Boki-Poki again.

19B—FOOD AD REPRISE

A seductive Female Announcer: Cram yourself with herrings, pickles, and all the old, acrid foods. You deserve no less than *The People's Delicatessen*.

SCENE 20—EXPLAINING THE LAW TO KWAME

Anchorman: Later tonight: *What Is a Child?* A special panel on Military Law and Children.

Legal Expert [elegantly dressed, composed manners]: In 2016, the youngest Palestinian girl ever, as far as we know, was imprisoned in Israel. D. was detained at the gateway of the Carmei-Tzur settlement with a knife hidden in her overcoat. She was found guilty of intent to cause death and sentenced to four and a half months in prison, to be served in an adult women's jail, or eight months if her parents failed to pay a fine [a short pause; she sniffs very discretely, clears her throat, and resumes talking]. Faced with this case, we may ask *What is a child?* And *How is she molded by the law?* But I'd like to tackle these questions today in a primary fashion, as if I were to explain the legal singularity of the occupation to a complete stranger, far removed in time and space; for example, to a young man from Ghana, seventy years from now [a short pause].

Childhood is a transitory state, and the law by which D. was tried was also conceived as temporary, being that the occupation is an interim state. Already before the 1967 war, Israel prepared itself

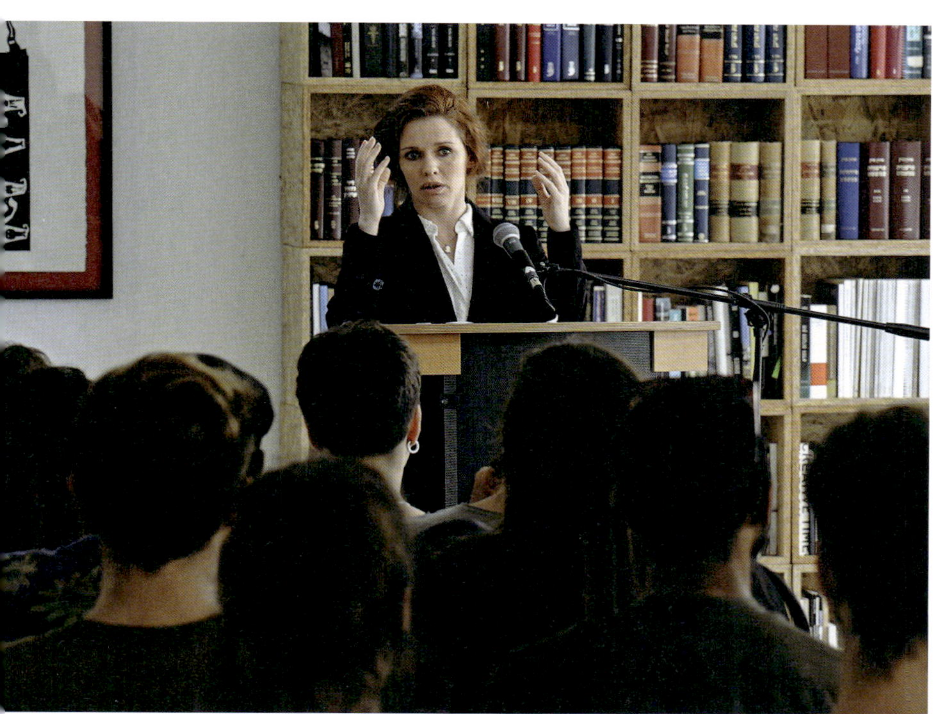

for territorial occupation so as to rule such areas in accordance with international law. Thus, some of the military governor's orders were written in advance. These are, in fact, Kwame, emergency regulations whose validity is extended from time to time. The precise duration of the Israeli occupation is unknown yet. Its age, however, happens to be close to mine: it is fifty years old. I am forty-eight years old [a short pause]; almost forty-nine. [Pause. Her expression clouds somewhat. She seems to be preoccupied by something else. She resumes.]

But I would need to explain to Kwame, that future veterinarian from Accra, capital of Ghana, that although the army rules the territories, not all those who live there are under its jurisdiction. Israeli Jews settle in the occupied territories in violation of international law, and they abide by Israeli civil law rather than military orders. Thus the same area has two kinds of law, and two types of childhood [while speaking, she occasionally turns her face towards her right armpit and the podium below it, as if searching for the source of a smell]. According to Israeli law, childhood ends at the age of eighteen. The Palestinian, however, ceases to be a child at the age of twelve. Order 1651 compiles dozens of earlier orders, many of which pertain to minors, and already in Clause 1 it clarifies that D. is not a child, but rather a youth, the legal category of a Palestinian between the ages of twelve and fourteen. Once a Palestinian turns fourteen, he becomes a tender adult, in legal terms, and remains so until the age of sixteen. In the past, the Palestinian became an adult at the age of sixteen. The military law amended the threshold of adulthood to eighteen, but it remains unclear, in the latest compendium of orders, if past sixteen the Palestinian is no longer a tender adult [reflective]. A *tender* adult [pause]. Clause 168B sets the progressively harsher punishments meted, and states that a youth such as D. may serve a maximum of six months in prison. The punishment of a tender adult, on the other hand ... [She abruptly falls silent and sniffs her armpit more conspicuously. Seemingly troubled, she kneels down, sniffing and looking for the source of the smell on the floor behind the podium. She stands up.]

I should probably apologize for what I said earlier, when I said ... [pause]. I am such a skilled public speaker, I'm nourished by it, I easily win over my listeners, it's like taking your regular route, the road you drive on every day. You are driving your private car, the car is your body, alone, late at night, your routine journey. It is dark. You are lecturing, but you are also alone in the dark, and the car is cozy and familiar, your body, which you always inhabit. You sink in thoughts, some of which may concern the lecture, that is to say, the road: the trees, bumps on the lane, Clause 93 prohibiting the disclosure of a detained minor's name, a small prison amongst the orchards, 1,638 minors detained in the occupied territories in 2015, the air perfumed by orange blossom, all is there, in the same spot as in any other night, rhetorical seduction, fervor, knowledge, hand gestures [she demonstrates a few gestures]. The way is so familiar that you could close your eyes. You wish to narrow them, at least, so as to ease the fatigue. You are driving and driving, lost in thoughts. Your mind wanders to other regions. You stare ahead, not really looking, one hand on the wheel ... Something troubles you, nags you, a disconcerting odor makes you fear you lost your way. You're in a foreign place. Lost. The car is still your body, but it is also alien, suddenly. Where is Kwame Ashanti and his glowing smile now, and where are you? The stench lingers in the air and it is unclear whether it emanates from you, within the car, or from the outside. You must have made a terrible mistake, you recklessly mixed unrelated issues, told an inappropriate joke, or committed a shameful factual error. The conceit that is yourself bursts at the seams, and you are left exposed, humiliated, and lost [pause]. But fortunately, it doesn't happen [she smiles a small, unconvincing smile of relief, and resumes her lecture].

The age division ascribed by military law, Kwame, does not exhaust the ambiguity and malleability of Palestinian childhood. As Hedi Viterbo had shown, often the judges themselves contest this division. Their inclination to apply independent criteria intensifies when faced with defendants whose bodies are small and frail, or whose development seems arrested, preserved as children although they are youth by age, or as youths despite having turned to tender adults.

Viterbo cites several cases in which a judge would rather trust his eyesb and decree that the child is more childish than his legal age, thus justifying leniency in punishment. [Slowly]: The judge's eyes relish the delicate little body and deem that the law errs in relation to this intimate sensitivity. On the other hand, there is the suspicion that the Palestinian would lie and claim to be younger so as to exploit the judge's compassion. [Pause, reflective, and a bit distracted]: In a different context we may ask why is compassion reserved for children ... While bodily fluids become diluted ... When you hug a child, do you turn your back on an adult, simply because he is an adult? ... What harms are caused by the urge to nurse a child? ... This issue is ... [absentmindedly fingers her ears] different.

It seems that as perplexing as the child's childhood may be, it will always be a mitigating point. But it turns out that childhood can also be an aggravating factor. Thus, for example, as early as 1967, military prosecutor Avraham Fechter argued that, in cases of

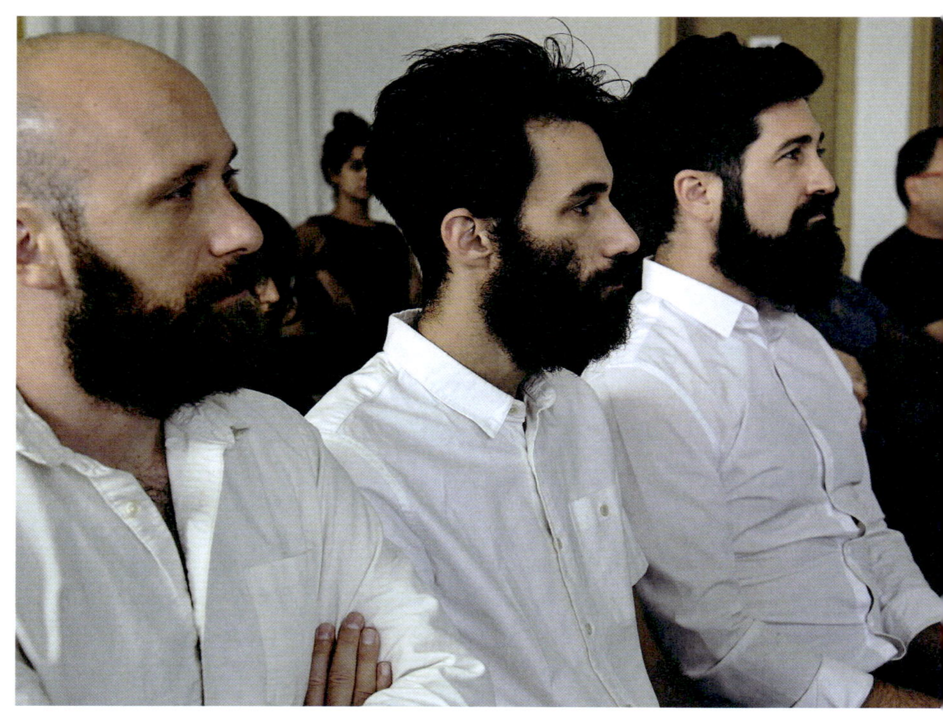

terror acts carried out by minors, the punishment should be harsher "in order to deter other young people of their age from being tempted by adventures of this sort." [A short pause.]

When I was young, my body odor seemed, to me at least, subtle and fruity, a peach, or perhaps a banana. But at age forty, the scent of sweat became more complex and piercing, guava. And then came those moments, during physical exertion or excitation, of a smell I thought emanated from someone else's body, outside the car, an odor similar to that of my ex-husband's sweat, akin to citrus peel, grapefruit perhaps, more bitter and sour. When I realized the smell was mine, I took it as a sign of a medical disorder, a food poisoning, or a virus. Not that the smell is bad, I *don't* find it bad. But it entails a message. It announces the next stage in the body's collapse. Your young girlfriend would sense the change and be repelled.

[She closes her eyes, hums a melancholy tune. Opens her eyes.]

If the occupation is a car, men of law like Fechter are the gas pedal. On the other hand, there are judges such as Meir Shamgar, who endowed the Palestinians with the right to appeal a military court's verdicts in front of Israel's supreme court. Shamgar personifies the military man of law for whom the law should not only enforce order, but also attain justice and defend the interests of the occupied. Thus, if Fechter is the gas pedal, Shamagar is the brake pedal of the occupation car [pause]. But it is important to understand that the brake pedal does not prevent the drive, but on the contrary, the car cannot operate without it. For the vehicle of the occupation's law to ride smoothly, you need both gas and brake: Fechter–Shamgar, Shamgar–Fechter, Fechter–Shamgar.

The orifices rot. The fluids flow, but the odor changes. She avoids me as if I were a sick animal, Plotkin's plump, sweet apprentice ... but there still remains the pleasant touch of the animal doctor.

[Pause. She kneels and raises her hands.] And yet, a small issue is left unresolved. [Pause] If I may reenact: when the guard sees D. at the settlement's gate, points his gun, and shouts at her to kneel and raise her hands, and she complies: does he reach himself to the inner pocket of her overcoat, or does he order *her* to open the coat and take out the knife? [Her arms reflect a wavering between the two options. A long pause, eyes shut, mouth open, a light whimper.]

I feel kicks inside [opens her eyes and stands up]. Like a pregnancy, but outside the womb, higher and behind, in the ribcage, the nape, more like a quiver, fish fins quivering inside. Something throws itself against the ribs as if tries to break bars, but it's unclear what this thing is, this incontrollable sexual heat, perhaps a new kind of desire, or a first cancerous mutation in the liver, or the stomach [she takes off her jacket].

And what led to D.'s incarceration in an adult women's prison, against the law? The simple explanation is that there is no facility in the territories for female juvenile delinquents. But what's more important, Kwame, is that the law is premised on its ability to contradict itself, *not to be one*, to allow the illegal from one angle to be legal from another [one of the young men grips the crotch of his neighbor]. You can pick and choose from different sets of laws to suit what you need sanctioned. Not only the military law is flexible, convulsive, and shapeshifting, but the entire Israeli law operates as a set of emergency measures, thus becoming a fluid jurisprudence, as Yoav Mehozay defined it; a convoluted panoply culled from five distinct statutes, whose contradictions allow reality to alter on demand.

The author of the 2015 *Third Compendium of Military Orders*, legal counsel Colonel Doron Ben-Barak, is well aware of this legal complexity, and writes [she reads from her papers]: "As is well known, the criminal law in Judea and Samaria consists of multiple layers, beginning with the laws of the British mandate, going through Jordanian legislation, and ending with security orders issued by the military governor since 1967. Moreover, the reality of life is ever-changing, and calls for constant, numerous adjustments of the law." But this spectacular legislative bounty, the colonel knows, has to be displayed in full light, with all its delicious intricacies and orgasmic twists. Ben-Barak quotes from an old verdict when he writes [the camera zooms on the pair of young men kissing passionately]: "Legislation done in secrecy and kept hidden is a trait of totalitarian regimes and cannot go hand in hand with the rule of law." He then continues, "These lofty words, in the spirit of Kafka's book, still hold true." [Pause.] It is unclear which of Kafka's books he's referring to. "Unconcealed legislation, not kept hidden ..."

I sit on the pavement's curb. I wish I could cease to be. I wish I could kill this sexual urge and remain alone, silent, and dry, free from the taxing grotesqueries of desire. But then, a shiny yellow car stops beside me. Kwame steps out and extends his arm to me. He is muscular, tall, my eyes are exactly the height of his nipples. His skin glistens with sweat, and I notice it is encrusted with sawdust and feathers. Perhaps he has operated on a miraculous African bird, or plain chickens, and he smells spicy, delectable. I realize that Kwame is here to take me. The present becomes the past, and thanks to the yellow car, the future is the present. I am 120 years old, perhaps 130, but that does not disturb the delight of our fresh romance, it does not bother Kwame at all, just as sometimes in dreams, age is undefined. [A slow zoom in until her face fills the screen.] He draws me to him. According to the new law, I am a child again.

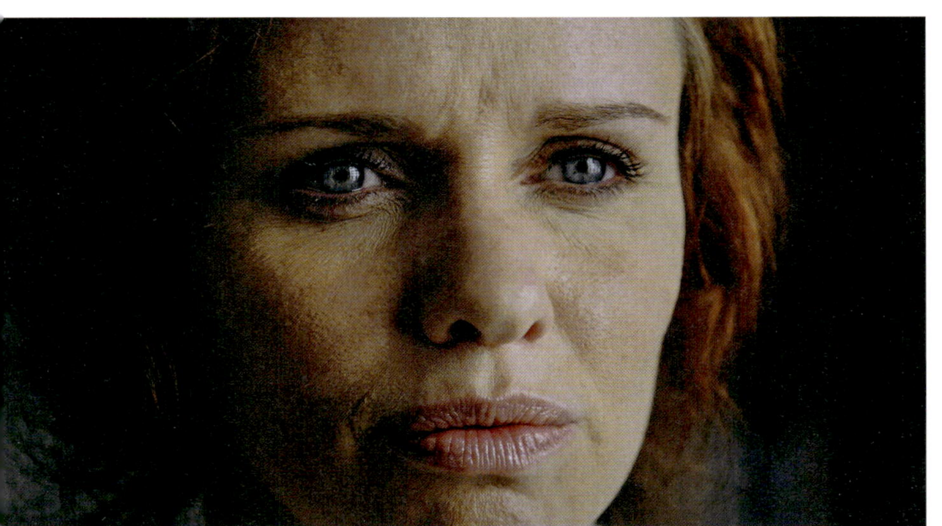

He ignites, and we drive upwards, or downwards, faraway in any case, and in that expanse the present shrinks into an ever-diminishing ball. The things that bothered me shrivel up, and so do all of you: shrivel, wither, ossify, and then crumble to dust. A space is freed: other suffering will trouble other people [instrumental prologue of the nursery rhyme begins]. His nipples are erect, like sensors ready to read my orders. The sight is alluring, but I'll resist until we arrive home, in Accra. You are dead. I lurch on a straw divan, spreadeagled. The animals growl and yelp in the garden. Kwame hovers above me, and lo'o=it becomes dark [closes her eyes; opens them].

SCENE 21—GOOD NIGHT

While the Legal Expert utters her last sentences, her face slowly cross-dissolves with that of the Child, seen from the top, in bed. The music is ongoing; the Storyteller is heard without being seen.

Storyteller: In the morning, the cleaning woman found the dead insect and dumped him in the dustbin. It was a lovely day. The sun was shining, and the family decided to take a day off from work. They packed a basket, and went for a picnic.

Child: Oh! Like the hunter, and grandma, and Red Riding Hood after they killed the wolf.

Storyteller: Yes.

Child: Only the wolf was very heavy, because his belly was filled with stones after he gave birth [pause]. A hard, old sausage.

Storyteller: What?

Child: Sausage, for the picnic.

Storyteller: Exactly. And now, it is time to sleep.

Kafka for Kids Nursery Rhyme

The song is shot as a top-view continuous zoom-out of the bedroom, beginning with the Child's face and ending with a full view of the bed, nightstands, and rugs on the floor. The angle is slightly diagonal to allow a view of the wall and of the objects on the nightstands. The music corresponds precisely to this gradual exposure: it begins with a solo by the Child, with voices joining, ending with the full Choir. The Singers appear as the different objects in the room, such as the Pillows and the Blanket, and they join in singing as they are revealed to the camera. When the verses are sung again, their melody will polyphonically interlace with a reprise of lines from *What Is a Child?* (Scene 9).

[Child]:
Am I alone, when I am alone, cuddled in my bed?
Do all the friends I see and hug reside inside my head?

[Pillows, and then Blanket, join in]:
The pillows press against my cheek, the blanket hugs me tight,
Will they protect and cuddle me if I am scared tonight?

[Bed joins in]:
And if I dream of growing up, will I remain the same?
And if I should grow old and tall, will I grow small again?

[Lamp and Ball on the nightstand join in]:
Perhaps my dreams are dreaming me, it's really hard to tell,
Perhaps I live inside their heads, but only for a spell.

Am I alone, when I am alone, cuddled in my bed?
Do all the friends I see and hug reside inside my head?
What is a child? What is a child? The smell is sweet and clean.
Perhaps one day she'll practice law and play the violin.

The pillows press against my cheek, the blanket hugs me tight,
Will they protect and cuddle me if I am scared tonight?
What is a child? What is a child? It's really hard to tell.
A child is ever growing, but only for a spell.

And if I dream of growing up, will I remain the same?
And if I should grow old and tall, will I grow small again?
Till when a child? Till when a child? Seven? Twelve? Fourteen?
When will it flip from plump and pink to wrinkled aubergine?

Perhaps my dreams are dreaming me, it's really hard to tell,
Perhaps I live inside their heads, but only for a spell.
A child is happy promises of futures spread ahead,
A treasure box inside of which lies someone old, then dead.

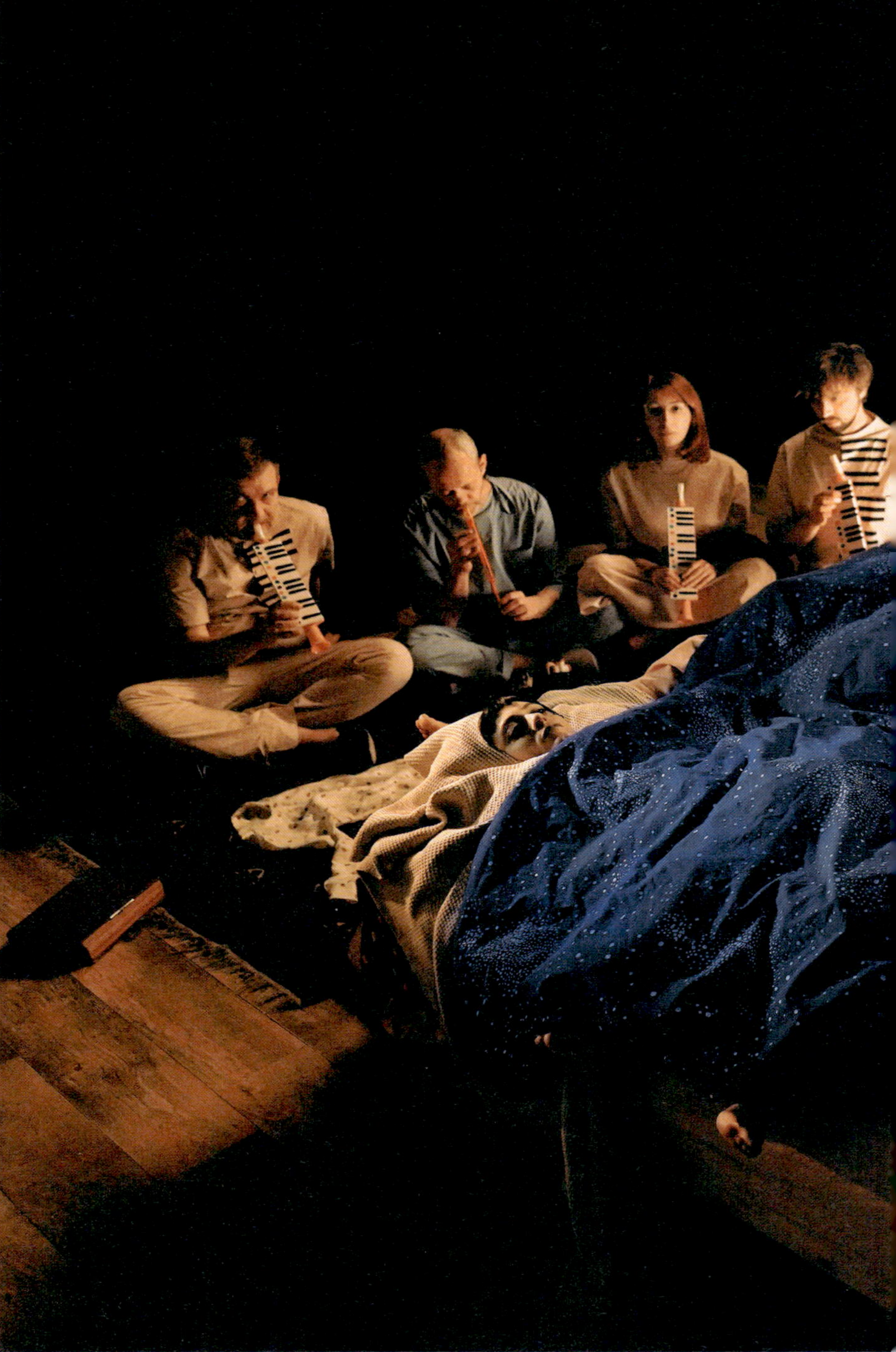

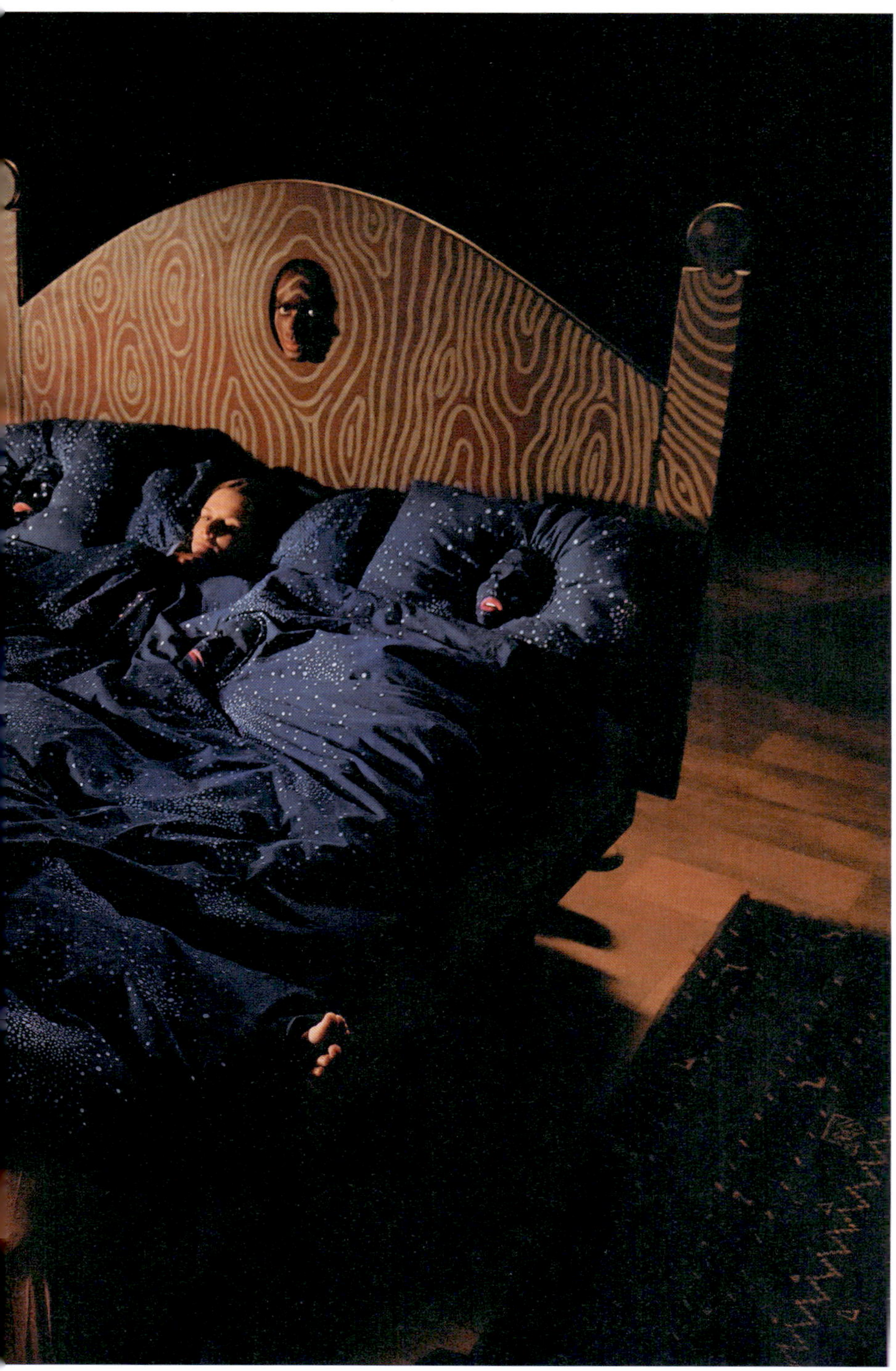

THE ESCALATION

FANNI FETZER

Maybe it's due to the many vowels, or perhaps the dual initials R.R.: at any event, Roee Rosen's name seems virtually impossible to fix to paper. The letters separate, are pulled magnetically toward one another and rearrange themselves: R to R, o to o, ee to e, s and n float freely over the sheet, dock here and there, pushing between the other letters. This strange phenomenon should be kept in mind when speaking about Roee Rosen and his work. Encountering Roee Rosen means also meeting Rose Rosen, Reese Noor, Enos Sneer, Roro Seeen, and many others.

Actually, the artist insinuates that it will be easier. In its title, the film *Kafka for Kids* implies that the intellectual great of modern literature will finally be presented in a way that is generally understandable. Roee Rosen wants to present Franz Kafka, of all people, with his contorted thought constructions, in a way that is even accessible to kids! But unfortunately, that's not how things turn out: the star writer of the educated middle class is not simplified, but his story becomes much more complex, corresponding to reality, for reality is more complicated than we like to represent using biaxial graphs. But first things first: *Kafka for Kids* is a 120-minute-long two-part film that in its use of the camera and professionalism refers to the film industry. But in terms of plot, dramaturgy, and structure, it is clearly a work of contemporary art. Is that so different? Yes, in fact it is very different. While films from the film industry are created to keep the audience from getting distracted, film in the context of artworks operate by the audience engaging and remaining engaged. In the first part of *Kafka for Kids*, an older man tells a girl Franz Kafka's story of Gregor

Samsa turning into a beetle in the midst of a vividly colorful, fully exaggerated setting. In the second part of the film, a law professor explains in a lecture the impact of military law in the territories occupied by Israel on the jurisdiction over juveniles. How is that related?

In Kafka's *Metamorphosis* and in the first part of the film, the parents no longer know whether they should treat their son Gregor Samsa like a human or a beetle. The end of the film is about Israel's treatment of juveniles facing trial in the Occupied Territories not like insects, but as young adults. Is this analogy not somewhat exaggerated? Perhaps. But before we judge Roee Rosen's film *Kafka for Kids* as over the top, let us recall the magically self-organizing letters in the name of the artist. Roee Rosen alias Eros Reno alias Orson Eerie shows us with this supposed exaggeration how shocking and confusing our world is, indeed Kafkaesque.

For Israel's intellectuals, it must be frustrating to see how their country is treated abroad. In arguments over the pros and contras of Boycott, Divestment, Sanctions (BDS), there is little space for differentiated debate. In efforts to overcome the dominant Western gaze and to subject our perspective to an anti-colonialist critique, the discussion quickly gets out of control. As usual, only very few are able to put up with ambivalence, and their voices are usually not the loudest. Perhaps these voices are as quiet as the letter F, that can easily be overheard. Just a breath that streams from our mouth. If we fail to hear the F, Kafka becomes "kaka." And Roee Rosen also demonstrates this in his childen's room: the chorus in the background sings fecal language for the star of modern literature. Outrageous! The artist takes things pretty far in any case. The girl being told Kafka's *Metamorphosis* and the extremely attractive law professor who holds a lecture on juvenile law in the Occupied Territories are played by the same actor. But why does she sweat so profusely while lecturing? Her perspiration is obscene and recalls Roee Rosen's work *Sweet Sweat* (the title once again playing with letters). On his website, the artist lists *Sweet Sweat* in the category of "artist books": the book contains a translation of Justine Frank's smut novel. But who is Justine Frank? Justine Frank is a fictional Belgian-Jewish painter who can be classified as a surrealist. In her brief lifetime (1900–43), her oeuvre did not receive any recognition. But for several years now, Roee Rosen has been maintaining her estate. But strangely, in one of the few extant photographs Justine Frank looks strikingly like Orna, Rosee Rosen's wife. The author of the preface of Justine Frank's first monograph was Joanna Führer-Ha'sfari. In a television interview, Führer-Ha'sfari strongly recalls Roee Rosen in facial expression and gestures.

Roee Rosen is thus underway in various systems and roles as a stowaway. Playfully and most importantly wonderfully self-ironically, he does not negate the complexity of the present, but takes it to the next level by exploring how everything is interlinked with everything else. He neither doubts the complexity of our reality, nor does he oversimplify to a fault. The artist alias Nurse Rosie alias Russ Nero adeptly juggles the interdependence. For Roee Rosen, silence is not an option in the face of the political situation, simple worldviews, or our being overtaxed. But he is not alone, with Noor Rees, Ross Ensor, Mort Error, Rrose Noser and a few others he enters a multilayered representation of reality that seduces us to be attentive and to think. The way Roee Rosen uses language as an artistic material, ably generating fiction that we all take at face value, makes the present bearable. The desire to become better acquainted with Soren Oreo and Ssorerrosen is just as great.

THE STANDARD EDITION
OF THE COMPLETE PSYCHOLOGICAL WORKS

ORION SEER

VOLUME XIX
(1923–1925)

The Kafka Companion to Wellness

with an Appendix on His Death

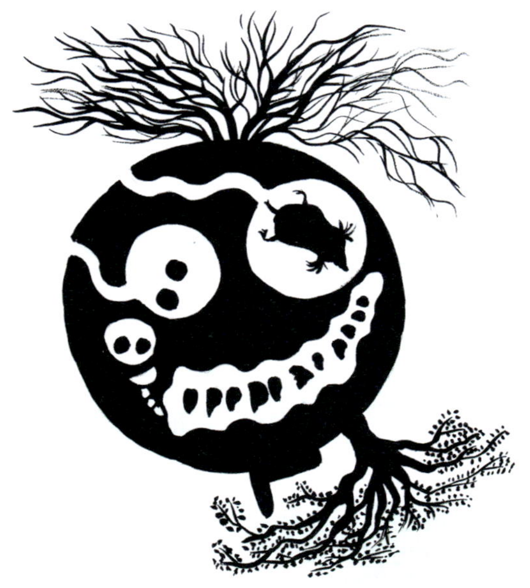

THE HOGARTH PRESS
AND THE INSTITUTE OF NUDE NUTRITION

Orion Seer
The Kafka Companion to Wellness,
with an Appendix on his Death, Illustrated
(The Standard Edition, vol. XIX, 1923–25), 2022
gouache on a digital print

THE STANDARD EDITION
OF THE COMPLETE PSYCHOLOGICAL WORKS OF

ENOS SNEER

VOLUME V
(1900–1901)

Memory Problems
Induced by Autobiographies

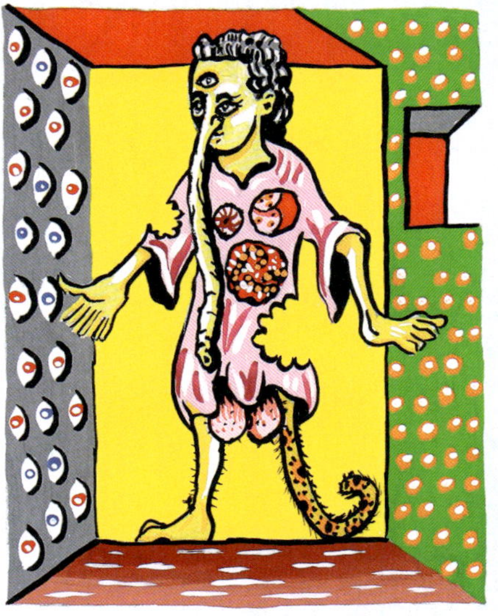

THE HOGARTH PRESS
AND THE INSTITUTE OF PSYCHO-ANALYSIS

Enos Sneer
Memory Problems Induced by Autobiographies, Illustrated
(The Standard Edition, vol. V, 1900–01), 2022
gouache on a digital print

ROEE ROSEN: LITERATURE, FICTIONALITY, AND BLINDNESS

SERGIO EDELSZTEIN

> "Being an agnostic means all things are possible, even God, even the Holy Trinity. This world is so strange that anything may happen or may not happen. Being an agnostic makes me live in a larger, a more fantastic kind of world, almost uncanny ..."
>
> —Jorge Luis Borges

Roee Rosen's interest in literature and its peripheral features are intrinsic to his oeuvre. From his earliest writings, he already developed some of the characteristics that define his works today: a tale of fictional characters, interchangeable in genre and age, always reflecting on the artist himself, and using media—drawing, video—as a means of expanding, deepening, and distorting the scope and meaning of the literary narrative.

Two of Rosen's earliest publications are "children's books": *Lucy* (1991–92) and *A Different Face* (2000). The latter is Rosen's only work actually intended for children: a story about a girl called Naomi Elvissa who constantly decides to change her face, switching her features—her eyes, mouth, ears, nose—with objects, animals, letters, and so on:

> "She selected nice mice as eyes,
> faucet for a nose, and a zipper mouth.
> The great headway was on the top of her head:
> an umbrella as hair!"

This graphic book follows Rosen's already-established use of both objects and body features and the animistic way in which these—and letters—morph and interchange.

None of his other books, however, or his films, such as *Kafka for Kids*, are in fact for children. In *Lucy*, even though the illustrations of both Lucy and his girlfriend Annie show them as children, Lucy is presented by the text—through his feelings and activities, including explicit and extreme sexual acts—as an adult male in his thirties. Representing the protagonists of his narrations both as adults and children is a constant in Rosen's work: in *Live and Die as Eva Brown* (1995–97) Hitler himself is depicted as a child with moustache. Significantly, the representations of both Lucy and Hitler are based on photos of Rosen as a toddler. In *Vladimir's Night* (2011–14), Putin is represented as a cross between a child and the adult political leader.

From the very first lines in *Lucy*, Rosen points to a complexity and morbidity that is not to be expected in a literary work for children:

> "The name of our hero might sound inappropriate and rather silly. Not only is our Lucy masculine, and 'Lucy' is a feminine name—our Lucy is Jewish, and 'Lucy' is the name of a Christian martyr."

In her hagiography, St. Lucy's eyes were gouged. In Christian iconography she is depicted exhibiting her eyeballs on a tray. Lucy, Rosen's alter ego, is blind. So too are many of his other "alter egos." In the film *The Confessions of Roee Rosen* (2007–8) the subjects of his monologues read "blindly" a text they do not under stand. Each one of the female foreign workers starts her speech with: "Hello, I am Roee Rosen." Likewise, Rosen's fictional character Efim Poplavsky (a Russian émigré who writes under the pseudonym Maxim Komar-Myshkin) and his artist collective, the Buried Alive Group, who insist on living in a culture that they despise and ignore, also resonate in blindness. So too does his comedian who "does not see" that his audience is annoyed by her improper jokes (in *Hilarious*, 2010). Blindness is also a by-product of being possessed (as in *Out*, 2010), being alienated from one's body and persona, or being abducted, as is prominently featured in *Killing Andrey Lev* (2014), a film by the Buried Alive Group.

Rosen's first blind alter-ego, however, is to be found in his *Blind Merchant* (1989–91), a re-telling of William Shakespeare's *Merchant of Venice*. The original play, rich with identity and gender shifts, and a pinch of torture and hints of cannibalism, makes it a fitting work for Rosen to tackle. But, prompted by the "Jewish question" that underlines the Shakespearean story, Rosen introduces a prologue to the play wherein, during a pogrom-like event, Shylock's wife, Leah, is brutally raped and murdered, and the merchant's eyes are gouged. The whole of the Shakespearean play develops page by page, side by side with illustrations done blindfolded by Rosen-Shylock, the Jew.

The motif of blindness defines Rosen's relationship with literature and fiction but, rather than expressing sightlessness as a punishment, as in the myth of Oedipus, Rosen's use of blindness would fit better the mythological oracle Tiresias (whose lack of sight was no obstacle to his prophesying and who, incidentally, was also transformed into a woman for seven years). For Rosen, the motif of blindness allows him to address his inherent distrust of the image. An iconoclast might destroy images, but Roee Rosen would more readily turn himself blind.

Blindness is an existential situation that entails constraint and imagination. The archetypal function of blindness is to demand intense introspection that might open the gates to fiction in literature. As Jorge Luis Borges reflects, for authors the loss of sight might be a gift:

> "No one should read self-pity or reproach
> into this statement of the majesty
> of God; who with such splendid irony
> granted me books and blindness at one touch."

This condition of sight deprivation explains the emphasis Rosen places on the other senses—smell above all. In fact, in Rosen's first novel (*Ziona*™, 2016) one of the many—and quite useless—superpowers of Ziona, the dysfunctional Jewish superheroine, is a highly developed sense of smell. In *Kafka for Kids* and *The Dust Channel* (2016) we find awkward moments where odors disrupt the narrative, too.

It is in his project *Justine Frank* (1998–2005) that Rosen makes his most complex comment on literature, its peripheral genres, and clichés. Justine Frank is a forgotten Belgian painter and writer whose life and work were meticulously created by Rosen. The reasons for her demise and oblivion are implanted in her biography: a Jewish woman among the male-dominated Surrealist movement in Paris, who, in her work, combined extreme sexuality and Jewish iconography. As the *coup de grace* to her oblivion, she emigrates to Israel,

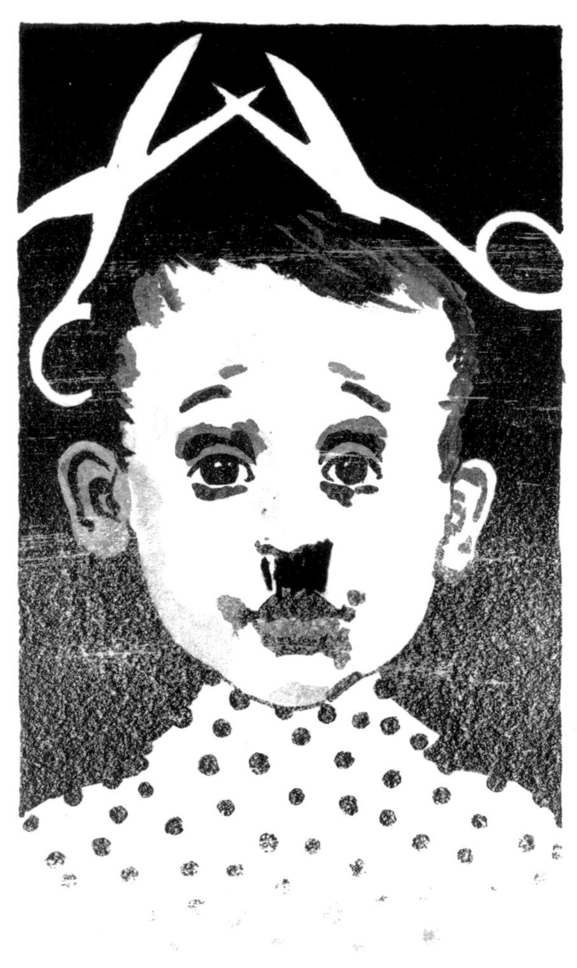

Roee Rosen
Live and Die as Eva Braun (number 2), 1995
mixed media on paper
(collection of the Israel Museum)

disappearing from the artistic scene in Europe and being totally alien, even offensive, to the minute cultural milieu of the Zionist settlement in 1940s British Palestine.

The whole Justine Frank cosmogony is literary in concept. It includes a biography of Frank, which masterfully alternates between fake, documentary and gossip, leaving mysterious gaps for speculation. In addition to Frank's surviving pictorial output, there is also an erotic novel titled *Sweet Sweat* (1931). Then there is a pseudo-academic and lengthy study of Frank (credited to Roee Rosen), in which she is presented either as a radical proto-feminist who claims for herself the signs and symbols of "Jewishness," or (no less radical) as a relative of the ominous Rabbi Jacob Frank, who promoted the discipline of redemption through sin. We also find the figures of several scholars of Frank, among them the translator of her novel to Hebrew, Joanna Führer-Ha'sfari (the choice of the name and the way it reflects her ethnic origin faithfully reflects academic, as well as wider cultural, clichés). Furthermore, Führer-Ha'sfari is the subject of a supposedly botched TV interview that resurfaces as the film *Two Women and a Man* (2005). In this video, the critic is represented by Rosen in a memorable drag appearance. In the interview, Führer-Ha'sfari takes the opportunity to thrash Roee Rosen because of his appropriation of Frank's legacy, thus bringing full circle the Justine Frank project as a reflection of the artistic and literary world, its mechanisms, and personal grudges.

The implementation of mediatic structures, and the use of specific language and conventions, is to be found in all of Rosen's works, whether literary, filmic, or pictorial. Whether creating operettas (*The Dust Channel*, *The Confessions of Roee Rosen*, or *Kafka for Kids*) or revisiting TV formats, interviews, and documentary film, Rosen always addresses the medium's inner structure. *The Confessions of Roee Rosen* comes with a trailer and a gag reel, while *The Dust Channel* and *Kafka for Kids* mimic TV formats, including advertisements, news, and more. This is the case also for the relationship between text and image, where Rosen implements a slew of generic precedents, from medieval illuminations, and the work of the British eighteenth-century poet and painter William Blake, to the history of comics and children's book illustrations.

For a later literary project, Rosen adopts a structure analogous to Justine Frank's, centering on his character Efim Poplavsky (writing under the pseudonym of Maxim Komar-Myshkin). In an album of verse and images entitled *Vladimir's Nights*, Poplavsky, who believed Putin had a personal vendetta against him, hallucinates his revenge: objects are animated so as to torture, rape, and eventually kill Putin. The plot, which at the time of publication in 2014 was deemed a paranoid delusion, looks today much like a prophetic reading of the Russian dictator's murderous character.

As was the case with Führer-Ha'sfari in Justine Frank, the committed fictional literary scholar Rosa Chabanova mediates Komar-Myshkin's work, exploring its complex, paranoiac web of references to Russian culture and politics. Her plate-by-plate annotations, presented as a long appendix to the album, turn out to be a macabre novel in disguise, with herself as one of the principal protagonists. In a world of blind artists, the external eye, the onlooker, interprets the literary work, adding layers of narratives that result in a kaleidoscope of views that violently conflict. Rosen's protagonists might not see, but they gain significance from being seen by others.

In addressing the gaps in the narrative rather than the obviously stated, Rosen touches upon another literary convention—the frontispiece of books. Taking advantage of the perception we might have of Sigmund Freud and his intrinsic ambivalence and psychological ambiguity, in his *Standard Edition* (2014–22), Rosen takes the universally accepted edition of Freud's works, and engages in a playful spree of deconstruction of the titles and subjects in his facsimile, reflecting on his own life and ongoing artistic concerns.

Rosen's engagement with a canonic work such as Franz Kafka's *The Metamorphosis*, then, comes hardly as a surprise. A masterpiece that tells the story of a person morphing into an insect, it could have come directly from Rosen's creative mind. By presenting the work as a piece for children, it falls in line with his other "children's books," as well as continuing his defiance of child/adult and male/female divides. Like the transformative qualities of the story it references, *Kafka for Kids* itself morphs from one thing into another. It is the translation of a book into an opera script and the transformation of a story for adults into a story for kids. As is to be expected, far from being adapted appropriately for a young audience, Kafka's story is literally dumped on a shocked child. The legal monologue towards the end of the film shows that the interest of the work is not in making Kafka's *Metamorphosis* palatable for children but rather to show how the "blind" Israeli justice system in the Occupied Territories creates truly Kafkaesque situations for detained children.

In *Lucy is Sick* (2020–ongoing), his most recent book, Rosen returns to his old alter-ego to tell the story of his own illness and recovery from bone cancer. The explicit pornography of the first *Lucy* is replaced by the no-less shocking and detailed description of the excruciating pain, medical procedures, and terminology that Rosen faces—all in the pleasant, recreational guise of a coloring book.

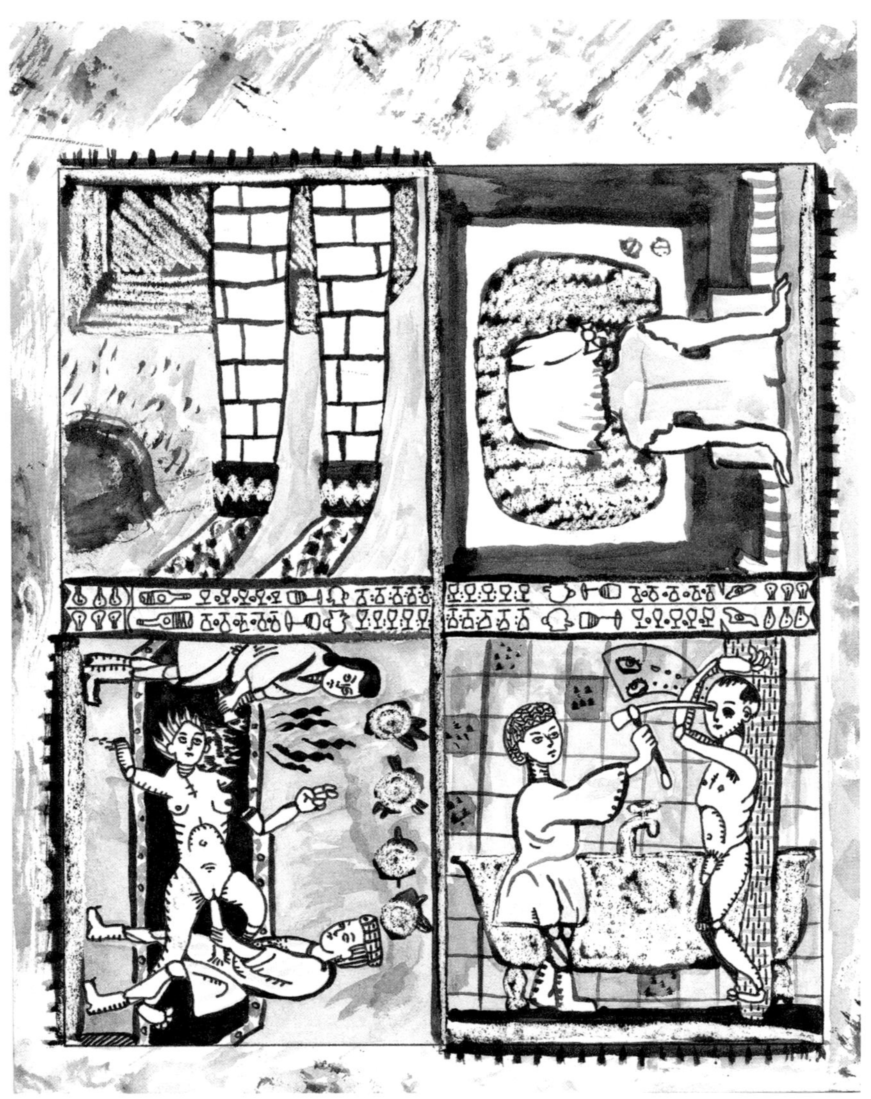

Roee Rosen
from *The Blind Merchant* (prologue, plate 6), 1989–91
pastel and watercolor on paper
(collection Centre Pompidou)

At the end of this book, confronted with the brutal reality of illness, Rosen manifests in the clearest way his use of fiction:

> "Throughout life, fictionality was Lucy's mighty superpower.
> Fictionality emancipated the body from its prescribed anatomy.
> Fictionality transported the past to the present and changed it.
> Fictionality revealed the truth in fantasies and exposed the fallacies of the real.
> Fictionality fought resiliently against excessive narcissism, heroism, self-pity, and authority. Fictionality was a superheroine with an infinite number of costumes and weapons."

Rosen's use of the word "fictionality" is unusual, and its meaning may seem ambiguous. Perhaps we can interpret the word "fictionality" as relating to "fiction," just as we understand "functionality" as relating to "function." Take, for instance, a Dyson DC07™ vacuum cleaner. As an appliance, the function of this object is to remove dust. Its functionality, though, lies rather in the metaphorical translation of that function—in this case, is to help get us rid of undesired objects, ideas, realities, or people—as reflected in *The Dust Channel*.

The term "fictionality," then, implies looking beyond mere fictional narrative to a palimpsest of cultural and tautological meta-narratives. Moreover, while fiction can only represent itself, fictionality also leaves room for the introduction of the real and concrete in the narrative. In so doing, fictionality always keeps alive the dilemma between reality and the imaginary—a dilemma that continually drives the work of the agnostic artist, Roee Rosen.

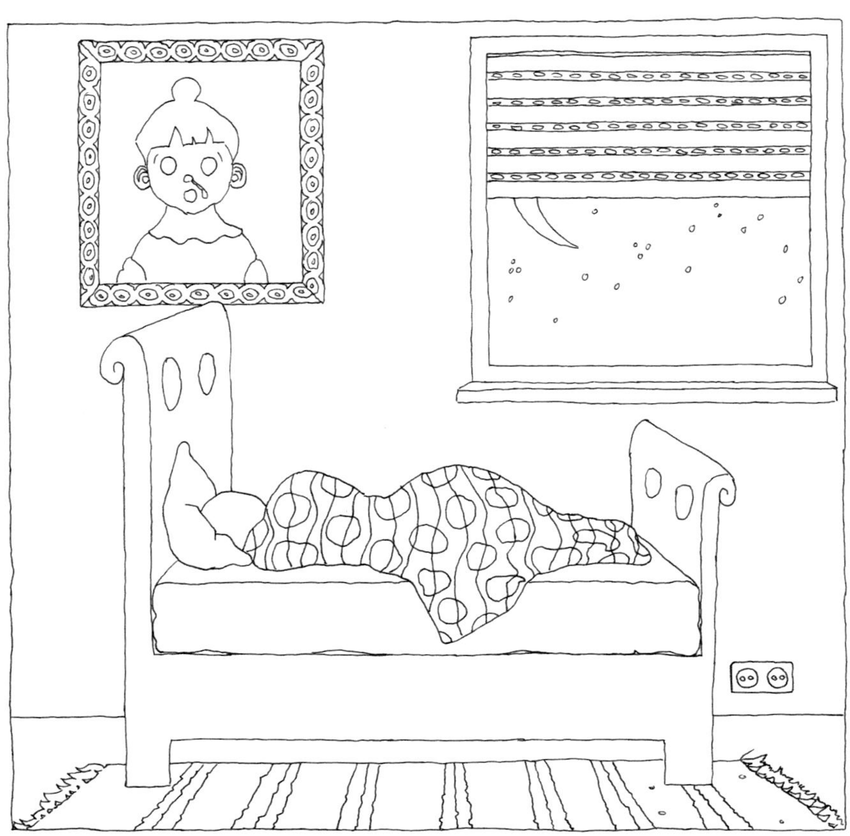

Roee Rosen
from the artist book *Lucy is Sick*, 2020–ongoing
pen on paper

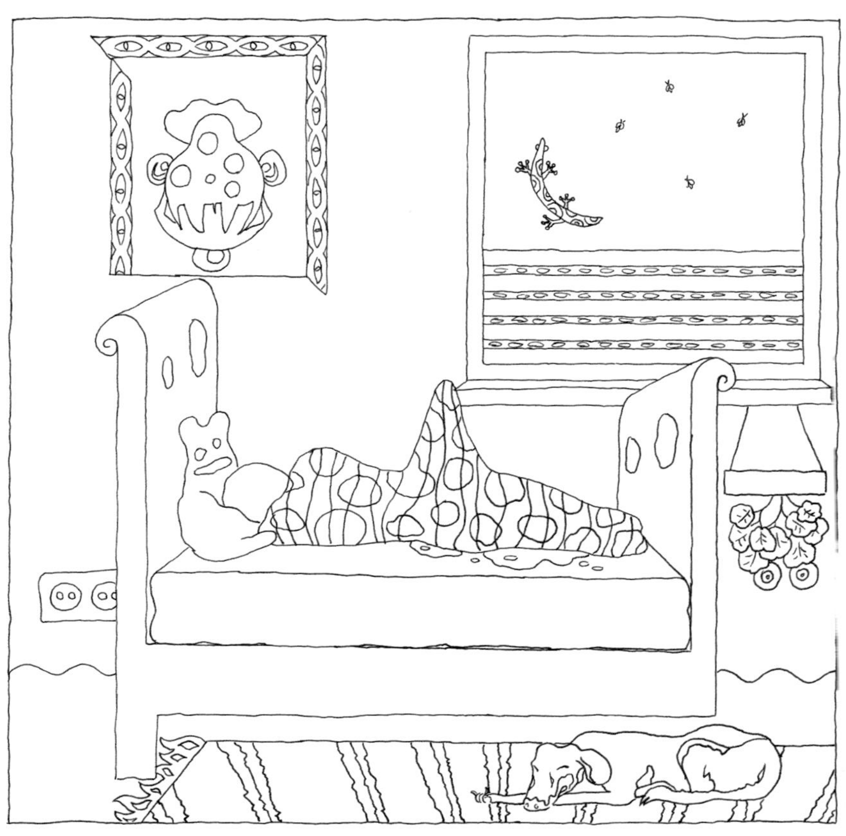

K. FOR KIDS

JEAN-PIERRE REHM

After "being" Justine Frank, Joanna Führer-Ha'sfari, Eva Braun, Anne Kastorp, Roee Rosen, Maxim Komar-Myshkin, Efim Poplavsky, Rosa Chabanova; after fashioning all these personas, all this novelistic manna, all these multicolored, intricate worlds—by turns and at once playful, clever, mordant, equivocal, unsettling, disturbing—here, with *Kafka for Kids*, Roee Rosen makes use of the authority of an antecedent signature. It is important to take the full measure of this gesture, which breaks with the *biographical production* at the heart of Rosen's work—work consisting until now of construction, of reinterpretation, of *possession*, as it is described in the trailer for *The Confessions of Roee Rosen*. This was already the case with one of Rosen's earliest works, *The Blind Merchant*, made between 1989 and 1991—an artist's book that reimagined *The Merchant of Venice* in 145 drawings. But in contrast with Shakespeare, to choose Kafka is to turn to an author who, in spite of his unparalleled impact, is not self-evident. After having been rather discreet during his lifetime, Kafka is presented as sulfurous. *Faut-il brûler Kafka?* (*Should Kafka be burned?*) was the provocative title of a 1946 survey by Pierre Fauchery in the communist weekly *Action*, in which he summarized the communist argument for discrediting an oeuvre deemed "suspect."[1] What this journalist judged to be cause enough to call for auto-da-fé, and just after the end of the war during which Kafka's texts were

1 Pierre Fauchery, "Faut-il brûler Kafka?," *Action*, no. 90 (24 May 1946); https://www.tandfonline.com/doi/abs/10.1080/00168890.2015.1039411?journalCode=vger20.

banned (not to mention the bundle of manuscripts seized and irremediably lost in 1933 after a raid by the Gestapo in the Berlin apartment of Kafka's last companion, Dora Diamant), is all the more sinister and violent because Kafka himself had charged his friend Max Brod with carrying out a similar obliteration. This order is notorious, set out in Kafka's will by the writer himself in the form of a folded note written in ink three years before his death in 1924 and later found among his other papers:

> "Dearest Max, my last request: Everything I leave behind me (in my bookcase, linen-cupboard, and my desk both at home and in the office, or anywhere else where anything may have got to and meets your eye), in the way of diaries, manuscripts, letters (my own and others'), sketches, and so on, to be burned unread; also all writings and sketches which you or others may possess; and ask those others for them in my name. Letters which they do not want to hand over to you, they should at least promise faithfully to burn themselves."[2]

Thus, after many threatened autos-da-fé Kafka's oeuvre endured, paradigmatically, in the mode of a *survivance*.[3] This question of survivance relates, in a far more general manner, to the nature of literature itself. Kafka himself, in striking terms, ceaselessly weaves a tangle of contradictions from the two "deaths": the death of the author, and his own death. Hence his abyssal letter to Max Brod on 5 July 1922:

> "I died my whole life long and now I will really die. My life was sweeter than other people's and my death will be more terrible by the same degree. Of course, the writer in me will die right away, since such a figure has no base, no substance, is less than dust. He is only barely possible in the broil of earthly life, is only a construct of sensuality. That is your writer

2 The English translation of this testament comes from Max Brod's afterword to Kafka's *The Trial*, trans. Willa and Edwin Muir (New York: Schocken, 1968), 265–6.

3 For the French theorist Jacques Derrida, the term "survivance" describes a way of survival that is life enhanced, more than one could imagine on the basis of the simple opposition between life and death. See: Jacques Derrida, *The Beast & the Sovereign*, vol. II (Chicago: University of Chicago Press, 2011), 130.

> for you. But I Myself cannot go on living because I have not lived, I have remained clay, I have not blown the spark into fire, but only used it to light up my corpse."[4]

It is striking to note that Kafka's image of the writer—without "base," without "substance"—corresponds to the qualities of the cartoon, that creature of animation that Agamben, in *The Coming Community*, associated with Limbo, the abode of children who died without being baptized. Also remarkable is the reconciliation between the medieval aesthetic mode and animated cartoons, as suggested by the critic Roberto Maria Dainotto in his discussion of Rosen's *Martyr Paintings*:

> "Cartoons, like martyrdom, are two sides of the same fantasy. Scene after scene, the cartoon hero is stabbed, blown off, minced, a steamroller flattens his body like a ribbon. Yet, in the next scene, he appears with his normal body. As an allegory, his body is indestructible, beyond the natural law of physics, of life and death. The role of painting—understood as a form of martyrdom and witness—must then be that of inventing an allegorical body."[5]

Roee Rosen previously staged his own survivance in his series of *Funeral Paintings* (2006–15) with cartoonish features and captions like" seen from his viewpoint, after being buried, with the ground transparent." It is a suite of eight tondi, a format traditionally based on the perfection of the circle, in service of the mode of allegorical representation known as *apotheosis*. Building on Sergei Eisenstein's laudatory remarks about Walt Disney that "Disney is an example (within the general formula of the comical) of a case of formal ecstasy!!!,"[6] let us take the hypothesis that animation's horizon, and the source of its jouissance ("a construct of sensuality,"[7] as Kafka said, or in French *l'appétit de jouir*), is precisely

4 In Franz Kafka, *Letters to Friends, Family, and Editors*, trans. Richard and Clara Winston (London: John Calder, 1978), 332–5, at 334.

5 Roberto Maria Dainotto, "Portrait of the Artist as a Blind Martyr," in *Roee Rosen: Martyr Paintings* (Ramat Gan, Israel: Ramat Gan Museum, 1994), 20.

6 In *The Eisenstein Collection*, ed. Richard Taylor (Kolkata: Seagull Books, 2006), 126.

7 In *Franz Kafka, Briefe. 1902–24*, ed. Max Brod (Frankfurt am Main: Fischer, 1975), 385.

apotheosis: the ascent into heaven, deliverance, the logical consequence of a metamorphic force free from any predetermined form and from all gravitational heaviness. A similar apotheosis was evoked in Scene 8 of *Live and Die as Eva Braun*: "You are actually flying! The childish renditions of the dead person leaving its body were almost true! Ascendance, chariots of cherubs, flight," Rosen's text says, before ending with the famous magical flight that concludes De Sica's 1951 film *Miracle in Milan*. Another apotheosis is in the photo of a bas-relief illustrating the celestial assumption of Elijah, brandished by Francisca Panikar in the second chapter of Rosen's *Confessions*. The use of cartoons is therefore not only the stylistic promise of a program *for children* and its necessary scenario; it would also be, *a priori*, a guarantee of emancipation from the finitude of mortality, a childhood art form that certifies general innocence.

There is the rub, however, and in multiple instances. There is, first of all, literally a tale of apotheosis in Kafka's story "The Bucket Rider"—a sublimity that Italo Calvino, in one of his last lectures, compared to medieval portrayals of witches on their broomsticks. But such apotheosis ends in a desert, a frozen hell, a hell all the more emphatic by being thus inverted (cold is punishment for those who freeze to death; for them the infernal flames would be an unseasonable luxury): "And with that I ascend into the regions of the ice mountains and am lost forever,"[8] turning the black of the coal bucket into the "sole dark spot" in the expanse of the "frozen whiteness,"[9] a single period on a blank page. In *Kafka for Kids*, the character of the miserable knight cries, *blinded*, his eyes pierced by frozen jets of tears.

Next is that the cartoon is not sheltered from corruption—moral or tangible. Boki-Poki, a summary figure in *Kafka for Kids*, at once farcical and unsettling, ends up appearing on screen in over-large pixels; the picture freezes at the exact moment the indictment is announced. Innocence is seriously doubted, and the animation seizes up to eliminate the possibility of any effigy.

Continuing among the innumerable links that are woven within Rosen's oeuvre, one would have to be blind not to note the similarity between the cartoons of *Kafka for Kids* and another work, *Lucy is Sick* (2020), his children's coloring

8 "The Bucket Rider," trans. Willa and Edwin Muir, in *Franz Kafka: The Complete Stories*, ed. Naum Glatzer (New York: Schocken, 1971), 412–14.

9 These two phrases appear only in some early versions of "The Bucket Rider" and in the French translation (as "unique tache sombre" and "gelée blanche") by Alexandre Vialatte and Marthe Robert in *Kafka: Œuvres Complètes*, vol. 2, ed. Claude David (Paris: Gallimard, 1980), 457, 460.

book with drawings in distinct black lines on white pages. Contemporary with the development of *Kafka for Kids*, this album with its pale pink cover is once again an autobiographical undertaking, a detailed log of extremely fragile health. The childlike innocence of the coloring book is an ineffectual and painful—and comical as a result—camouflage for a dreadful chronicle, that of a metamorphosis inflicted by a deadly illness. Thus, it resonates completely differently from the macabre joke, of which Rosen is still fond, in his invitation to *A Guided Journey Inside My Grave* (2014).

Here's where the "magic carpet" of the animated image is pulled out from under the feet of the certainty of a supposed childhood tranquility, in order to put it into relation with the harmful forces of metamorphosis. The animation has contaminated with its incredible power the very nature of presence on the entire stage, since the furnishings find themselves haunted by actors who are roughly made up to blend into the set. It is in a context of such indecisiveness (intently imitated according to the tradition of musical comedy, where artifice never bothers with verisimilitude but, quite the opposite, flaunts its anti-naturalism, an assurance of enchantment), between the living and the inanimate, that one must consider that Titorelli's painting be declared a counterfeit by The Bearer of Bad News. The picture reveals an absence of innocence: being a copy, a fake; lying; being an outlaw—this is inherent to its nature.

In a sense, this is evidence of the very decisiveness of the project of *Kafka for Kids*. For Max Brod is no longer the only one to defy Kafka's interdiction; Rosen also capitalizes on it in authorizing himself to represent Gregor Samsa metamorphosed into an insect. As recalled by *Kafka for Kids*' The Bearer of Bad News character's threatening to interrupt the broadcast, Kafka gave strict instructions against attempts to pictorially represent *The Metamorphosis*'s vermin. On 25 October 1915, a very worried Kafka wrote to his editor Kurt Wolff:

> "You recently mentioned that Ottomar Starke is going to do a drawing for the title page of *Metamorphosis*. [...] This prospect has given me a minor and perhaps unnecessary fright. It struck me that Starke [...] might want to draw the insect itself. Not that, please not that! I do not want to restrict him, but only to make this plea out of my deeper knowledge of the story. The insect itself cannot be depicted. It cannot even be shown from a distance. [...] I would be very grateful if you would pass along my request and make it more emphatic. If I were to offer suggestions for an illustration, I would choose such scenes as the following: the parents and the head clerk in front of the locked door,

or even better, the parents and the sister in the lighted room, with the door open upon the adjoining room that lies in darkness."[10]

It is of course interesting to note that Kafka himself got out ahead of this drive for figuration (and to forestall it) and added a magnificent focal precision that trumped the illustrator's potential play of depicting the insect indistinctly from afar. It's equally compelling to see him imagine, instead of the insect, a sort of theater dictated by space, the staging of open and closed doors, and the distribution of light and shadow. Even if Orson Welles would follow this vein for his adaptation of *The Trial*, Roee Rosen does not retain this direction. One could call this moment suggested by Kafka expressionist *avant la lettre* (and Hanns Zischler's beautiful book *Kafka Goes to the Movies* pays particular attention to the writer's love of going to the cinema, about which Kafka said in 1913: "The people should rise up for the movie theaters and not let themselves be *tricked* and *seduced* [...] by the 'psychological clowns' of literature!"[11]); Rosen prefers the spotlight of the TV set, as well as the depthless surface of an animation: a cinema without the effect of illusion. Exemplarily, in the animated passages—with the remarkable exception of the framed portrait of the Venus in furs (let's call her that) on the wall of Gregor's bedroom—the faces of the protagonists emphatically display their abstraction, a playful and mobile citation from cubism, contemporary with the writing of the short story (Titorelli presents, moreover, as feminized, a caricature of Picasso). Such cinema leaves no place for drama other than that opened up by the voice of the narrator inside this "théâtre de l'écoute", this theater of the ear, of listening. The device here, announced by the title and methodically stated (without forgetting the interludes for advertisements), is that of the children's educational broadcast. The space of the book is open: the quiet roughness of a text to be deciphered alone is replaced by the ritual of bedtime reading before going to sleep. The multivalent theater of the ear, like the lecturer of *What is a Child?*, speaks to an evident variety of listeners: the little girl's active listening; the furniture's listening (tables, lamps, paintings, etc.), precisely embodied by obviously attentive actors; even the *Toy Orchestra* musicians' listening as they're always present, even when they are off-screen, even when they are not playing.

10 In *Franz Kafka: Letters to Friends, Family, and Editors*, 114–15.

11 Cited in Hanns Zischler, *Kafka Goes to the Movies*, trans. Susan H. Gillespie (Chicago: University of Chicago Press, 2003), 127.

There is a clear distinction between, on the one hand, the messages of the interludes which directly address the spectator and, on the other hand, everything that is recounted, questioned, explained, sung, played, and mediated each time by the general device of hearing. In this sense, the animated passages are completely silent. This is exemplified by the sole moment when Gregor tries to express himself and only produces rumblings that are unintelligible—except for to us, because they are written directly on the image, because they are translated *as* images, as block letters. This is how *Kafka for Kids* avoids being merely *The Metamorphosis* translated for a child audience—Kafka reduced, simplified, metamorphosed to a format supposedly appropriate to a supposedly identified target, like *Dust Channel* presented itself as a television program aimed at an audience of vacuum cleaners. It's exactly this theater of the ear that Kafka, in his autobiographical sketches, describes as anything but familiar:

> "A boy, for instance, who is in the middle of reading an exciting story in the evening, will never be made to realize, merely by an argument bearing solely upon himself that he must stop reading and go to bed. [...] But the main thing was that the condemnation with which my peculiarity of reading for a long time had met I Myself now extended, by my own means, to the peculiarity, which I kept concealed, of dereliction of duty."[12]

Cited by Bataille (an author who we know is of seminal importance to Rosen's Justine Frank) in the chapter devoted to Kafka in his text *Literature and Evil*, this supports what he calls his "childishness"—a consistency upheld by the titles of several of the chapters in Bataille's essay: "Kafka's Perfect Puerility," "The Sustenance of the Infantile Situation," "The Child's Happy Exuberance [...]."[13] This childishness is not guilelessness; it is, on the contrary, the manifestation of incongruity, the outrage of the *sans-droit*—those without rights.

With *Kafka for Kids*, Rosen makes the metamorphosis, and Kafka, as its best vector, touches childhood. *K. for Kids*, like Welles's title *F. for Fake*: Kafka is projected not *towards* the children but rather, so to speak, *in their place*—the children's; and this in a double movement exemplified by the chiasmus at work in Kafka's story. On the one hand, this is the Goethean idealism of improving and completing an

12 "Fragments from Note-Books and Loose Pages," in Franz Kafka, *Wedding Preparations in the Country and Other Posthumous Prose Writings*, trans. Ernst Kaiser and Eithne Wilkins (London: Secker and Warburg, 1954), 222–24.

13 Georges Bataille, "Kafka," in *Literature and Evil*, trans. Alastair Hamilton (London: Marion Boyars, 1973), 149–71.

initial form. Goethe, for whom the *Journal* of Kafka is testament to assiduous reading, writes in *The Metamorphosis of Plants*: “you began to grow and thrive / according to the law, which made you appear. / That way you must be, you cannot escape yourself / […] No power and no time is able to destroy / such imprinted form, which develops while living.”[14] Such is the case for Grete, Gregor’s sister, so much so that these are the final words of Kafka’s *The Metamorphosis*: “In spite of [the beauty creams] which had made her cheeks pale, [Grete] had bloomed into a pretty girl with a good figure. […] [She] sprang to her feet first and stretched her young body.”[15] Grete, the only other character besides her brother to be given a first name in Kafka’s story (and one similar to his), is the one who, from the start, tries to understand her brother’s new disposition and takes care of him; she is also the one who changes her mind, gets tired of her transformed brother, and convinces the family to get rid of him. What’s more, Grete blossoms and passes from child to soon-to-be-married woman over the course of the story. Gregor, on the other hand, is struck by regression. The story begins with his difficulty in leaving his bed, his difficulty in retaining bodily autonomy. Decomposition is in the making and disappearance is at work in Gregor’s body. His final state is that of a “completely flat and dry”[16] corpse, somewhat resembling a cartoon; then, carried away by the cleaning lady, his remains literally vanish from the story: “‘Oh,’ said the charwoman, giggling so amiably that she could not at once continue, ‘just this, you don’t need to bother about how to get rid of the thing next door. It’s been seen to already.’”[17] The change of form is so radical that it passes from form to formless, then to the volatilization of all form.

In *Kafka for Kids*, if indeed Gregor vanishes as he should, what about Grete? Besides her animated characterization, Grete is also, without a doubt, the “little girl”

14 Cited in Giorgio Agamben, *The Adventure*, trans. Lorenzo Chiesa (Cambridge, MA: MIT Press, 2018), 8–9. The poem first was published as *Urworte. Orphisch* (*Primal Words. Orphic*), see: "Urworte, Orphisch," in *Johann Wolfgang Goethe. Werke in 2 Bänden*, (Gütersloh: Bertelsmann Club GmbH, 1982), vol. 2, 126.

15 *The Metamorphosis*, trans. Willa and Edwin Muir, in *Franz Kafka: The Complete Stories*, ed. Naum Glatzer, p. 139. [Translator’s Note: The Muirs’ translation differs from the French translation that Rehm cites in his essay, which comes from Kafka’s *Récits* (Paris: Gallimard, coll. "La Pléiade," 1980), 244. Instead of "the beauty creams" that make Grete’s cheeks pale in the Gallimard translation, the Muir translation begins, "In spite of all of the sorrow of recent times, which had made her cheeks pale."]

16 *The Metamorphosis*, trans. Willa and Edwin Muir, 137.

17 Ibid. 138.

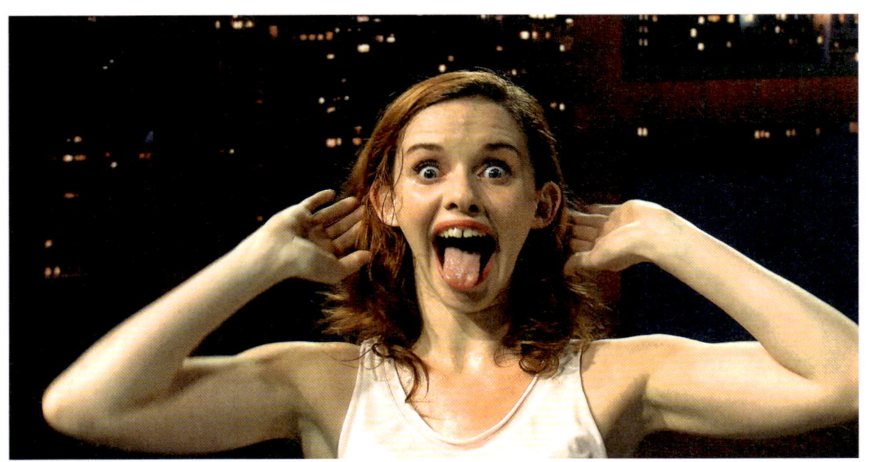

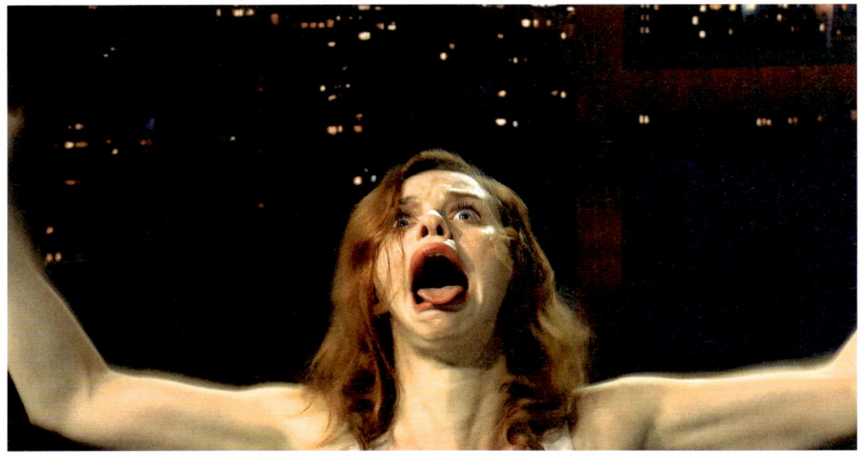

Roee Rosen
Hilarious, 2010
HD video, 21 minutes

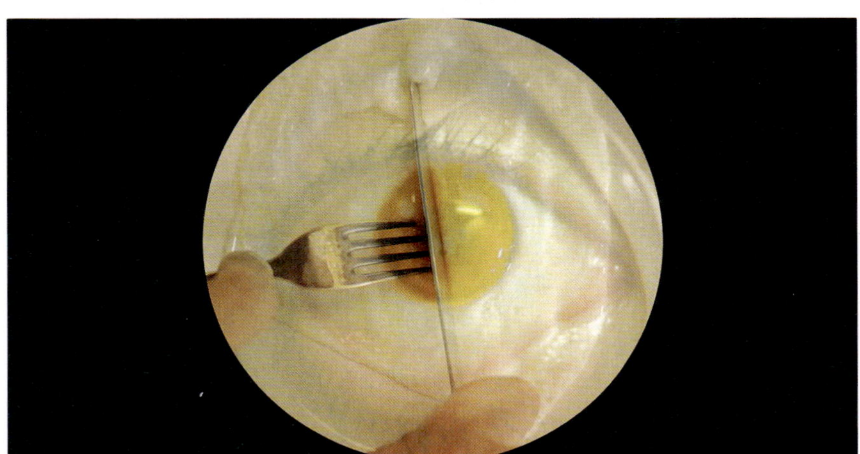

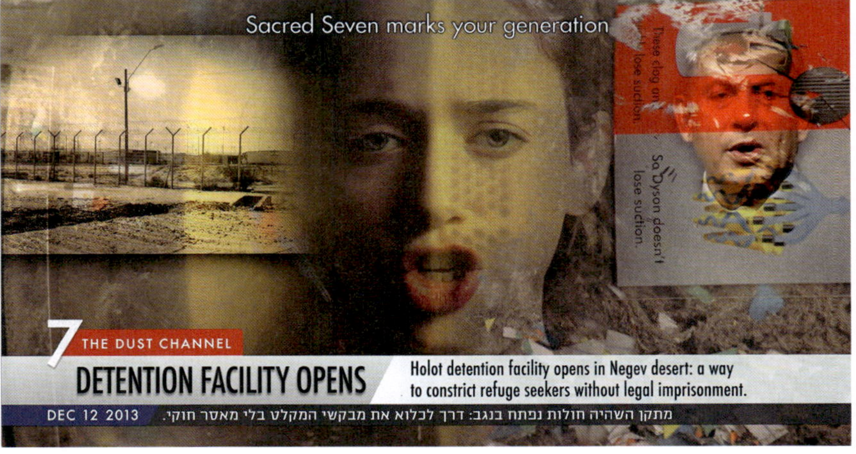

Roee Rosen
The Dust Channel, 2016
2K Video, 23 minutes

in the audience with sadistic impulses expressed plainly, snickering at the word "nude," stumbling over a rather sinister illustration of the metamorphosis, ready to welcome the end of the show, keen to lick the author's shoe, delighted at the prospect of killing the painting, etc. Transformed into an adult, Grete might also be *Kafka for Kids*' lecturer, a law expert who is portrayed by the very same actress as the young audience member, the fabulous Hani Furstenberg. And one must not forget "D.," the 12-year-old Palestinian to whom the lecturer makes her arguments and whose age and criminal status are subject to change. It goes without saying that setting this long educational insert at the end of Rosen's film overturns all the meaning of the scenes that preceded it. On the one hand, the contemporary meaning of exposing Israeli policy on punishment of children in the Occupied Territories appears as a counter-effect to curb any possibility of credulity when it comes to yet another "cultural" adaptation of Kafka. On the other hand, the lecturer herself doubles and troubles the clarity of her political analysis by confiding autobiographical secrets: About the aging of the body and its various mutations, including olfactory ones (crucial for Gregor). About the projection in space (in Accra) and in time (in a century) of an encounter with Kwame, a Ghanaian (like Haddy, the third Roee Rosen of the *Confessions*) and the fictitious addressee of the explanation of Israeli criminal law and its contradictions that make the very law a transitional text, a metamorphic text. There is not enough room here to unfold all the formidable and staggering complexities at play in this piece of bravery, but the fact remains that its heart is not *only* the rigorous commentary on military law (described as "flexible, convulsive, shapeshifting") but, in a more decisive manner, that its "contradictions allow reality to alter on demand."

Both of them subject to state-of-exception laws (which allow the sovereign to abrogate personal rights and the rule of law under exceptional circumstances), neither Gregor nor Grete are free from its effects. Neither are those who are subjected to it, nor those who denounce it, nor even the fabrications that expose it. Kafka may well be a "doctor of law," but he cannot cure it either, it is explained to the little girl in the audience. Metamorphosis, the law of generalized corruption, is mixed up in everything. Thus, can we understand one of *Kafka for Kids*' advertising inserts, "The People's Delicatessen." In a 30 October 1911 journal entry, Kafka writes, with hints of the fantastic, a confession that echoes the repugnant gluttony of the new Gregor:

> "This craving that I almost always have, when for once I feel my stomach is healthy, to heap up in me notions of terrible deeds of daring with

food. I especially satisfy this craving in front of pork butchers. If I see a sausage that is labeled as an old, hard sausage, I bite into it in my imagination with all my teeth and swallow quickly, regularly, and thoughtlessly, like a machine. [...] I shove the long slabs of rib meat unbitten into my mouth, and then pull them out again from behind, tearing through stomach and intestines. I eat dirty delicatessen stores completely empty. Cram myself with herrings, pickles, and all the bad, old, sharp foods."[18]

Such an obsessional alimentary consumerism, whose signature is a predilection for the spoiled, the filthy, and the suspect, reveals no immediate reason. In other words, that there is proximity here between Franz and Gregor produces no further clarification—apart from the proof of evident circulation between Kafka's diaries and *The Metamorphosis*—of a potential, supposedly autobiographical, referent between the writer's dietary predilections and the eating habits of a woodlouse. (In Kafka's journal entry, the physiological firmness of the speaker's *I* is particularly mangled—bizarrely swallowed, digested, devoured, regurgitated.) Recall that at the end of a 17 November 1912 letter addressed to Félice Bauer, Kafka (after having mentioned his great difficulty in extricating himself from his couch) alludes to "a little story that came to my mind in the desolation of my bed and which is overwhelming me to the core," here also drawing a parallel between the circumstances of the start of the writing and the beginning of *The Metamorphosis* itself. The metamorphosis makes it possible, in the scene after the first visit by The Bearer of Bad News, to slide on a play of sonorities from *Kafka's shoe* to *Kafka's Jew*—from a patchwork kind of prohibition on formal representation, to its paradoxical authorization by Kafka's being Jewish—and all by the strange telephone that the shoe represents (which comes perhaps from Chaplin, in addition to the shoe's fetishist function ["May I lick it?"]); this is what alerts us to any certainty as regards the force that is metamorphosis. It permits the forbidden; it permits itself to *use* the forbidden; it makes mute the "law beyond the law"—without forgetting that it is an object of desire.

***

The only time the word *metamorphosis* appears in a title of Rosen's is, unless I'm mistaken, *The Metamorphosis of a Woman-Assassin*, the last of many self-portraits

18 *The Diaries of Franz Kafka, 1910–1913*, trans. Joseph Kresh, ed. Max Brod (London: Secker & Warburg, 1948), 122.

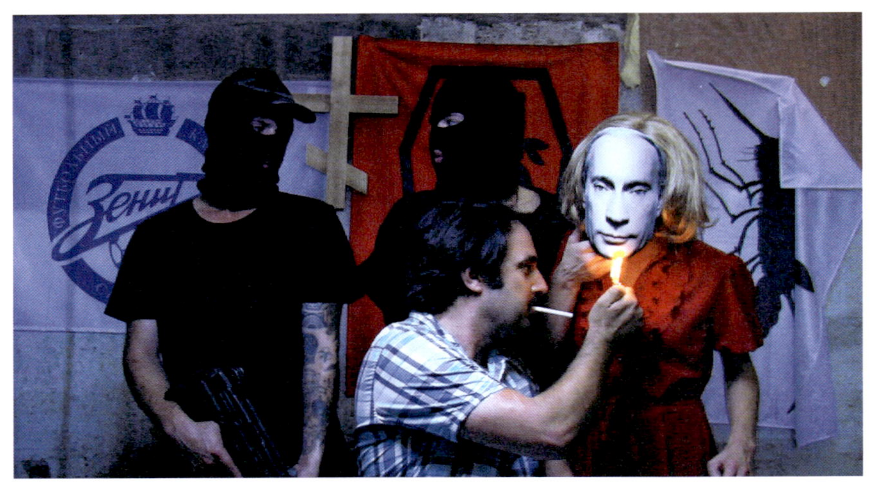

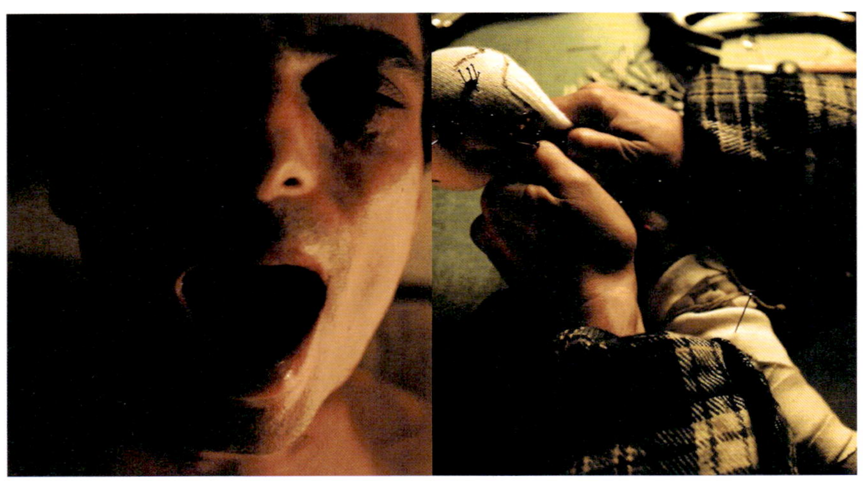

Roee Rosen
The Buried Alive Videos, 2013
HD video, 36 minutes

by Justine Frank, an oil on canvas given the date 1940–41. Incidentally, recall that the first name of the pseudonym with which Justine Frank signs her only novel is none other than Gregoire, which in this tableau rather emphasizes a decided and declared kinship between Justine and the protagonist of the famous novella, even ignoring what is signified by the proximity between the names *Frank* and *Franz K.* The last in a series, *The Metamorphosis of a Woman-Assassin* presents itself as a silhouetted quadruple portrait cut out in profile, black on a bluish white background, then red stained with white. The tradition of these profiles in silhouette goes back a long way, but it was so widespread in Europe in the middle classes from the 18th century onward that some call it the ancestor of photography in its actual and symbolic use. For Frank, reviving this practice is a way of attacking, of ruining, a kind of figuration that is connected with the Enlightenment, both historically and in the binary principle of its production. From the first profile to the last in *The Metamorphosis of a Woman-Assassin*, increasing hairiness degrades the silhouette's delicate initial contours to the point of transforming the young woman into a caricature of a witch or an unsettling Janus with the hair itself becoming a grotesque profile, or even disfiguring a face to make it fertile ground for the roots of some tuber that has already buried Justine alive and is now extending itself underground. Justine, a kind of vermin without borders: her devouring hairiness is in contradiction with the expectations of the technique of silhouette, which is characterized by its true edge, not its growths or branches or static. The silhouette emerges distinctly from the surface while the metamorphic hairy being, scribbled with excrescences, plunges back into the abyss of underground works, back into the indiscernibility of the rhizome. The "woman-assassin" of the portrait's title can be understood as a reference to the pseudoscience of physiognomy, liable to purportedly reveal the soul and the idiosyncrasies of the portrait subject: here, a murderess. But it also represents the assassination, in painting, of Justine by Justine, a gradual execution, and the evident "metamorphosis" that the title specifies. Between 1941 and 1942 it will be followed, unsurprisingly, by Justine's final oil paintings: metamorphosed apotheoses, images that hide demonic self-portraits, celestial but depraved visions, tableaus of pathological and perverted heavens: *Sick Heaven*, *Shit Heaven*, and *A Portrait of Thieving Skies*.

***

The use of the filmic medium in Roee Rosen's work is anything but incidental. It is part of a strategy of authentication insofar as the film serves as proof of a subject each time: the self-portrait (*Dr Cross*; *The Confessions ...*), the taking of hostages (*Buried Alive Videos*), scientific discourse (*Two Women and a Man*; *Explaining the Law to Kwame*), televised stand-up (*Hilarious*), documentary evidence (*Out*). It can be confirmed, based on *Dust Channel*, that it is a question of doing the (perhaps contradictory) publicity, of polishing the (perhaps deceptive) advertisement, of producing the (perhaps scandalous) marketing *for a subject*. For the first time, perhaps, with *Kafka for Kids*, it is a question of letting the metamorphic principle act as a principle of ruin—or worse, of assassination. The assassination of childhood, the assassination of law, of a nation, of art, etc. And it is indeed an interment that we attend in *Kafka for Kids*' wonderful finale seen from above, seen from the perspective of those who have had an apotheosis, where Grete and all the protagonists of the film (one also glimpses figures from other films) sing a lullaby that bids adieu to childhood, to their fictional being, to themselves.

ROEE ROSEN

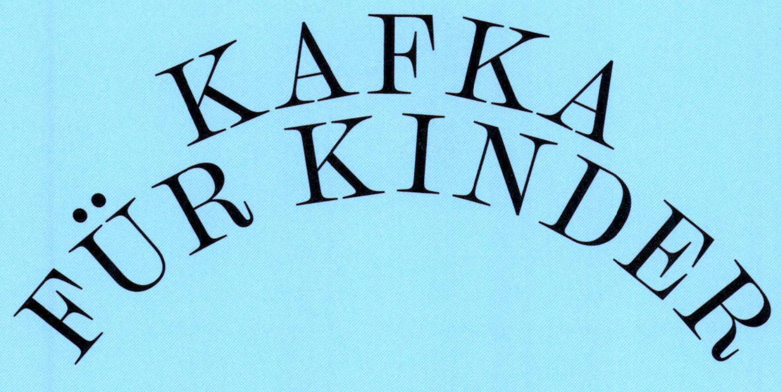

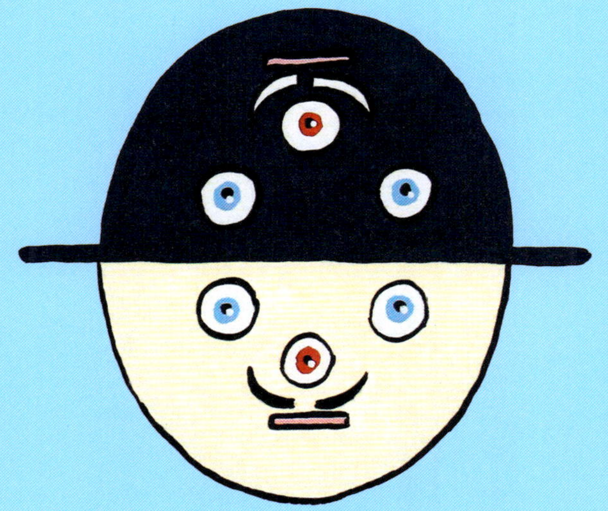

DAS SKRIPT

BESETZUNG

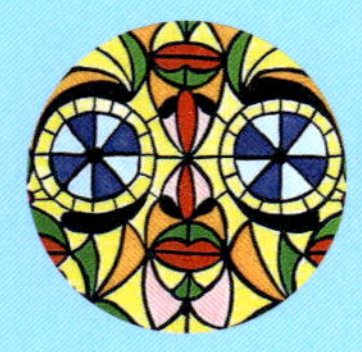

Geschichtenerzähler – Jeff Francis
Kind/Rechtsexpertin – Hani Furstenberg
Der Überbringer schlechter Nachrichten – Eli Gorenstein

Chor:

Im Wohnzimmer:

Herr Tisch (als *Prokurist*) – Hillel Rosen
Frau Schrank (als Stimme der *Bedienerin*) – Nadya Kucher
Frau Lampe (als Stimme von *Grete*) –Yifeat Ziv
Herr Ball (als Stimme des *Vaters*) – Yiftach Mizrahi
Herr Stuhl (als Stimme des *Zimmerherren*)/Sprecherin – Ayelet Robinson
Frau Stuhl (als Stimme der *Mutter*) – Orna Katz
Titorellis Gemälde – Yum Umi

Im Schlafzimmer:

Fräulein Linkes Kissen – Ayelet Robinson
Fräulein Rechtes Kissen – Nadya Kucher
Fräulein Decke – Yifeat Ziv
Herr Bett – Hillel Benjamin Rosen
Herr Ball – Yiftach Mizrahi
Fräulein Hellblaue Decke – Yum Umi
Fräulein Rosa Decke – Orna Katz

Musiker:innen des Toy Orchestra

PROLOG

1. SZENE – IM MAGISCHEN GESCHICHTENHAUS

Der Geschichtenerzähler und das Kind sitzen an einem Tisch, auf dem das Buch wartet. Viele der Gegenstände im Raum sind Schauspieler:innen, deren Gesichter (bemalt, passend zu den Gegenständen) durch Löcher sichtbar sind; anwesend sind Herr und Frau Stuhl, Frau Lampe, das Gemälde an der Wand („Titorelli") und die anderen Mitglieder des Chores.

Geschichtenerzähler: Guten Morgen.
Kind [*winkt schüchtern*]**:** Hallo.
Geschichtenerzähler: Weißt du noch, was wir heute tun wollten?
Kind: A-ha.
Geschichtenerzähler [*Kind nickt*]**:** Aufregend, oder? Heute werden wir erstmals ... [*Wartet, dass Kind den Satz vollendet.*]
Kind: A-ha.
Geschichtenerzähler: Du weißt weshalb?
Kind: A-ha.
Geschichtenerzähler: Weshalb wir alle aufgeregt sind?
Kind: A-ha.
Geschichtenerzähler: Wir sind aufgeregt, weil wir heute die Geschichten von ...
Kind [*nach einer Pause*]**:** A-ha.
Geschichtenerzähler [*sanft*]**:** Du kannst den Namen sagen, Schatz.
Kind [*kann sein Glück kaum glauben*]**:** Kann ich?
Geschichtenerzähler: Los, sag' all deinen Freund:innen im magischen Geschichtenhaus [*zeigt herum*], und sogar unseren Freund:innen da draußen, wie den Landwirt:innen, den Ärzt:innen, ...
Kind: ... den Steinen, den Pilot:innen, den Zwergen, den Mäusen, den Fenstern, den Türen, den Steinen ...
Geschichtenerzähler: ... und den Kindern, den Rechtsexpert:innen – erzähl' allen, dass wir eine der erstaunlichsten, lustigsten und manchmal gruseligsten [*führt eine fröhliche Zitterbewegung aus*] Geschichten lesen werden, von ...
Kind [*leise*]**:** Fr-hanz Ka-fka.
Geschichtenerzähler: Franz Kafka! [*Musikalische Untermalung*] Viele Jahre hat Franz Kafka Erwachsenen viel Glück und Freude

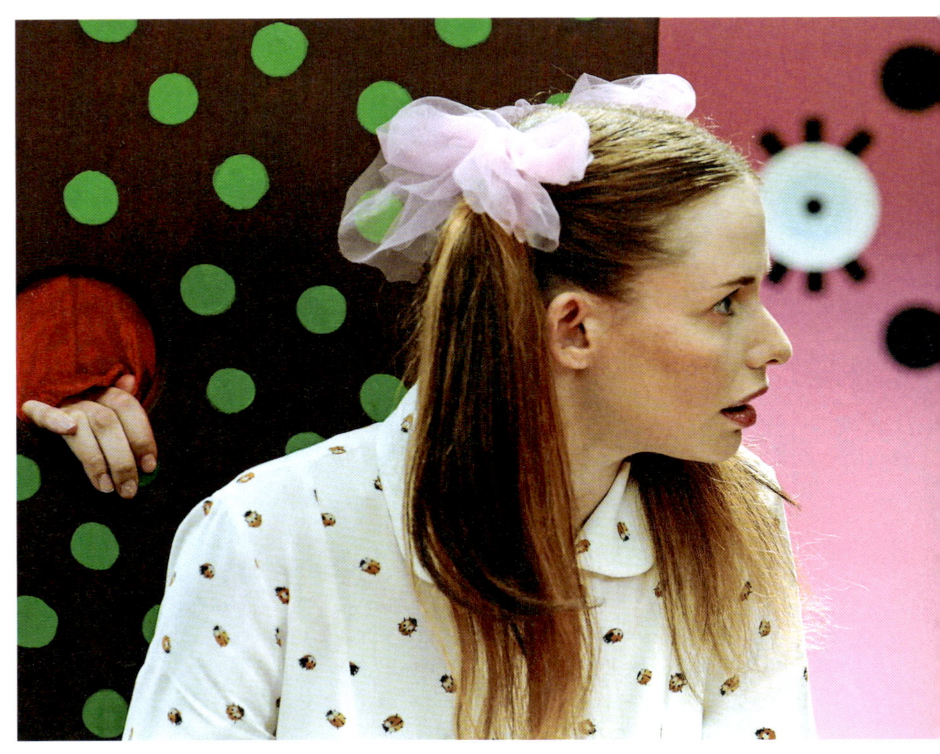

gebracht und jetzt sollen auch Kinder Anteil an dem Spaß haben. Und heute beginnen wir mit einer von Kafkas berühmtesten Erzählungen. Sie ist manchmal lustig, manchmal seltsam, und manchmal sogar gruselig [*beide zittern*], aber zum Schluss gibt es ...

Kind [*zögerlich*]**:** Ein Happy End?

Geschichtenerzähler: Genau. Wie fast alle von Kafkas Geschichten, hat auch diese hübsche Geschichte ein Happy End. [*Öffnet das Buch*] Die Geschichte heißt *Die Verwandlung.*

Kind: Die *was*?

Geschichtenerzähler: Hört sich kompliziert an, ist aber ganz einfach: Bei einer Verwandlung wird eine Sache zu einer anderen. Verstehst du?

Kind: Oh, klar. Wie wenn man ein Ei kocht.

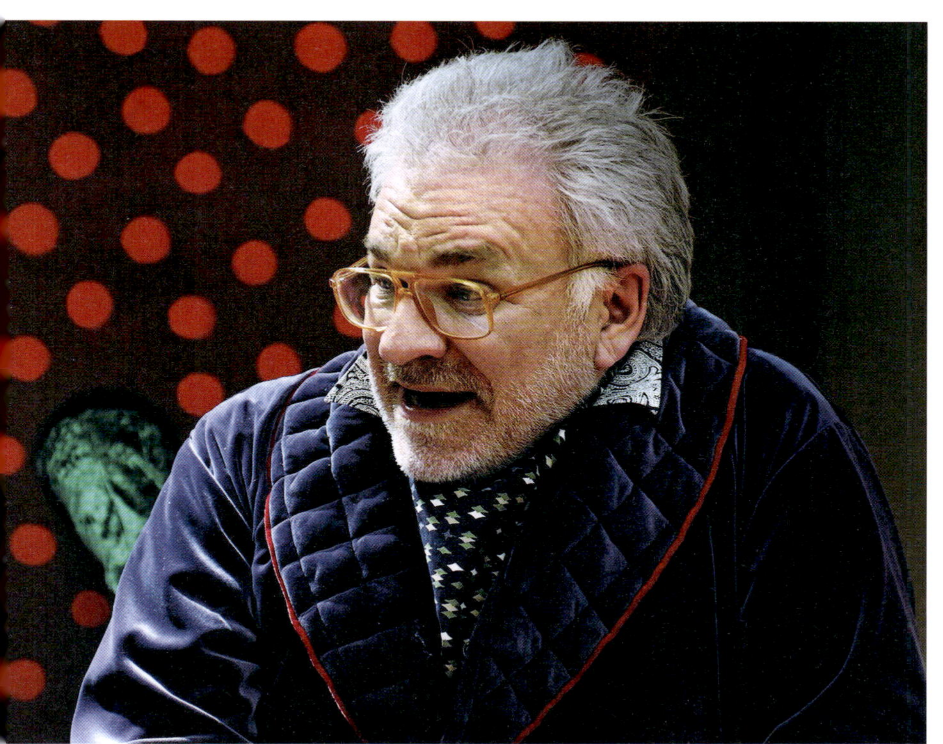

Geschichtenerzähler [*fröhlich*]**:** OK! Oder ...?

Kind: Und das Ei ist dann drinnen nicht mehr feucht, man kann es in der Hand halten und essen.

Geschichtenerzähler: OK. ... Fällt dir noch ein Beispiel für eine Verwandlung ein?

Kind: Ich hab' mal drei gekochte Eier gegessen. Drei! [*Hebt vier Finger*]

Geschichtenerzähler: Sehr gut ... aber fällt dir eine weitere Verwandlung ein?

Kind [*nach einer kurzen Pause*]**:** Wenn ein:e Pilot:in zu einem harten Ei wird. [*Pause.*] Oder wenn ein:e Landwirt:in stirbt.

Geschichtenerzähler [*fröhlich*]**:** Na dann! Eine Verwandlung! Also lass uns beginnen.

Eröffnungslied *Kafka für Kinder*

Ein fröhlicher zweiteiliger Kanon, vorgetragen vom Chor, während die Buchstaben des Kafka-Alphabets über den Bildschirm tanzen, ihn ausfüllen und sich zum Filmtitel zusammensetzen.

Ka, Ka,
Ka, Ka,
Ka ka ka ka ka,
Ka ka ka ka ka,
Ka-*Wow*, Ka-*Wie*, Ka-*Bumm*,
Ka-*Oh*, Ka-*Oi*, Ka-*Uuh*!
Das ist Kafka,
Kafka für Kinder.

KAPITEL

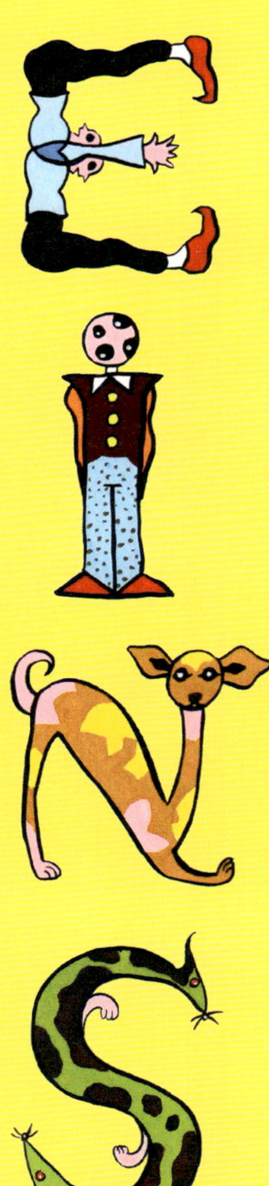

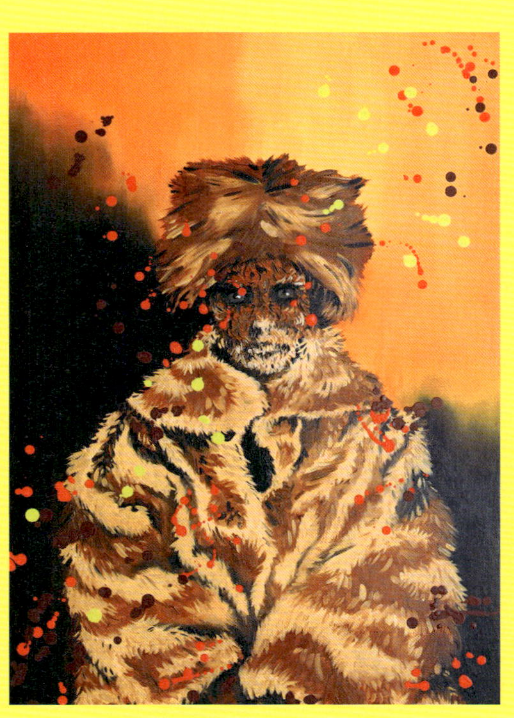

2. SZENE – ERWACHEN

Ein gemaltes Muster erscheint auf dem Bildschirm; die Kamera schwenkt langsam nach links, die Musik hört auf und der Geschichtenerzähler fährt fort.

Geschichtenerzähler: Eines Morgens erwachte ein Mann namens Gregor Samsa aus seinen Träumen und fand sich zu einem ungeheuren Ungeziefer verwandelt. [*Das Muster gehört zu der Decke, die Gregors Körper bedeckt und die Kamera zeigt jetzt sein Gesicht.*]

Kind [*erfreut*]**:** Wow! Ich würde mich auch gerne in ein riesiges Ungeziefer verwandeln können!

Geschichtenerzähler: Genau! Zuerst dachte Gregor er würde nur träumen, aber es war kein Traum. [*Animiertes Standbild: die Kamera zoomt aus Gregors Gesicht und zeigt sein Bett, die Wände und den Boden des Zimmers in der Totale. Ein ständiges Schwenken zur Linken bietet eine 360°-Tour der vier Wände und zeigt Details, die mit der Erzählung übereinstimmen.*] „Wie wäre es, wenn ich noch ein wenig weiterschliefe", dachte Gregor, „und alle Narrheiten vergäße. Dies frühzeitige Aufstehen macht einen ganz blödsinnig."

Kind [*kichert*]**:** „Blödsinnig."

Geschichtenerzähler: Aber es sollte nicht sein. Gregor blickte aus dem Fenster und sah, dass es draußen hell war. Er sah zum Wecker auf der Kommode und war erstaunt: Er hatte ihn auf vier Uhr eingestellt und es war schon halb sieben! [*Der Wecker ist zu sehen.*] Gregor war ein vielbeschäftigter Handelsreisender. Er musste jeden Tag früh aufstehen und hart arbeiten, weil sein Vater seinem Chef viel Geld schuldete und es zurückzahlen musste. Auf dem Tisch lagen Stoffmuster und darüber hing das Bild einer schönen Frau im Pelz, die ihren Arm ausstreckte. Gregor gefiel es so gut, dass er es gerahmt hatte. [*Der Schwenk stoppt für einen Augenblick, während die Kamera auf dem Bild verharrt.*] Aber es war so spät! Sein Chef würde sich Sorgen machen und jemanden schicken, der nach ihm sieht. Er musste sich beeilen. Außerdem war Gregor sehr hungrig. [*Der Schwenk ist vollendet, das Insekt ist wieder zu sehen; die Decke liegt nun auf dem Boden*] Und – sein Bauch juckte. [*Ein Blick zum Bauch, der mit weißen Flecken übersät ist.*] Dann hörte er seine Mutter aus dem Nebenzimmer rufen.

Mutter (Frau Stuhl) [*Animiertes Standbild als Zwischenschnitt zwischen der geschlossenen weißen Doppeltüre und Gregor*]**:** „Gregor? Es ist dreiviertel sieben. Wolltest du nicht wegfahren?“

Geschichtenerzähler [*wie Gregor*]**:** „Danke Mutter, ich stehe schon auf.“ [*Mit seiner normalen Stimme*] Dann hörte er seinen Vater.

Vater (Herr Ball) [*Zwischenschnitt gleiche Türe*]**:** „Gregor! Was ist denn?“

Geschichtenerzähler: Und an der anderen Türe rief seine Schwester.

Grete (Frau Lampe) [*zweite Türe im Zwischenschnitt mit Gregor*]**:** „Gregor? Ist dir nicht wohl? Brauchst du etwas?“

Geschichtenerzähler [*Gregors Stimme*]**:** „Bin schon fertig!“ [*Normale Stimme*] Er musste sich nun wirklich herumrollen und aus dem Bett kommen. Aber wie rollen sich Insekten herum?

3. SZENE – AUS DEM BETT KOMMEN

Dynamische Animation: Gregor wiegt sich hin und her. Die Bewegung wiederholt sich ständig und ist einfach, abgesehen vom komplexeren Zucken der acht Beine. Ein 2/4 Rhythmus; Musikinstrumente fallen in ein Crescendo ein, doch der Text wird eher rhythmisch gesprochen als gesungen.

Geschichtenerzähler: Gregor rollte sich von einer Seite zur anderen – eins, zwei! Wieder rollte er sich und versuchte, sich zu drehen –

Geschichtenerzähler und Kind: Eins, zwei!

Geschichtenerzähler: Schaukelt, schaukelt den ganzen Körper –

Geschichtenerzähler und Kind [*enthusiastischer*]**:** Eins, zwei!

Herr und Frau Stuhl [*das erste Mal hinter den nach hinten gelehnten Rücken von Kind und Geschichtenerzähler zu sehen*]**:** Tanz nur weiter, schmutziger Schatz! –

Geschichtenerzähler, Kind und Stühle: Eins, zwei!

Herr Ball und Frau Lampe: Weiter schaukeln, gruseliger Krabbler –

Geschichtenerzähler, Kind, Stühle, Herr Ball und Frau Lampe: Eins, zwei!

Frau Schrank und Titorelli: Auf mit dir, die Uhr sagt sieben –

Geschichtenerzähler, Kind und ganzer Chor: Eins, zwei!

Herr Ball und Frau Lampe: Das macht Spaß, es ist wie ein Spiel.

Geschichtenerzähler, Kind und Chor: Eins, zwei!

Herr und Frau Stuhl: Schaukeln, rollen, Panzerkäfer –

Geschichtenerzähler, Kind und Chor: Eins, zwei!

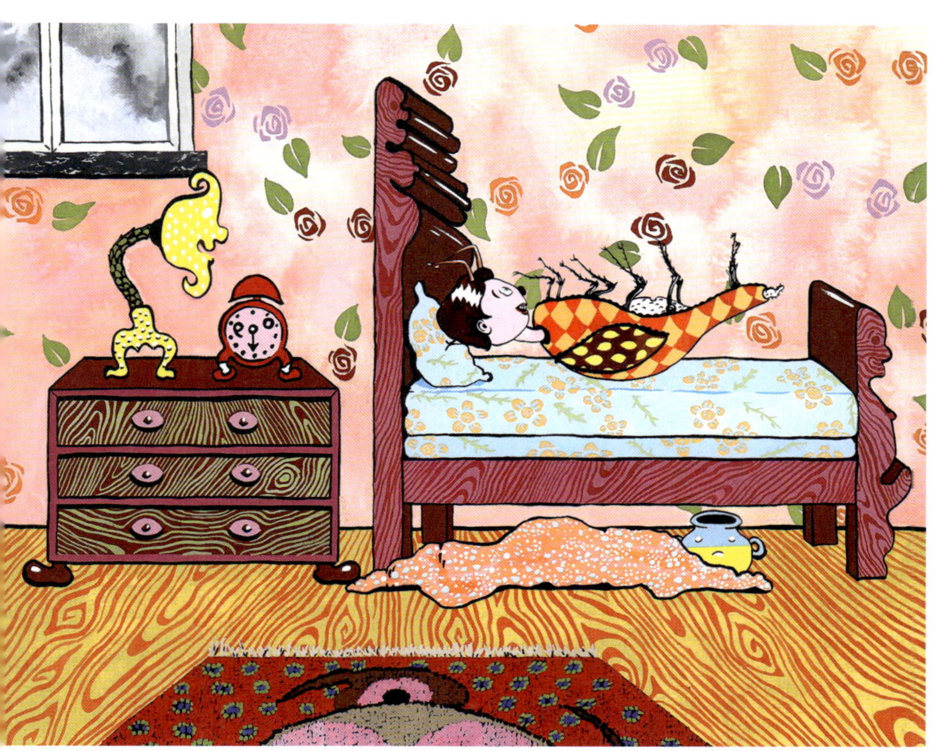

Herr Tisch: Gib acht, dass du dir die Fühler nicht zerdrückst –

Geschichtenerzähler, Kind und Chor [*enthusiastisch; Glockengeläut betont die Worte*]**:** Eins, zwei!

Geschichtenerzähler [*reagiert auf die Türglocke*]**:** Oh nein, die Türglocke läutet!

Chor: Oh nein! Wer ist da?

Geschichtenerzähler: Los, los, ein Schubs noch –

Geschichtenerzähler, Kind und gesamter Chor: Einer, einer!

Geschichtenerzähler [*während die Musik stoppt*]**:** Und KABUMM! Gregor schwang sich aus dem Bett! Doch gerade, als Gregor auf dem Boden landete, hörte er die Stimme des Prokuristen, der vom Chef des Büros geschickt wurde, um zu sehen, weshalb Gregor so spät war.

Herr Tisch: Da ist etwas runtergefallen, in Gregor Samsas verschlossenem Zimmer. [*Pause. Es läutet erneut.*]

Frau Schrank: Oh nein, der Prokurist ist hier! [*Ein weiteres, nachdrücklicheres Läuten.*]

Titorelli: Du liebe Güte – der Prokurist ist hier!

Kind [*verwirrt*]**:** Schon wieder die Glocke? Aber der Prokurist ist doch schon hier! Er hat gehört, wie das Tier aus dem Bett gefallen ist. [*Ein weiteres Läuten.*] Wer läutet da also?

Chor: Es ist er, er, er. Hört mit der Geschichte auf!

Kind: Wer? Wer? Wer?

Chor: Es ist der Überbringer schlechter Nachrichten! [*Das Lied des Überbringers schlechter Nachrichten erklingt, als er eintritt, in einen weißen Ärztekittel gekleidet, mit einem Stethoskop, einem Hammer und einer Zange, die um seinen Hals hängen.*]

4. SZENE – DER ÜBERBRINGER SCHLECHTER NACHRICHTEN

Lied des Überbringers schlechter Nachrichten

Das rote Rad, das Becky will,
Steht sicher niemals vor dem Tor,
Und in dem Autounfall im April,
Verlor ihre Schwester ein Handy, ihr Vater sein Ohr.

Doris – Alice lässt dich im Regen stehen,
Einsamer Lee, du kriegst keinen Brief.
Wer freundlich ist, wird Bosheit sehen.
Und der kleine Bruder Abed im Gefängnis schlief.

Ich bin der traurigste Kerl, echt:
Meine Nachrichten sind immer schlecht!

[Chor:]
Da hat er leider ziemlich recht,
seine Nachrichten sind immer schlecht!

Meine Arbeit ist gar nicht nett,
ich bliebe viel lieber in meinem Bett.
[Chor:]

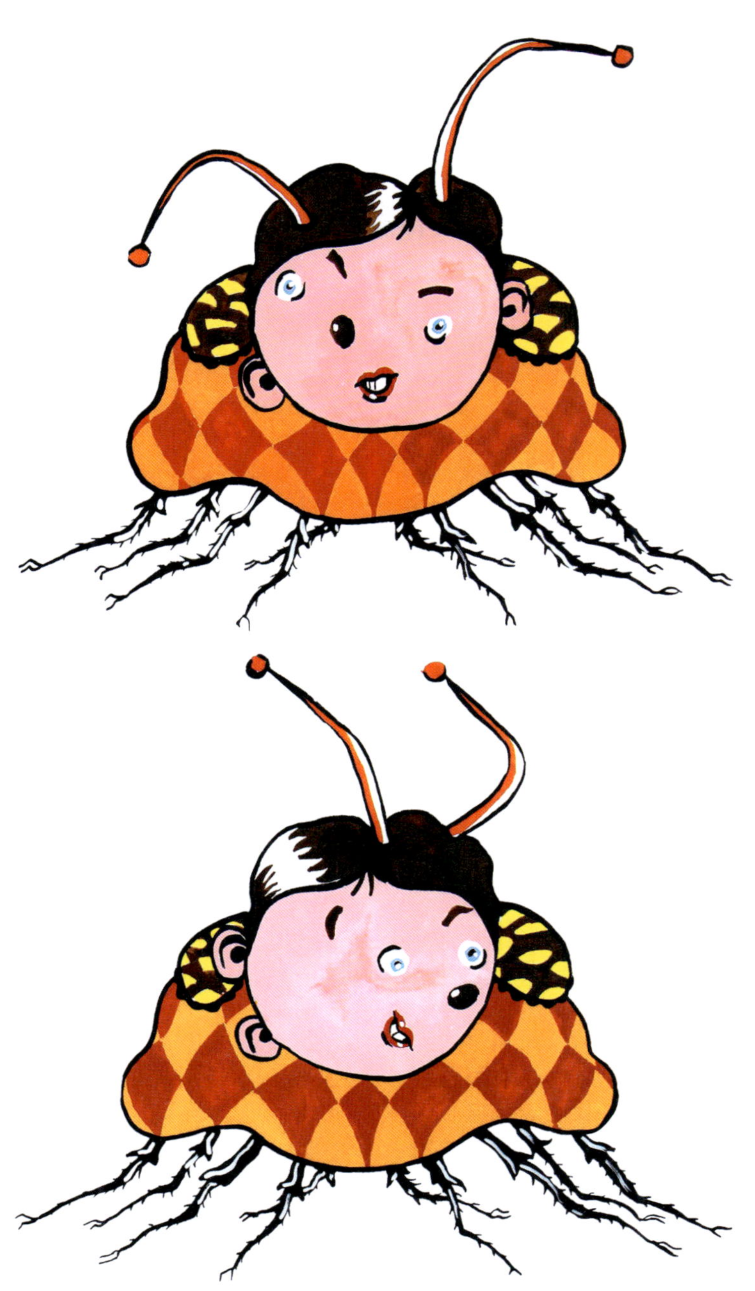

Wirklich gar nicht nett,
wir blieben auch viel lieber im Bett.

Seht ihr die glückliche Frau Taylor am Fenster stehen?
Lächelt ohne jede Not.
Ich muss zur Nachbarin Eve Katz hingehen,
die jetzt Witwe ist, denn ihr Mann ist tot.

Doch auch Frau Taylor lacht nicht mehr,
weder aus Schadenfreude noch Humor,
Weil ich ihr sage, bitte sehr,
das ist kein Knoten, sondern ein tödlicher Tumor.

Ich weine viel, den ganzen Tag,
weil ich meinen Job nicht mag!

[Chor:]
Wir weinen viel, den ganzen Tag,
weil er seinen Job nicht mag.

Ich will nur einmal, das wär' schön,
Frau Katz und Frau Taylor in Freudentränen sehen.

[Chor:]
Lauf weg, liebe Frau Taylor,
Es ist der Überbringer schlechter Nachrichten!

Der Überbringer schlechter Nachrichten!
Der Überbringer schlechter Nachrichten!

Der Überbringer: Hallo Kinder. Ich hoffe, die Geschichte gefällt euch. Es tut mir so leid, dass ich der Überbringer schlechter Nachrichten bin, aber wie ihr wisst, *bin* ich nun mal der Überbringer schlechter Nachrichten.
Kind: A-ha.
Geschichtenerzähler: Das wissen wir, und wir lieben dich trotzdem.
Kind: A-ha.
Der Überbringer: Danke. Das bedeutet mir so viel. [*Sie umarmen*

einander. Der Überbringer wischt sich Tränen aus dem Gesicht und schnäuzt sich.]

Geschichtenerzähler [*lächelt mitfühlend*]: Und welche schlechten Nachrichten hast du heute für uns?

Der Überbringer: Ich fürchte, die schlechten Nachrichten sind sehr schlecht. [*Pause*] Womöglich müssen wir die Geschichte abbrechen und das Programm streichen!

Kind: Die Geschichte abbrechen? Nein! Nein!

Chor [*erfreut; der gezeigte Titorelli lächelt*]: Das Programm streichen Ja! Ja!

Kind: Die Geschichte abbrechen? Warum? Weshalb? Wir haben doch gerade erst angefangen! [*Das Kind klatscht zweimal und führt einen kleinen einfachen Tanz im Kreis auf, klatscht noch zweimal und setzt sich hin.*]

Der Überbringer: Ich weiß. Mir geht's genauso. [*Singt, wie für sich selbst, und erhält eine leise Antwort von Titorelli, wobei beide sich nicht allzu traurig anhören.*] *Ich weine viel, den ganzen Tag, weil ich meinen Job nicht mag!*

Titorelli: *Wir weinen viel, den ganzen Tag, weil er seinen Job nicht mag.*

Geschichtenerzähler: Aber was ist das Problem, warum sollen wir die Geschichte abbrechen?

Der Überbringer: Wisst ihr, vor vielen Jahren, als *Die Verwandlung* erstmals als Buch gedruckt wurde, hörte Kafka, dass es ein Bild auf dem Umschlag geben würde, und er schrieb sofort an seinen Verleger, Herrn Meyer [*zieht ein Stück Papier aus der Tasche*], und in dem Brief schreibt Kafka [*er liest*]: „Das Insekt selbst kann *nicht* gezeichnet werden. Es kann noch nicht einmal von der Ferne aus gezeigt werden."[1]

Kind und Chor: Oh nein!

Der Überbringer: Oh ja. Kafka selbst verbot jede Zeichnung des Insekts, und wir haben *viele* Zeichnungen des Insekts in unserem Programm. Es ist eindeutig falsch, vielleicht sogar illegal, Kafkas Wünsche nicht zu befolgen. Man darf niemals sehen, wie das Insekt aussieht. Es ist nicht nur illegal,

1 Franz Kafka, Brief an Georg Heinrich Meyer, 25. Oktober 1915, zit. in: Peter-André Alt, *Franz Kafka: der ewige Sohn. Eine Biographie*, München: C.H. Beck, 2008, S. 339.

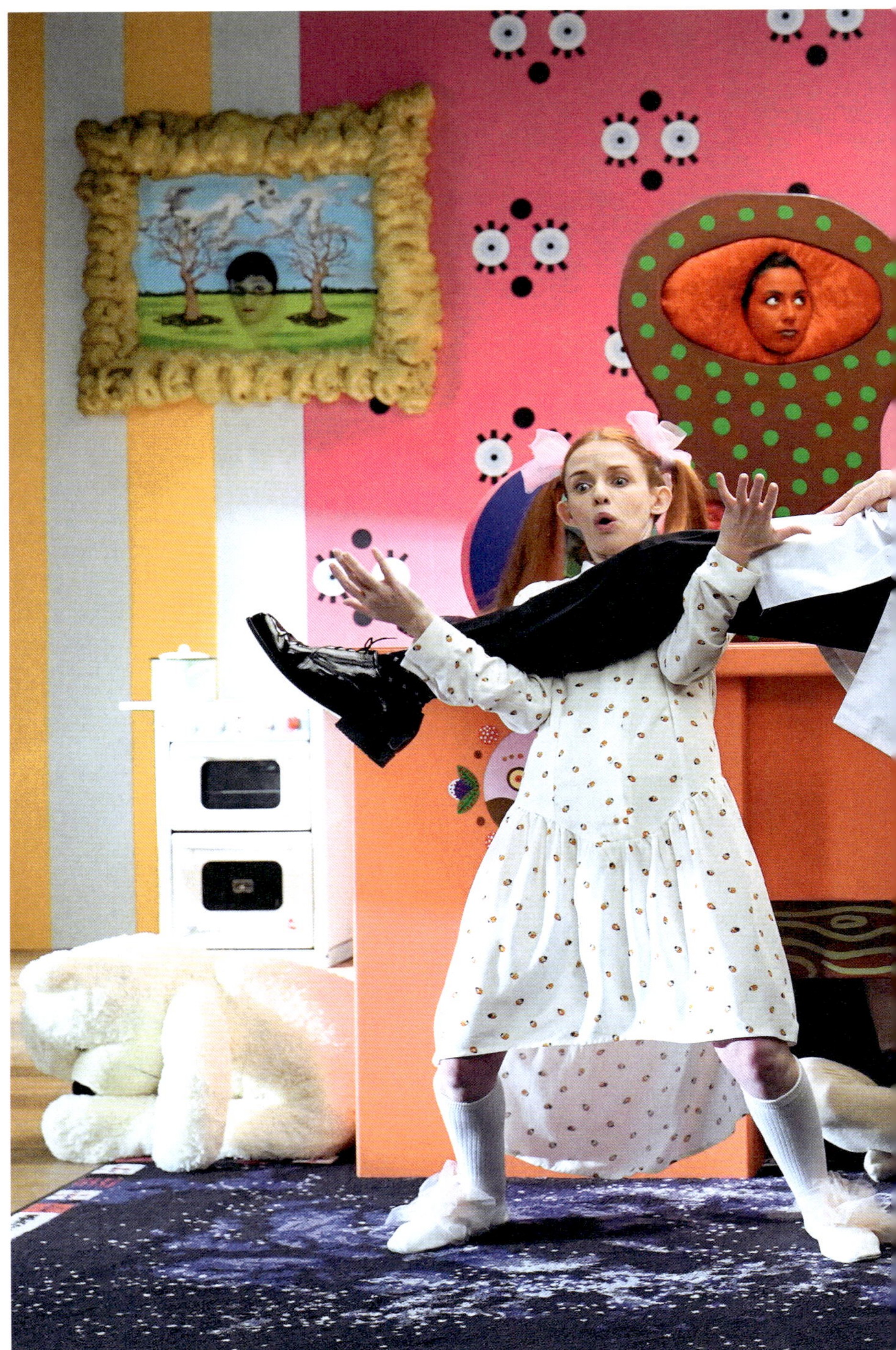

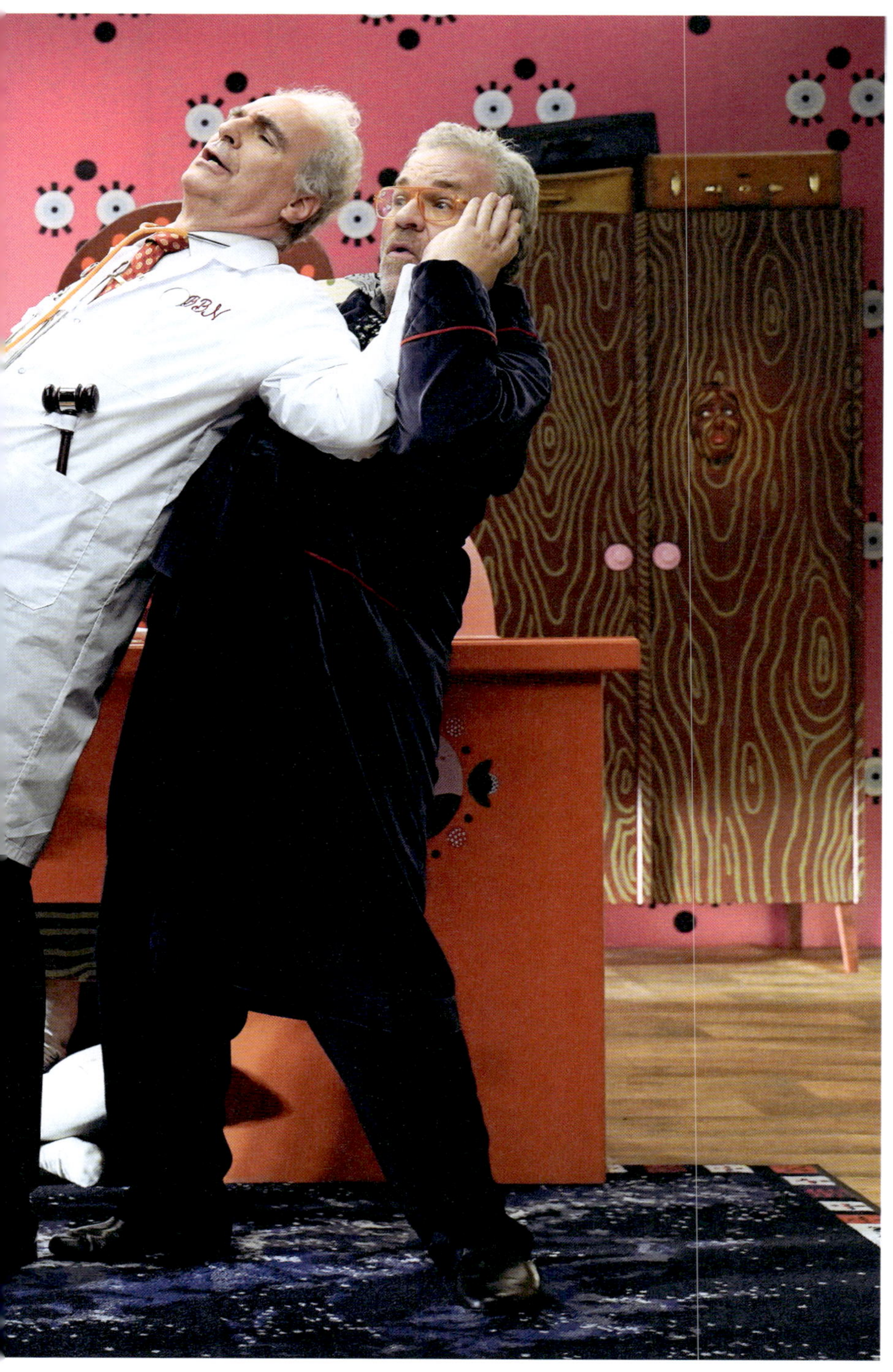

es ist sogar schlecht! [*Blickt auf sein Handy.*] Aber ich muss laufen. Und noch mehr schlechte Nachrichten, viele, viele schlechte Nachrichten an andere Freund:innen überbringen. [*Anmaßend:*] Adieu!

Geschichtenerzähler [*zum Kind*]**:** Das heißt „Auf Wiedersehen". [*Abgang des Überbringers*]

Kind und Geschichtenerzähler: Adieu! [*Sie winken, während das Motiv des Überbringers erklingt.*]

Kind: Also, was tun wir? Was tun wir, was tun wir? Was tun wir? Was sollen wir bloß tun? Was werden wir tun? Was müssen wir tun? *Chto Dyelat?* Was nun? Und wie? Wir können keine Geschichte ohne Bilder erzählen. Wir müssen doch wissen, was in der Geschichte passiert! Und wir haben das Insekt ja schon gesehen! Das sind schlechte Nachrichten. [*Pause. Blickt gedankenverloren auf seine* Hände.] Ich frage mich, ob meine Hände mir gehören. Sind meine Hände nur geliehen? Muss ich sie eines Tages zurückgeben? [*Sieht zum Geschichtenerzähler.*]

Geschichtenerzähler: Ich sage dir, was wir tun müssen. Der Überbringer schlechter Nachrichten ist nicht unser einziger Freund. Weißt du, an wen wir uns in schwierigen Situationen wenden, wenn es kompliziert wird?

Kind und Chor: An wen?

Geschichtenerzähler: Wir suchen den Rat unseres klügsten Freundes, jemand der Kafka im echten Leben sehr, sehr nahe stand. Wer findet einen Ausweg, selbst wenn alles verloren scheint? Wer ist der klügste Freund in unserem ganzen magischen Geschichtenhaus? Wer weiß am meisten, besonders über Franz Kafka?

Kind und Chor: Wer? Wer?

Geschichtenerzähler [*nach einer Pause*]**:** Unser weiser, gottgleicher Freund ist … Kafkas Schuh! [*Kind und Chor ringen nach Luft, als der Geschichtenerzähler hinter dem Schreibtisch einen Herrenschuh hervorholt. Das Motiv des Schuhliedes erklingt.*]

5. SZENE – KAFKAS SCHUH

Lied von Kafkas Schuh

Kafkas Schuh, Kafkas Schuh,
Gibt's Probleme, bewährt er sich im Nu.

Kafkas Schuh, Kafkas Schuh,
Ein wahrer Freund, was sagst du.

Du schlauer Jude, Kafkas Schuh,
Sag' mir, was ich denn jetzt tu'.

Schuh-Jud', -tschu- Jud', -Schuh- dudu,
Sag mir, was ich denn jetzt tu'.

Kind: Ist das wirklich Kafkas Schuh?

Geschichtenerzähler: Natürlich ist er das. Ein klassisch geschnittener linker Schuh, für den linken Fuß. Kafka trug ihn und ging damit jeden Tag in sein Büro, wo er sich darüber freute, ein großer Rechtsexperte zu sein. Tatsächlich war er sogar ein Doktor des Rechts.

Chor [*erstaunt*]**:** Ein Doktor für das Recht?

Titorelli: Hat er das Recht behandelt, als das Recht krank war?

Geschichtenerzähler: In gewisser Weise ja, richtig, sein Spezialgebiet war die Arbeitsunfallversicherung. Kafka war ein guter und erfolgreicher Doktor des Rechts, obwohl er auch Jude war ...

Chor: Ein Jude!

Geschichtenerzähler: Ein Jude wie sein Schuh ...

Chor: Sein Schuh!

Geschichtenerzähler: Und für Schuhe, ich meine für Juden, waren die Geschäfte damals sehr eingeschränkt. Jedenfalls liebte Kafka diesen Schuh sehr. Er war beinahe ein Teil seines Körpers.

Kind: Er ist so ... schwarz.

Geschichtenerzähler: Ja. Es ist ein schwarzer Schuh. [*Pause*]

Kind: Ist er viel Geld wert?

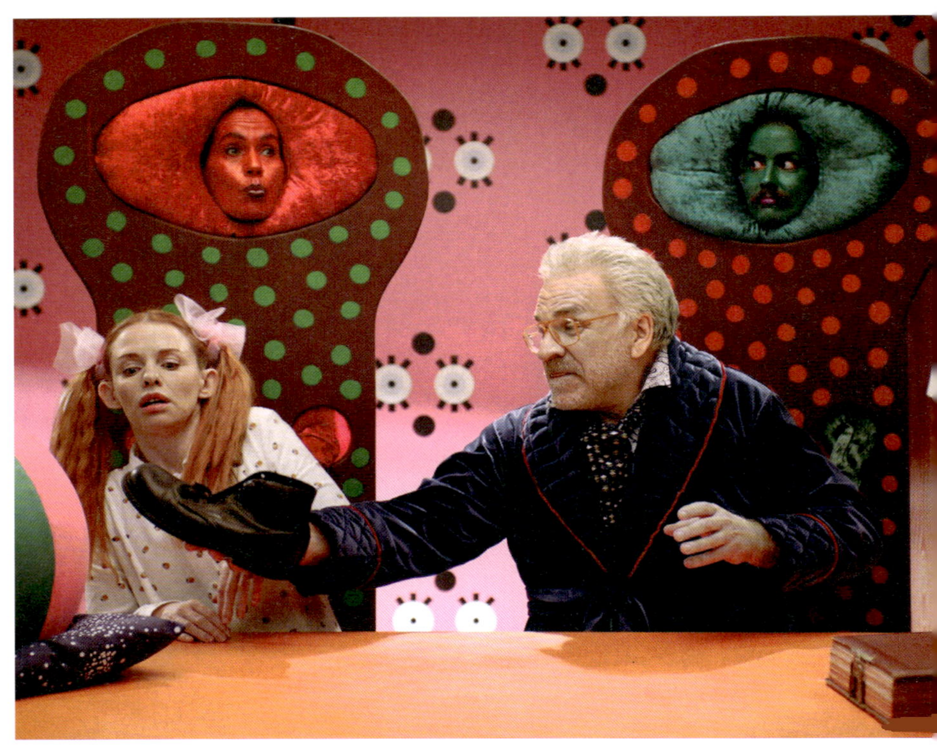

Geschichtenerzähler: Unglaublich viel. [*Kind und Chor ringen nach Luft.*] Alles, was mit Kafka zu tun hat, ist sehr gut verkäuflich. Aber wir werden ihn niemals verkaufen.

Kind: Kann ich ...

Geschichtenerzähler: Was denn, Schatz?

Kind [*schüchtern*]**:** Kann ich an Kafkas Schuh riechen?

Geschichtenerzähler: Ja, kannst du! [*Sieht zustimmend zu, wie das Kind bedächtig und gründlich an dem Schuh riecht.*]

Kind: Er riecht so gut!

Geschichtenerzähler: Ja, das tut er, oder? Das finde ich auch! Woran erinnert dich der Geruch?

Kind: Ich bin mir nicht sicher. Vielleicht an Schnitzel?

Frau Stuhl: Hm! Schnitzel! [*Sie leckt sich die Lippen.*]

Kind: Kann ich ... Darf ich an Kafkas Schuh lecken?

Geschichtenerzähler [*besorgt*]**:** Nein. Du kannst an Kafkas Schuh riechen, aber du darfst nicht daran lecken. Jedenfalls – erinnerst du dich, warum wir den Schuh geholt haben?

Kind [*Pause. Das Kind hat Schwierigkeiten die Sache in Worte zu fassen und gestikuliert mit den Händen, während es denkt und spricht*]**:** A-ha. Kakerlake ... Bild ...

Geschichtenerzähler: Das stimmt! Kafka hat die Darstellung des Ungeziefers verboten und wir befürchten, dass die Show abgesagt werden muss. Und jetzt hören wir ganz genau auf Kafkas Schuh und der Schuh sagt uns, ob wir weitermachen können oder nicht. [*Er hält den Schuh zwischen ihnen hoch. Gespannte Musik im Hintergrund. Die Kamera geht näher heran.*]

6. SZENE – WOHNZIMMERSUITE

6A – PROBLEM GELÖST

Geschichtenerzähler und Kind hören dem Schuh aufmerksam zu. Gespannte Hintergrundmusik. Ein Lächeln erscheint auf dem Gesicht des Geschichtenerzählers. Die Musik stoppt.

Geschichtenerzähler: Ja! Ja!

Chor: Hurra! Hurra! Der Schuh sagt Ja!

Geschichtenerzähler: Kafkas Schuh erlaubt uns, die Bilder des Ungeziefers zu benutzen! Du erinnerst dich sicher, wie Gregor von Vater, Mutter und Grete gedrängt wurde, die Tür zu öffnen. Der Prokurist verlor die Geduld und ärgerte sich – und so versuchte Gregor, ihn zu beruhigen ...

6B – LIED DER TIERSTIMMEN

Im Lied wird Gregors unverständliche Stimme durch ein misstönendes, kreischendes Saiteninstrument wiedergegeben. Die Worte erscheinen wie auf einem Karaoke-Bildschirm. Animiertes Standbild: Vorderansicht von Gregor, mit seinem sich bewegenden Mund, der abwechselnd mit Reaktionen von Vater, Prokurist, Mutter, Grete und Chormitgliedern zu sehen ist. Jedes Mal, wenn Gregor im Bild ist, sind seine Gesichtszüge anders zusammengesetzt.

***** ****** ****, *** *** *** ***** *****, *** *** *** ***** ********.

(Bitte lieber Herr, ich war ein wenig krank, mir war ein wenig schlecht.)

**** ***'* *** ****** ***, ********, **** *** *****.

(Bald geht's mir wieder gut, aufrecht, wohl und recht.)

***** *** **** ** ****** ******, ***** ****,

(Seien Sie nett zu meinen Eltern, bitte sehr,)

****** ***** *** ****** *** **** ***.

(Gleich komme ich selbst zur Türe her.)

***** *** *** ****, *** ****' *** **** ** ***,

(Sagen Sie dem Chef, ich komm' nie mehr zu spät,)

**** *** *** ****** *** ******, *** ****** *****, ** ****.

(Bald bin ich wieder ich selbst, Sie werden sehen, es geht.)

6C – GREGOR ERSCHEINT

Eine andere, dramatische Melodie entwickelt sich aus dem vorherigen Lied. Ansicht des vorderen Zimmers. Vater, Mutter und Prokurist rahmen Gregors Türe ein.

Prokurist (Herr Tisch): Haben Sie auch nur ein Wort verstanden?

Mutter (Frau Stuhl): Um Gottes willen, er ist vielleicht schwer krank! Grete, liebe Tochter!

Chor: Beeilung Grete! Beeilung Grete!

Grete (Frau Lampe) [*rechts aus dem Off*]**:** Mutter? Mutter?

Mutter: Du musst augenblicklich zum Arzt!

Chor: Augenblicklich zum Arzt!

Vater: Seine Tür ist versperrt – Anna! Anna!

Chor: Beeilung, schlecht bezahltes Dienstmädchen – Anna! Anna!

Anna (Frau Schrank) [*rechts aus dem Off*]**:** Herr? Herr?

Vater (Herr Ball): Sofort einen Schlosser holen!

Anna und Grete: Ich eile! Ich eile! [*Beide Mädchen kommen von rechts ins Bild und verschwinden dann mit raschelnden Röcken links, während der nächste Satz gesungen wird.*]

Prokurist (Herr Tisch) [*ruhig und unheilvoll*]**:** Er klingt wie ein Tier. Das war eine Tierstimme!

Chor [*wiederholt spöttisch die Zeile und imitiert dabei Gregors Piepsen*]**:** ** ****** *** *** ****. *** *** **** **********!

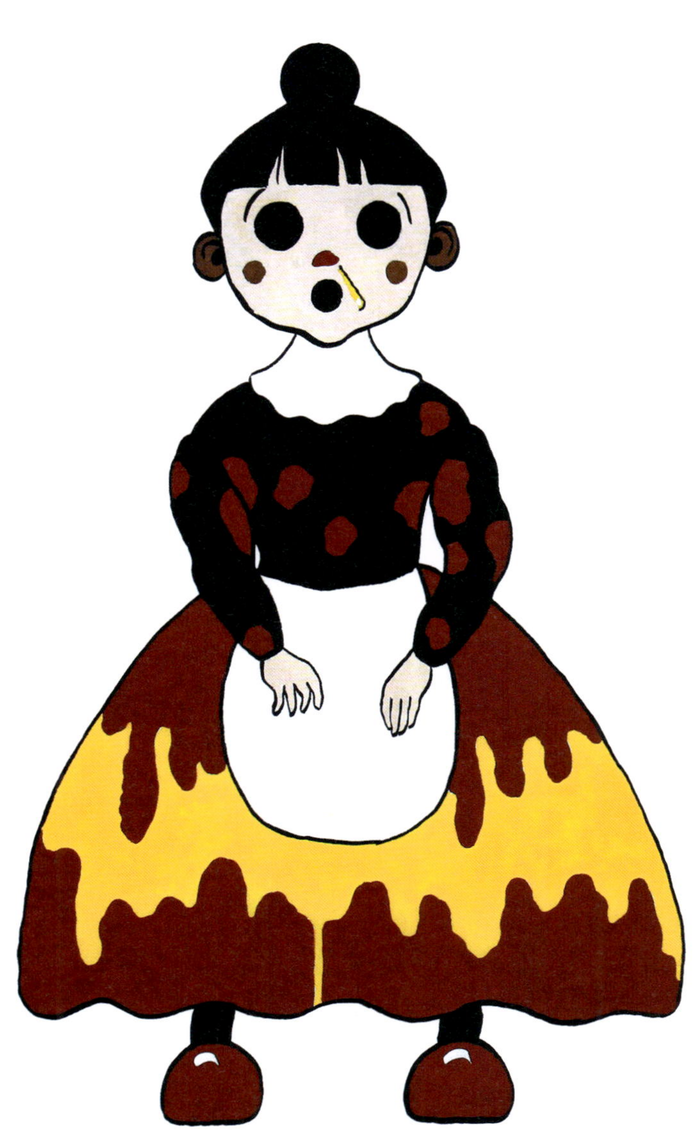

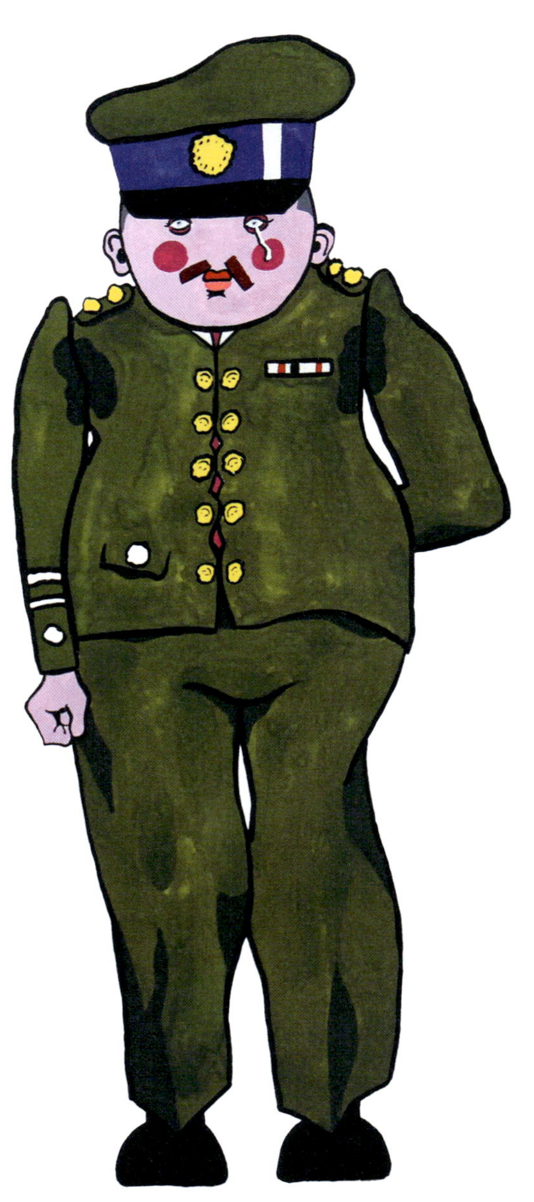

Geschichtenerzähler [*rezitiert*]: Gregor strengte sich an, den Schlüssel mit seinem Kiefer zu drehen. Er bemühte sich so sehr!

Chor: Wie sehr?

Geschichtenerzähler: So sehr, dass er sich verletzte, denn eine braune Flüssigkeit kam ihm aus dem Mund, doch schließlich konnte er die Türe öffnen. [*Die weiße Türe öffnet sich langsam, die Musik behält das Tempo bei, doch ein Diminuendo verdeutlicht die Spannung. Gregor blickt zwischen den Türflügeln hervor. Die Musik gelangt zu voller Kraft, wobei die Melodie das Motiv von* Kafka für Kinder *wiederholt.*]

Prokurist: Ka-Oh!

Mutter (Frau Stuhl) [*ruft*]: Ka-Aj!

Vater (Herr Ball) [*schüttelt die Faust*]: Ka-Uh!

Chor: Ka-Ah, Ka-Oi, Ka-Uh!

Mutter, Vater, Prokurist: Kaf-Ah, Kaf-Oi, Kaf-Uh!

Geschichtenerzähler [*imitiert Gregors Stimme*]: ** ******** *** **** *** **** *** ***** *** **** ** ****.

[*Ich zieh' mir Hemd und Hose an und komme nie mehr zu spät.*]

Geschichtenerzähler: Gregor wollte seinen nackten Körper nicht zeigen.

Kind [*kichert*]: Nackt!

Geschichtenerzähler: Aber als er sah, dass der Prokurist gehen wollte, vergaß Gregor seine Vorsicht und sprang aus dem Zimmer! [*Gregor ist komplett zu sehen. Der entsetzte Prokurist verlässt rasch den Raum.*]

Prokurist: Ka- Oh! Oh! Oh!

Mutter: Ka-Aj! Aj! Aj! [*Die Mutter springt zweimal hoch in die Luft und bricht dann am Tisch zusammen. Während sie fällt, fliegt ihr Rock hoch und ihre Unterwäsche ist zu sehen.*]

Vater: Ka-Uh! Ka-Uh! [*Er schnappt sich einen Gehstock.*]

Geschichtenerzähler: Vater wollte Gregor in sein Zimmer zurücktreiben. Gregor hatte Angst, sich umzudrehen.

Chor: Schaben können nicht rückwärtsgehen!

Geschichtenerzähler: Doch schließlich hatte er sich umgedreht und Vater gab ihm von hinten einen starken Stoß und Gregor flog, heftig blutend, weit in sein Zimmer hinein. Die Tür wurde noch mit dem Stock zugeschlagen, dann war es endlich still.

Ende des 1. Kapitels

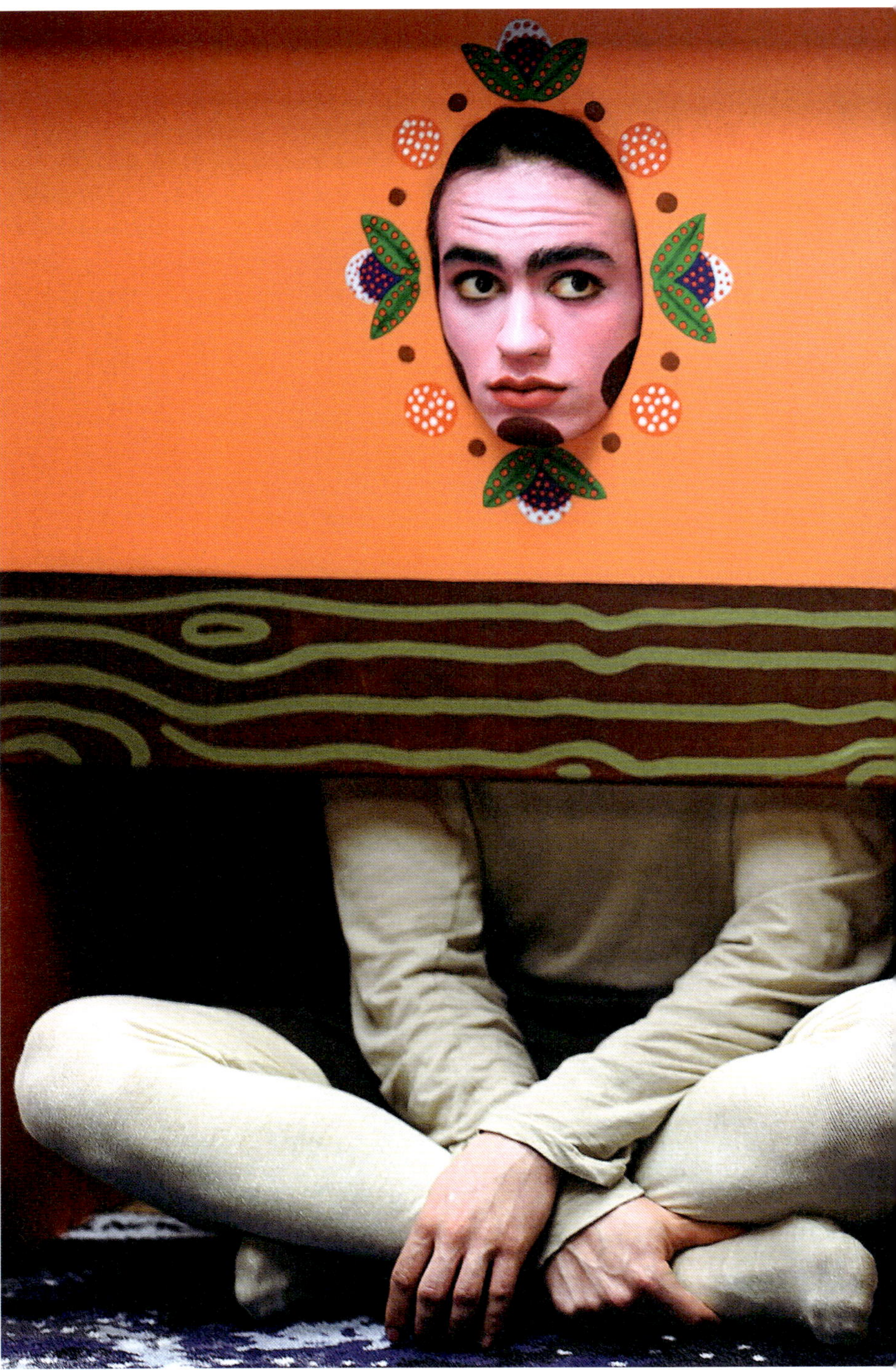

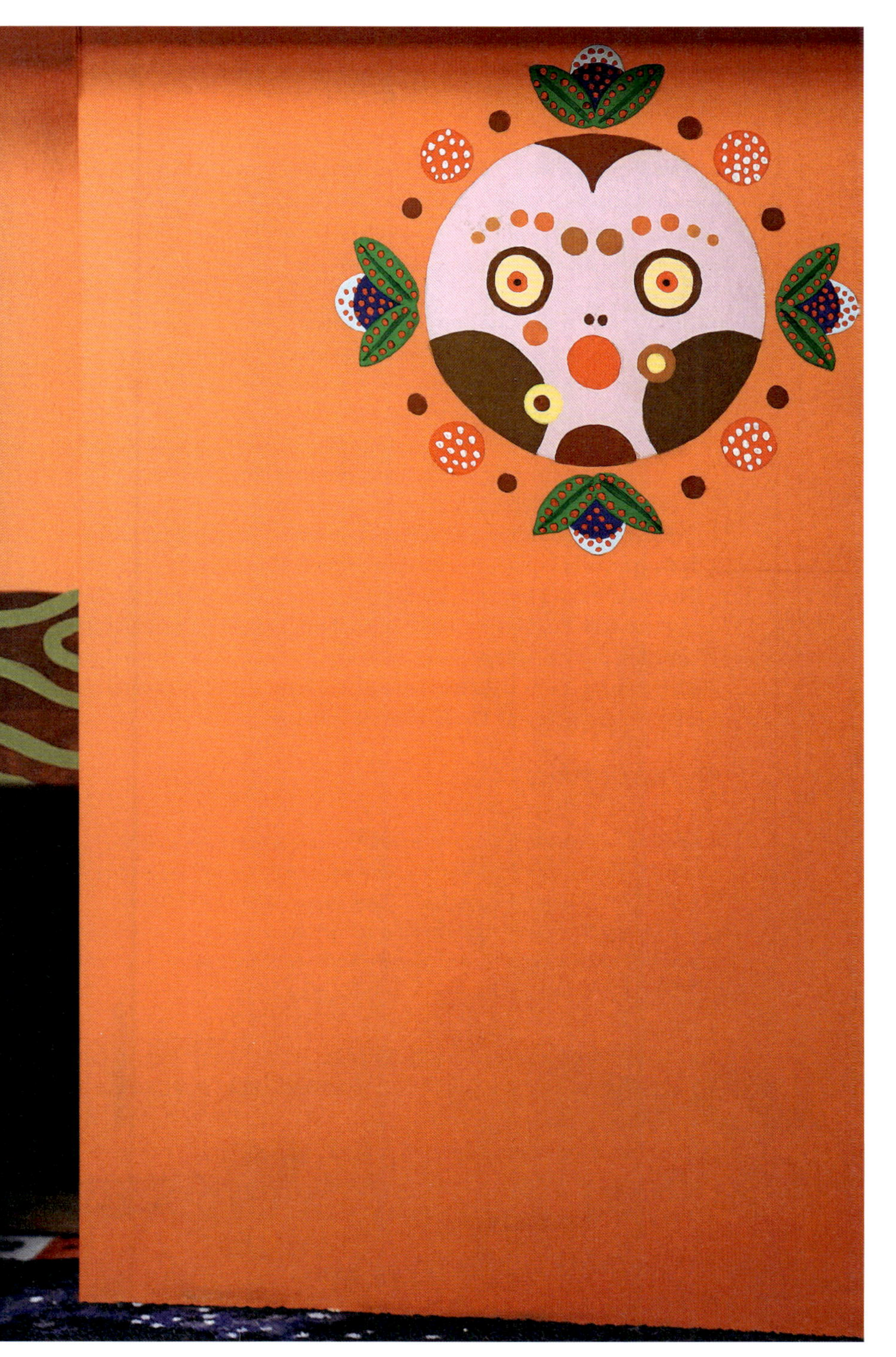

7. SZENE – ERSTE WERBEUNTERBRECHUNG

7A – ESSEN

Vogelperspektive auf einen Teller mit Essen. Himmlische Musik. Die Kamera zoomt langsam heran und bietet eine extreme Nahaufnahme der Textur des Essens. Bilder anderer Speisen werden darübergelegt und erzeugen eine nicht identifizierbare, jedoch äußerst greifbare Masse.

Verführerische weibliche Sprecherin: Hmmmmm ... dieses Verlangen, das du fast immer hast, wenn es deinem Magen gut geht, sich mit leckerem Essen vollzustopfen – und es zu wagen, schreckliche Dinge zu tun. Genieß' zuerst das Etikett einer alten, harten Wurst, beiß' mit allen Zähnen hinein, mmmhhh ... aahhh ... und schlucke nun rasch, regelmäßig und gedankenlos wie eine Maschine. Mach weiter. Steigere deine Eile. Schiebe dir die langen Scheiben rohen Rippenfleisches, ohne zu kauen in den Mund und ziehe sie von hinten wieder heraus, indem du sie durch Magen und Darm reißt. Stopf' dich mit Heringen, Essiggurken und all den alten, scharfen Speisen voll. Ein Hagelsturm aus Bonbons ergießt sich aus Blechdosen in deinen Mund. Du bist ein braves, liebes Kind. Papa liebt dich ... mmmmhh ... du wirst nie alleine sein ... ahhh! Du verdienst nichts Geringeres als *The People's Delicatessen*.[2]

7B – BOKI-POKI

GIF-ähnliche Animation: schnelle, rhythmische Musik begleitet den rundgesichtigen, glücklich-verrückten Boki-Poki, der dem Gesicht auf Gregors Teppich ähnelt. Boki-Poki rollt die Augen und streckt die Zunge heraus, alles zum Rhythmus der Musik. Der Hintergrund zeigt eine schwindelerregende und ständige Abfolge konzentrischer Kreise, deren Farben in grellen Kombinationen blinken. Auch Boki-Poki verändert die Farbe.

Chor [*gemeinsam, zum Rhythmus der Musik*]**:** Boki-Poki! Boki-Poki! Boki-Poki! Boki-Poki! Boki-Poki! Boki-Poki! Boki-Poki! Boki-Poki! Boki-Poki!

Ein fröhlicher Ansager: Morgen, auf dem besten Kinderkanal.

2 Basierend auf einem Eintrag in Kafkas *Tagebüchern*, 30. Oktober 1911.

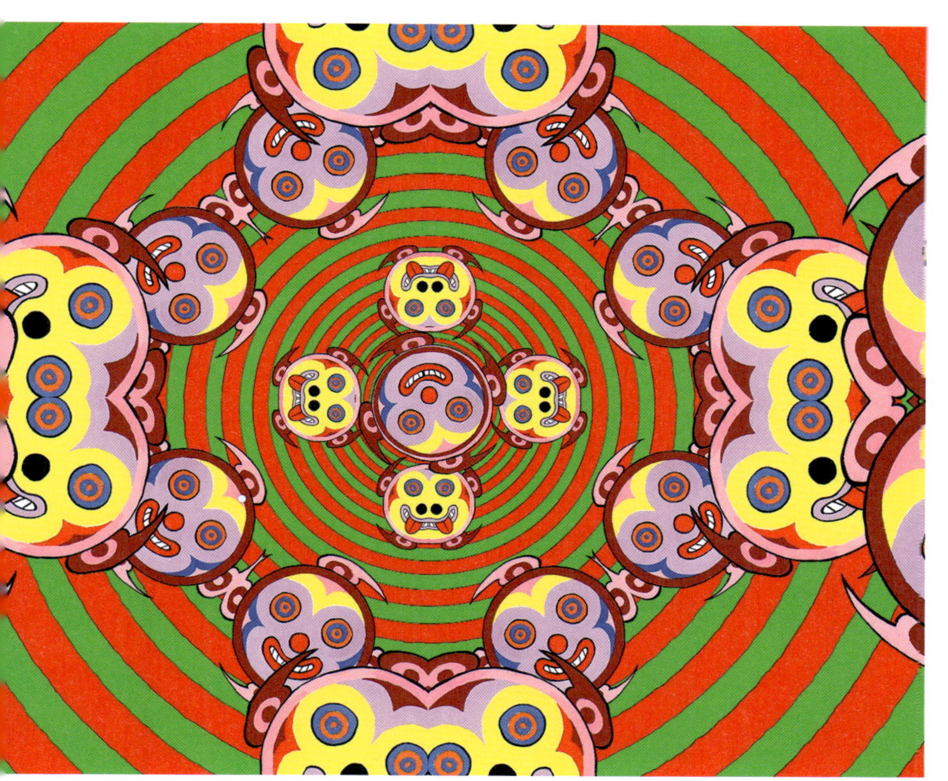

7C – DEMNÄCHST BEI KAFKA FÜR KINDER: DER KÜBELREITER[3]

Animiertes Standbild mit Zwischenschnitten von Reaktionen des Kindes, des Geschichtenerzählers und der Chormitglieder.

Verführerischer Ansager: In den nächsten Folgen von *Kafka für Kinder …*

Geschichtenerzähler: Es war so kalt! Auf der Suche nach Kohle, reite ich auf dem Kübel hin, die Hand oben am Griff,

3 Basierend auf „Der Kübelreiter", in: *Franz Kafka, Sämtliche Erzählungen*, Frankfurt am Main: S. Fischer 1993 (1970), S. 195f.

dem einfachsten Zaumzeug, unten aber steigt mein Kübel auf, prächtig, prächtig!

Kind [*reitet auf einem Eimer, die Hände wie Flügel gespreizt im Versuch sich nach vorne zu bewegen, während es so tut, als würde es fliegen*]**:** Wiiiiiiii! Wiiiiii!

Chor [*reagiert ohne Begeisterung*]**:** Wiiiii! Wiiiiii!

Geschichtenerzähler: Ich fliege auf meinem Kübel durch die eisige Luft, bis ich vor der Tür des Kohlenhändlers ankomme und rufe: „Kohlenhändler! Kohlenhändler! Gib mir ein wenig Kohle. Sobald ich kann, bezahl ich's."

Kohlenhändler (Herr Stuhl): Hör ich recht? Kundschaft!

Kohlefrau (Frau Schrank): Was hast du, Mann? Niemand ist es! Die Gasse ist leer; wir können schlafen gehen.

Geschichtenerzähler: „Aber ich sitze doch hier auf dem Kübel, und mir ist sehr kalt. Bitte gebt mir doch eine Schaufel voll Kohle." [*Tränenströme fließen aus den Augen des Reiters. Motiv* Kafka für Kinder *erklingt und das Logo des Programms füllt den Bildschirm.*]

KAPITEL

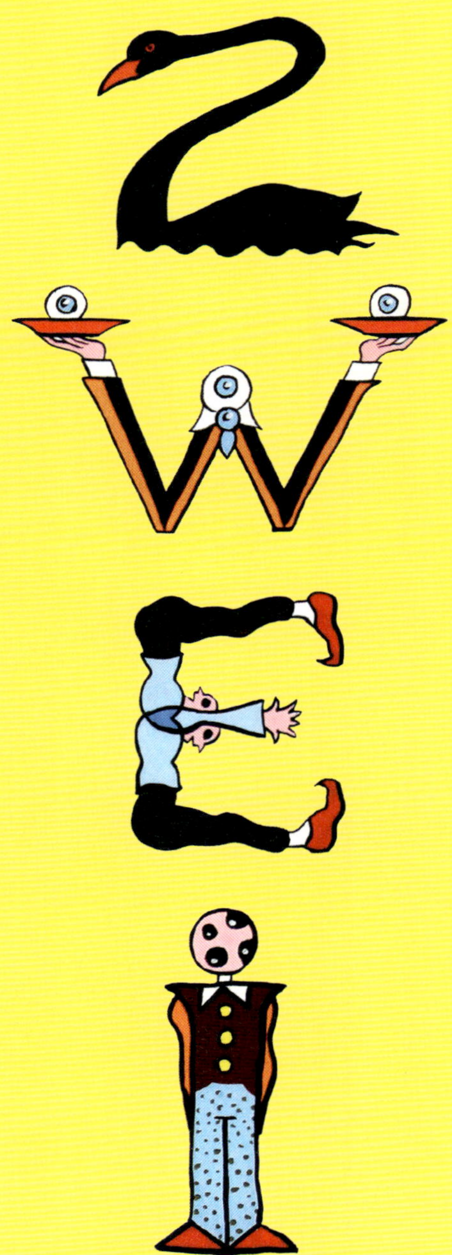

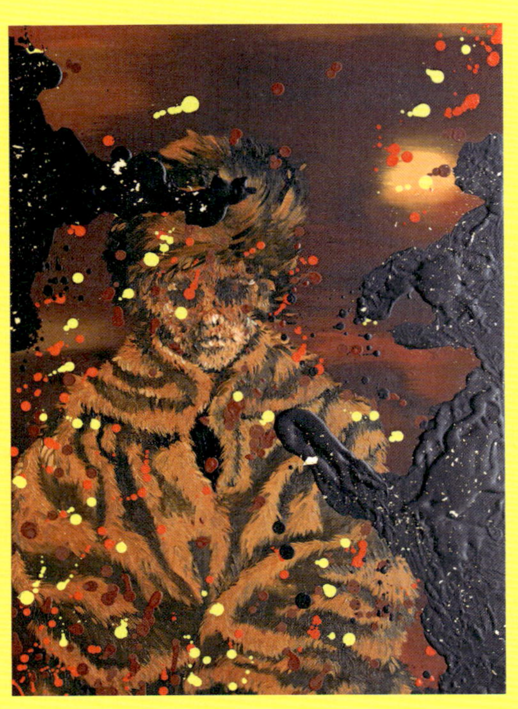

8. SZENE – MÜLLBROT

Mit ein paar Anpassungen wird das Wohnzimmer des Geschichtenhauses zu einer provisorischen Küche. Nahaufnahme der Hände des Geschichtenerzählers während er klebrigen Teig knetet, in dem widerliche Stückchen zu erkennen sind. Während die Kamera wegzoomt zeigt sich, dass der Tisch teilweise von einem weißen Tischtuch bedeckt ist und Herrn Tischs Gesicht zur Hälfte bedeckt.

Geschichtenerzähler: Bist du nicht froh, dass wir mit dem ersten Kapitel fertig sind?

Kind [*abgelenkt von den emsigen Händen des Geschichtenerzählers*]: A-ha.

Geschichtenerzähler: Aber auch ein bisschen traurig?

Kind [*eine kurze Pause*]: A-ha.

Geschichtenerzähler: Ein bisschen traurig, weil die Geschichte bald zu Ende ist.

Kind: Ja, ich bin traurig, weil die Geschichte zu Ende sein wird.

Geschichtenerzähler: Kein Grund traurig zu sein, Dummerchen! Kafka schrieb so viele Geschichten! Und ich werde dir alle vorlesen, jede einzelne!

Kind: Aber du wolltest, dass ich sage, ich sei traurig. [*Leise zu sich selbst:*] So ein Mist! [*Das Kind starrt wieder auf den Teig:*] Was ist das?

Geschichtenerzähler: Ich mache ein spezielles Müllbrot. Weißt du, im zweiten Kapitel geht es vor allem ums Essen. Gregor war sehr hungrig, und die einzige Person, die das begriff, war die, die er am meisten liebte.

Titorelli: Wer? Wer?

Frau Lampe [*als Grete, süßlich*]: Seine hübsche kleine Schwester, Grete.

Geschichtenerzähler [*energisch knetend, während er spricht*]: Das stimmt. Grete war es, die es schließlich wagte, in das Zimmer des Insekts zu kommen und ihm Essen zu bringen. Gregor spürte, dass er zu widerlich aussah, um gesehen zu werden, und versteckte sich rasch unter dem Kanapee. Grete brachte eine Schüssel seines Lieblingsgetränks – warme Milch – und ging schnell hinaus, damit er sie in Ruhe trinken konnte. Doch sobald die Milch seinen Kiefer berührte, spürte er nur Widerwillen!

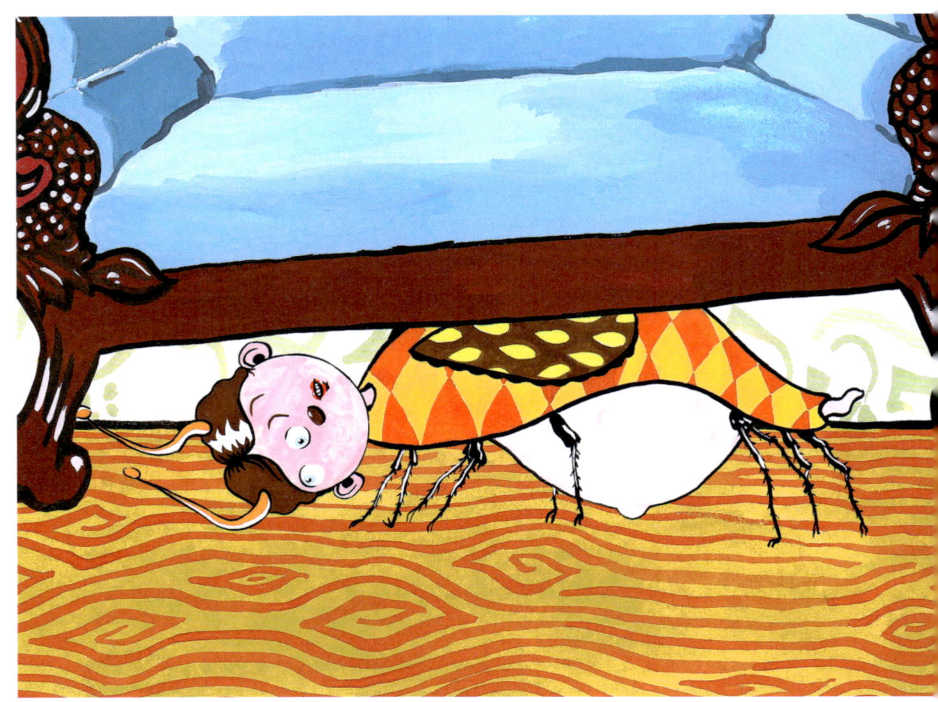

Chor: Er mochte keine warme Milch! Er mochte keine warme Milch!

Geschichtenerzähler [*hört auf zu kneten*]**:** Was stellte Grete also am nächsten Abend statt der Milch auf den Boden?

Chor: Was? Was ?

Geschichtenerzähler: Sie brachte ihm eine ganze Auswahl, alles auf einer alten Zeitung ausgebreitet. Dann entfernte sie sich eiligst und drehte sogar den Schlüssel um, damit das Insekt von der Auswahl probieren konnte. [*Der Geschichtenerzähler wendet sich einer Reihe von Produkten zu, die auf dem Tischtuch aufgereiht sind.*] Es gab halbverfaultes Gemüse, Knochen vom Nachtmahl mit festgewordener weißer Sauce ... [*Der Geschichtenerzähler schöpft die Sauce in den Teig. Etwas Sauce spritzt über das Gesicht von Herrn Tisch, der bereits wegen des Tischtuchs verstimmt ist.*]

Herr Tisch [*leise zu sich selbst*]**:** So ein Mist! [ausrufend]: Das ist so ein Mist!

Geschichtenerzähler: ... ein paar Rosinen und Mandeln, einen ungenießbaren alten Käse, ein trockenes Brot, eine Scheibe Brot mit Butter und ein gesalzenes Butterbrot. Gregor stürzte sich gierig auf den schimmeligen Käse.

Chor [*jeweils mit einem anderen begeisterten Ausruf*]**:** Hmmmmm! Köstlich! Schimmelig! Oooohh!

Geschichtenerzähler: Begeisterung! Und er fraß auch das halbverfaulte Gemüse. [*Der Geschichtenerzähler fügt das Gemüse seinem Teig hinzu. Die Teigkugel wird sichtbar größer.*]

Chor [*gemeinsam*]**:** Hmmmmm! Köstlich, hau rein!

Geschichtenerzähler: Und Gregor liebte auch die eklige alte Sauce.

Chor: Hmmmm! Aaaaahhhh!

Geschichtenerzähler: Die frischen Speisen dagegen schmeckten Gregor nicht, er vertrug nicht einmal ihren Geruch.

Titorelli [*Das Gemälde kaut lebhaft und spuckt dann mit übertrieben angewidertem Gesicht Speisereste aus.*]**:** Frische Speisen – Gott bewahre uns!

Geschichtenerzähler: Es wird Zeit, den Teig in unseren Geschichtenhaus-Super-Speed-Turbo-Ofen zu stecken. [*Stellt den Teig in den Ofen.*] Gregor war jetzt richtig satt. Sein Bauch war ein wenig gerundet. [*Animiertes Standbild: Gregors Bauch schwillt so sehr an, dass die meisten seiner Beine ganz gestreckt sein müssen, um zum Boden zu reichen, während die kürzeren in der Luft baumeln.*] Gregor war so fett, dass er kaum unter das Kanapee kam, als er hörte, wie Grete den Schlüssel umdrehte.

Herr Stuhl: Jetzt wusste Grete genau, was ihm schmeckt und sie kam jeden Tag, um ihn zu füttern.

Frau Stuhl [*zum Kind*]**:** So süß, die kleine Grete – so wie du!

Chor: So wie du!

Kind [*dreht sich zu den Chormitgliedern*]**:** Wie ich?! Wie das?

Herr Ball: Tja, sie war auch ein kleines Kind.

Frau Schrank: Hübsch, aber zerbrechlich ...

Titorelli: Glücklich, aber sensibel ...

Frau Lampe: Talentiert, aber verwirrt ...

Herr Ball: Klein, aber nicht zu klein ...

Chor: Ein Kind! Ein Kind!

Frau Stuhl: Erst Siebzehn!

Kind: Wartet, was? Siebzehn? Siebzehn ist ein Kind? [*Lied beginnt.*]

9. SZENE – WAS IST EIN KIND?

Ein sanfter Walzer. Während des letzten Verses, der nur vom Chor gesungen wird, scheint das Kind einzuschlafen. Animation: Während die Instrumente pausieren taucht Grete dreimal auf. Einmal ist ihr ganzer Körper sichtbar, wie sie verzückt im Himmel schwebt. Beim zweiten Mal taucht ihr Gesicht in einer Nahaufnahme auf, in jedem Auge drehen langsam drei Pupillen wie in alten Bildschirmschonern. Das dritte Mal füllt ein Auge den gesamten Bildschirm mit denselben Bildschirmschoner-ähnlichen Bewegungen.

Was ist ein Kind? Was ist ein Kind? Der Duft ist süß und rein,
Doch eines Tags studiert sie Recht und spielt die Geige fein.

Was ist ein Kind? Was ist ein Kind? Das ist gar nicht so leicht.
Ein Kind wächst ständig weiter, bis es einmal reicht.

Bis wann ein Kind? Bis wann ein Kind? Sieben? Zwölf? Vierzehn?
Wann wechselt es von prall und pink zu altem, hartem Lehm?

Ein Kind ist von Versprechen reich, da ist noch alles drin,
Ein Schatzkästchen, da liegt jemand, erst ziemlich alt, dann hin.

10. SZENE – ROUTINE, GELD

Ein Alarm weckt das schlafende Kind.

Geschichtenerzähler: Das Brot ist fertig! [*Er nimmt ein perfektes, appetitliches Brot aus dem Ofen. Freudig bricht er ein Stückchen ab, beißt hinein und spuckt sofort wieder aus.*] Das ist widerlicher, vergammelter Mist! [*Verschiedene Chor- und Orchestermitglieder sind zu sehen, wie sie Brot ausspucken.*] Und so gingen die Tage dahin. Gregor lauschte neugierig den Gesprächen der Familie im anderen Zimmer und erfuhr einige erfreuliche Überraschungen. Davor, als er noch ein Mann war, hatte er gedacht, das gesamte Vermögen seines Vaters sei verloren und das Geld, das Gregor jeden Monat ablieferte, würde rasch ausgegeben. Nun erfuhr er aber, dass sein Vater einige Ersparnisse angehäuft hatte und dass es auch Zinsen auf dieses Geld gab.

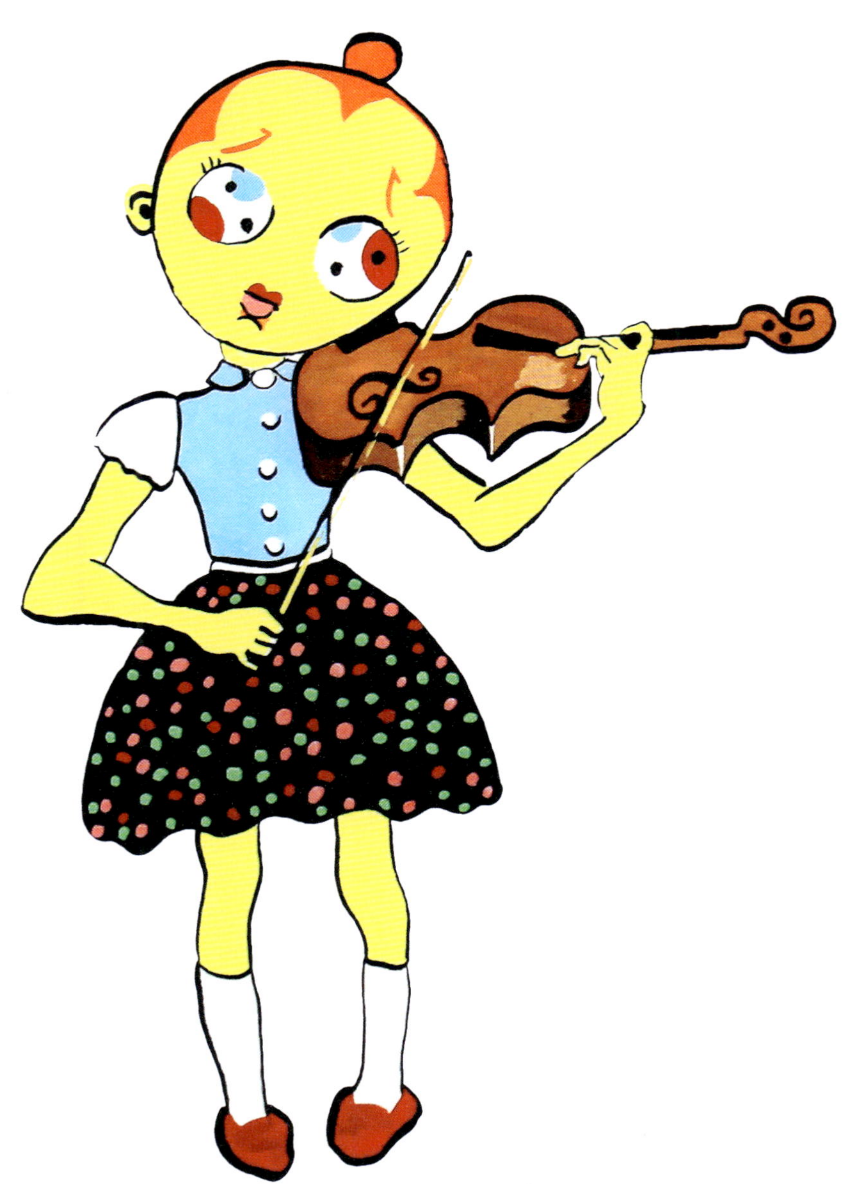

Herr Ball: Zinsen sind eine Belohnung, die Menschen mit Geld dafür bekommen, dass sie Geld haben, und die Belohnung ist mehr Geld.

Geschichtenerzähler: Es war kein Vermögen. Mutter, Vater und Grete mussten nun alle arbeiten, aber die Dinge standen gar nicht so schlecht! Sie fanden eine angenehme Arbeit: Mutter nähte Kleider und Vater – [*Animiertes Standbild des Vaters*] wurde Bankpförtner.

Chor: Bankpförtner! [*In der Zeichnung erscheint ein kleines Lächeln auf Vaters mürrischem Gesicht, das sofort wieder verschwindet.*]

Geschichtenerzähler: Und hatte eine herrliche Uniform.

Chor: Uniform!

Geschichtenerzähler: Mit goldenen Knöpfen.

Chor: Gold!

Titorelli: Gold! Ich kippe um! Haltet mich! Sonst falle ich von der Wand!

Geschichtenerzähler: Jetzt, wo der Vater eine so prächtige Uniform hatte, zog er sie nie mehr aus. Ja, es gab aufregende Veränderungen in der Familie. Doch um nichts weniger aufregend waren die Veränderungen, die Gregor durchmachte. Er entwickelte sich immer weiter. [*Das Lied vom übermütigen Ungeziefer beginnt.*]

11. SZENE – DAS LIED VOM ÜBERMÜTIGEN UNGEZIEFER

Das Lied wird von einer dynamischen Animation begleitet, die sich sehr von der bisherigen lethargischen Animation unterscheidet. Gregor tanzt und wirbelt an der Wand und hinterlässt dabei eine grüne Spur. Diese grünen Linien verändern sich rhythmisch und abstrakt und Gregors Körper vervielfältigt sich, zuckt elastisch und ändert sich im Rhythmus der Musik zu abstrakten, tanzenden Formen. Das im Text erwähnte Erbrochene der Schwester ist in dieser Sequenz als abstraktes malerisches Element zu sehen, ebenso wie die nasenlochartigen schwarzen Ovale, Sardinen und andere Elemente. Aber die Hauptfigur ist Gregor, der mit großer Geschwindigkeit in Kreisen über die Wand huscht.

[Gregor:]
Als die Schwester mich roch, wurde ihr schlecht, es kam ihr hoch.
Ich stank nach Kacke, dreckigen Latrinen, und glitschigen grünen Sardinen.

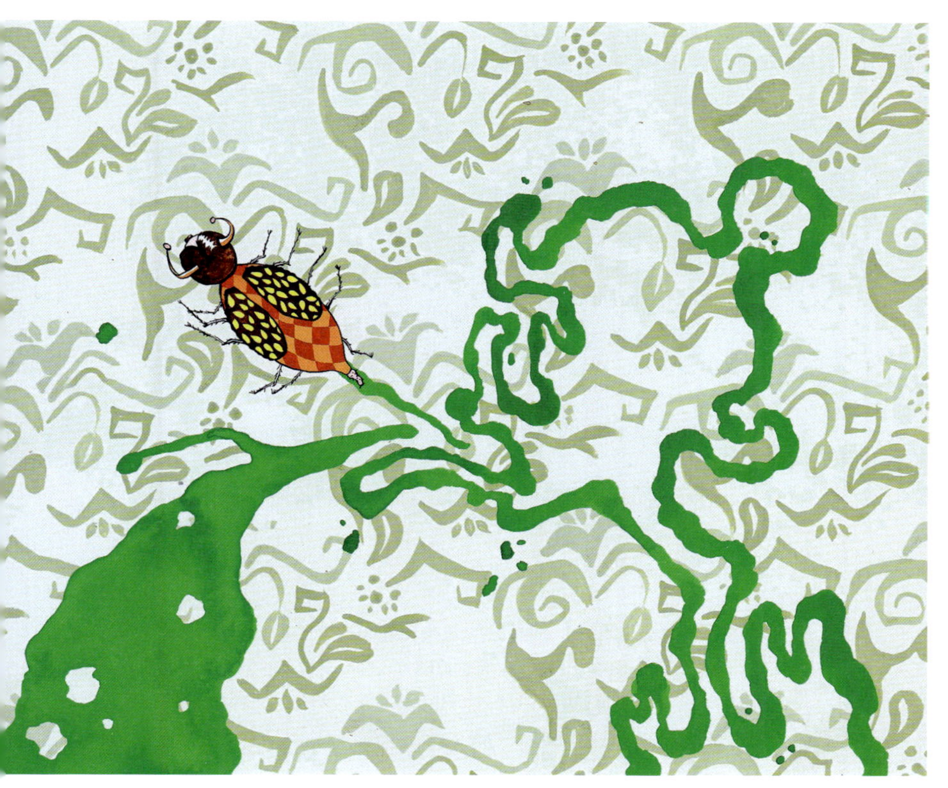

Ihr Ekel war nicht nett, doch ich hielt still, kroch unter's Bett.
Denn im stinkenden Königreich, und das ist nicht wenig, bin ich der stinkende König.

[Chor:]
Er ist ein unglaublich übermütiges Ungeziefer,
Unglaublich übermütiges Ungeziefer,
Wir sind grün vor Neid,
Auf den schnüffelnden stinkenden König.

[Gregor:]
Als die kleine Schwester mich sah, wurde sie grün und fiel fast um,
Und während ich immer weniger sehe, rieche ich alles um mich herum.

Egal, wenn ich erblinde, Sehkraft ist doch nichts wert.
Gestank ist eine herzliche Umarmung, Sehkraft eine Dirne, ganz ausgezehrt.

[Chor:]
Er ist ein unglaublich übermütiges Ungeziefer,
Unglaublich übermütiges Ungeziefer,
Kurzsichtigkeit ist ein Segen,
Nicht mehr viel zu sehen.

[Gregor:]
Ich tanze frei die Wand entlang, leicht häng ich von der Decke,
Und hinterlasse unter mir klebrige Spuren von grünlich-flüssigem Drecke.
Sie würgt, vielleicht ist es die Eifersucht, die sie würgen lässt.
Ihre Augen wandern hoch – doch am Boden steckt sie fest.

[Chor:]
Er ist ein unglaublich übermütiges Ungeziefer,
Unglaublich übermütiges Ungeziefer,
Erhebt sich frei, steigt ganz leicht, und wir, wir stecken fest.

12. SZENE – MÖBEL

Geschichtenerzähler: Gregors Zimmer war jetzt *so* schleimig. Grete kam so selten wie möglich herein, und wenn, dann riss sie sofort das Fenster auf. Natürlich bemerkte sie Gregors sich überkreuzende grüne Spuren auf Boden und Decke.

Titorelli [*ruft*]: Eklig! Eklig!

Kind [*schüttelt den Finger in Richtung Titorelli*]: Titorelli, still!

Geschichtenerzähler: Und so dachte sich Grete: Warum nicht einige der großen Möbelstücke aus Gregors Raum entfernen, damit er mehr Platz hat, sich zu bewegen, vor allem den Schreibtisch und den Schrank?

Herr und Frau Stuhl: Ein Insekt braucht keine Stühle!

Frau Tisch: Ein Tausendfüßler braucht keinen Schreibtisch!

Frau Schrank: Eine Küchenschabe braucht keinen Wandschrank!

Herr Ball: Ein Käfer braucht weder einen Schrank noch einen Ball.

Titorelli: Beschissener Scheiß-Käfer!

Chor [*außer Titorelli*]**:** Titorelli, still!

Herr und Frau Stuhl: Was für eine Ausdrucksweise!

Herr Ball: Was ist heute los mit dir, Titorelli? Weißt du nicht, dass Gemälde still sein sollten?

Frau Stuhl: Ja, gute Gemälde brauchen keine Worte!

Herr Stuhl [*wichtigtuerisch*]**:** Echte Gemälde stehen über Worten!

Titorelli: Beschissen, Scheiße, Scheiße.

Chor: Titorelli, still!

Geschichtenerzähler: Nun, Grete war nicht imstande, solche schweren Möbelstücke alleine zu bewegen. Den Vater wagte sie nicht um Hilfe zu bitten. So wartete sie, bis er zur Arbeit gegangen war und bat dann ihre dämliche Mutter um Hilfe. [*Animiertes Standbild der beiden Frauen.*]

Mutter (Frau Stuhl): Ja! Ich werde helfen und endlich meinen hübschen Sohn wieder sehen. [*Mutter lächelt.*]

Geschichtenerzähler: Doch sobald die Türe offen war, bekam sie ein wenig Angst. [*Mutters Gesichtsausdruck wird besorgt.*]

Grete (Frau Lampe): Keine Angst, Mutter, man sieht ihn nicht; er versteckt sich immer unter dem Sofa.

Geschichtenerzähler: Und so begannen die beiden, die Möbel durch Drücken und Schieben hinauszuschaffen. [*Eine Variation der Musik aus der 3. Szene, als Gregor versuchte, sich umzudrehen.*]

Chor: Eins, zwei!

Frau Lampe: Drücken, Schieben.

Chor: Eins, zwei!

Frau Stuhl: Ich krieg' keine Luft.

Chor: Eins, zwei!

Frau Lampe: Immer weiter.

Chor: Eins, zwei!

Geschichtenerzähler: Doch der Schrank war so schwer! [*Musik hört auf.*] Als er in der Mitte des Zimmers stand, kamen der Mutter Bedenken.

Mutter (Frau Stuhl): Ist es nicht so, als ob wir durch die Entfernung der Möbel zeigten, dass wir jede Hoffnung auf Besserung aufgegeben haben? Es wäre das Beste, wir lassen das Zimmer in dem Zustand, in dem es war.

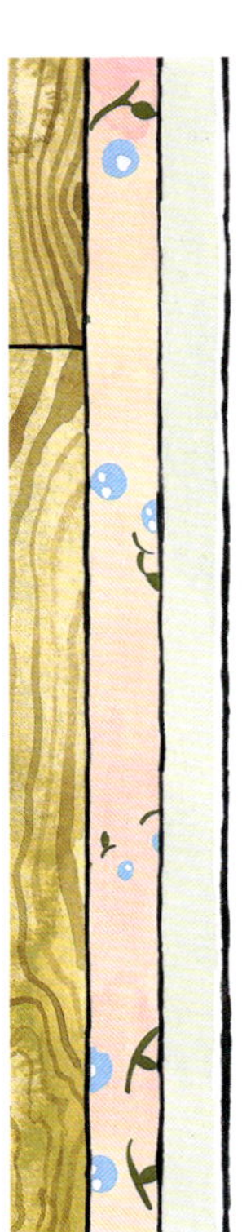
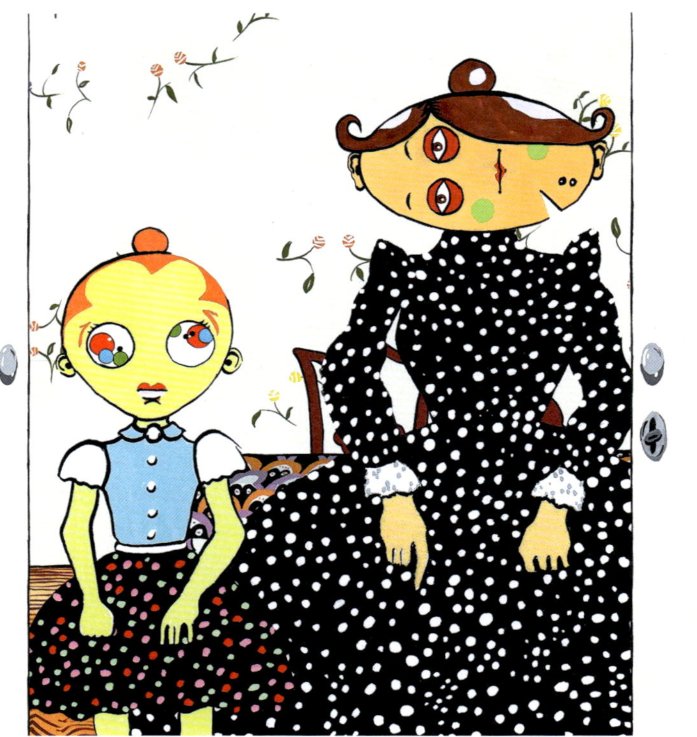

Geschichtenerzähler: Als Gregor diese Worte hörte, begannen zwei Stimmen in seinem Kopf zu streiten. [*Gregors Gesicht ist jetzt in der Mitte des Bildschirms zu sehen; zwei Kreise erscheinen an den Seiten seines Kopfes und zeigen die angehenden Chor-Mitglieder, die für den inneren Konflikt stehen.*]

Herr Stuhl [*für die Insektenseite*]**:** Ich brauche mehr Platz, um zu tanzen und die glückliche Schabe zu sein, die ich bin: Wuuuu! Wiiii! Waaaa! Rundherum, räumt den Krempel weg und verbrennt ihn!

Frau Stuhl [*für die menschliche Seite*]**:** Wie könnte ich vergessen, dass ich ein Mensch bin? Oi! Aj! Wej! Ich brauche ein vernünftiges Schlafzimmer, keine Höhle!

Herr Ball [*Insektenseite*]**:** Kein Zimmer, kein Zimmer! Ihr stört mich, geht weg! Macht euch davon, raus hier, ich will spielen!

Herr Tisch [*Menschenseite*]**:** Sie können nicht nehmen, was mir gehört, meinen Tisch und meinen Stuhl! Es ist ungehörig, es ist unzivilisiert, es ist unrechtmäßig – es ist nicht fair!

Frau Schrank [*Insektenseite*]**:** Weg mit dem Dreck – Es ist die Höhle des stinkenden Königs!

Geschichtenerzähler: Ja, Gregor war durch die Worte seiner Mutter sowohl alarmiert als auch gerührt. Aber Grete war von Mutters idiotischen Gedanken genervt und entschlossener denn je, das Zimmer zu räumen.

Chor: Alles muss raus!

Geschichtenerzähler: Die beiden Frauen gingen ins Nebenzimmer, um ein wenig zu verschnaufen. Gregor sah, dass er alleine war, rannte hin und her, um seine Gedanken zu sammeln. Dann fiel sein Blick auf seinen wertvollsten Schatz ...

Chor: Seine Frau im Pelz!

Herr Stuhl: Er kann nicht zulassen, dass sie sie wegnehmen! [*Das musikalische Motiv der Frau im Pelz erklingt; es ist auch in der folgenden Szene zu hören: Die Frau im Pelz verändert sich langsam in Überblendung von zweiter zu dritter Phase, dann zu vierter, wird dabei schmutziger, dunkler und pelziger. Abblende.*]

13. SZENE – ZWEITE WERBEUNTERBRECHUNG

13A – BOKI-POKI

Ein fröhlicher Ansager: Morgen, hier, auf dem besten Kinderkanal. *Animiertes Standbild: Bokis Musik und seine verrückt-fröhliche Figur ist wie in der ersten Werbeunterbrechung zu sehen, jetzt jedoch dynamischer. Sein Gesicht wirbelt herum, nähert sich und entfernt sich wieder, vervielfacht sich und ändert die Farben. Rahmen erscheinen und verschwinden im Bild, jeder zeigt unzusammenhängende Kinderprodukte: ein farbiges Stiftetui, Mädchenschuhe, einen Lollipop und ein Spielzeugeinhorn,* ähnlich der beharrlichen Logik *nutzer:innenorientierter Werbeanzeigen im Netz.*

Ein fröhlicher Sänger: Boki-Poki! Boki-Poki! Boki-Poki! Boki-Poki! Boki-Poki! Boki-Poki! Boki-Poki! Boki-Poki! Boki-Poki!

13B – WIEDERHOLUNG DER LEBENSMITTELWERBUNG

Du bist ein braves, liebes Kind. Papa liebt dich … mmmm … du wirst nie alleine sein … ahhh! Du verdienst nichts weniger als *The People's Delicatessen*.[4]

13C – DER ECHTE UND DER FALSCHE TITORELLI

Animiertes Standbild von Joseph K. und dem Maler Titorelli.

Verführerischer Ansager: In einer demnächst ausgestrahlten Episode von *Kafka für Kinder …*

Herr Ball (als Maler): In der Tat, Herr K., Sie werden vom Gericht beschuldigt, doch seien Sie versichert, dass ich, der Maler Titorelli, der mehr Zeit als jeder andere darauf verwendet hat, Kläger:innen im Gericht zu porträtieren, Ihnen alles sagen werde, was Sie über Ihre Chancen auf Freispruch wissen müssen …

Geschichtenerzähler [*zum Kind*]**:** Das heißt „nicht schuldig".

Herr Ball (als Maler): Aber zunächst – möchten Sie nicht eines meiner Landschaftsbilder kaufen? [*Zeigt ein Bild mit zwei Bäumen, ähnlich dem Charakter Titorellis.*]

Herr Tisch (als K.): Gut. Da ich wissen will, wie ich meinen Prozess beenden kann, ist es wohl sinnvoll, ein Landschaftsbild zu kaufen.

Herr Ball (als Maler): Oder vielleicht zwei? [*Die beiden Figuren werden mit zwei identischen Gemälden hinter sich gezeigt.*]

Herr Tisch (als K.): Ich finde sicher Platz für zwei Landschaftsbilder an meiner Wand.

Herr Ball (als Maler): Fast umsonst! Für nicht viel mehr – eine ganze Serie? [*Gesamtansicht mit der Wand dahinter, die vollgehängt ist mit identischen Gemälden. Eine kurze Pause.*] Also ausgemacht. Und nun zum Freispruch: Sie stehen vor Gericht und Sie sind unschuldig, also leuchtet es ein, dass Sie freigesprochen werden wollen. Aber ich muss Sie fragen: Welche Art von Freispruch wollen Sie? Es gibt nicht einen, sondern drei, drei Arten

4 Basierend auf einem Eintrag in Kafkas *Tagebüchern*, 30. Oktober 1911.

von Freispruch: erstens, den wirklichen Freispruch! [*Musikalische Unterstreichung*] Dann gibt es den scheinbaren Freispruch! [*Musikalische Unterstreichung*] Und schließlich gibt es die Verschleppung. [*Musikalische Unterstreichung*]

Chor: Verschleppung!

Der Überbringer [*tritt mit einem eingepackten Bild in der Hand ein*]:
Ich bin der traurigste Kerl, echt:
Meine Nachrichten sind immer schlecht!

[Chor:]
Da hat er leider ziemlich recht,
Seine Nachrichten sind immer schlecht!

[Der Überbringer:]
Ich weine viel, den ganzen Tag,
Weil ich meinen Job nicht mag!

[Chor:]
Wir weinen viel, den ganzen Tag,
Weil er seinen Job nicht mag.

Der Überbringer legt das eingepackte Bild auf den Ofen neben dem Orchester, so dass es etwas unterhalb von Titorelli liegt.

Der Überbringer: Meine Freund:innen, ich befürchte, dass ich schlechte Nachrichten habe. [*Pause*] Euer Titorelli-Gemälde [*Nahaufnahme des Gemäldes, als es den Überbringer sichtbar alarmiert beäugt.*] ... ist eine Fälschung!

Chor, Geschichtenerzähler, Kind: Oh!!!

Geschichtenerzähler: Bist du dir da völlig sicher?

Der Überbringer: Als Beweis habe ich einen *echten* Titorelli mitgebracht. Ihr werdet sofort den Unterschied zwischen schöner Kunst und Fälschung erkennen. [*Der Überbringer legt eine dramatische Pause ein, ehe er den echten Titorelli enthüllt.*
Er ist nahezu identisch, der Kopf auf dem Bild steht allerdings auf dem Kopf. Er hängt das Gemälde „falsch“ herum auf, damit das Gesicht gerade erscheint, der Boden unten ist und der Himmel oben. Das Kind betrachtet beide Gemälde sorgfältig.]

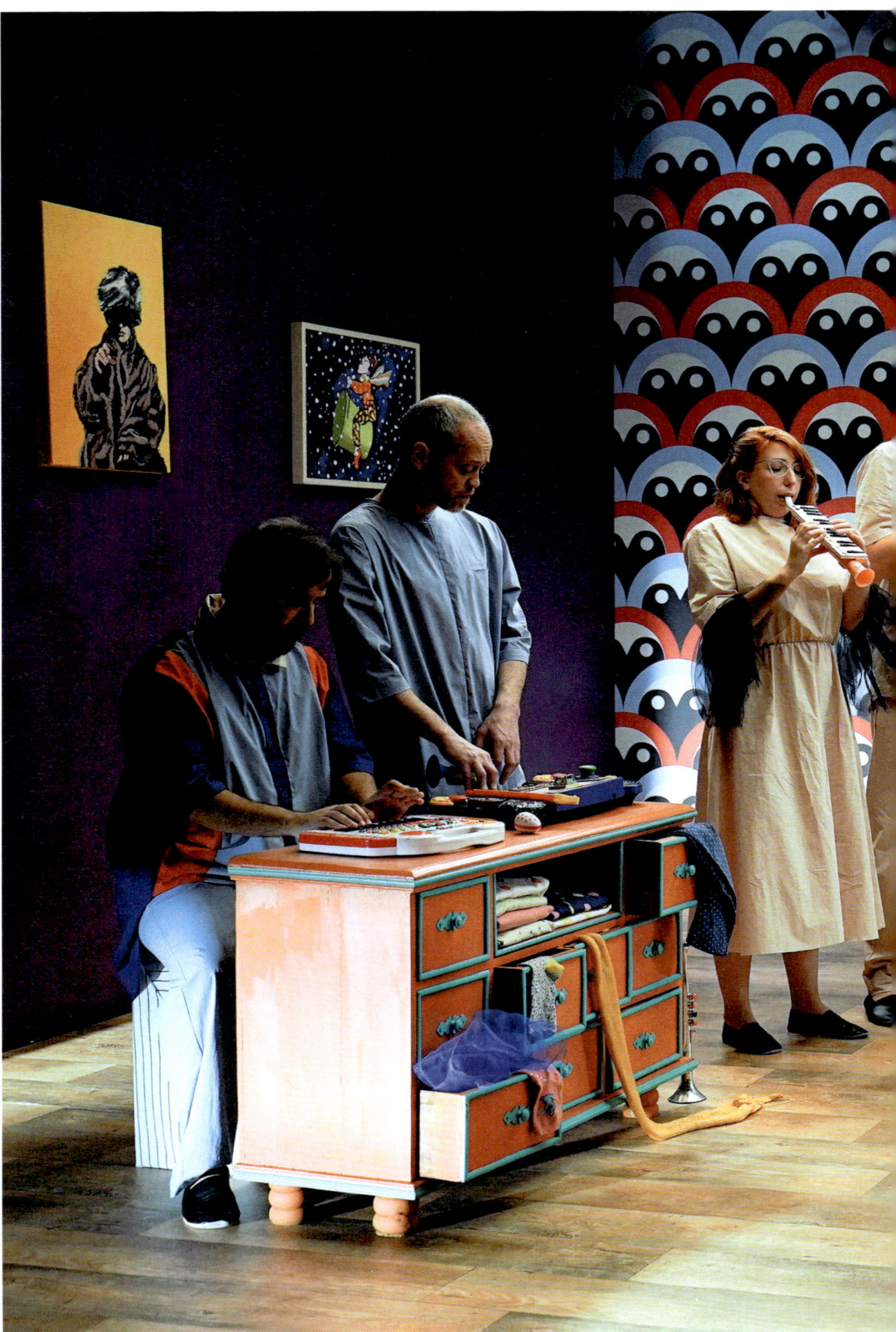

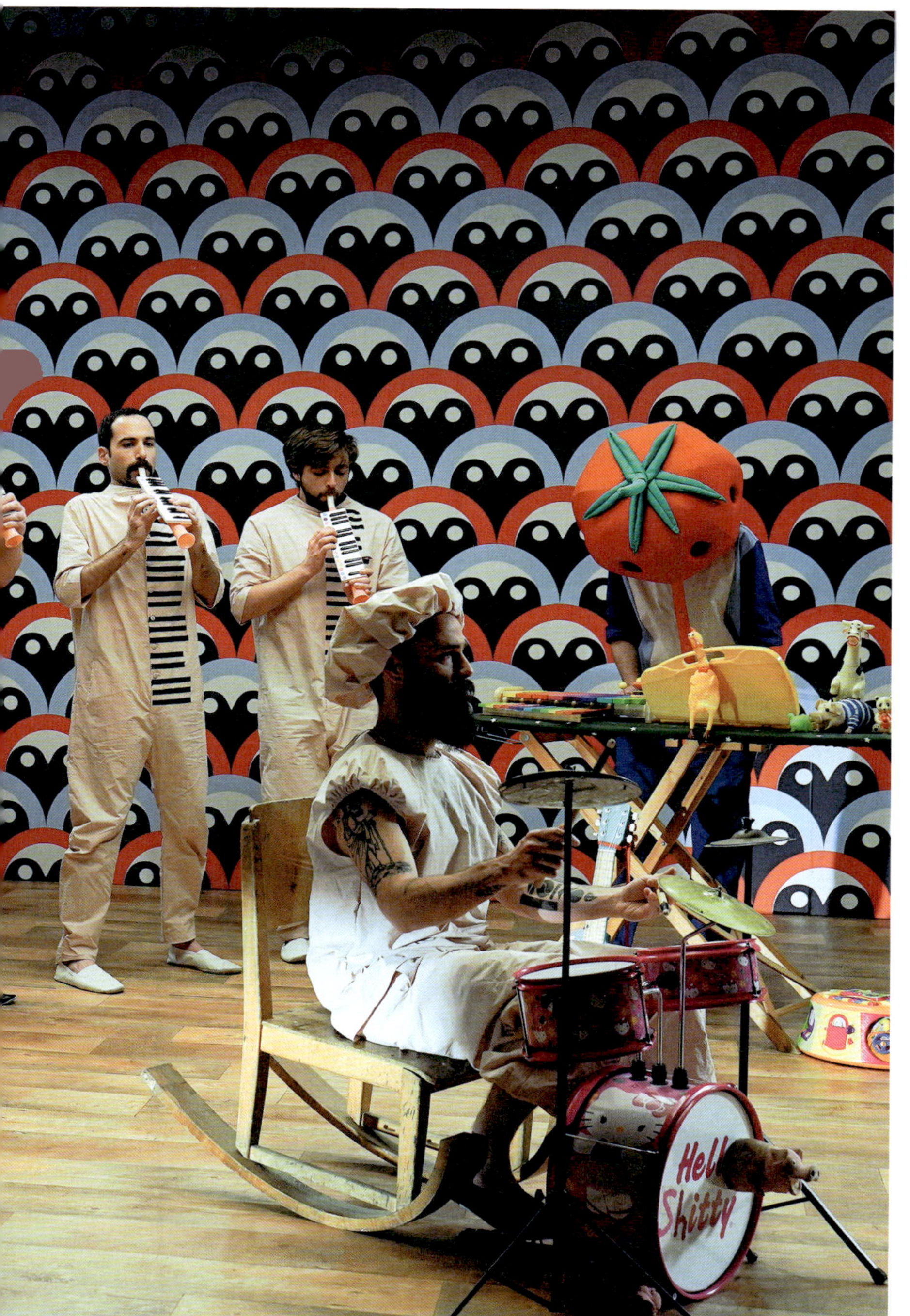
Hell
Shitty

Kind: Ich sehe keinen Unterschied. [*Das Kind untersucht die Gemälde weiter. Die Kamera folgt ihm dabei und wechselt zwischen den Bildern*] Sie sind genau gleich.

Der Überbringer: Es kommt dir nur so vor, weil du ein süßes, unschuldiges Kind bist, nicht vertraut mit Diebstahl und Betrug. Ich weiß ja, dass ihr alle in der Zeit, die ihr miteinander verbracht habt, den alten, falschen Titorelli liebgewonnen habt. Er ist fast schon ein Familienmitglied. Aber die schlechten Nachrichten sind, dass er bestraft werden muss, und die noch schlechteren Nachrichten sind, dass es keine andere Wahl als die härteste Bestrafung gibt. [*Pause*] Dies ist eine schwere Straftat. Und die schlimmsten Nachrichten sind, dass der falsche Titorelli ... [*Pause*] verbrannt werden muss!

Chor: Feuer! Feuer! Feuer!

14. SZENE – MUTTER UND DIE FRAU IM PELZ

Die Frau im Pelz ist in ihrer schmutzigsten und pelzigsten Verkörperung zu sehen.

Chor: Seine Frau im Pelz!

Herr Stuhl: Gregor wird nicht zulassen, dass sie sie entfernen! *[Eine Reihe von Nahaufnahmen. Das Kind betrachtet Titorelli unheilverheißend. Das Gemälde erwidert den Blick stumm. Das Kind schüttelt den Kopf. Titorelli ist entsetzt durch die Geste. Das Kind signalisiert mit dem Finger ein Kopfabschneiden, dann ein am Genick aufhängen und macht schließlich das Erwürgen nach und weitere Todesdrohungen. Titorelli weint ausgiebig, seine Tränen sind als verlaufende Schminke auf seinen Wangen sichtbar. Durchgehende Aufnahme, während der Geschichtenerzähler selbstvergessen mit der Geschichte fortfährt.]*

Geschichtenerzähler: Seine geliebte Frau im Pelz? Keinesfalls! Gregor würde nicht zulassen, dass sie seine Freundin entfernten, [*das Bild ist auf der Rückwand mit Blumentapete in Gregors Zimmer zu sehen*] und so kroch er eilends die Wand hinauf – und ... [*Gregors Körper bedeckt das Bild fast vollständig.*]

Chor: PLUPP!

Herr Tisch: Das kalte Glas fühlte sich so gut an und tat seinem heißen Bauch wohl.

Chor [*ausgenommen Titorelli, der völlig außer sich vor Freude scheint*]**:** Hmmmmm! Ooooooh!

Herr Ball: Oh, wie gut sich dieses Bild anfühlte! Es ist *gut*, am Leben zu sein!

Chor: Hmmmmm! Ooooh!

Titorelli: Am Leben zu sein! Am Leben! [*Bricht wieder in Tränen aus.*]

Geschichtenerzähler: ... und nun – kamen die beiden Frauen zurück ins Zimmer, Grete als erste. Da kreuzten sich ihre Blicke mit jenen Gregors. [*Zwischenschnitte als die beiden einander anstarren. Gretes Augen verändern sich von zerstreut zu fokussiert. Ihr Gesicht zittert vor Ärger.*]

Grete (Frau Lampe): Komm, wollen wir nicht lieber einen Augenblick zurück ins Wohnzimmer gehen, liebe Mutter?

Geschichtenerzähler: Nun, Mutter war, wie ihr bereits wisst, ein bisschen blöde – aber sie war keine komplette Närrin, und Gretes Worte ließen sie erst recht auf das blicken, was ihr Kind sie nicht sehen lassen wollte ... und sie war schockiert!

Chor [*in einer spöttischen – Kichern ist zu hören – irgendwie chaotischen Imitation von Mutters Antwort*]**:** Schockiert! Schockiert! Oy vey! [*Mutter fällt auf das Sofa, als würde sie das Bewusstsein verlieren, wieder wird ihre Unterwäsche sichtbar.*]

Geschichtenerzähler: Das Mädchen eilte in die Küche, um irgendeine Essenz zu finden, mit der sie die Mutter aus ihrer Ohnmacht wecken könnte. Gregor sah, dass es seiner Mutter schlecht ging, wollte auch helfen und riss sich mit Gewalt von der Frau im Pelz, was gar nicht so einfach war, denn sein Bauch klebte wegen all des grünen Glibbers, den er absonderte, am Glas fest. Doch schließlich fiel er zu Boden und eilte aus dem Zimmer hinaus der Schwester nach. Grete, die Arme voller Fläschchen, bemerkte ihn gar nicht. Eine Flasche fiel auf den Boden und zerbrach, ein Splitter verletzte Gregor im Gesicht. Dann rannte Grete zurück in Gregors Zimmer, die Tür schlug sie mit dem Fuß zu und ließ ihn ganz alleine im Wohnzimmer zurück.

Chor: Ganz allein! Zuerst drinnen eingesperrt – dann draußen gefangen!

Herr Ball: Gregor begann zu kriechen.

Chor: Hin und her.

Stühle: Boden, Teppiche ...
Herr Ball, Frau Lampe, Herr Tisch: ... Wände, Zimmerdecke ...
Geschichtenerzähler: Schließlich fiel er in seiner Verzweiflung mitten auf den großen Tisch und lag ermattet da.

15. SZENE – ÄPFEL

Pause. Ein Läuten ist zu hören.

Chor [*Plötzlich ertönt als Reaktion auf das Läuten ein Lied*]:
Lauf weg, liebe Frau Taylor,
Es ist der Überbringer schlechter Nachrichten!
Der Überbringer schlechter Nachrichten!
Der Überbringer schlechter Nachrichten!

Geschichtenerzähler [*vorwurfsvoll*]: Nein! [*Chormitglieder mit verwirrtem Gesichtsausdruck*] Diesmal war es *nicht* der Überbringer schlechter Nachrichten, ihr liegt *falsch*! [*Verschämter Ausdruck einiger Chormitglieder.*]

Herr Stuhl: Es war Titorellis Schuld!

Chor: Titorelli! Feuer! Feuer! Feuer! [*Lynchjustiz liegt in der Luft.*]

Geschichtenerzähler: Bitte, Leute, Ruhe. Jemand hatte geläutet und Grete öffnete die Tür.

Grete (Frau Lampe) [*Animiertes Standbild: niedergeschlagen*]: Hallo Vater. Wie war's bei der Arbeit? Gregor ist ausgebrochen. Mutter ist in Ohnmacht gefallen.

Vater (Herr Ball) [*mit wachsender Entrüstung*]: Ich habe es ja erwartet. Aber ihr Frauen wolltet nicht hören. Ich habe es euch ja immer gesagt. Ich habe es euch immer gesagt. Ich habe es euch immer gesagt. Ich habe es euch immer gesagt.

Geschichtenerzähler: Um zu zeigen, dass er die beste Absicht habe, flüchtete sich Gregor zur geschlossenen Tür seines Zimmers und blieb dort stehen, damit klar war, dass er nur wieder zurück in sein Zimmer wollte. [*Animiertes Standbild des Vaters.*]

Vater (Herr Ball): Ah-ha!

Geschichtenerzähler: Diesmal hatte Vater keinen Krückstock, mit dem er Gregor stoßen konnte, aber er fand etwas noch Besseres.

Chor: Was? Was?

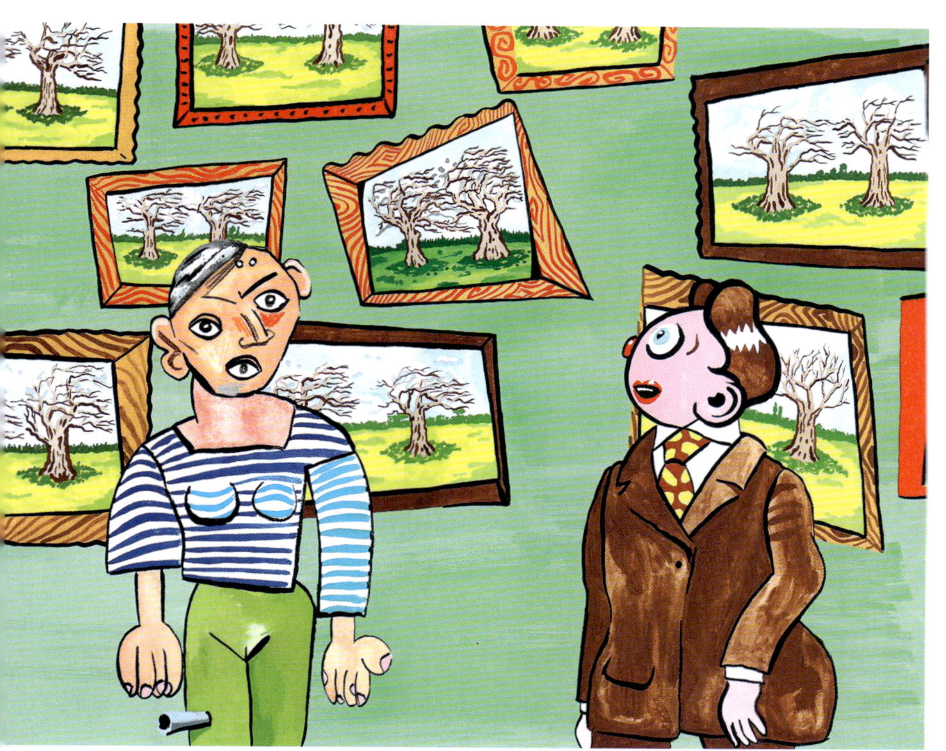

Geschichtenerzähler: Eine Obstschale mit Äpfeln! Und er begann, Gregor mit Äpfeln zu bombardieren, Apfel für Apfel …
Herr und Frau Stuhl: Bäng! Puff! Padam!
Chor [*glücklich*]**:** Bäng! Puff! Padam!
Chor und Kind [*beschwingt*]**:** Bäng! Puff! Padam!
Geschichtenerzähler: Gregor wusste einfach nicht mehr, wohin er laufen sollte und die Äpfel flogen immer weiter!

Apfellied

Herb und hart, wenn grün,
Süß und saftig, wenn rot,
Gekuschelt in die Schale,
Stellen sie sich tot.

Äpfel beißen, Äpfel schmeißen,
Aus Angst vor dem Gegessen werden, stellen sie sich tot.

Iss ihn, wenn er klein,
Von grün und rot ein Happs,
Iss' nen Apfel-Sohn,
Eh er schrumpelt wie dein Paps.

Äpfel schälen, Äpfel spülen,
Besser kleine Äpfel schälen als spülen den miesen Paps.

Geschichtenerzähler [*während die Musik spielt und das Kind immer noch tanzt*]**:** Vater war vielleicht stark und hatte herrliche Goldknöpfe, aber er war nicht sehr gut bei dem Spiel. Er verfehlte Gregor immer wieder. Die Äpfel rollten überall auf dem Boden herum. Dann gelang Vater ein wahrlich fabelhafter Wurf: Er traf Gregor so fest, dass der Apfel tief in Gregors Rücken drang und dort stecken blieb. [*Musik hört auf; Geschichtenerzähler und Kind sitzen; Aufnahme des Apfels, der in Gregors Rücken steckt.*]

Frau Stuhl: Und das Letzte, was Gregor sah, ehe er das Bewusstsein verlor, war die Mutter, im Hemd, die sich auf den Vater warf, um ihn aufzuhalten. [*Animiertes Standbild: Mutter mit hochgerutschtem Rock auf dem Vater. Musikalisches Motiv der Frau im Pelz.*]

Ende des 2. Kapitels

KAPITEL

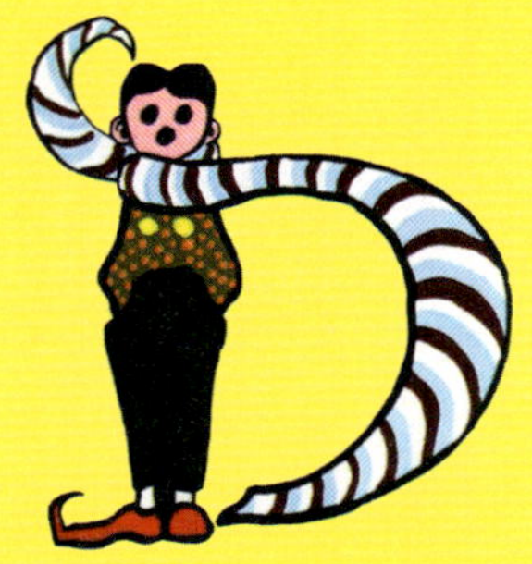

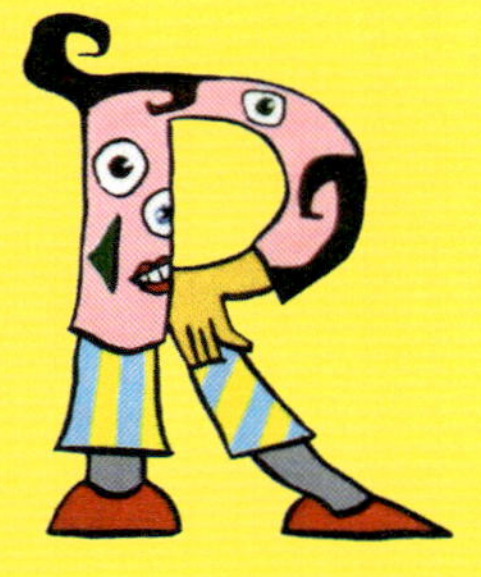

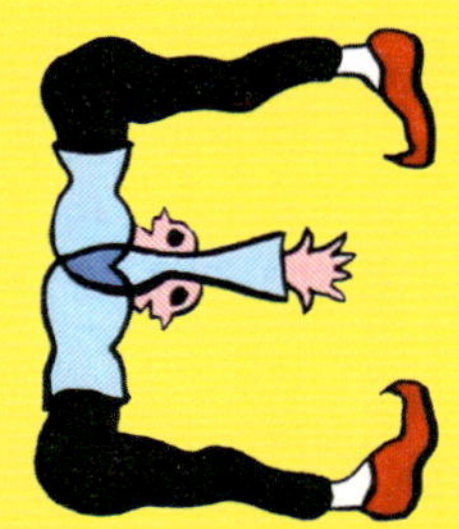

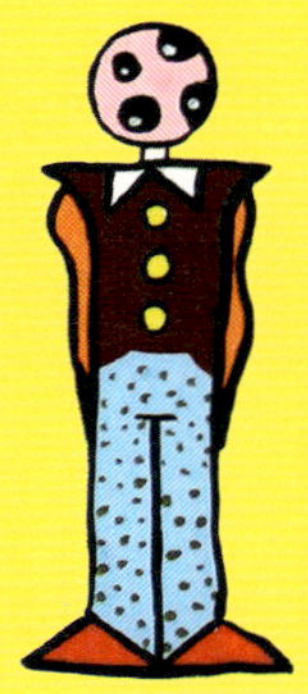

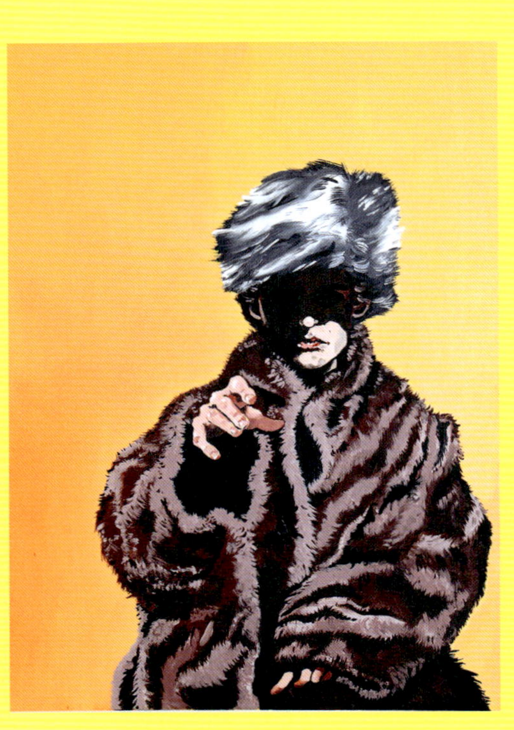

16. SZENE – FAMILIENGESCHÄFT

Nahaufnahme: Die letzte, dunkelste und schmutzigste Phase der Frau im Pelz. Animiertes Standbild: Gregor.

Geschichtenerzähler: Der Apfel, der Gregor getroffen hatte, blieb lange in seinem Fleisch stecken. Er ging jetzt sehr langsam. An Kriechen in der Höhe war nicht zu denken. Doch es war nicht alles schlecht. Seine Türe wurde nun am Abend immer geöffnet, damit er seine liebe Familie beobachten konnte. Der Haushalt war ein geschäftiges kleines Unternehmen: Grete arbeitete in einem Laden, Mutter nähte feine Damenwäsche, Vater legte seine Uniform nie ab und ab und zu wurde ein Schmuckstück verkauft. Gregor beobachtete all das wie ein stiller Teilhaber; schließlich war er einmal der einzige Versorger der Familie gewesen.

Kind: Was ist ein:e Versorger:in?

Herr Ball: Ein:e Versorger:in ist eine Person, die das Geld nachhause bringt, um die Dinge zu kaufen, die eine Familie braucht oder will.

Kind: Aber ...

Herr Ball: Aber was?

Kind: Aber das ergibt keinen Sinn.

Herr Ball [*nach einer Pause*]**:** Du hast Recht, irgendwie. Es gibt viele Fragen zu Versorgung und Arbeit wie: Warum sollte jemand zugunsten von anderen arbeiten, selbst wenn diese vielleicht alte, geschwächte Eltern oder kleine Kinder sind. Es gibt andere komplizierte Themen – wie soll zum Beispiel das zur Verfügung gestellte Geld aufgeteilt werden – was zufällig ein Thema ist, für das Kafka als Doktor des Rechts, der mit Versicherungen zu tun hatte, ein großer Experte war. Du hast also Recht, wenn du meinst, dass es nicht ohne Weiteres Sinn ergibt, ein:e Versorger:in zu sein.

Kind: Nein, ich meine, dass es keinen Sinn ergibt, dass Gregor Geld verdiente.

Herr Ball: Warum nicht?

Kind: Es ergibt überhaupt keinen Sinn. [*Pause. Das Kind kichert, als käme ihm eine offensichtliche Absurdität in den Sinn.*]

Herr Ball: Und warum nicht?

Kind: Weil er eine Kakerlake ist. Eine Kakerlake kann kein Geld verdienen. [*Pause*] Es sei denn, man verkauft sie. [*Pause*] Aber selbst dann verdient jemand anderes das Geld.

Geschichtenerzähler [*nach einer Pause, sanft aber ein wenig entmutigt*]**:** Aber du erinnerst dich ... oder?

Kind: Woran?

Geschichtenerzähler: Dass Gregor nicht immer ein Insekt war.

Kind [*zweifelnd*]**:** Was?

Geschichtenerzähler: Er wurde zu Beginn der Sendung eine Frau, ich meine ein Ungeziefer.

Kind: OK.

Herr Ball: OK, also!

Kind: Wenn du das sagst. [*Herr Ball lächelt. In einem plötzlichen Ausbruch von Rebellion und Wut nimmt das Kind den Ball mit beiden Händen und wirft ihn. Der Effekt ist der einer Enthauptung. Der Ball schreit, während er durch die Luft fliegt. Er trifft die Wand und fällt auf den Boden. Der Geschichtenerzähler hebt ihn auf, wischt mit der Fußsohle einen Blutfleck vom Boden und legt den Ball zurück auf den Tisch.*]

Geschichtenerzähler: Gregors Zimmer war seit Wochen nicht geputzt worden. Gregor versuchte Grete auf all den Schmutz aufmerksam zu machen, indem er sich vorwurfsvoll in die schmutzigste Ecke stellte, doch sie ignorierte ihn. Einmal kam seine Mutter herein, um zu putzen. Sie verbrauchte einige Kübel Wasser dafür. Als Grete von der Arbeit nachhause kam – oh, wie wütend war sie da!

Vater (Herr Ball) [*sichtbar lädiert und verletzt*]**:** Dieser Unsinn kann so nicht weitergehen. Wir werden eine Bedienerin einstellen.

17. SZENE – DIE BEDIENERIN

Geschichtenerzähler: Und so stellten sie eine Bedienerin ein, und es wurde sogar noch besser. Wenn sie ins Zimmer kam, sagte sie freundlich zu Gregor ...

Frau Schrank: Komm mal herüber, alter Mistkäfer!

Geschichtenerzähler: Oder sie sagte ...

Frau Schrank: Seht mal den alten Mistkäfer!

Geschichtenerzähler: Eines Tages ging Gregor auf sie los, um zu sehen, ob er sie erschrecken könne. Aber er war schon so geschwächt, dass sein Laufen nur mehr ein langsames Hinken und Humpeln war. Die Bedienerin hob bloß einen Stuhl mit ihren starken Armen und Gregor bekam es mit der Angst. Diese kleinen Spielchen konnten sie nun jeden Tag spielen. Sie war natürlich arm, schmutzig und wegwerfbar wie Klopapier. Doch diese Bedienerin war großartig.

Das Lied der Bedienerin

Ein würdevoller Gesang, der mit einem Sänger beginnt, als Duett mit den Frauen weitergeht und in einem Diminuendo endet. Nach oben wandernd zeigt das Bild, beginnend bei den Beinen, den Körper der Bedienerin. Sobald ihr Gesicht zu sehen ist, schrumpfen und erweitern sich ihre Gesichtsöffnungen (Augen, Mund, Nasenlöcher) und verändern langsam ihre Position.

Eine tolle Frau, die alles kennt,
Eine tolle Frau mit buschiger, weißer Mähne,
Eine tolle Frau, viele Jahre alt,
Eine tolle Frau, mit echten Falten,
Eine tolle Frau, aufrecht und groß,
Eine tolle Frau, mit langem Schatten,
    Sie weiß, wie man den Besen schwingt,
Eine tolle Frau, mit muskulösen Schenkeln,
    Sie weiß, wie man den Mopp auswringt,
Eine tolle Frau, mit würzigem Duft,
    Sie weiß, wie man den Stecken hält,
Eine tolle Frau, mit breiten Schultern,
    Sie weiß, wie man den Dreck beherrscht,
Eine tolle Frau, mit stechend-schwarzem Blick,
    Sie weiß, wie man den Staub besiegt,
Eine tolle Frau, mit einer Stimme, die betört,
    Sie weiß, wie man den Feger schwenkt,
    Sie weiß alles über Borsten und Zinken,
    Sie weiß, wie man den Schwamm ausdrückt,
    Sie weiß, wie man die Stühle hebt,

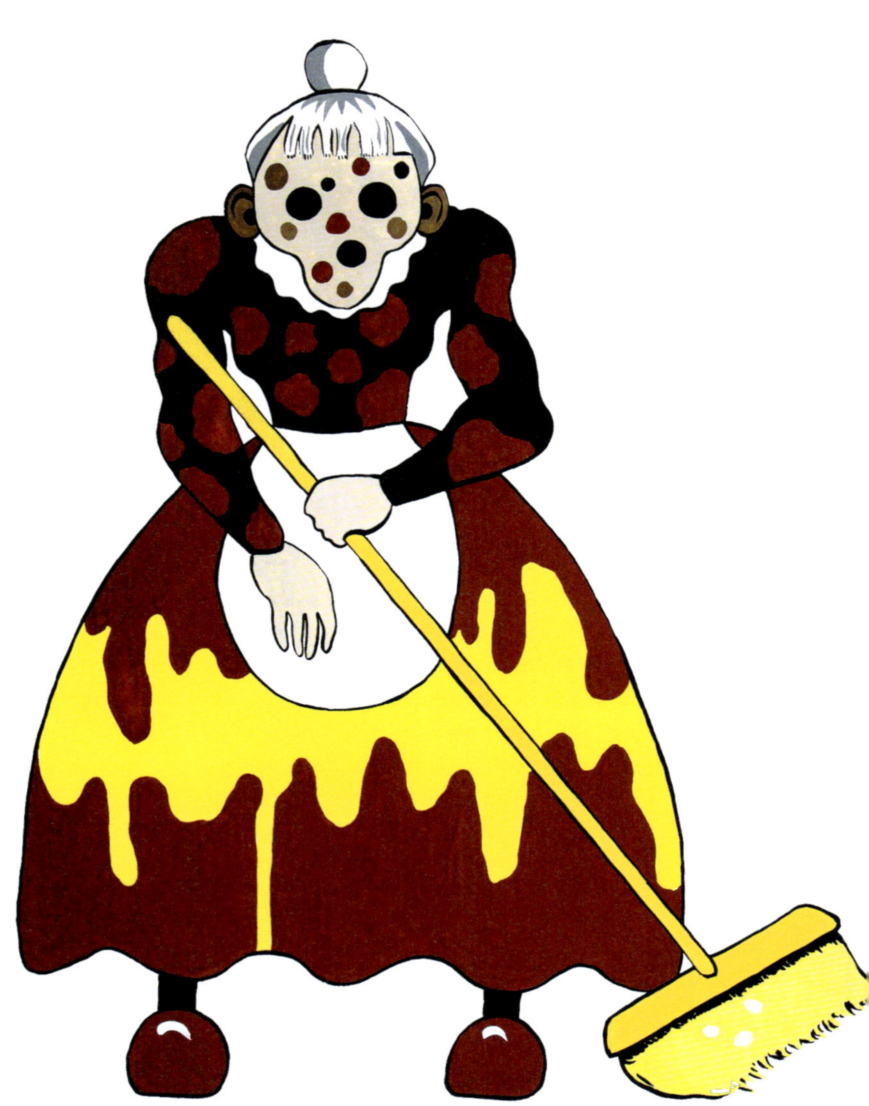

Sie weiß, wie man den Mist zähmt,
Sie weiß alles über Ungeziefer und so,
Sie weiß, wie sie dein Herz zerquetscht,
Sie weiß, wie sie deine Seele knetet,
Sie weiß, wie man den Besen schwingt,
Sie weiß, wie man den Besen schwingt,
Sie weiß, wie man den Besen schwingt.

18. SZENE – DIE DREI ZIMMERHERREN

Geschichtenerzähler: Jetzt, wo Gregor sich kaum mehr bewegte, konnte die Familie alle möglichen Dinge in seinem Zimmer unterstellen: zerbrochene Stühle, ausrangierte Erbstücke, abgenutzte Teppiche. Gregor aß nun fast gar nichts mehr. Manchmal nahm er einen Bissen in den Mund, hielt ihn dort stundenlang und spuckte ihn dann wieder aus, wenn die Betreuungsperson nicht hinsah.

Kind: Wir sind alle Abfall.

Frau Stuhl: Abfall.

Frau Lampe: Abfall.

Geschichtenerzähler [*ignoriert die Unterbrechung*]**:** Nachdem nun all der Müll bei Gregor untergebracht war, wurde ein kleines Zimmer frei und die Familie konnte extra Geld verdienen, indem sie dieses an drei Zimmerherren vermietete. Es waren drei Angestellte, die drei Betten und drei kleine Lampen mitbrachten. Da die Zimmerherren gerne zuhause speisten, blieb Gregors Türe für gewöhnlich verschlossen. Doch eines Abends vergaß die Bedienerin, sie zu schließen, und Gregor sah die drei Zimmerherren, die im Wohnzimmer saßen und aßen. [*Entsprechendes animiertes Standbild der Zimmerherren am Tisch mit erhobenen Messern und Gabeln*]

Grete (Frau Lampe): Die Kartoffeln – weich genug?

Zimmerherr (Frau Stuhl): Weich genug. [*Vater erscheint im Bild.*]

Vater (Herr Ball): Das Fleisch – mürbe genug?

Zimmerherr (Herr Stuhl): Mürbe genug. [*Vater verschwindet aus dem Bild. Das Essen verschwindet. Eine Zeitung erscheint. Sie lesen. Der Klang einer Violine ertönt schwach und verführerisch; er erinnert an Gregors Stimme im 1. Kapitel.*]

Vater (Herr Ball): Meine Tochter übt Violine. Ist den Herren das Spiel vielleicht unangenehm?

Zimmerherr (Herr Stuhl): Im Gegenteil, möchte sie nicht zu uns hereinkommen und hier im Zimmer spielen? Meine Kollegen und ich schätzen Kultur. [*Grete erscheint. Sie beginnt zu spielen, die Melodie ist die gleiche wie Gregors Rede im 1. Kapitel.*] Wir sind enttäuscht. Wir finden die Musik keineswegs unterhaltsam.

Geschichtenerzähler: Gregor hingegen war sehr ergriffen von den Klängen. [*Animiertes Standbild: Nahaufnahme von Gregors ziemlich schmutzigem Gesicht*] Er hatte Grete seit sehr langer Zeit nicht spielen gehört. Er beschloss, hinüber zu kriechen und sie zu ermutigen, sie vielleicht sogar einzuladen, in seinem Zimmer zu spielen. Und so machte er sich auf den Weg, obwohl es schwierig für ihn war und er eine Spur aus stinkendem Dreck hinterließ – er war kaum mehr als ein kleiner Haufen Schmutz.

Chor: Wir sind alle Abfall.

Geschichtenerzähler: Gregor kroch langsam ins Wohnzimmer, den ganzen Weg bis zu Grete.

Zimmerherr (Herr Stuhl) [*zeigt mit dem Finger*]**:** Herr Samsa! Angesichts dieser widerlichen Verhältnisse, der schmutzigen Wohnung ...

Chor: Abfall, Abfall!

Zimmerherr (Herr Stuhl): ... und der unzuträglichen Familie, erkläre ich hiermit, dass ich mein Zimmer augenblicklich kündige.

Chor [*rufend*]**:** Auch wir kündigen augenblicklich.

Zimmerherr (Herr Stuhl): Ich werde natürlich für die Tage, die ich hier gewohnt habe, nicht das Geringste bezahlen.

Chor [*glücklich rufend*]**:** Auch wir werden natürlich für die Tage, die wir hier gewohnt haben, nicht das Geringste bezahlen.

Herr Stuhl (Zimmerherr): Dagegen werde ich es mir noch überlegen, ob ich nicht mit irgendwelchen Forderungen an Sie herantreten werde! [*Die Zimmerherren verschwinden. Vater, Mutter und Grete* hängen *niedergeschlagen in ihren Stühlen.*]

Frau Lampe (Grete) [*nach einer Pause*]**:** Wir müssen versuchen, es loszuwerden.

Herr Ball (Vater): Was sollen wir aber tun?

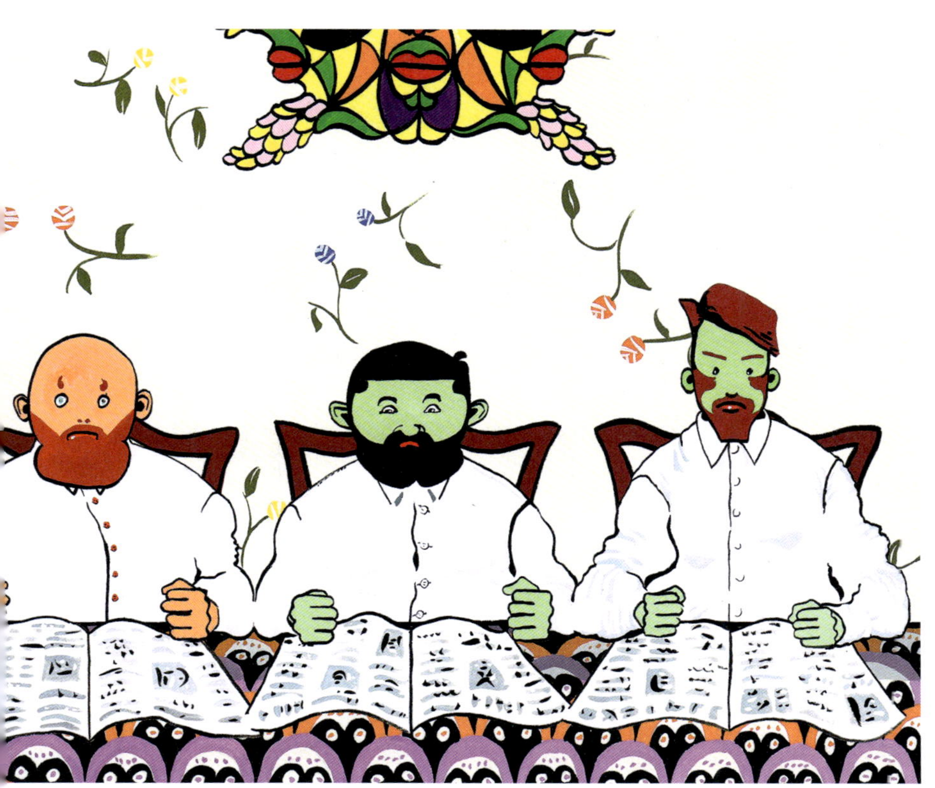

Frau Lampe (Grete): Wir müssen es loszuwerden versuchen.
Herr Ball (Vater): Du hast Recht, aber was können wir tun?
Frau Lampe: Sieh nur, er fängt schon wieder an!
Geschichtenerzähler: Tatsächlich bewegte Gregor sich nun ein wenig. Er wollte bloß in sein Zimmer zurückwandern, aber der Weg zurück – jetzt, da er so dünn und schwach war – war sehr lang. Kaum war er innerhalb seines Zimmers, wurde die Tür eiligst zugedrückt, verriegelt und versperrt. Und so schloss das Ungeziefer seine Augen zum allerletzten Mal.
Kind [*gähnend*]**:** Ich bin auch müde.
Geschichtenerzähler [*schaut das Kind liebevoll an*]**:** Ich bringe dich zu Bett, und wir beenden die Geschichte dort, ehe wir Gute Nacht sagen.

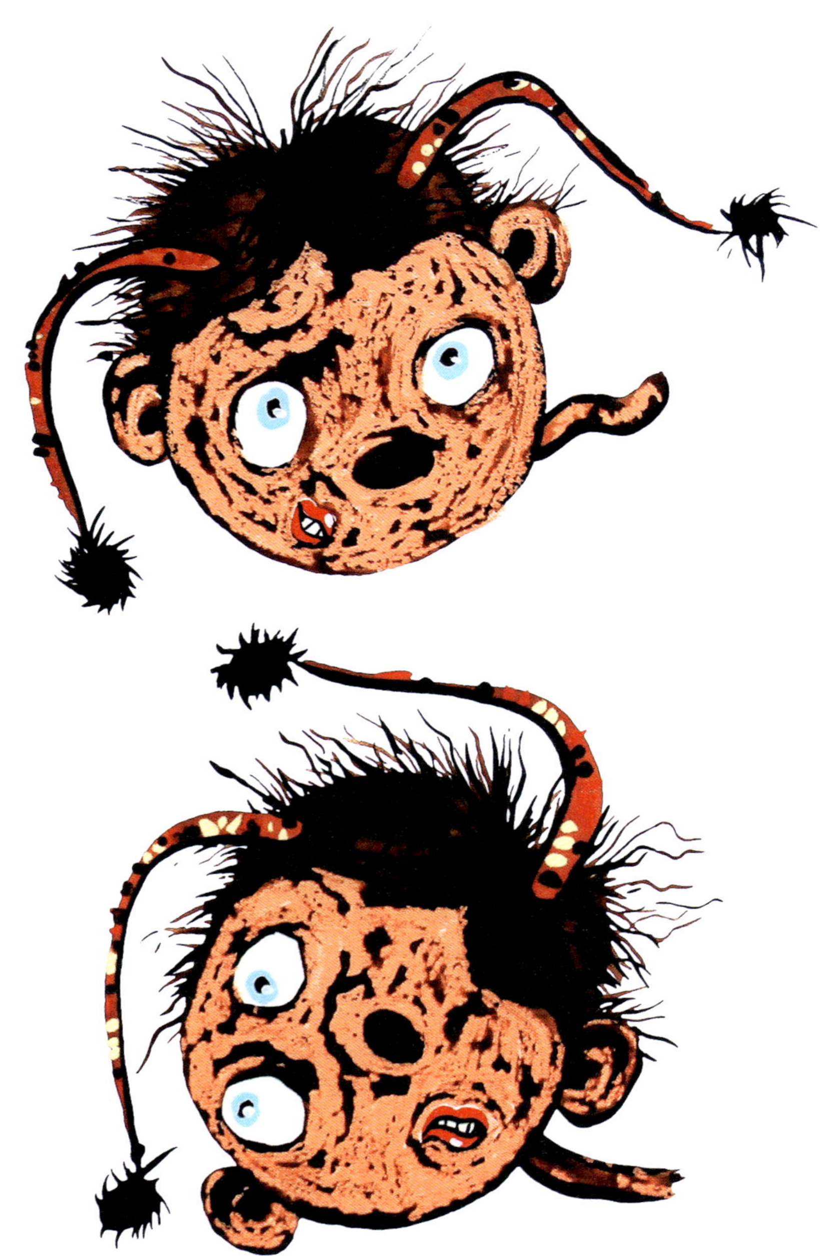

19. SZENE – DRITTE WERBEUNTERBRECHUNG

19A – BOKI-POKI GESTRICHEN

Boki-Pokis Gesicht erscheint in verminderter, schlechter Auflösung und ohne Musik.

Ansager [*ein wenig besorgt*]: Aufgrund der Umstände wird Boki-Poki morgen nicht gesendet. Wir sind alle in der Hoffnung vereint, dass alle Anschuldigungen gegen Boki-Poki fallen gelassen werden, Boki-Poki freigelassen wird und sich wieder zu uns gesellt. Folge bitte unserem Programm, um zu erfahren, wann du Boki-Poki wieder sehen kannst.

19B– WIEDERHOLUNG DER LEBENSMITTELWERBUNG

Stopf dich voll mit Heringen, Essiggurken und all den alten, scharfen Speisen. Du verdienst nichts Geringeres als *The People's Delicatessen*.[5]

20. SZENE – KWAME DAS RECHT ERKLÄREN

In der gleichen Kulisse angesiedelt wie in der Vorschau für die Diskussion über Kinder und das Militärgesetz (Szene 13c), erscheint dieser Monolog zunächst wie eine weitere kurze Ankündigung für das gleiche Programm, ehe das Publikum allmählich begreift, dass der Film ein anderer ist.

Rechtsexpertin [*elegant gekleidet und äußerst gefasst*]: Guten Tag! 2016 wurde ein zwölfjähriges Mädchen, bekannt unter dem Kürzel D., soweit wir wissen, zum jüngsten palästinensischen Mädchen, das jemals in Israel verhaftet wurde. D. wurde am Tor der Siedlung Carmei-Tzur mit einem in ihrem Mantel versteckten Messer angehalten. Man befand sie des Vorsatzes schuldig, töten zu wollen, und verurteilte sie zu viereinhalb Monaten Gefängnis, die sie in einer Einrichtung für erwachsene Frauen verbüßen musste. Ihre Strafe sollte auf acht Monate verlängert

5 Basierend auf einem Eintrag in Kafkas *Tagebüchern*, 30. Oktober 1911.

werden, wenn ihre Eltern eine Geldstrafe nicht zahlten. [*Kurze Pause. Sie schnieft sehr zurückhaltend, räuspert sich und spricht weiter.*] Angesichts dieses Falles könnte man sich fragen: *Was ist ein Kind?* Und: Wie wird es durch das Recht geformt? Das sind komplexe Fragen, die ich heute nur kurz behandeln möchte, als müsste ich einem völlig Fremden, jemandem, der zeitlich und räumlich weit entfernt ist – wie zum Beispiel ein junger Mann aus Ghana, in siebzig Jahren – die rechtlichen Rahmenbedingungen der Besetzung erklären. [*Kurze Pause*]

Kindheit ist ein vorübergehender Zustand und auch das Gesetz, auf dessen Grundlage D. verurteilt wurde, war zeitlich begrenzt konzipiert, da die Besetzung ein vorläufiger Zustand ist. Bereits vor 1967 hatte sich Israel auf eine territoriale Besetzung vorbereitet und auf die Notwendigkeit, diese Gebiete in Übereinstimmung mit dem Völkerrecht zu regieren. So wurden einige der Befehle des Militärgouverneurs bereits im Voraus festgelegt. Und dabei, Kwame, handelt es sich eigentlich um Notstandsverordnungen, die regelmäßig erneuert werden müssen. Die genaue Dauer der israelischen Besetzung ist derzeit unbekannt. Ihr Alter jedoch, das meinem zufällig ähnelt, beträgt fünfzig Jahre. Ich bin achtundvierzig [*kurze Pause*]; fast neunundvierzig. [*Pause. Ihr Gesicht verdunkelt sich ein wenig. Sie wirkt zerstreut. Sie fährt fort.*]

Aber ich müsste Kwame – dem zukünftigen Tierarzt aus Accra, der Hauptstadt Ghanas – erklären, dass die Armee zwar über die Hoheitsgewalt in den Territorien verfügt, jedoch nicht alle, die dort leben, unter ihre Gerichtsbarkeit fallen. Israelische Jüd:innen siedeln in den besetzten Gebieten unter Verletzung des Völkerrechts, sie unterliegen jedoch dem israelischen Zivilrecht und nicht dem Militärrecht. Es gibt also zwei Arten von Recht in ein und demselben Gebiet – und damit auch zwei Arten von Kindheit. [*Während sie spricht, wendet sie das Gesicht gelegentlich zu ihrer rechten Achselhöhle und dem Podium darunter, als suchte sie nach dem Ursprung eines Geruches.*] Israelischem Recht zufolge endet die Kindheit mit achtzehn Jahren. Die Palästinenser:innen hören jedoch im Alter von zwölf Jahren auf, Kinder zu sein. Verordnung 1651 fasst Dutzende früherer Verordnungen zusammen, die sich vielfach auf Minderjährige beziehen, und bereits Abschnitt 1 stellt klar, dass D. kein

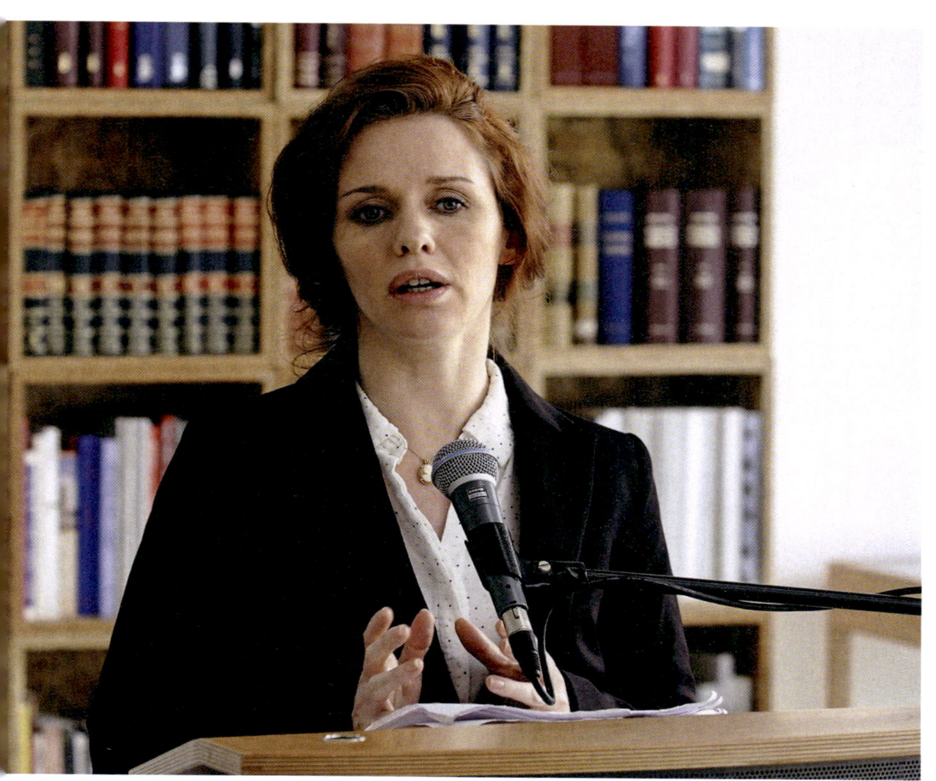

Kind ist, was das Alter betrifft, sondern eine Jugendliche, die rechtliche Kategorie von Palästinenser:innen im Alter zwischen zwölf und vierzehn Jahren. Wird ein:e Palästinenser:in vierzehn Jahre alt, ist sie oder er dem Gesetz zufolge bis zum sechzehnten Lebensjahr ein junger Erwachsener. Früher wurden Palästinenser:innen mit sechzehn Jahren erwachsen. Das Militärrecht änderte die Grenze zur Volljährigkeit auf Achtzehn, studiert man jedoch das jüngste Kompendium an Verordnungen, bleibt unklar, ob Palästinenser:innen nach Vollendung des sechzehnten Lebensjahres tatsächlich aufhören, junge Erwachsene zu sein. [*Überlegend*] Junge Erwachsene. [*Pause*] Abschnitt 168/B definiert die zunehmend strengeren Strafen für die verschiedenen Altersgruppen und besagt, dass Jugendliche wie D. höchstens sechs Monate im Gefängnis verbringen dürfen. Die Strafe für einen jungen Erwachsenen hingegen … [*Sie verstummt abrupt und riecht auffällig an ihrer Achsel. Scheinbar beunruhigt kniet sie nieder, schnüffelt und sucht nach dem Ursprung eines Ge-ruches auf dem Boden hinter dem Podium. Sie steht auf.*]

Ich sollte mich wahrscheinlich für das entschuldigen, was ich vorhin gesagt habe, als ich sagte … [*Pause*] Ich bin eine so talentierte öffentliche Rednerin, es erfüllt mich, mühelos gewinne ich mein Publikum für mich. Es ist so, als würde man einen vertrauten Weg entlangfahren, die Straße, die man jeden Tag nimmt. Du fährst in deinem eigenen Auto, das Auto ist dein Körper, du bist alleine, mitten in der Nacht, auf deiner gewohnten Strecke. Es ist dunkel. Du hältst einen Vortrag, aber gleichzeitig bist du ganz alleine auf dieser unbeleuchteten Straße und das Auto ist gemütlich und vertraut, dein Körper, den du stets bewohnst. Du versinkst in Gedanken und deine Gedanken wandern – einige davon betreffen den Vortrag, das heißt die Straße: Bäume, Unebenheiten auf der Fahrbahn, Abschnitt 93, der die Bekanntgabe des Namens eines inhaftierten Minderjährigen untersagt, ein kleines Gefängnis, fast versteckt zwischen den Obstgärten, 1638 inhaftierte Minderjährige im Jahr 2015 in den besetzten Gebieten, die Luft erfüllt vom Duft der Orangenblüten, alles ist an seinem Platz, an exakt der gleichen Stelle wie in jeder anderen Nacht, rhetorische Arten des Flirtens, Leidenschaft, Erkenntnis, Handzeichen [*führt einige Handzeichen aus*]. Die Straße ist so vertraut, dass du die Augen schließen könntest. Du würdest sie wenigstens gerne zusammenkneifen, um die Müdigkeit zu vertreiben. Du fährst und fährst, in Gedanken versunken. Deine Gedanken schweifen in andere Regionen ab. Du starrst vor dich hin, ohne wirklich zu sehen, eine Hand am Lenkrad … Etwas beunruhigt dich, ein irritierender Geruch wird stärker und du scheinst dich verirrt zu haben. Du bist an einem fremden Ort. Verloren. Das Auto ist immer noch dein Körper, aber plötzlich fühlt es sich fremd an. Wo sind Kwame Ashanti und sein strahlendes Lächeln jetzt, wo bin ich? Der Gestank liegt in der Luft und es ist unklar, ob er von dir ausgeht, im Auto, oder ob er von außen kommt. Während des Vortrags muss dir ein schrecklicher Fehler unterlaufen sein: Leichtsinnigerweise hast du unzusammenhängende Themen vermischt, einen unpassenden Witz erzählt oder einen peinlichen Sachfehler begangen. Der Hochmut der du selbst bist, platzt aus allen Nähten. Du bist bloßgestellt, gedemütigt und verloren. [*Pause*] Doch zum Glück ist das nicht passiert. [*Lächelt ein kleines, wenig überzeugendes, erleichtertes Lächeln und fährt in ihrem Vortrag fort.*]

Die vom Militärrecht vorgeschriebenen Alterskategorien, Kwame, reizen die Ambivalenz und Formbarkeit einer palästinensischen Kindheit nicht aus. Wie Hedi Viterbo aufzeigte, sind es oft die Richter:innen selbst, die diese Altersklassifizierungen anfechten. Ihre Neigung, unabhängige Kriterien anzuwenden, verstärkt sich beispielsweise, wenn sie es mit Angeklagten zu tun haben, die klein und zerbrechlich sind oder deren Entwicklung vermindert scheint, die als Kinder eingestuft werden, obwohl sie eigentlich Jugendliche sind, oder die als Jugendliche eingestuft werden, obwohl sie junge Erwachsene sind.

Viterbo führt mehrere Fälle an, in denen ein:e Richter:in lieber dem eigenen Blick vertraute und entgegen der schriftlichen Verordnung entschied, dass ein Kind kindlicher ist als sein gesetzliches Alter, was eine mildere Strafe rechtfertigt. [*Langsam*] Die richterlichen Augen finden Gefallen am zarten kleinen Körper und befinden, dass das Gesetz im Verhältnis zum persönlichen Gespür irrt. Andererseits besteht der Verdacht, dass Palästinenser:innen lügen und behaupten könnten, sie wären jünger, als sie tatsächlich sind, um das Mitleid auszunutzen. [*Pause, überlegend und ein wenig abgelenkt*] In einem anderen Kontext könnten wir uns fragen, warum Mitleid Kindern vorbehalten sein sollte ... Während die Körperflüssigkeiten sich verdünnen ... Wenn du dich vorbeugst, um ein Kind zu umarmen, kehrst du dann einem Erwachsenen den Rücken zu, nur weil er ein Erwachsener ist? Welcher Schaden entsteht durch diesen Drang, ein Kind zu verteidigen? ... Diese Frage ist ... [*Fasst sich gedankenverloren ans Ohr*] eine andere.

So verwirrend der genaue Status der Kindheit des Kindes auch sein mag, so wird sie doch immer ein mildernder Faktor sein. Es zeigt sich jedoch, dass Kindheit auch ein erschwerender Faktor sein kann. So argumentierte Militärstaatsanwalt Avraham Fechter bereits 1967, dass in Fällen von Terrorakten, die von

Minderjährigen verübt wurden, die Strafe härter ausfallen sollte, „um andere junge Menschen in dem Alter davon abzuhalten, sich von solchen Abenteuern verleiten zu lassen." [*Pause*]

Als ich jung war, erschien mir – also zumindest mir selbst – mein Körpergeruch subtil und fruchtig, wie ein Pfirsich oder vielleicht eine Banane. Doch mit Vierzig wurde der Geruch von Schweiß komplexer und durchdringender, mehr nach Guave. Und dann kamen diese Momente körperlicher Anstrengung oder Erregung, in denen ich einen Geruch wahrnahm, der von einem anderen Körper auszugehen schien, außerhalb des Autos, ein Geruch ähnlich des Schweißes meines Ex-Mannes, ähnlich wie Zitrusschalen, Grapefruit vielleicht, aber bitterer und säuerlicher. Als ich merkte, dass dieser Geruch von mir stammte, hielt ich ihn zunächst für das Anzeichen einer Erkrankung – etwa einer Lebensmittelvergiftung oder eines Virus. Nicht, dass der Geruch schlecht wäre, ich finde ihn nicht schlecht. Aber er trägt eine Botschaft. Er kündigt die nächste Stufe des körperlichen Verfalls an. Deine junge Freundin würde die Veränderung spüren und angewidert sein. [*Sie schließt die Augen und summt eine melancholische Melodie. Sie öffnet die Augen wieder.*]

Die Besetzung ist wie ein Auto. Und man könnte sagen, dass Jurist:innen wie Fechter das Gaspedal dieses Autos sind. Auf der anderen Seite gibt es auch Richter:innen wie Meir Shamgar, der den Palästinenser:innen das Recht einräumte, gegen ein Urteil des Militärgerichts vor dem Obersten Gerichtshof Israels in Berufung zu gehen. Shamgar verkörpert den militärischen Mann des Gesetzes, für den das Recht nicht nur Ordnung aufrechterhalten, sondern auch für Gerechtigkeit sorgen und die Interessen der Besetzten vertreten soll. Wenn also Fechter das Gaspedal ist, dann ist Shamagar die Bremse des Autos der Besetzung. [*Pause*] Man muss jedoch begreifen, dass die Bremse das Fahrzeug nicht am Fahren hindert. Ganz im Gegenteil, das Fahrzeug kann ohne die Bremse unmöglich fahren; damit also das Gesetz zur Besetzung reibungslos funktioniert, braucht man beides, Gaspedal und Bremse: Fechter–Shamgar, Shamgar–Fechter, Fechter–Shamgar.

Die Körperöffnungen verrotten. Die Flüssigkeiten fließen, aber der Geruch ändert sich. Sie meidet mich, als wäre ich ein krankes Tier – plumper, süßer Lehrling … aber es bleibt die angenehme

Berührung des Tierarztes. [*Pause. Sie kniet nieder und hebt die Arme.*] Und doch bleibt ein kleines Problem ungelöst. [*Pause*] Wenn ich das noch einmal wiederholen darf: Als die Wache am Tor der Siedlung D. sieht und die Waffe zieht und sie auffordert, sich hinzuknien und die Hände zu heben, was sie auch tut: greift er dann in die Innentasche ihres Mantels, oder befiehlt er *ihr*, den Mantel zu öffnen und das Messer herauszunehmen? [*Ihre Arme zeigen ein Wanken zwischen den zwei Optionen an. Eine lange Pause, Augen geschlossen, Mund geöffnet, ein leises Wimmern.*]

Ich fühle Tritte in meinem Innern [*öffnet die Augen und steht auf*]. Wie eine Schwangerschaft, aber außerhalb der Gebärmutter, höher und hinten, im Brustkorb, im oberen Rücken, mehr wie ein Zittern, Fischflossen, die im Innern zittern. Etwas wirft sich gegen die Rippen, als wolle es Gitterstäbe durchbrechen, aber es ist unklar, was dieses Ding ist, diese unkontrollierbare sexuelle Hitze. Das Feuer im Schambein ist nur ein Symptom von etwas, das sich in meinem Körper abspielt, eine neue Art von Verlangen vielleicht, oder eine erste Krebsmutation in der Leber oder im Magen. [*Zieht die Jacke aus.*]

Und was führte zu D.s Inhaftierung in einem Frauengefängnis für Erwachsene, in Missachtung des Gesetzes? Die einfache Erklärung lautet, dass es in den Gebieten keine Einrichtung für jugendliche Straftäter:innen gibt. Aber noch wichtiger, Kwame, ist, dass das Gesetz auf seiner Fähigkeit beruht, sich selbst zu widersprechen, nicht eins zu sein, das Illegale von einem Blickwinkel aus legal sein zu lassen. [*Einer der jungen Männer greift seinem Nachbarn in den Schritt.*] Man kann aus verschiedenen Gesetzen wählen, je nachdem, was gerade ansteht, und nach Belieben sanktionieren oder Milde walten lassen. Das israelische Recht agiert als eine Reihe ständiger Notfallmaßnahmen und wird so zu einer fließenden Jurisprudenz, wie Yoav Mehozay es definierte – ein unübersichtliches Sammelsurium von Verfügungen aus fünf verschiedenen Statuten, deren Widersprüche es zulassen, dass die Realität nach Bedarf verändert wird.

Der Verfasser des *Dritten Kompendiums der Militärverordnungen* von 2015, Oberst Doron Ben-Barak, ist sich dieser rechtlichen Komplexität durchaus bewusst und schreibt [*liest aus ihren Unterlagen vor*]: „Wie allgemein bekannt, besteht das Strafrecht in Judäa und Samaria aus mehreren Ebenen, beginnend mit den Gesetzen des britischen Mandats, über die jordanische Gesetzgebung und weiter mit den Sicherheitsverordnungen des Militärgouverneurs seit 1967. Zudem ändert sich die Lebensrealität ständig, manchmal sehr schnell, und erfordert zahlreiche, kontinuierliche Anpassungen des Gesetzes." Aber der Oberst weiß, dass diese spektakuläre Gesetzgebung mit all ihren köstlichen Verwicklungen und orgastischen Wendungen ins rechte Licht gerückt werden muss. Ben-Barak zitiert ein altes Gerichtsurteil [*die Kamera zoomt auf ein Paar junger Männer, die einander leidenschaftlich küssen*]: „Eine Gesetzgebung, die im Geheimen erfolgt und im Verborgenen gehalten wird, ist ein Merkmal totalitärer Regime und kann nicht Hand in Hand mit der Rechtsstaatlichkeit gehen." Er fährt fort: „Diese erhabenen Worte, im Geiste von Kafkas Buch, sind immer noch gültig." [*Pause*] Es ist unklar, auf welches von Kafkas Büchern er sich bezieht. „Unverhüllte Gesetzgebung, nicht im Geheimen gehalten ..."

Ich sitze an der Bordsteinkante. Ich wünschte, ich könnte aufhören zu sein. Ich wünschte, ich könnte diesen sexuellen Drang töten und alleine bleiben, still und trocken, frei von den anstrengenden Grotesken der Intimität. Aber dann hält ein glänzendes gelbes Auto neben mir. Kwame steigt aus und streckt seinen Arm nach mir aus. Er ist muskulös, groß, meine Augen sind genau auf Höhe seiner Brustwarzen. Seine Haut glänzt vor Schweiß, und ich bemerke, dass sein Körper von Sägemehl und Federn verklebt ist. Vielleicht hat er einen wundersamen afrikanischen Vogel operiert, vielleicht auch nur ein Huhn. Er riecht würzig, köstlich. Mir wird klar, dass Kwame hier ist, um mich mitzunehmen. Die Gegenwart wird zur Vergangenheit und dank des gelben Autos ist die Zukunft die Gegenwart. Ich bin hundertzwanzig Jahre alt, vielleicht hundertdreißig, aber das beeinträchtigt die Freude an unserer frischen Romanze nicht. Es stört Kwame überhaupt nicht, wie in einem Traum, in dem das Alter manchmal undefiniert ist. [*Ein langes Hinzoomen, bis ihr Gesicht den Bildschirm ausfüllt.*] Er zieht mich an sich. Dem neuen Gesetz zufolge bin ich wieder ein Kind. Er dreht den Schlüssel um und wir fahren hinauf, oder hinunter, auf jeden Fall weit weg, und in dieser Weite schrumpft die Gegenwart zu einem immer kleiner werdenden Ball. Die Dinge, die mich einst

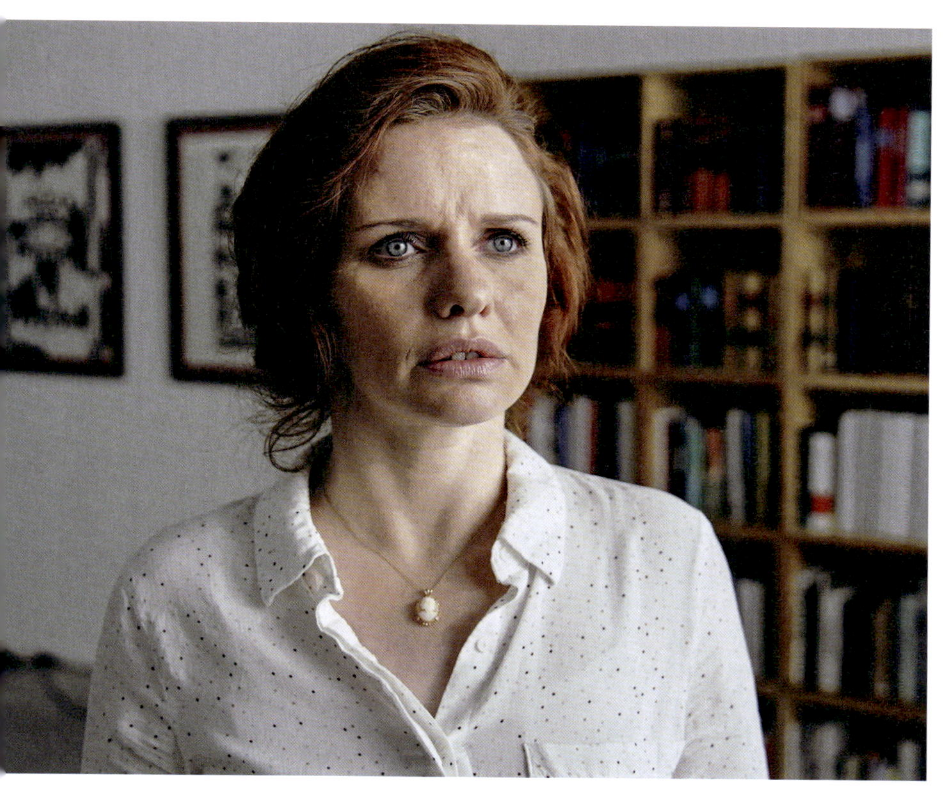

störten, schrumpfen zusammen und auch ihr schrumpft alle, verwelkt, verknöchert und zerfallt dann zu Staub. Der Raum wird frei: Anderes Leid wird andere belasten. [*Instrumentaler Prolog des Schlafliedes setzt ein.*] Seine Brustwarzen sind steif, wie Sensoren, bereit, meine Befehle zu lesen. Der Anblick ist verführerisch, aber ich widerstehe, bis wir zu Hause sind, in Accra. Ihr seid alle tot. Ich liege auf einem Bett aus Heu, mit gespreizten Beinen. Im Garten knurren und kläffen die Tiere. Kwame schwebt über mir und alles wird dunkel. [*Schließt die Augen und öffnet sie wieder.*]

21. SZENE – GUTE NACHT

Während die Rechtsexpertin ihre letzten Sätze spricht, wird ihr Gesicht von oben gesehen, im Bett liegend mit dem des Kindes überblendet. Die Musik erklingt weiterhin. Der Geschichtenerzähler ist zu hören, jedoch nicht zu sehen.

Geschichtenerzähler: Am Morgen fand die Bedienerin das tote Insekt und warf es in den Mülleimer. Es war ein herrlicher Tag. Die Sonne schien und die Familie beschloss, den Tag frei zu nehmen. Sie packten einen Korb und machten sich auf zu einem Picknick.

Kind: Oh! Wie der Jäger und die Großmutter und Rotkäppchen, nachdem sie den Wolf getötet haben.

Geschichtenerzähler: Ja.

Kind: Nur, dass der Wolf sehr schwer war, weil sein Bauch mit Steinen gefüllt war, nachdem er geboren hatte. [*Pause*] Eine harte alte Wurst.

Geschichtenerzähler: Was?

Kind: Wurst für das Picknick.

Geschichtenerzähler: Genau. Und jetzt ist es an der Zeit zu schlafen.

Kafka-für-Kinder-Schlaflied

Das Lied wird von oben gesehen als stufenloses Wegzoomen aus dem Schlafzimmer gefilmt, beginnend mit dem Gesicht des Kindes und endend mit einer Gesamtansicht von Bett, Nachtkästchen und Teppichen auf dem Boden. Der Winkel ist leicht diagonal, damit die Wand und die Gegenstände auf den Nachtkästchen zu sehen sind. Die Musik entspricht präzise dieser stufenweisen Präsentation: Sie beginnt mit einem Solo des Kindes, Stimmen setzen ein, dann folgt der komplette Chor. Die Sänger:innen erscheinen als Gegenstände im Raum, so wie Kissen und Decke. Sie setzen ein, sobald die Kamera sie zeigt. Sobald die Verse wieder gesungen werden, überschneidet sich die Melodie mit einer Reprise von Zeilen aus Was ist ein Kind? *[Szene 9].*

[Kind]:
Bin ich allein, wenn ich allein bin, tief in mein Bett vergraben?
Die Freund:innen, die ich seh' und umarme, soll ich im Kopf nun haben?

[*Kissen und dann Decke setzen ein*]:
Die Kissen fest an mein Gesicht, die Decke wärmt mich sacht,
Sind sie noch warm und kuschelig, wenn ich mich fürcht' heut
Nacht?

[*Bett setzt ein*]:
Und wenn ich träum', ich wäre groß, bin ich die Gleiche dann?
Und wenn ich einmal alt und groß, werd' wieder klein ich
irgendwann?

[*Lampe und Ball auf dem Nachtkästchen setzen ein*]:
Die Träume träumen vielleicht mich, das ist gar nicht so leicht,
Vielleicht leb' ich in ihrem Kopf, bis es einmal reicht.

Bin ich allein, wenn ich allein bin, tief in mein Bett vergraben?
Die Freunde, die ich seh' und umarme, soll ich im Kopf nun haben?

Was ist ein Kind? Was ist ein Kind? Der Duft ist süß und rein,
Doch eines Tags studiert sie Recht und spielt die Geige fein.

Die Kissen fest an mein Gesicht, die Decke wärmt mich sacht,
Sind sie noch warm und kuschelig, wenn ich mich fürcht' heut' Nacht?

Was ist ein Kind? Was ist ein Kind? Das ist gar nicht so leicht.
Ein Kind wächst ständig weiter, bis es einmal reicht.

Und wenn ich träum', ich wäre groß, bin ich die Gleiche dann?
Und wenn ich einmal alt und groß, werd' wieder klein ich
irgendwann?

Bis wann ein Kind? Bis wann ein Kind? Sieben? Zwölf? Vierzehn?
Wann wechselt es von prall und pink zu altem, hartem Lehm?

Die Träume träumen vielleicht mich, das ist gar nicht so leicht,
Vielleicht leb' ich in ihrem Kopf, bis es einmal reicht.

Ein Kind ist von Versprechen reich, da ist noch alles drin,
Ein Schatzkästchen, da liegt einer, erst ziemlich alt, dann hin.

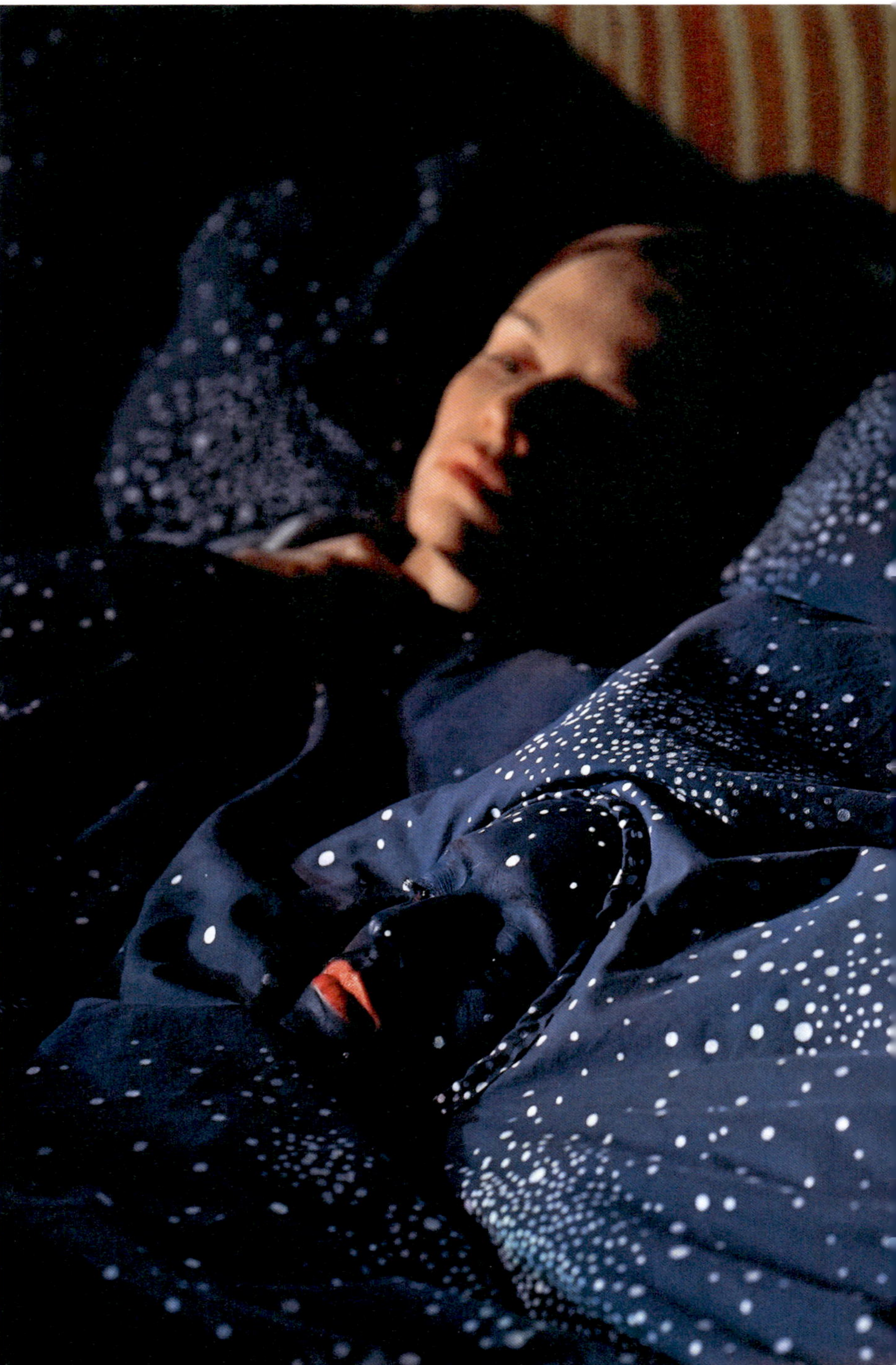

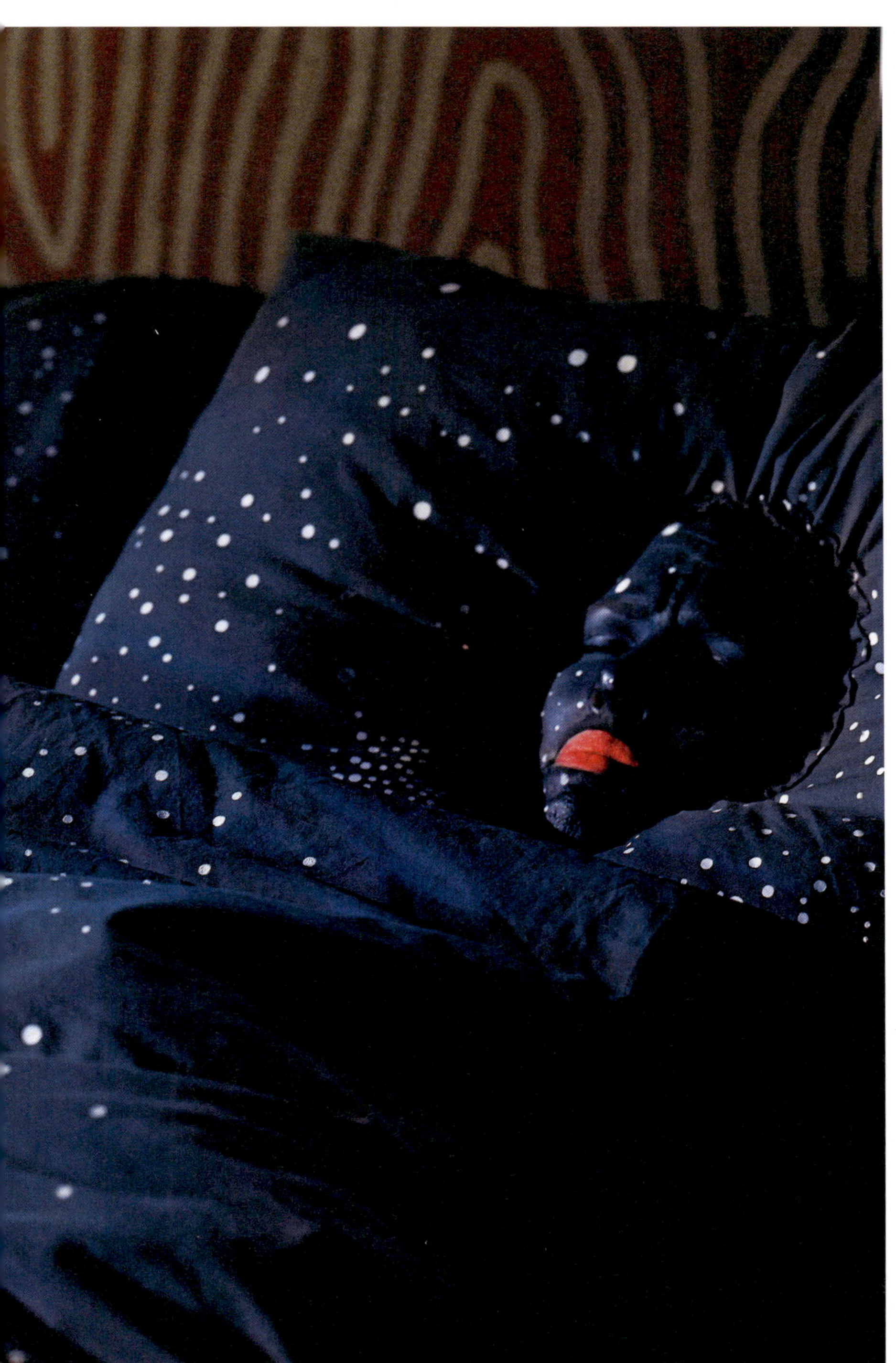

DIE STEIGERUNG

FANNI FETZER

Vielleicht liegt es an den vielen Vokalen, möglicherweise auch am Doppelinitial R.R., jedenfalls scheint Roee Rosens Name kaum auf Papier fixiert werden zu können. Die Buchstaben lösen sich, streben magnetisch angezogen aufeinander zu und sortieren sich: R zu R, o zu o, ee zu e, s und n schweben frei übers Blatt, docken einmal hier und einmal da an, drängeln sich zwischen die anderen Buchstaben. Dieses seltsame Phänomen sollten wir im Hinterkopf behalten, wenn wir über Roee Rosen und sein Werk sprechen. Roee Rosen zu begegnen, bedeutet eben, auch Rose Rosen, Reese Noor, Enos Sneer, Roro Seeen und viele andere kennenzulernen.

Eigentlich insinuiert der Künstler, dass es einfacher wird. Sein Film *Kafka for Kids* (*Kafka für Kinder*) impliziert im Titel, dass der intellektuelle Weltstar der modernen Literatur endlich allgemeinverständlich präsentiert wird. Ausgerechnet Franz Kafka mit seinen verschlungenen Gedankengebäuden will Roee Rosen auf eine selbst für Kinder zugängliche Weise zeigen! Aber leider ist es anders: Der Starautor des Bildungsbürgertums wird nicht vereinfacht, sondern die Geschichte wird noch viel komplexer – entsprechend der Wirklichkeit. Denn die Realität ist komplizierter, als wir sie mit zweiachsigen Diagrammen gerne darstellen. Doch der Reihe nach: *Kafka for Kids* ist ein 120 Minuten langer, zweiteiliger Film, der in Kameraführung und Professionalität auf die Filmindustrie verweist. Aber bezüglich Plot, Dramaturgie und Struktur ist er eindeutig der zeitgenössischen Kunst zuzuordnen. Ist das so anders? Ja, es ist sogar sehr anders. Während Filme aus der Filmindustrie darauf angelegt sind, dass das Publikum nicht aussteigt, funktioniert das Medium Film im Kontext der Kunst so, dass das Publikum einsteigt und dann hängenbleibt. Im ersten Teil von *Kafka for Kids* erzählt ein älterer Herr einem Mädchen inmitten eines knallbunten, völlig übertriebenen Settings Franz Kafkas Geschichte von Gregor Samsa, der sich in einen Käfer verwandelt. Gegen Ende des Films erläutert eine Rechtsprofessorin in einer Vorlesung die Auswirkungen des Kriegsrechts in den von Israel besetzten Gebieten auf die Rechtsprechung bei Delikten von Kindern und Jugendlichen. Was hat das miteinander zu tun?

In Kafkas *Verwandlung* und im ersten Teil des Films wissen die Eltern nicht mehr, ob sie ihren Sohn Gregor Samsa wie einen Menschen oder wie einen Käfer behandeln sollen. Der zweite Teil des Films verhandelt, dass Israel Minderjährige in den besetzten Gebieten, sofern sie vor Gericht gestellt werden, zwar nicht als Insekten, aber als junge Erwachsene einstuft. Ist diese Analogie nicht etwas übertrieben? Vielleicht. Aber bevor wir Roee Rosens Film *Kafka for Kids* als überzogen verurteilen, erinnern wir uns an die sich magisch selbstorganisierenden Buchstaben im Namen des Künstlers. Roee Rosen alias Eros Reno alias Orson Eerie zeigt uns durch diese vermeintliche Übertreibung, wie krass und verwirrend unsere Welt ist. Kafkaesk im besten Sinne.

Für Israels Intellektuelle muss es frustrierend sein, wie ihr Land von außen verhandelt wird. Zwischen pro und kontra Boykott, Deinvestition, Sanktionen (BDS) bleibt wenig Aufmerksamkeit für eine differenzierte Debatte. Im Bemühen, den dominanten westlichen Blick zu überwinden und die eigene Perspektive einer antikolonialistischen Kritik zu unterziehen, entgleitet die Diskussion. Wie immer wird Ambivalenz nur von ganz wenigen ausgehalten, deren Stimmen allerdings meist nicht zu den lautesten gehören. Vielleicht sind diese Stimmen so leise wie der Buchstabe F, der ausgesprochen leicht überhört werden kann. Ein Wind nur, der aus unserem Mund strömt: Überhören wir das F einfach und schon wird aus „Kafka" „Kaka". Auch das macht uns Roee Rosen in seinem Kinderzimmer vor: Der Chor im Hintergrund singt Fäkalsprache für den Star der modernen Literatur. Unerhört! Sowieso treibt es der Künstler weit: Die Schauspielerin, der als Mädchen vom Geschichtenonkel im Kinderzimmer Kafkas *Verwandlung* erzählt wird, spielt auch die äusserst attraktive Rechtsprofessorin, die zum Kinder- und Jugendrecht in den durch Israel besetzten Gebieten referiert. Aber warum bloß schwitzt sie bei ihrem Vortrag dermaßen heftig? Ihr Schweiß ist obszön und erinnert an Roee Rosens Werk *Sweet Sweat* (*Süßer Schweiß*; schon wieder ein Spiel mit Buchstaben!). Auf seiner Website führt der Künstler *Sweet Sweat* unter „Künstler:innenbücher";

angeblich enthält das Buch zwei Auszüge aus Justine Franks Novelle. Aber wer ist Justine Frank? Justine Frank ist eine fiktive belgisch-jüdische Malerin, die dem Surrealismus zuzurechnen ist. In ihrem kurzen Leben (1900–1943) erfuhr ihr Werk keine Anerkennung. Doch seit einigen Jahren kümmert sich Roee Rosen um ihren Nachlass. Nur seltsam, dass Justine Frank auf den wenigen erhaltenen Fotos auffällig Orna gleicht, Roee Rosens Frau. Die Verfasserin des Vorworts von Justine Franks erster Monografie heißt übrigens Joanna Führer-Ha'sfari. In einem Fernsehinterview erinnert Führer-Ha'sfari in Gestik und Mimik stark an Roee Rosen.

Roee Rosen ist also als blinder Passagier in verschiedenen Systemen und Rollen unterwegs. Spielerisch und vor allem auch wunderbar selbstironisch negiert er die Komplexität der Gegenwart nicht, sondern steigert sie noch, indem er die Abhängigkeiten und Verflechtungen von allem mit allem thematisiert. Weder verzweifelt er an der Komplexität unserer Wirklichkeit, noch vereinfacht er die Dinge unzulässig. Der Künstler alias Nurse Rosie alias Russ Nero jongliert die Interdependenzen gekonnt. Für Roee Rosen ist Verstummen angesichts der politischen Verhältnisse, der simplen Weltanschauungen oder der Überforderung von uns allen keine Option. Aber er ist ja auch nicht alleine, zusammen mit Noor Rees, Ross Ensor, Mort Error, Rrose Noser und ein paar anderen steigert er sich in eine vielschichtige Darstellung der Realität, die uns verführt, aufmerksam zu sein und nachzudenken. Wie Roee Rosen Sprache als künstlerisches Material verwendet, wie er Fiktion so gekonnt erzeugt, dass wir alles für bare Münze nehmen, macht uns die Gegenwart erst erträglich. Die Lust, auch noch Soren Oreo und Ssorerrosen kennenzulernen, ist groß!

THE STANDARD EDITION

O O OO O

EROS RENO

VOLUME XII

(1911–1913)

Armpits and Genitalia Physiognomy

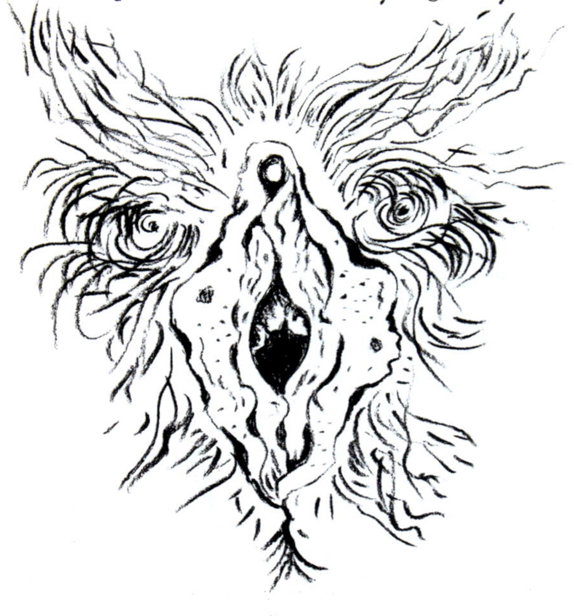

THE HOGARTH PRESS

AND THE INSTITUTE OF PSYCHO-ANALYSIS

Eros Reno
Armpits and Genitalia Physiognomy, Illustrated, 2022
(The Standard Edition, volume XII, 1911-1913)
charcoal on digital print

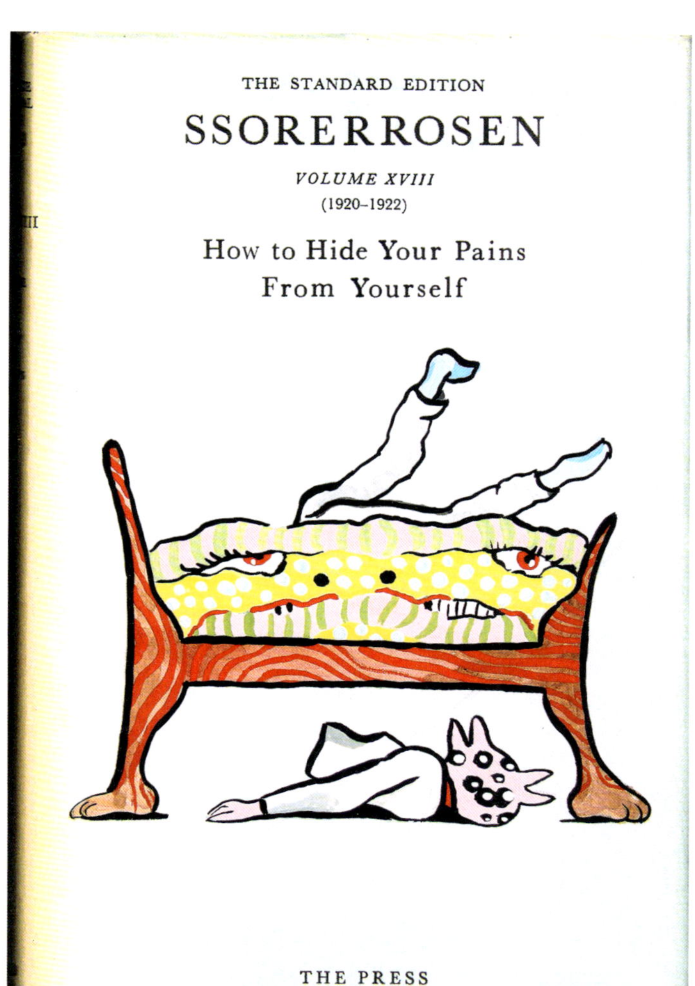

Ssorerrosen
How to Hide Your Pains From Yourself, Illustrated, 2022
(The Standard Edition, volume XVIII, 1923-1925)
gouache on digital print

ROEE ROSEN: LITERATUR, FIKTIONALITÄT UND BLINDHEIT

SERGIO EDELSZTEIN

> „Ein Agnostiker zu sein, bedeutet, dass alles möglich ist, sogar Gott, sogar die Heilige Dreifaltigkeit. Diese Welt ist so seltsam, dass alles geschehen könnte, oder auch nicht geschehen könnte. Ein Agnostiker zu sein, lässt mich in einer größeren, fantastischeren, beinahe unheimlichen Art von Welt leben …"
>
> Jorge Luis Borges

Roee Rosens Interesse an Literatur und deren Randerscheinungen ist ein ganz wesentliches Element seiner Arbeiten. Bereits in seinen frühesten Texten entwickelt er einige der charakteristischen Eigenschaften, die seine Werke bis heute definieren: eine Erzählung mit fiktiven Charakteren, austauschbar was Genre und Alter anbelangt, stets mit Überlegungen zu dem/der Verfasser:in selbst, unter Einsatz von Medien – Zeichnung, Video – als Instrument, um Zweck und Bedeutung des literarischen Narrativs zu erweitern, zu vertiefen und zu verfälschen.

Zwei von Rosens frühesten Publikationen sind „Kinderbücher": *Lucy* (1991–1992) und *A Different Face* (*Ein anderes Gesicht*, 2000). Letztere ist Rosens einzige Arbeit, die tatsächlich auch für Kinder gedacht ist: Eine Geschichte über ein Mädchen namens Naomi Elvissa, die ständig ihr Gesicht verändert und die einzelnen Charakteristika ihres Gesichtes – Augen, Mund, Ohren, Nase – mit Gegenständen, Tieren, Buchstaben etc. vertauscht:

> „Sie wählte niedliche Nager als Augen,
> einen Wasserhahn als Nase, und einen Reißverschluss als Mund.
> Die Hauptsache befand sich ganz oben auf ihrem Kopf:
> Ein Schirm als Haare!"

In dem grafisch gestalteten Buch setzt Rosen erneut auf seine bereits etablierte Praxis des Einsatzes von Gegenständen und Körperteilen sowie auf Animation, mit der diese – und die Buchstaben – verschmelzen und miteinander vertauscht werden.

Keines seiner anderen Bücher oder seiner Filme wie *Kafka for Kids* (*Kafka für Kinder, 2022*), ist jedoch tatsächlich für Kinder gedacht. In *Lucy* wird, obwohl sowohl Lucy als auch seine Freundin Annie als Kinder gezeigt werden, der Hauptprotagonist – durch seine Gefühle und Aktivitäten, darunter explizite und extreme sexuelle Praktiken – als männlicher Erwachsener in seinen Dreißigern dargestellt. Die Protagonist:innen von Rosens Erzählungen sowohl als Erwachsene wie auch als Kinder zu zeigen, ist eine Konstante in seinem Werk: In *Live and Die as Eva Brown* (*Leben und Sterben als Eva Brown*, 1995–1997) ist Hitler selbst als Kind mit Schnurrbart dargestellt. Bezeichnenderweise basiert sowohl die Darstellung von Lucy als auch von Hitler auf Fotos von Rosen als Kleinkind. In *Vladimir's Night* (*Vladimirs Nacht*, 2011–2014) wird Putin als Mischung aus Kind und erwachsenem politischem Anführer wiedergegeben. Schon mit den ersten Zeilen in *Lucy* lässt Rosen eine Komplexität und Morbidität erkennen, die in einem literarischen Werk für Kinder nicht zu erwarten sind:

> „Der Name unseres Helden mag unpassend oder sogar dumm erscheinen. Nicht nur, dass unser Lucy männlich und ‚Lucy' ein Frauenname ist – unser Lucy ist auch noch jüdisch und ‚Lucy' [bzw. Lucia, Anm. d. Üb.] ist der Name einer christlichen Märtyrerin."

Ihrer Vita zufolge wurden der Heiligen Lucia die Augen ausgestochen, weshalb sie in der christlichen Ikonografie oftmals mit einem Tablett dargestellt wird, auf dem sich ihre Augen befinden. Lucy, Rosens Alter Ego, ist blind. Ebenso wie viele seiner anderen „Alter Egos". Im Film *The Confessions of Roee Rosen* (*Die Geständnisse des Roee Rosen*, 2007–2008) lesen die Protagonist:innen seiner Monologe

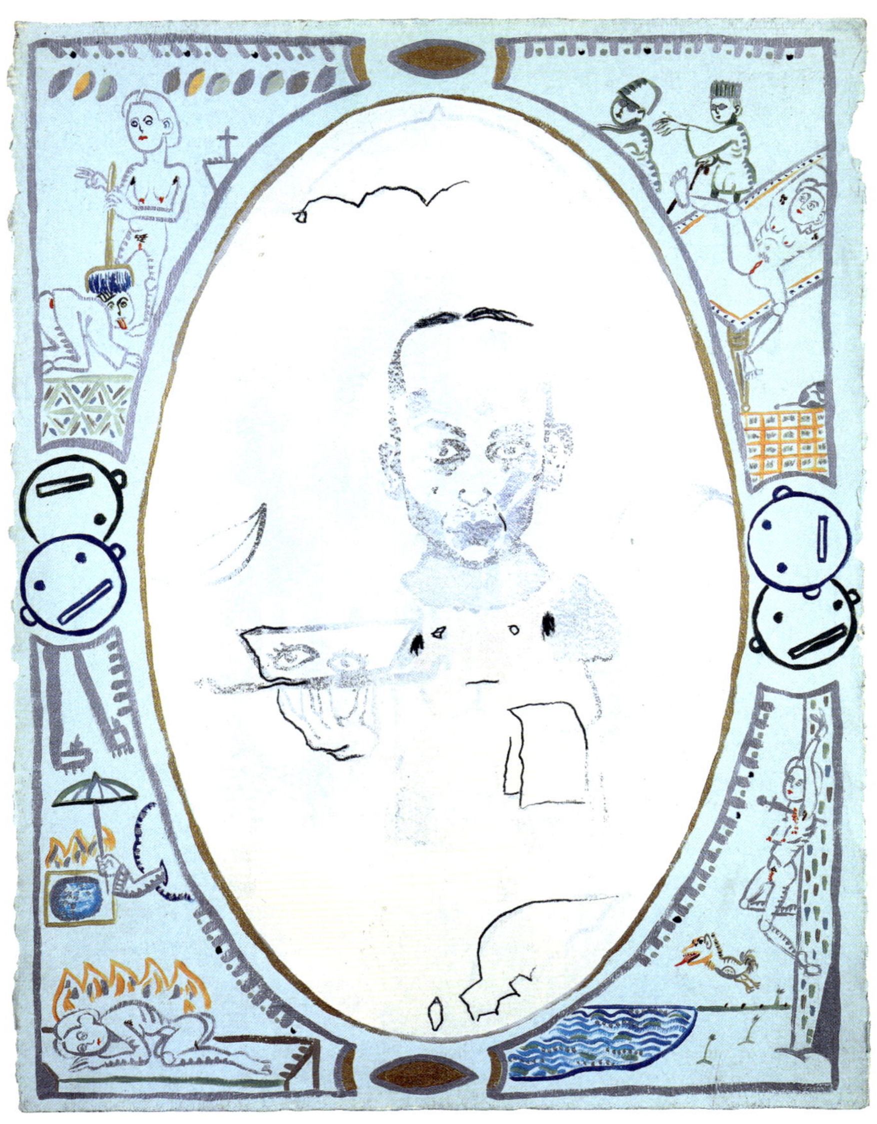

Roee Rosen
Martyr Lucy, 1991
oil, gesso and pastel on paper
(collection The Tel Aviv Museum of Art)

einen Text „blind“ vor, den sie nicht verstehen. Die Gastarbeiter:innen beginnen ihre Ansprache mit: „Hallo, ich bin Roee Rosen.“ Auch Rosens fiktionaler Charakter Efim Poplavsky (ein russischer Emigrant, der unter dem Pseudonym Maxim Komar-Myschkin schreibt) und sein Künstler:innenkollektiv, Buried Alive Group agieren blind, die darauf bestehen, in einer Kultur zu leben, die sie verachten und ignorieren. Ebenso wie seine Kabarettistin, die „nicht sieht“, dass ihr Publikum sich über ihre unpassenden Witze ärgert (in *Hilarious* [*Urkomisch*, 2010]). Die Blindheit ist auch ein Nebenprodukt der Besessenheit (wie in *Out* [*Raus, 2010*]), der Entfremdung vom eigenen Körper und der eigenen Person, oder der Entführung, wie es in *Killing Andrey Lev* (*Andrey Lev töten*, 2014), einem Film der Buried Alive Group, so markant dargestellt wird.

Rosens erstes blindes Alter Ego findet sich jedoch in seinem *Blind Merchant* (*Der blinde Kaufmann*, 1989–1991), einer Art Nacherzählung von William Shakespeares *Kaufmann von Venedig.* Das ursprüngliche Stück, reich an Identitäts- und Geschlechterverschiebungen, sowie mit einer Prise Folter und Andeutungen von Kannibalismus garniert, bildet die perfekte Vorlage für Rosens Bearbeitung. Angespornt durch die „Judenfrage“, die Shakespeares Erzählung zugrunde liegt, führt Rosen einen Prolog zu dem Stück ein, in dem Shylocks Frau Leah während eines Pogroms brutal vergewaltigt und ermordet wird und die Augen des Kaufmanns ausgestochen werden. Die Gesamtheit des Shakespear'schen Stückes entwickelt sich Seite für Seite, neben Illustrationen, die vom Juden Rosen-Shylock mit verbundenen Augen ausgeführt wurden.

Das Motiv der Blindheit definiert Rosens Beziehung zu Literatur und Fiktion, doch anstatt fehlende Sehkraft als Strafe darzustellen, wie im Mythos von Ödipus, passt Rosens Einsatz von Blindheit besser zum mythologischen Orakel Tiresias (dessen Verlust des Augenlichts seine Prophezeiungen nicht beeinträchtigte und der übrigens auch sieben Jahre lang in eine Frau verwandelt lebte). Das Motiv der Blindheit erlaubt es Rosen, das ihm innewohnende Misstrauen dem Bild gegenüber zu thematisieren. Ein Ikonoklast würde die Bilder vielleicht zerstören, doch Rosen würde es wohl vorziehen zu erblinden.

Blindheit ist ein existenzieller Zustand, der mit Einschränkung und erhöhter Vorstellungskraft einhergeht. Die archetypische Funktion von Blindheit ist die Forderung nach intensiver Introspektion, die die Tore zur Fiktion in der Literatur zu eröffnen vermag. Wie Jorge Luis Borges meint, kann der Verlust des Sehens für Schriftsteller:innen auch ein Geschenk bedeuten:

> „Niemand sollte Selbstmitleid oder Vorwürfe
> in diese Bekundung der Erhabenheit

Gottes hineindeuten; der mir mit solch herrlicher Ironie Bücher und Blindheit zugleich gestattete."

Dieser Zustand fehlender Sehkraft erklärt die Bedeutung, die Rosen anderen Sinnen zukommen lässt – vor allem dem Geruchssinn. Tatsächlich ist in Rosens erstem Roman (*Ziona*™, 2016) eine der vielen – und ziemlich nutzlosen – Superkräfte der dysfunktionalen jüdischen Superheldin Ziona ein hochentwickelter Geruchssinn. In *Kafka for Kids* und *The Dust Channel* (*Der Staubkanal*, 2016) finden wir ebenfalls merkwürdige Augenblicke, in denen Gerüche die Erzählung unterbrechen.

In seinem Projekt *Justine Frank* (1998–2005) tätigt Rosen seinen komplexesten Kommentar zur Literatur, ihren Randgenres und Klischees. Justine Frank ist eine vergessene belgische Malerin und Schriftstellerin, deren Leben und Arbeiten akribisch von Rosen erschaffen wurden. Die Gründe für ihren Untergang und ihr Vergessenwerden sind in ihrer Biografie zu finden: eine jüdische Frau in der von Männern dominierten Surrealismus-Bewegung von Paris, die in ihren Arbeiten extreme Sexualität und jüdische Ikonografie miteinander verbindet. Als Gnadenstoß ihrer Nichtbeachtung emigriert sie nach Israel, verschwindet aus der europäischen Kunstszene und steht dem kulturellen Milieu der zionistischen Siedler:innen im britischen Palästina der 1940er-Jahre völlig fremd, sogar offensiv gegenüber.

Die gesamte Justine-Frank-Kosmogonie ist, was das Konzept anbelangt, literarisch. Sie umfasst eine Biografie von Frank, die meisterhaft zwischen fingierter Dokumentation und Klatsch wechselt und die rätselhafte Lücken zum Spekulieren lässt. Zusätzlich zu Franks erhaltenem malerischem Werk gibt es auch einen erotischen Roman mit dem Titel *Sweet Sweat* (1931). Zudem findet sich eine ausführliche pseudo-akademische Studie zu Frank (Roee Rosen zugeschrieben), in der sie entweder als radikale Proto-Feministin dargestellt wird, die für sich selbst die Zeichen und Symbole des „Jüdischseins" beansprucht, oder (um nichts weniger radikal) als Verwandte des unheilvollen Rabbi Jacob Frank, der die Disziplin der Wiedergutmachung durch Sünde vertrat. Wir finden außerdem die Figuren verschiedener Expert:innen zu Frank, darunter auch die Übersetzerin ihres Romans ins Hebräische, Joanna Führer-Ha'sfari (die Wahl des Namens und die Art und Weise, in der dieser ihre ethnische Herkunft widerspiegelt, verdeutlicht gewissenhaft sowohl wissenschaftliche als auch umfassendere kulturelle Klischees). Des Weiteren ist Führer-Ha'sfari Gegenstand eines vermeintlich verpfuschten Fernsehinterviews, das als Film *Two Women and a Man* (*Zwei Frauen und ein Mann*, 2005) wieder auftaucht.

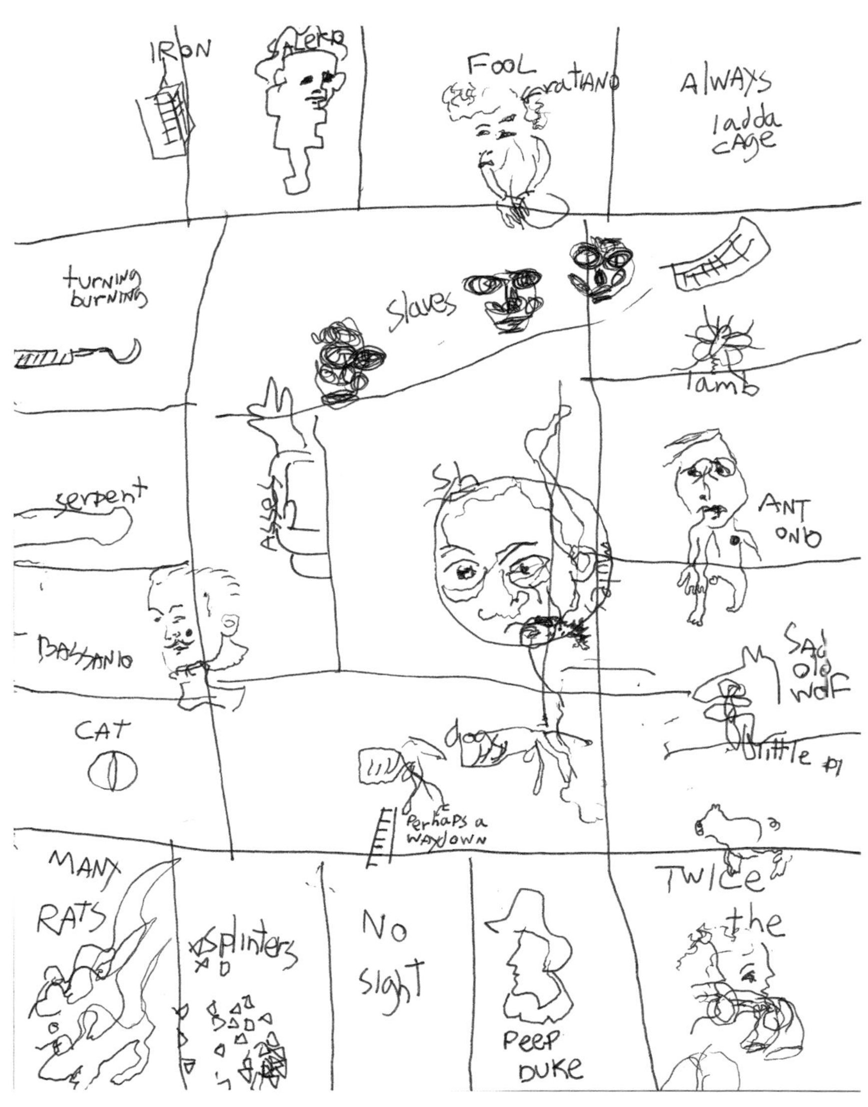

Roee Rosen
from *The Blind Merchant* (act 4, scene 1, plate 5), 1989-1991
a blind pen drawing
(collection Centre Pompidou)

In diesem Video wird die Kritikerin von Rosen selbst in einem bemerkenswerten Auftritt in Frauenkleidern dargestellt. Im Interview ergreift Führer-Ha'sfari die Gelegenheit, Roee Rosen aufgrund seiner Aneignung von Franks Erbe zusammenzustauchen, wodurch sich der Kreis des Justine-Frank-Projekts schließt als Reflexion der künstlerischen und literarischen Welt, ihrer Mechanismen und des persönlichem Grolls.

Die Einführung medialer Strukturen und der Einsatz spezifischer Sprache und Konventionen finden sich in sämtlichen Arbeiten Rosens, ob literarisch, filmisch oder bildhaft. Ob er nun Operetten ersinnt (*The Dust Channel, The Confessions of Roee Rosen* [*Die Bekenntnisse von Roee Rosen*] *oder Kafka for Kids*) oder TV-Formate, Interviews und Dokumentationen aufgreift, Rosen thematisiert stets die innere Struktur des Mediums. *The Confessions of Roee Rosen* umfasst zudem einen Trailer und Outtakes, während *The Dust Channel* und *Kafka for Kids* TV-Formate imitieren, inklusive Werbung, Nachrichten und vielem mehr. Dies gilt auch für die Beziehung von Text und Bild, bei der Rosen eine ganze Menge an exemplarischen Vorbildern einsetzt, von mittelalterlicher Buchmalerei und den Arbeiten des Dichters und Malers William Blake aus dem 18. Jahrhundert, bis hin zur Geschichte von Comics und Kinderbuchillustrationen.

Für ein späteres Literaturprojekt greift Rosen eine Struktur auf, die mit jener von Justine Frank vergleichbar ist, und in deren Mittelpunkt Efim Poplavsky steht (der unter dem Pseudonym Maxim Komar-Myschkin schreibt). In einem Album aus Versen und Bildern mit dem Titel *Vladimir's Night* halluziniert Poplavsky, der überzeugt ist, dass Putin einen persönlichen Rachefeldzug gegen ihn führt, seine Vergeltung: Die Gegenstände werden animiert, so dass sie Putin foltern, vergewaltigen und schlussendlich töten können. Der Inhalt, der 2014 zur Zeit der Veröffentlichung als paranoide Wahnvorstellung gelten konnte, wirkt heute eher wie eine prophetische Interpretation des mordlüsternen Charakters des russischen Diktators.

Wie schon im Fall von Führer-Ha'sfari bei Justine Frank, analysiert hier die engagierte fiktive Literaturwissenschaftlerin Rosa Chabanowa Komar-Myschkins Arbeit und erkundet deren komplexes, paranoides Netz von Anspielungen auf russische Kultur und Politik. Ihre Anmerkungen zu jeder Tafel, die als langer Anhang zum Album präsentiert werden, erweisen sich als verkappter makabrer Roman, mit ihr selbst als einer Hauptprotagonistin. In einer Welt blinder Künstler:innen interpretiert das äußere Auge, das Publikum, das literarische Werk, fügt narrative Ebenen hinzu, die ein Kaleidoskop von Blickwinkeln hervorbringen, die in heftigem Widerstand zueinander stehen. Rosens Protagonist:innen sehen es vielleicht nicht, aber sie gewinnen an Bedeutung, weil sie von anderen gesehen werden.

Indem Rosen eher die Lücken in der Erzählung thematisiert als das, was offensichtlich ist, spricht er eine weitere literarische Konvention an – das Frontispiz von Büchern. Er bedient sich der Wahrnehmung, die wir womöglich von Sigmund Freud, seiner spezifischen Ambivalenz und seiner psychologischen Ambiguität haben, und zieht in seiner *Standard Edition* (*Standardausgabe* 2014–2022) die allgemein anerkannte Ausgabe von Freuds Werk heran, um sie in seinem Faksimile einer spielerischen Tour der Dekonstruktion von Titeln und Themen zu unterziehen, wobei er auch sein eigenes Leben und aktuelle künstlerische Belange miteinbezieht.

Rosens Auseinandersetzung mit einer kanonischen Arbeit wie Franz Kafkas *Verwandlung* ist also kaum überraschend. Das Meisterwerk, das die Geschichte eines Menschen erzählt, der sich in ein Insekt verwandelt, könnte auch direkt Rosens kreativem Geist entsprungen sein. Indem er das Werk als Stück für Kinder präsentiert, fügt er es in die Reihe seiner anderen „Kinderbücher" ein, setzt jedoch auch seine Missachtung der Trennung von Kind/Erwachsener und Mann/Frau fort. Wie die transformativen Eigenschaften der Geschichte, auf die es sich bezieht, verändert auch *Kafka for Kids* selbst die Gestalt. Es ist die Übertragung eines Buches in ein Opernlibretto und die Umwandlung einer Geschichte für Erwachsene in eine Erzählung für Kinder. Wie zu erwarten, wird Kafkas Geschichte, die sich natürlich keineswegs für ein junges Publikum eignet, buchstäblich einem geschockten Kind übergekippt. Der juristische Monolog gegen Ende des Films zeigt, dass das Interesse an der Arbeit nicht darin liegt, Kafkas *Verwandlung* Kindern zugänglich zu machen, sondern vielmehr darin, aufzuzeigen, wie das „blinde" israelische Rechtssystem in den besetzten Gebieten wahrlich kafkaeske Situationen für inhaftierte Kinder heraufbeschwört.

In *Lucy is sick* (*Lucy ist krank*, 2020–unvollendet), seinem jüngsten Buch, kehrt Rosen zu seinem alten Alter Ego zurück, um die Geschichte seiner eigenen Erkrankung an Knochenkrebs und seiner Genesung zu erzählen. Die explizite Pornografie des ersten *Lucy* wird durch die nicht weniger schockierende Beschreibung der qualvollen Schmerzen, der medizinischen Prozeduren und Terminologie, mit denen Rosen konfrontiert ist, ersetzt – alles in der gefälligen, unterhaltenden Verpackung eines Malbuches.

Gegen Ende dieses Buchs offenbart Rosen sehr deutlich, konfrontiert mit der brutalen Realität der Krankheit, seinen Einsatz von Fiktion:

> „Im Laufe des Lebens war Fiktionalität Lucys geheime Superkraft. Fiktionalität emanzipierte den Körper von seiner vorgegebenen Anatomie. Fiktionalität transportierte die Vergangenheit in die Gegenwart und veränderte sie.

> Fiktionalität enthüllte die Wahrheit in Fantasien und entlarvte die Täuschungen des Realen.
> Fiktionalität focht unverwüstlich gegen exzessiven Narzissmus, gegen Heldentum, Selbstmitleid und Autorität.
> Fiktionalität war eine Superheldin mit einer unendlichen Anzahl an Kostümen und Waffen."

Rosens Einsatz des Wortes „Fiktionalität" ist ungewöhnlich und die Bedeutung erscheint womöglich unklar. Vielleicht können wir das Wort „Fiktionalität" in Zusammenhang mit „Fiktion" interpretieren, wie wir auch „Funktionalität" in Zusammenhang mit „Funktion" verstehen. Nehmen wir zum Beispiel einen Dyson DC07™ Staubsauger. Als Haushaltsgerät ist die Funktion dieses Gegenstandes das Entfernen von Schmutz. Seine Funktionalität liegt jedoch eher in der metaphorischen Übertragung dieser Funktion – in diesem Fall soll es dabei helfen, uns von unerwünschten Objekten, Vorstellungen oder Menschen zu befreien, wie in *The Dust Channel* verdeutlicht.

Der Begriff „Fiktionalität" impliziert damit einen Blick über das rein fiktionale Narrativ hinaus, auf ein Palimpsest kultureller und tautologischer Meta-Narrative. Während die Fiktion nur sich selbst darstellen kann, lässt die Fiktionalität auch Raum für die Einführung des Realen und Konkreten in die Erzählung. Damit hält die Fiktionalität immer auch das Dilemma zwischen Realität und Imaginärem am Leben – ein Dilemma, das die Arbeit des agnostischen Künstlers Roee Rosen beständig antreibt.

K. WIE KINDER

JEAN-PIERRE REHM

Er „war“ Justine Frank, Joanna Führer-Ha’sfari, Eva Braun, Anne Kastorp, Roee Rosen, Maxim Komar-Myshkin, Efim Poplavsky, Rosa Chabanova und hat nun, nach all diesen Figuren, nach diesem ganzen wundervollen romanesken Reigen, all den bunten, vielschichtigen, heiteren, kunstvollen, maliziösen, zweideutigen, verstörenden, verwirrenden Welten, die er erschaffen hat, mit *Kafka for Kids* (*Kafka für Kinder*) auf einen Schriftsteller rekurriert, der ihm darin vorangegangen ist. Es ist wichtig, die ganze Dimension dieser Geste zu erfassen, die einen Bruch mit der biografischen Produktion darstellt, die bisher im Mittelpunkt von Rosens Arbeit stand, einer Arbeit, die – wie es im Trailer zu *The Confessions* (*Die Bekenntnisse*) heißt – durch Konstruktion, Verfremdung und Besessenheit gekennzeichnet war. Dies war jedoch bereits in einem der ersten Werke der Fall, dem zwischen 1989 und 1991 entstandenen *The Blind Merchant* (*Der blinde Kaufmann*), in dem der Künstler in 145 Zeichnungen Shakespeares *Kaufmann von Venedig* neu interpretierte. Doch im Unterschied zu Shakespeare war die Wahl Kafkas trotz dessen singulärer Wirkung keine Selbstverständlichkeit, wurde der zu seinen Lebzeiten eher unauffällige Schriftsteller doch als Teufel dargestellt. *Faut-il brûler Kafka?* (*Soll man Kafka verbrennen?*), lautete 1946 die provokante Überschrift eines Artikels von Pierre Fauchery, in dem dieser in der Wochenzeitung *Action* die kommunistischen Standpunkte resümierte und dazu aufforderte, ein als zweifelhaft geltendes Werk in Misskredit zu bringen.[1] Dass

1 Pierre Fauchery, "Faut-il brûler Kafka?," in: *Action*, Nr. 90 (24. Mai 1946); https://www.tandfonline.com/doi/abs/10.1080/00168890.2015.1039411?journalCode=vger20.

es dem Journalisten angebracht schien, zum Autodafé aufzurufen – und das unmittelbar nach dem Ende des Krieges, in dem Kafkas Bücher verboten waren (und die Gestapo 1933 bei einer Hausdurchsuchung in der Berliner Wohnung seiner letzten Lebensgefährtin Dora Diamant ein Konvolut mit Manuskripten beschlagnahmte, das unwiederbringlich verloren ging), ist umso furchtbarer und grausamer, weil Kafka selbst seinen Freund Max Brod mit einer ähnlichen Vernichtung beauftragt hatte. Die vom Schriftsteller eigenhändig mit Tinte geschriebene testamentarische Verfügung, die er drei Jahre vor seinem Tod im Jahr 1924 verfasst hatte und die man als gefaltetes Schriftstück zwischen anderen Papieren entdeckte, ist berühmt:

> „Liebster Max, meine letzte Bitte: alles was sich in meinem Nachlass (also im Bücherkasten, Wäscheschrank, Schreibtisch zuhause und im Bureau, oder wohin sonst irgendetwas vertragen worden sein sollte und Dir auffällt) an Tagebüchern, Manuscripten, Briefen, fremden und eigenen, Gezeichnetem u.s.w. findet restlos und ungelesen zu verbrennen, ebenso alles Geschriebene oder Gezeichnete, das Du oder andere, die Du in meinem Namen darum bitten sollst, haben. Briefe, die man Dir nicht übergeben will, soll man wenigstens selbst zu verbrennen sich verpflichten.“[2]

Nachdem ihm mehrfach die Verbrennung drohte, existiert Kafkas Werk also in einem Modus der „Survivance“.[3] Die Frage des Über- und Weiterlebens berührt jedoch ganz allgemein das Wesen der Literatur. Kafka selbst wurde nicht müde, die beiden Tode – derjenige des Schriftstellers und sein eigener – auf bewegenden Seiten in einem Wirrwarr von Widersprüchen miteinander zu verflechten. Nachdrücklich macht dies der Brief an Max Brod vom 5. Juli 1922 deutlich:

> „Mein Leben lang bin ich gestorben und nun werde ich wirklich sterben. Mein Leben war süßer als das der andern, mein Tod wird um so schreck-

2 Max Brod, Franz Kafka, *Eine Freundschaft. Briefwechsel,* hg. v. Malcolm Pasley, Frankfurt a.M. 1989, S. 365.

3 Für den französischen Theoretiker Jacques Derrida beschreibt der Begriff „survivance" eine Art des Überlebens, die das Leben bereichert, mehr als man sich auf der Grundlage des einfachen Gegensatzes zwischen Leben und Tod vorstellen kann. Vgl. Jacques Derrida, *The Beast & the Sovereign,* Volume II, Chicago: University of Chicago Press, 2011, S. 130.

> licher sein. Der Schriftsteller in mir wird natürlich sofort sterben, denn eine solche Figur hat keinen Boden, hat keinen Bestand, ist nicht einmal aus Staub; ist nur im tollsten irdischen Leben ein wenig möglich, ist nur eine Konstruktion der Genußsucht. Dies ist der Schriftsteller. Ich selbst aber kann nicht weiterleben, da ich ja nicht gelebt habe, ich bin Lehm geblieben, den Funken habe ich nicht zum Feuer gemacht, sondern nur zur Illuminierung meines Leichnams benützt."[4]

Bemerkenswerterweise deckt sich diese Beschreibung des Schriftstellers als „Figur ohne Boden, die keinen Bestand hat" mit dem Wesen des *Toon*, der Zeichentrickfigur, die Giorgio Agamben in seinem Buch *Die kommende Gemeinschaft* mit der Welt des Limbus,[5] dem Ort für die Seelen der ungetauft verstorbenen Kinder, assoziiert. Bemerkenswert ist auch die Parallele, die der Kritiker Roberto Maria Dainotto im Zusammenhang mit Rosens *Martyr Paintings* (*Märtyrergemälde*) zwischen mittelalterlichem Stil und Animation zieht:

> „Cartoons sind, wie Martyrien, zwei Seiten ein und derselben Fantasie. Szene für Szene wird der Protagonist durchbohrt, durch die Luft gewirbelt, in Stücke gerissen oder sein Körper wird von einer Dampfwalze platt gedrückt. Und doch erscheint er in der folgenden Szene wieder mit seinem normalen Körper. Als Allegorie ist sein Körper unzerstörbar, jenseits des Naturgesetzes der Physik, von Leben und Tod. Die Aufgabe der Malerei – als Form des Martyriums und als Zeugnis verstanden – muss in diesem Fall in der Erfindung eines allegorischen Körpers bestehen."[6]

Sein eigenes Überleben hat Roee Rosen bereits im Zyklus der *Funeral Paintings* (*Beerdigungsgemälde*, 2006–2015) in Szene gesetzt, der Züge eines Cartoons trägt und beschrieben wird als „nach dem Begräbnis von seinem Blickpunkt aus durch einen transparenten Boden gesehen". Es handelt sich dabei um eine Serie von acht Tondi, die aufgrund der Perfektion des Kreises traditionell für allegorische Darstellungen verwendet und als Apotheose bezeichnet werden. Nehmen wir einmal an, um an die Lobreden Eisensteins in Bezug auf Walt Disney anzuknüpfen – „Disney ist (in der Kategorie der Komödie) ein Fall von

4 Franz Kafka, *Briefe 1902–1924*, zit. nach: https://www.odaha.com.

5 Vgl. Giorgio Agamben, *Die kommende Gemeinschaft*, Berlin 2003.

6 Roberto Maria Dainotto, "Portrait of the Artist as a Blind Martyr", in: *Roee Rosen: Martyr Paintings*, Ramat Gan, Israel: Ramat Gan Museum, 1994, S. 20.

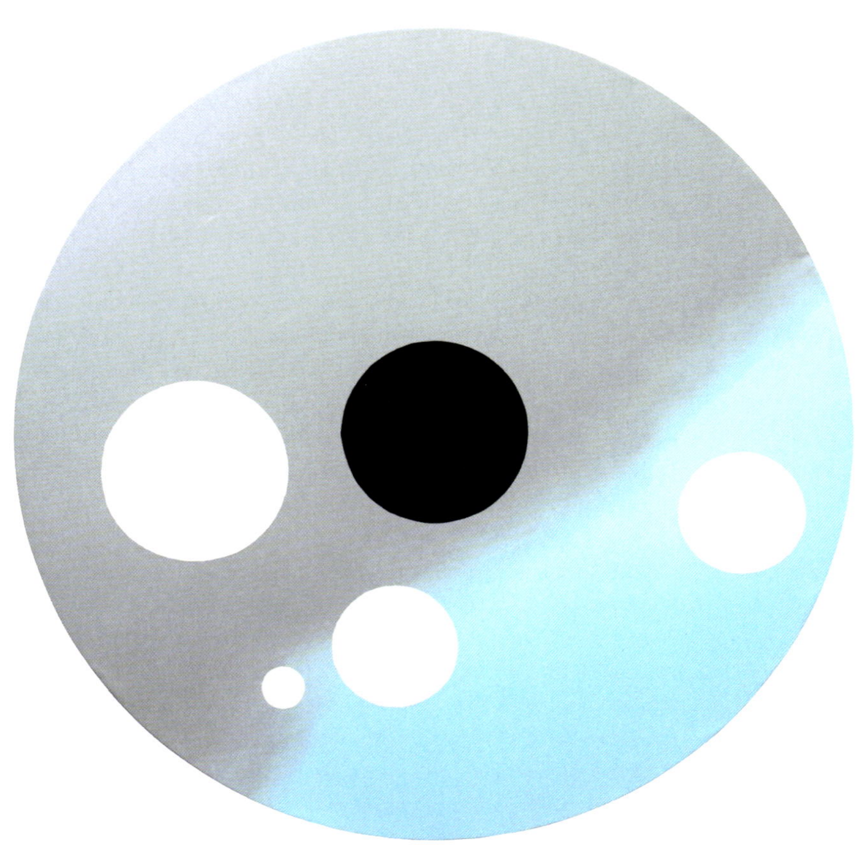

Roee Rosen
The Fourth Funeral of Roee Rosen, seen From His Own Viewpoint After Being Buried, With the Ground Transparent, 2015
oil on canvas, two circles, 160 cm diameter each
(collection Walter Kuna, Berlin)

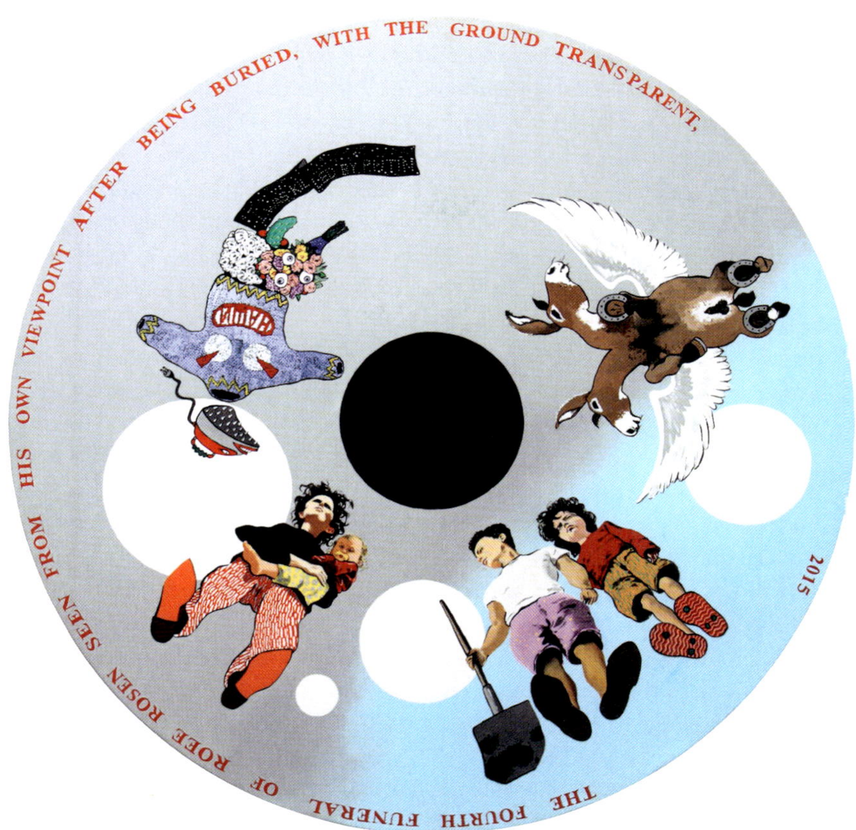
THE FOURTH FUNERAL OF ROEE ROSEN SEEN FROM HIS OWN VIEWPOINT AFTER BEING BURIED, WITH THE GROUND TRANSPARENT,
2015

formaler Ekstase!!"[7] –, die Apotheose sei der Horizont der Animation und die Quelle ihres Genusses („eine Konstruktion der Genußsucht"[8], wie es Kafka ausdrückte): die Auffahrt in den Himmel, die Erlösung, die logische Konsequenz einer von jeder vordefinierten Form und jeder Schwer- und Anziehungskraft losgelösten metamorphischen Kraft. Eine ähnliche Apotheose wird bereits in Sequenz 8 von *Live and Die as Eva Braun* (*Leben und Sterben als Eva Braun*, 1995–1997) evoziert: „Du fliegst wirklich! Die kindlichen Darstellungen der toten Person, die ihren Körper verlässt, waren beinahe wahr! Aufstieg, Triumphwagen mit Engeln, Flug", ist dort zu lesen, bevor die Sequenz mit der Schlussszene, dem berühmten magischen Flug aus de Sicas *Das Wunder von Mailand* endet. Eine Apotheose zeigt auch das Foto eines Flachreliefs, in dem die Entführung des Propheten Elias und seine Himmelfahrt dargestellt sind, das Francisca Panikar im zweiten Kapitel der *Confessions* schwenkt. Die Verwendung der Animation ist also nicht nur der stilistische Garant einer Sendung *für Kinder* und ihre unabdingbare Voraussetzung, sondern, *a priori*, der Beweis für eine Befreiung von der Endlichkeit des Sterblichen, der Verbündete einer Form von Kindheit der Kunst, der sich für eine allgemeine Unschuld verbürgt.

Dennoch drückt genau hier der Schuh und das gleich in mehrfacher Hinsicht. Da ist zunächst die als Einspielung gezeigte Szene, bei der es sich im wahrsten Sinn um die Erzählung einer Apotheose handelt – die des *Kübelreiters* –, ein Flug, den Italo Calvino in einem seiner letzten Vorträge mit den mittelalterlichen Darstellungen auf Besen reitender Hexen verglich. Eine solche Apotheose aber endet in einer Wüste, einer Eishölle, in einer Hölle, die umso drastischer ist, als sie in ihr Gegenteil verkehrt wird (die Kälte ist die Strafe derer, die obendrein vor Kälte sterben. Die Flammen der Hölle wären für sie ein Luxus außerhalb der Jahreszeit): „Und damit steige ich in die Regionen der Eisgebirge und verliere mich auf Nimmerwiedersehen"[9] und dabei kippt er den schwarzen Kohlenstaub in einem „einzigen dunklen Fleck" mitten auf die „weisse Eisfläche",[10] bizarrer Schlusspunkt auf einer unbeschriebenen Seite. In *Kafka for Kids* weint die Figur des bedauernswerten Reiters, *blind* von den Eistränen, die ihm wie Wasserstrahlen aus den leeren Augenhöhlen schießen.

7 In: *The Eisenstein Collection*, hg. v. Richard Taylor, Kolkata: Seagull Books, 2006, S. 126.

8 In: *Franz Kafka: Briefe. 1902–1924*, hg. v. Max Brod, Frankfurt a.M.: Fischer, 1975, S. 385.

9 Franz Kafka, „Der Kübelreiter", in: ders., *Sämtliche Erzählungen*, Köln 2007, S. 301.

10 Diese zwei Sätze erscheinen nur in frühen Versionen des *Kübelreiters*.

Darüber hinaus ist die Animation, weder moralisch noch konkret, gegen Verfälschungen gefeit – welcher Art sie auch sein mögen.

Ein weiterer Einschub ist Boki-Poki, eine gleichermaßen lustige wie verstörende Figur, die am Ende nur noch in Form überdimensionaler Pixel erscheint und die im Augenblick der Ankündigung ihrer Anklage erstarrt. Die Unschuld wird ernstlich in Zweifel gezogen und die Animation verschwimmt mehr und mehr, bis schließlich gar kein Bild mehr zu erkennen ist.

Verfolgt man die zahllosen Bezüge, die Rosen in seinem Werk unermüdlich herstellt, müsste man blind sein, würde man die Ähnlichkeit zwischen den Zeichentricksequenzen in *Kafka for Kids* und den Bildtafeln in seinem Kindermalbuch *Lucy is Sick* (*Lucy ist krank*, 2020–unvollendet) nicht erkennen, einem Malbuch mit in klaren schwarzen Linien auf weißem Grund gezeichneten Motiven. Auch dieses Album mit dem zartrosa Umschlag, das während der Arbeit an *Kafka for Kids* entstand, ist eine autobiografische Arbeit, das detaillierte Tagebuch einer angegriffenen Gesundheit. Die kindliche Unschuld des Malbuchs ist die wirkungslose, schmerzliche und infolgedessen komische Tarnung einer Schreckenschronik, einer durch eine tödliche Krankheit verursachten Verwandlung. Deshalb ist die Einladung zu *A Guided Journey Inside My Grave* (*Eine geführte Reise in mein Grab*, 2014) alles andere als ein makaberer Scherz, zu dem Rosen stets aufgelegt ist.

Und schon wird der fliegende Teppich der Animation unter den Füßen einer vermeintlichen kindlichen Gewissheit weggezogen und mit den unheilvollen Mächten der Metamorphose konfrontiert. Die fantastische Wirkungskraft der Animation hat sich auf das Wesen aller auf der Bühne anwesenden Personen und Gegenstände übertragen, wird doch das gesamte Mobiliar von Schauspieler:innen beherrscht, die so geschminkt sind, dass sie damit verschmelzen. In diesem (in der Tradition der Operette und des Musicals, in denen Glaubwürdigkeit bei Bühnentricks nie eine Rolle spielt, sondern die ganz im Gegenteil einen Antinaturalismus zur Schau stellen, der für ihren *Zauber* garantiert) zwischen lebendig und unbelebt schwankenden Kontext ist es zu verstehen, dass der Überbringer das Titorelli-Gemälde für eine Fälschung erklärt. Das Bild offenbart die Abwesenheit seiner Unschuld: Es ist seinem Wesen inhärent, eine Kopie, eine *Fälschung*, gesetzlos zu sein.

Davon zeugt in gewissem Sinn auch der Charakter des Projekts *Kafka for Kids*. Denn nicht nur Max Brod setzte sich über Kafkas Verbot hinweg, auch Rosen hat davon profitiert, indem er sich gestattete, den in ein Insekt verwandelten Gregor Samsa darzustellen. Hatte Kafka doch verbindliche Anweisungen gegeben, wie die Figur des Überbringers in *Kafka for Kids* bei ihrem Besuch mahnt und deshalb sogar mit dem Abbruch der Sendung droht, um die bildliche Darstellung des Insekts zu verhindern. Äußerst beunruhigt schrieb Kafka am 25. Oktober 1915 an seinen Verleger Kurt Wolff:

> „Sie schrieben letzthin, daß Ottomar Starke ein Titelblatt zur Verwandlung zeichnen wird. Nun habe ich einen kleinen, allerdings soweit ich den Künstler aus ‚Napoleon' kenne, wahrscheinlich sehr *überflüssigen Schrecken bekommen. Es ist mir nämlich, da Starke doch tatsächlich illustriert,* eingefallen, er könnte etwa das Insekt selbst zeichnen wollen. Das nicht, bitte das nicht! Ich will seinen Machtkreis nicht einschränken, sondern nur aus meiner natürlicherweise bessern Kenntnis der Geschichte heraus bitten. Das Insekt selbst kann nicht gezeichnet werden. Es kann aber nicht einmal von der Ferne aus gezeigt werden. Besteht eine solche Absicht nicht und wird meine Bitte also lächerlich – desto besser. Für die Vermittlung und Bekräftigung meiner Bitte wäre ich Ihnen sehr dankbar. Wenn ich für eine Illustration selbst Vorschläge machen dürfte, würde ich Szenen wählen, wie: die Eltern und der Prokurist vor der geschlossenen Tür oder noch besser die Eltern und die Schwester im beleuchteten Zimmer, während die Tür zum ganz finsteren Nebenzimmer offensteht."[11]

Interessant ist, dass Kafka selbst die Versuchung einer bildlichen Darstellung vorausahnte und, um zu verhindern, dass man auf diese List zurückgreifen könnte, die großartige Präzisierung „nicht einmal von der Ferne" hinzufügte. Ebenso interessant ist, dass er anstelle des Insekts eine durch den Raum vorgegebene, durch geöffnete und geschlossene Türen und die Verteilung von Licht und Schatten in Szene gesetzte Bühne entwarf. Während Orson Welles bei seiner Adaption des *Prozesses* dieser Linie folgte, schlug Rosen eine andere Richtung ein. Diesem Register, das man zur damaligen Zeit als expressionistisch hätte bezeichnen können (und Hanns Zischlers wundervolles Buch *Kafka geht ins Kino*, das Kafkas Liebe zum Kino besondere Aufmerksamkeit schenkt, wo dieser oft hingeht und 1913 sagt: „Das Volk soll sich erheben für die Kinotheater und sich nicht […] beschwatzen und betören lassen, von den ‚psychologischen Clowns' der Literatur!"[12]), zog Rosen das Leuchten des Fernsehbildschirms und die eindimensionale Oberfläche des Zeichentricks vor: ein Kino ohne Illusionseffekt. Die

11 Franz Kafka, *Briefe 1902–1924,* zit. nach: https://www.odaha.com.

12 Zit. nach: Hanns Zischler, *Kafka geht ins Kino,* Berlin 2017, S. 99.

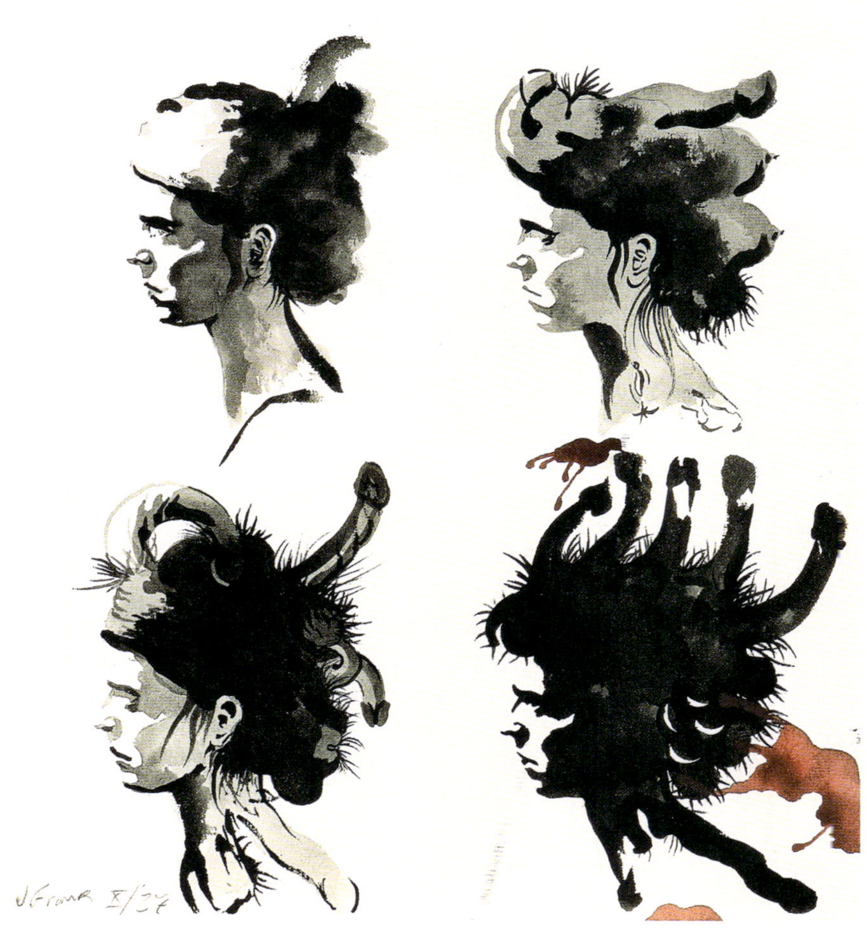

Justine Frank
from *The Stained Portfolio*, 1927-1928
gouache on paper

Gesichter der Protagonist:innen in den animierten Passagen tragen deutliche Züge der Abstraktion – eine bemerkenswerte Ausnahme bildet hier das gerahmte Porträt der Venus im Pelz (wie wir sie nennen) an der Wand in Gregors Zimmer –, eine lebendige, verspielte Anspielung auf den Kubismus, dem zur Zeit der Entstehung der Erzählung zeitgenössischen Stil (wie die Karikatur einer Picasso-Figur wirkt im Übrigen auch die feminisierte Darstellung Titorellis). Ein solches Kino lässt dem Drama keinen anderen Raum als denjenigen, den die Stimme des Vorlesers innerhalb der Studiobühne eröffnet. Angelegt ist das Ganze, wie im Titel angekündigt und einschließlich der Werbeeinblendungen systematisch durchdekliniert, als Wissenssendung für Kinder, die den Raum des Buches öffnet, indem das nüchterne, einsame lautlose Entziffern eines Textes durch das Ritual der vor dem Einschlafen vorgelesenen Gutenachtgeschichte ersetzt wird. Das Publikum auf dieser Bühne ist vielfältig und auch die Vortragende von *Was ist ein Kind?* wendet sich an ein offensichtlich heterogenes Publikum. Neben dem Mädchen als aktiver Zuhörerin lauscht auch das von Schauspieler:innen verkörperte Mobiliar (Tisch, Lampe, Bild etc.) mit aufmerksamen Mienen. Zum Publikum zählen außerdem die Musiker:innen des *Toy Orchestra*, die stets präsent sind, selbst wenn sie nicht im Bild sichtbar sind und nicht spielen.

Es gibt eine klare Trennung zwischen den Botschaften der Zwischenspiele, die sich unmittelbar an das Publikum richten, und all dem, was erzählt, gefragt, erklärt, gesungen, gespielt wird und das jedes Mal über das Hören vermittelt wird. In diesem Sinn sind die Zeichentricksequenzen durchweg stumm. Dies veranschaulicht der einzige Moment, in dem Gregor sich mitzuteilen versucht und nur unverständliche krächzende Laute hervorbringt. Nur wir verstehen, was er sagt, weil seine Worte auf den Bildern erscheinen, weil sie *als* Bilder, als Zierbuchstaben übertragen werden. Deshalb handelt es sich bei *Kafka for Kids* nicht um die für ein kindliches Publikum bestimmte *Verwandlung,* einen reduzierten, vereinfachten, in das vermeintlich adäquate Format für eine vermeintlich bekannte Zielgruppe umgewandelten Kafka – so wie sich *Dust Channel* (*Staubkanal*, 2016) als Fernsehsendung für ein Publikum von Staubsaugern präsentierte. Ein solches Hörtheater ist genau das, was Kafka in dem Fragment „Skizze einer Autobiografie" als alles andere als wohlbekannt beschrieb:

> „Man wird [...] einem Jungen, der abends mitten im Lesen einer aufregenden Geschichte ist, niemals durch eine bloß auf ihn eingeschränkte Beweisführung begreiflich machen können, dass er das Lesen unterbrechen und schlafen gehn muss. [...] Die Hauptsache aber war, dass ich die Verurteilung, die meine Eigentümlichkeit des langen Lesens erfahren

> hatte, nun mit eigenen Mitteln auf die verborgen gehaltene Eigentümlichkeit der Pflichtversäumnis weiterführte und dadurch zu dem niederdrückendsten Ergebnis kam."[13]

Ein Zitat, das Georges Bataille (ein Autor, der bekanntermaßen von herausragender Bedeutung für Justine Frank war) in dem Kafka gewidmeten Kapitel seines Essays *Die Literatur und das Böse* zur Untermauerung dessen heranzieht, was er als Kafkas „Kinderei" bezeichnet und deren Kohärenz durch die Überschriften der einzelnen Abschnitte – „Die vollkommene Kindlichkeit Kafkas", „Die Aufrechterhaltung der kindlichen Situation", „Der glückliche Überschwang des Kindes ..."[14] – untermauert wird. Diese Kinderei ist hier alles andere als etwas Unschuldiges, sondern ist im Gegenteil die Manifestation der Ungehörigkeit, die Empörung des Rechtlosen.

Mit *Kafka for Kids* bringt Rosen die Verwandlung – und Kafka als ihren besten Vermittler – mit der Kindheit in Berührung. *K. for Kids,* das lässt an Orson Welles' *F. für Fälschung* denken: *Kafka for Kids*, nicht Kafka zu den Kindern, für die Kinder, sozusagen Kafka, die Kinder. Und dies in einer zweifachen Bewegung, die den Chiasmus veranschaulicht, der in Kafkas Erzählung am Werk ist. Da ist einerseits das Goethe'sche Ideal der Perfektionierung und Vollendung einer Ursprungsform. Goethe, dessen Werke Kafka, wie wir aus seinen *Tagebüchern* wissen, mit Begeisterung gelesen hat, schreibt in seinem Gedicht *Die Metamorphose der Pflanzen*: „Bist alsobald und fort und fort gediehen / Nach dem Gesetz wonach du angetreten. / So mußt du sein, dir kannst du nicht entfliehen, [...] / Und keine Zeit und keine Macht zerstückelt / Geprägte Form, die lebend sich entwickelt."[15] Dies ist der Fall bei Gregors Schwester Grete, von der es am Ende der Erzählung heißt: „[...] wie sie in letzter Zeit trotz aller Plage, die ihre Wangen bleich gemacht hatte, zu einem schönen und üppigen Mädchen aufgeblüht war. [...] die Tochter als erste sich erhob und ihren jungen Körper dehnte."[16] Grete, die abgesehen von ihrem Bruder Gregor einzige Figur des Textes, die ei-

13 Georges Bataille, *Die Literatur und das Böse,* Berlin 2011, S. 125.

14 Ebd., S. 123, 126, 134.

15 Zit. nach Georgio Agamben, *Das Abenteuer. Der Freund*, Berlin 2018, S. 7. Das Gedicht erschien zuerst unter dem Titel *Urworte, Orphisch*, vgl. Johann Wolfgang Goethe, *Urworte, Orphisch*, in: ders., Werke in 2 Bänden, Gütersloh 1982, Bd. 2, S. 126.

16 Franz Kafka, *Die Verwandlung,* in: ders., *Sämtliche Erzählungen,* Köln 2007, S. 150.

nen Vornamen – und zudem einen dem seinen ähnlichen – hat, ist diejenige, die zu Beginn versucht, seine neue Wesensart zu verstehen, die sich um ihn kümmert. Sie ist aber auch diejenige, die ihre Meinung ändert, die dessen überdrüssig wird und die Familie davon überzeugt, sich seiner zu entledigen. Grete blüht im Verlauf der Erzählung auf, wächst vom Kind zur heiratsfähigen Frau heran, während sich Gregor zurückentwickelt. Zu Beginn der Erzählung gelingt es ihm nur mit Mühe das Bett zu verlassen und er hat Schwierigkeiten seinen Körper zu beherrschen. Bei ihm bahnt sich der Verfall an, er ist im Sterben begriffen. Am Ende befindet er sich im Zustand eines Leichnams, der – „vollständig flach und trocken“[17] – an einen *Toon* erinnert. Seine von der Haushälterin beseitigte Hülle hat sich – jenseits der Erzählung – im wahrsten Wortsinn in Luft aufgelöst: „[...] also darüber, wie das Zeug von nebenan weggeschafft werden soll, müssen Sie sich keine Gedanken machen. Es ist schon in Ordnung.“[18] Die Veränderung der Gestalt ist so radikal, dass sie von einer Form in die Unförmigkeit und schließlich in den Verlust jeglicher Form übergeht.

In *Kafka for Kids* verschwindet Gregor tatsächlich. Wie sieht es aber mit Grete aus? Sie begegnet uns nicht nur als Zeichentrickfigur, sondern sie ist ohne Zweifel auch „das Mädchen“, die Zuhörerin, die ganz offen ihren sadistischen Neigungen Ausdruck verleiht, die sich über das Wort „nackt“ amüsiert, die über eine eher erschreckende Illustration der Verwandlung stolpert, die das Ende der Sendung begrüßt, die am Schuh des Vorlesers lecken möchte, die sich an der Vorstellung erfreut, das Gemälde zu ermorden etc. Und Grete ist vermutlich auch, nunmehr in eine Erwachsene verwandelt, die von derselben Schauspielerin – der großartigen Hani Furstenberg – verkörperte Rechtsprofessorin. Und nicht zu vergessen D., die zwölfjährige Palästinenserin, deren Alter und Strafrechtsstatus Veränderungen unterworfen sind und über die die Professorin referiert. Die Platzierung dieses langen pädagogischen Einschubs am Ende des Films verändert natürlich die Bedeutung des gesamten zuvor Gezeigten. Einerseits erscheint die – aktuelle – Bedeutung einer Darlegung der israelischen Politik in der strafrechtlichen Verfolgung von Kindern in den besetzten Gebieten wie ein Umkehreffekt, um jeder eventuellen Leichtgläubigkeit im Hinblick auf eine x-te „kulturelle“ Adaption Kafkas Einhalt zu gebieten. Andererseits wird die politische Analyse der Professorin uneindeutig und verliert an Klarheit durch ihre autobiografischen Bekenntnisse bezüglich des Alterns ihres Körpers und seinen diversen – auch olfaktorischen (was im Zusammen-

17 Kafka, *Die Verwandlung*, S. 146.

18 Ebd., S. 149.

hang mit Gregor von besonderer Bedeutung ist) – Veränderungen, bezüglich einer räumlichen (nach Accra) und zeitlichen Projektion (in ungefähr hundert Jahren), über eine Begegnung mit Kwame, der ghanaischer Herkunft ist (wie Haddy, „die" dritte Roee Rosen der *Confessions*), dem fiktiven Adressaten der Ausführungen zum israelischen Strafrecht und zu seinen Widersprüchen, die auch dieses Gesetz zu einem Übergangstext machen, einem metamorphischen Text. Es ist hier aus Platzgründen nicht möglich, auf all die ungeahnten und furchtbaren Verwicklungen einzugehen, die in diesem Bravourstück im Spiel sind, dennoch ist es im Kern nicht *nur* der schonungslose Kommentar eines als „flexibel, konvulsiv, metamorph" beschriebenen Militärgesetzes, sondern, was noch entscheidender ist, seine „Widersprüche lassen es zu, die Realität auf Verlangen zu verändern."

Da sowohl Gregor als auch Grete dem Ausnahmegesetz unterworfen sind, sind beide von seinen Auswirkungen betroffen. Und dies gilt ebenso sowohl für diejenigen, die es ertragen, wie für diejenigen, die es anprangern, und sogar für die Fiktionen, die sich damit auseinandersetzen. Mag Kafka auch „Doktor der Rechte" sein, auch er wäre dagegen machtlos, wird dem Mädchen erklärt. Die Verwandlung, das Gesetz der allgemeinen Zersetzung, dringt überall ein. In diesem Sinn ist *People's Delicatessen* (*Volksdelikatessen*), eine der Werbeeinblendungen in *Kafka for Kids,* zu verstehen. Ein Bekenntnis, das an die ekelerregende Gefräßigkeit des neuen Gregor denken lässt, findet sich im Tagebucheintrag vom 30. Oktober 1911, in dem Kafka mit fantastischen Anklängen notiert:

> „Dieses Verlangen, das ich fast immer habe, wenn ich einmal meinen Magen gesund fühle, Vorstellungen von schrecklichen Wagnissen mit Speisen in mir zu häufen. Besonders vor Selchereien befriedige ich dieses Verlangen. Sehe ich eine Wurst, die ein Zettel als eine alte, harte Hauswurst anzeigt, beiße ich in meiner Einbildung mit ganzem Gebiß hinein und schlucke rasch, regelmäßig und rücksichtslos, wie eine Maschine. [...] Die langen Schwarten von Rippenfleisch stoße ich ungebissen in den Mund und ziehe sie dann von hinten, den Magen und die Därme durchreißend, wieder heraus. Schmutzige Greislerläden esse ich vollständig leer. Fülle mich mit Heringen, Gurken und allen schlechten alten scharfen Speisen an."[19]

19 Franz Kafka, *Die Tagebücher,* zit. nach https://www.projekt-gutenberg.org.

1

ВЛАДИМИР В СВОЕМ ЛЕТНЕМ ОСОБНЯКЕ.

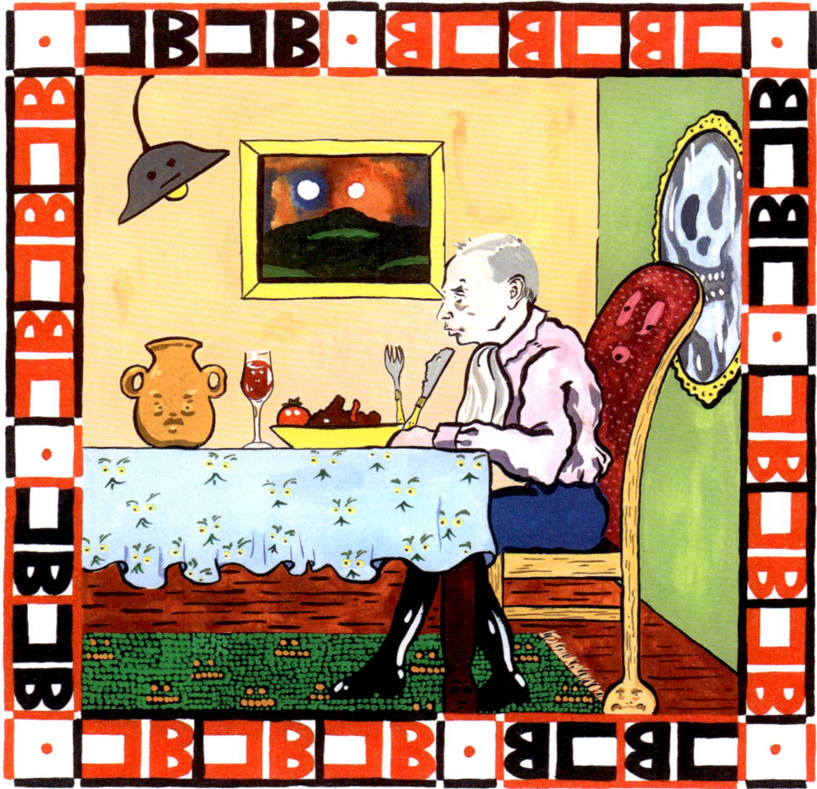

ОН УЖИНАЕТ.

Maxim Komar-Myshkin
from the album *Vladimir's Night* (plates 1 and 2), 2011–2014
gouache on paper

22

НАШ ТРУД ПРИНЕС ПЛОД, РАСПЕВАЮТ ДОБРЫЕ ПОВИТУХИ,

В ТО ВРЕМЯ, КАК ВОЛОДИНА ДУША, ВЕЛИКОЛЕПНЫЙ КОМАРМЫШ,

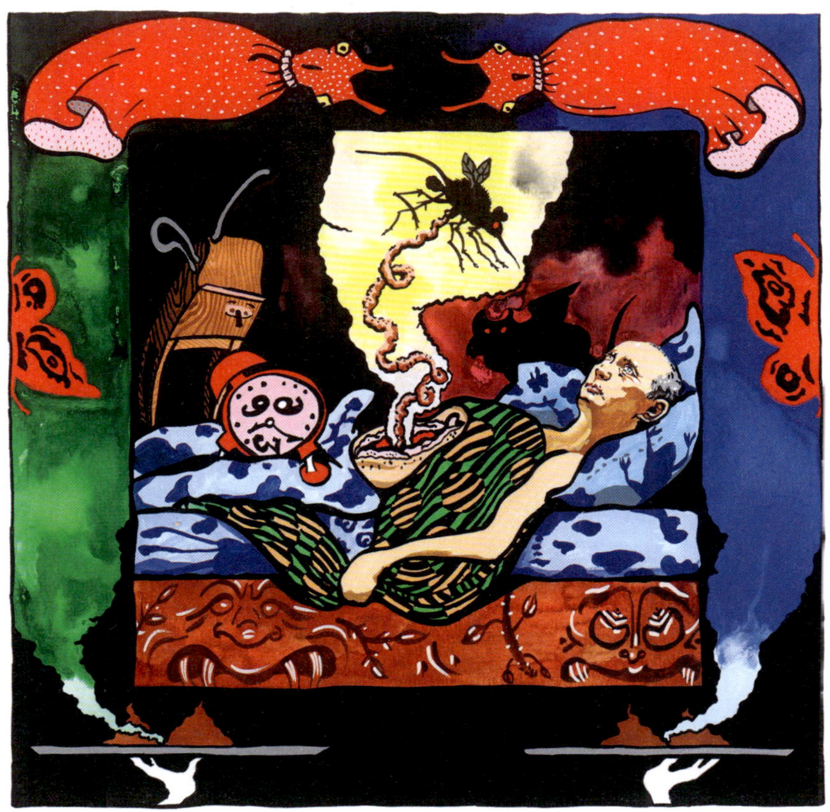

НАКОНЕЦ ВЫЛЕТАЕТ НА СВОБОДУ ИЗ СВОЕГО БРЕННОГО КОКОНА.

Ein derartiger, von der Vorliebe für das Verdorbene, Schmutzige und Ekelerregende geprägter obsessiver Nahrungsmittelkonsum ist nicht unmittelbar verständlich. Mit anderen Worten: Selbst wenn es hier eine Parallele zwischen Franz und Gregor gibt, liefert dies keinen weiteren Aufschluss, außer dass sie Ausdruck einer offensichtlichen Zirkulation von einem Text zum anderen, von einer möglichen Figur (vermutlich „autobiografisch", doch die physiologische Konsistenz eines *Ichs* wird hier besonders schlecht behandelt, bizarr zu sich genommen, verdaut, verschlungen, wieder erbrochen) zu einer anderen (die kulinarische Vorliebe einer Kellerassel). Wir erinnern uns, dass Kafka am Ende eines Briefes, den er am 17. November 1912 an Felice Bauer schrieb und in dem er zuvor schilderte, wie schwer es ihm gefallen sei, aus dem Bett aufzustehen, „eine kleine Geschichte, [...] die mir in den [sic!] Jammer im Bett eingefallen ist und mich innerlichst bedrängt"[20] erwähnt und damit auch dort eine Parallele zwischen dem Beginn des Schreibens und dem Anfang der Erzählung zieht. Die Verwandlung, die es, in der Szene nach dem ersten Besuch des Überbringers möglich macht, durch ein Spiel mit ähnlich klingenden Lauten aus „Kafka's shoe" („Kafkas Schuh"), „Kafka's Jew" („Kafkas Jude") zu machen, von einem mosaischen Bilderverbot zu dessen paradoxer Aufhebung durch Kafkas Jüdischsein, und all dies mithilfe des seltsamen Telefons in Gestalt des Schuhs – der, abgesehen von seiner Funktion als Fetisch („Darf ich lecken?"), möglicherweise von Chaplin kam –, das uns bewusst macht, dass es im Hinblick auf die Macht, die die Metamorphose darstellt, keine Gewissheit gibt. Sie erlaubt das Verbotene, sie beruft sich auf das Verbotene, sie macht stillschweigend Gesetze jenseits von Gesetzen – und nicht zu vergessen – sie ist Objekt der Begierde.

***

Wenn ich mich nicht irre, erscheint das Wort „Verwandlung" beziehungsweise „Metamorphose" bei Rosen lediglich in einem Titel, nämlich im letzten der zahlreichen Selbstporträts von Justine Frank, einem auf die Zeit von 1940–1941 datierten Ölgemälde mit dem Titel *The Metamorphosis of a Woman-Assassin* (*Die Verwandlung einer Frauenmörderin*). Am Rande sei hier daran erinnert, dass in dem Pseudonym, unter dem Justine Frank ihren einzigen Roman verfasste, just der Vorname Gregoire auftaucht, ein Umstand, der, abgesehen von der Ähnlichkeit von *Frank* und *Franz K.*, hinreichend eine deutliche, unzweifelhafte Verwandtschaft zwischen Justine und dem Protagonisten der berühmten

20 Franz Kafka, *Briefe an Felice*, zit. nach https://www.odaha.com.

Erzählung unterstreicht. Dieses letzte Bild einer Serie zeigt viermal ein Scherenschnitt-Profilbild, schwarz auf bläulich weißem beziehungsweise rotem Grund mit weißen Flecken. Diese Scherenschnittprofile haben eine lange Tradition und waren in der europäischen Mittelschicht seit dem 18. Jahrhundert so weit verbreitet, dass man sie im Hinblick auf ihre tatsächliche und symbolische Verwendung gelegentlich als Vorläufer der Fotografie bezeichnet. Diese Praxis für Frank wieder aufleben zu lassen, ist eine Art der Ermächtigung einer bildlichen Darstellung – mit dem Ziel diese zu vernichten –, die sowohl historisch als auch hinsichtlich ihrer Herstellungsweise einen Bezug zu den Brüdern Lumière hatte. Zwischen dem ersten und dem letzten Profilbild werden ursprünglich feine Konturen Justine Franks durch eine zunehmende Behaarung verunstaltet, bis sich die junge Frau schließlich in die Karikatur einer Hexe oder eines furchterregenden Januskopfs verwandelt hat, bei dem selbst die Frisur zu einem grotesken Profil wird oder bis ein ganzes Gesicht entstellt und zum Humus einiger Wurzelknollen geworden ist. Kurz: die bereits begrabene Justine („lebendig begraben"), die sich selbst unter der Erde ausdehnt. Justine als eine Art randloses Insekt: Ihre alles verschlingende Behaarung steht im Widerspruch zu dem, was man bei der Technik des Scherenschnitts erwartet: einen klaren Schnitt ohne Wucherungen, Verzweigungen oder andere störende Elemente. Die Silhouette hebt sich von der Oberfläche ab, während das behaarte oder durch Wucherungen verunstaltete metamorphe Wesen wieder in die Abgründe einer unterirdischen Arbeit, in die Gleichförmigkeit des Rhizoms eintaucht. Die titelgebende *Mörderin* kann als Bezug auf die Pseudowissenschaft der Physiognomik verstanden werden, die vermeintlich in der Lage ist, die Seele und die Schwächen der Porträtierten – in diesem Fall einer Mörderin – zu offenbaren. Doch es ist auch die Ermordung, in der Malerei, Justines durch Justine, die nach und nach umgebracht wird, eine unbestreitbare Verwandlung, die der Titel präzisiert. Es überrascht nicht, dass zwischen 1941 und 1942 letzte Ölgemälde folgten, metamorphosierte Apotheosen, im Bild versteckte dämonische Selbstporträts, himmlische, aber pervertierte Visionen, Bilder morbider, entstellter Himmel: *Sick Heaven*, *Shit Heaven* (*Kranker Himmel, Scheiss-Himmel*) und *A Portrait of Thieving Skies* (*Porträt eines diebischen Himmels*).

***

Der Einsatz des Mediums Film ist bei Rosen alles andere als unwesentlich. Er ist Teil einer Authentifizierungsstrategie, insofern als der Film jedes Mal der Dokumentation eines Sujets dient: des Selbstporträts (*Dr Cross* [*Dr. Kreuz*],

The Confessions …), der Geiselnahme (*Buried Alive Videos* [*Lebendig begrabene Videos*]), des wissenschaftlichen Diskurses (*Two Women and a Man* [*Zwei Frauen und ein Mann*]), *Explaining the Law to Kwame* [Kwame das Gesetz erläutern]), der TV-Stand-up-Comedy (*Hilarious* [*Urkomisch*]), des Dokumentarfilms (*Out* [*Raus*]). Mit Bezug auf Rosens *Dust Channel* kann man behaupten, dass es darum geht, Werbung mit all den darin enthaltenen Widersprüchen zu machen, der Reklame den letzten Schliff zu geben – Werbung, und sei sie auch haarsträubend, *für ein Sujet* zu machen. Zum vielleicht ersten Mal geht es bei *Kafka for Kids* darum, das metamorphe Prinzip als Prinzip des Untergangs, schlimmer noch der Auslöschung – Auslöschung der Kindheit, Auslöschung des Rechts, einer Nation, der Kunst etc. – wirken zu lassen. Und es ist tatsächlich eine Bestattung, der man in dem fulminanten – von oben, aus der Sicht derer, die eine Apotheose erleben durften, gesehenen – gesungenen Finale beiwohnt, in dem „Grete" und sämtliche Protagonist:innen des Films (es sind sogar Figuren aus anderen Filmen zu erkennen) einen Abschiedsgesang auf die Kindheit, auf ihr fiktionales Dasein und auf sich selbst anstimmen.

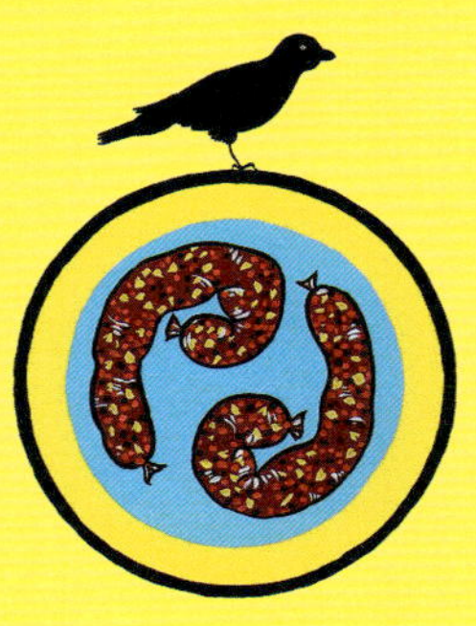

This book is published on the occasion of the exhibition *Roee Rosen. Kafka for Kids & Other Troubling Tales* at Kunstmuseum Luzern, 26.11.2022–05.02.2023.

Roee Rosen: *Kafka for Kids*

Editor: Kunstmuseum Luzern, Sternberg Press
Texts: Sergio Edelsztein, Fanni Fetzer, Jean-Pierre Rehm, Roee Rosen
Managing editors: Laura Breitschmid, Beni Muhl
Translation:
German–English: Brian Currid,
French–English: Sarah Wolberg,
French–German: Barbara Holle,
English–German:
Alexandra Titze-Grabec
Copyediting:
German: Fanni Fetzer,
Beni Muhl
English: Blanche Craig, Sternberg Press; the Kolenda Group
Proofreading:
German: Nina Mentrup
English: the Kolenda Group
Design: Alicja Kobza
Prepress: Krzysiek Krzysztofiak
Printing: Argraf Sp. z o. o, Warszawa

ISBN 978-3-95679-662-3

Distributed by The MIT Press, Art Data, Les presses du réel, and Idea Books

Image credits:

Roee Rosen, *Kafka for Kids*, video stills, cinematographer: Avner Shahaf

Roee Rosen, *Kafka for Kids*, gouaches, 43 cm × 50 cm / 50 × 43 cm, 2019–2020, Woman in Fur oil paintings, 75 cm × 50 cm each, 2017, all photos and scans by the artist

Roee Rosen, *Kafka for Kids*, still photography: Goni Riskin

Photography and scans of all other artworks by Roee Rosen. All images courtesy of the artist and Rosenfeld Gallery

Every effort has been made to contact the rightful owners with regards to copyrights and permissions. We apologize for any inadvertent errors or omissions.

This publication is supported by:

LANDIS & GYR STIFTUNG

Fondation
Jan Michalski

ארטיס أرتيس
artis

Published by

Sternberg Press

Sternberg Press
71–75 Shelton Street
UK–London WC2H 9JQ
www.sternberg-press.com

Exhibition curated by Sergio Edelsztein, Fanni Fetzer
Director: Fanni Fetzer
Research associate: Susanne Gerber
Communication: Beni Muhl, Eveline Suter
Head of administration: Gabriele Froning
Administration: Daniel C. Müller
Bookkeeping: Deborah Morozzi
Head of art education: Brigit Meier
Art education: Angela Erni, Ursula Helg
Head of art handling and registrar: Tobias Oehmichen
Restoration: Johanna Elebe
Technical team: Daniel Amhof, Steven Tod
Art handling: Samuli Blatter, Tobias Bühlmann, Tatjana Erpen, Raphael Muntwyler, Benedikt Notter, Anita Zumbühl
Head of museum services: Judith Wartenweiler
Front desk: Fabienne Immoos, Yvonne Zorzi

Museum services: Ursula Ambauen, Gabi Andres, Lisa Blaser, Lucia Ferrari Piazza, Sandra Harmath-Cerutti, Karin Eigenmann, Ivana Janackovic, Elisabeth Kaufmann, Silvana Liniger, Maya Mrak, Aline Peter, Katharina Schulik, Christian Sterchi, Yvonne Zorzi

Kunstmuseum Luzern

Kunstmuseum Luzern
Europaplatz 1
6002 Luzern, Switzerland
www.kunstmuseumluzern.ch

Main Credits for *Kafka for Kids*

Written, Directed and Painted by Roee Rosen
Music Composed and Arranged by Igor Krutogolov
Produced by Roee Rosen & Max Lomberg
Co-produced by Michel Balagué, Volte Films
Director of Photography: Avner Shahaf
Editor: Max Lomberg
Animation: Ofeq Shemer & Ada Rimon
Costume Design: Maya Bash
Choreography: Renana Raz
Props: Gal Melnick
MakeUp Artist: Orly Ronen
Gaffer: Nir Rachmin
Set Design: Roee Rosen

Musicians:
Igor Krutogolov: Toy clarinet, toy keyboards, toy guitar, toy effects, toy voice
Amir Buxbaum: Toy clarinet
Mihai Cernea: Toy clarinet
Roy Chen: Toy drums
Neil Kalman: Toy keyboards
Victor Levin: Toy clarinet
Niv Majar: Toy glockenspiel, toy xylophone
Naomi Rosin: Toy clarinet